Translated by Leslie Lonsdale-Cooper and Michael Turner
Renewed Art copyright © 1991 by Casterman, Belgium
Text Copyright © 1999 by Egmont UK Ltd.
American Edition © 2007 by Little, Brown and Company.

Little, Brown and Company
Hachette Book Group
1290 Avenue of the Americas, New York, NY 10104
Visit us at lb-kids.com
casterman.com
tintin.com

Little, Brown and Company is a division of Hachette Book Group, Inc.
The Little, Brown name and logo are trademarks of Hachette Book Group, Inc.

The publisher is not responsible for websites (or their content) that are not owned by the publisher.

First U.S. Edition: September 2007
ISBN: 978-0-316-00374-2
19 18 17 16 15 14 13 12 11 10
Published pursuant to agreement with Editions Casterman. Not for sale in the British Commonwealth.
Printed in China

THE ADVENTURES OF
TINTIN
REPORTER FOR "LE PETIT VINGTIÈME„
IN THE LAND OF
THE SOVIETS

BY HERGÉ

LITTLE, BROWN AND COMPANY
New York Boston

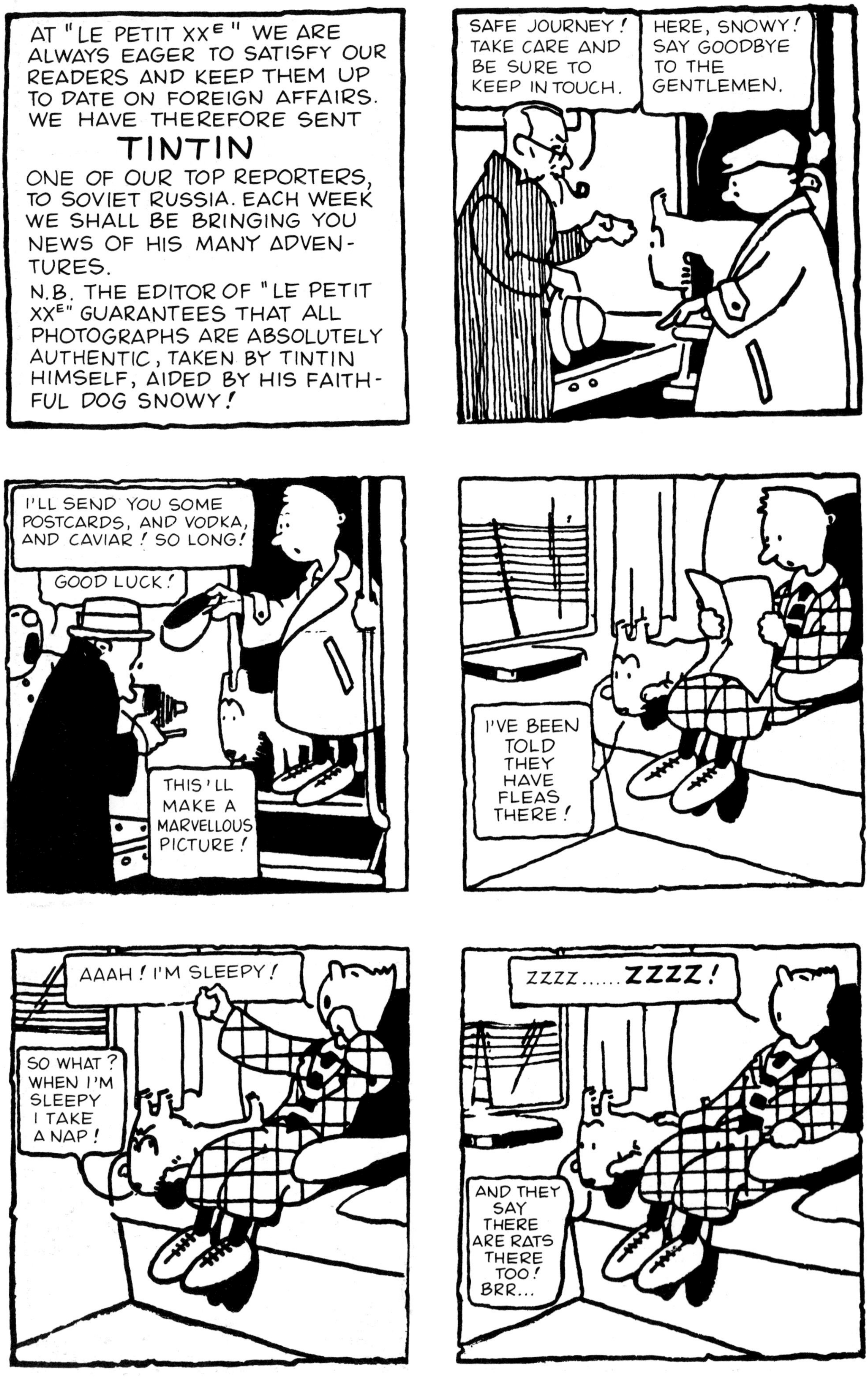
AT "LE PETIT XXE" WE ARE ALWAYS EAGER TO SATISFY OUR READERS AND KEEP THEM UP TO DATE ON FOREIGN AFFAIRS. WE HAVE THEREFORE SENT
TINTIN
ONE OF OUR TOP REPORTERS, TO SOVIET RUSSIA. EACH WEEK WE SHALL BE BRINGING YOU NEWS OF HIS MANY ADVENTURES.
N.B. THE EDITOR OF "LE PETIT XXE" GUARANTEES THAT ALL PHOTOGRAPHS ARE ABSOLUTELY AUTHENTIC, TAKEN BY TINTIN HIMSELF, AIDED BY HIS FAITHFUL DOG SNOWY!
SAFE JOURNEY! TAKE CARE AND BE SURE TO KEEP IN TOUCH.
HERE, SNOWY! SAY GOODBYE TO THE GENTLEMEN.
I'LL SEND YOU SOME POSTCARDS, AND VODKA, AND CAVIAR! SO LONG!
GOOD LUCK!
THIS'LL MAKE A MARVELLOUS PICTURE!
I'VE BEEN TOLD THEY HAVE FLEAS THERE!
AAAH! I'M SLEEPY!
SO WHAT? WHEN I'M SLEEPY I TAKE A NAP!
ZZZZ...... ZZZZ!
AND THEY SAY THERE ARE RATS THERE TOO! BRR...

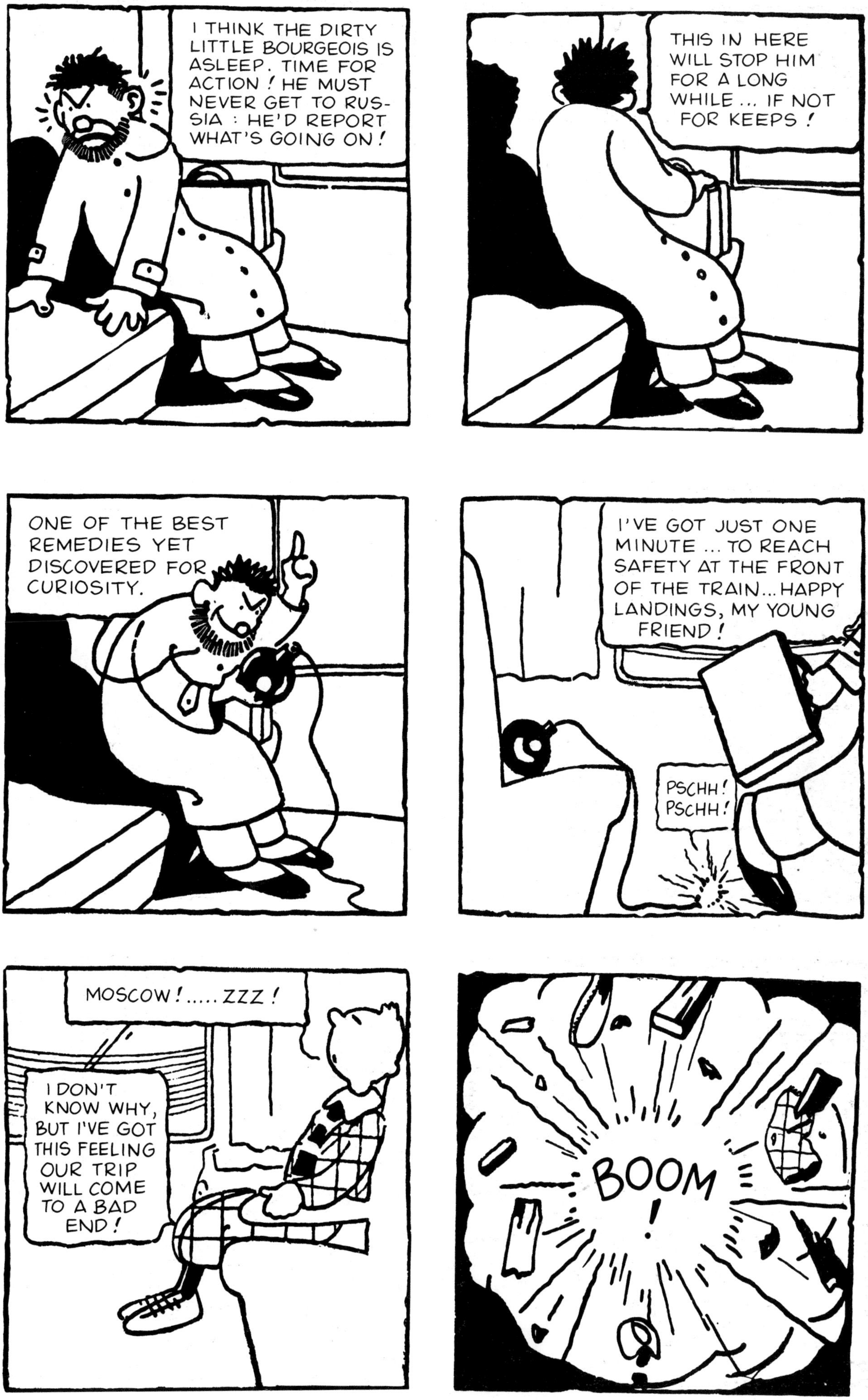
I THINK THE DIRTY LITTLE BOURGEOIS IS ASLEEP. TIME FOR ACTION! HE MUST NEVER GET TO RUSSIA: HE'D REPORT WHAT'S GOING ON!
THIS IN HERE WILL STOP HIM FOR A LONG WHILE ... IF NOT FOR KEEPS!
ONE OF THE BEST REMEDIES YET DISCOVERED FOR CURIOSITY.
I'VE GOT JUST ONE MINUTE ... TO REACH SAFETY AT THE FRONT OF THE TRAIN... HAPPY LANDINGS, MY YOUNG FRIEND!
PSCHH! PSCHH!
MOSCOW! ..... ZZZ!
I DON'T KNOW WHY, BUT I'VE GOT THIS FEELING OUR TRIP WILL COME TO A BAD END!
BOOM!

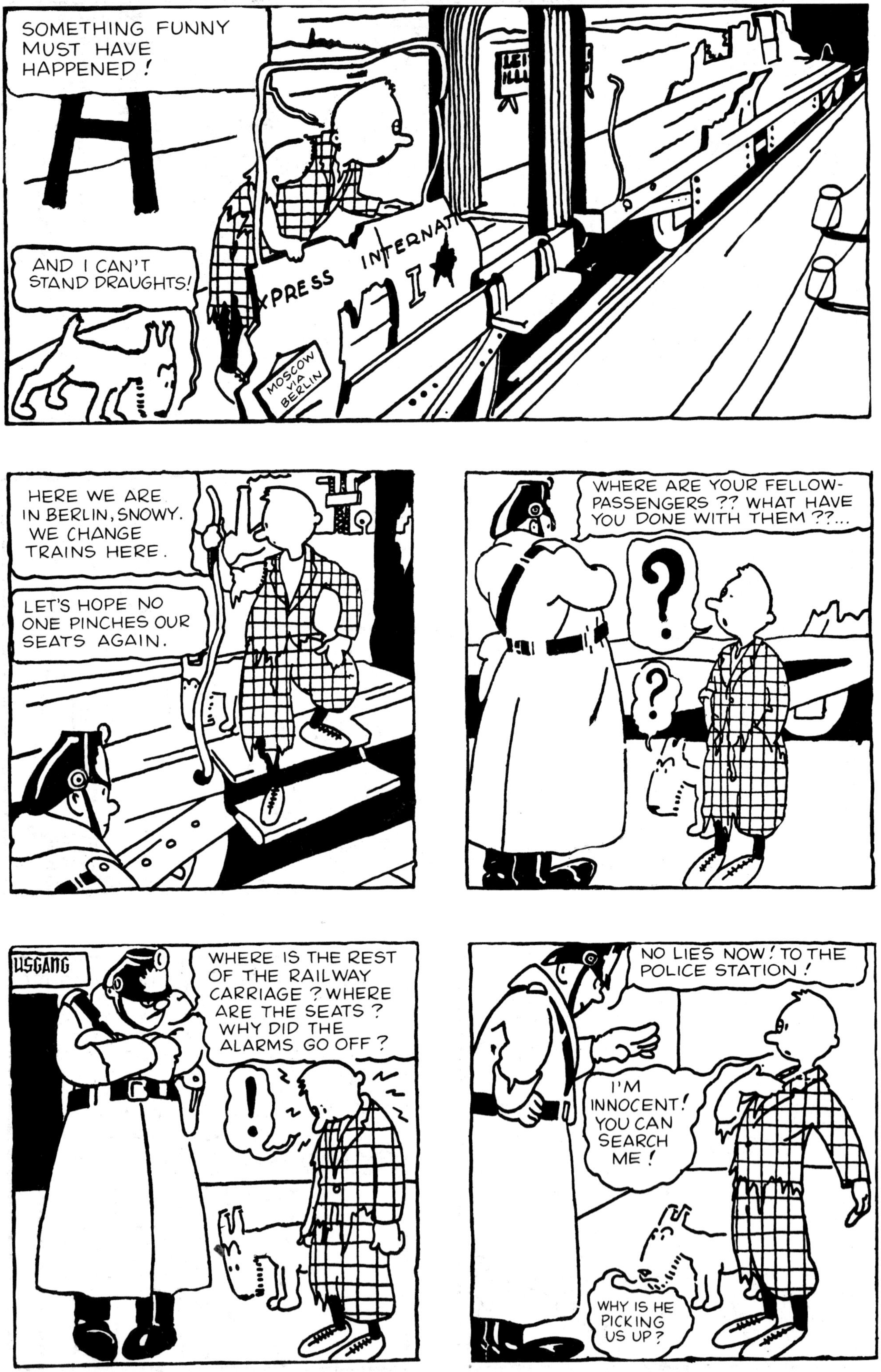
SOMETHING FUNNY MUST HAVE HAPPENED!
AND I CAN'T STAND DRAUGHTS!
XPRESS INTERNAT
MOSCOW VIA BERLIN
HERE WE ARE IN BERLIN, SNOWY. WE CHANGE TRAINS HERE.
LET'S HOPE NO ONE PINCHES OUR SEATS AGAIN.
WHERE ARE YOUR FELLOW-PASSENGERS ?? WHAT HAVE YOU DONE WITH THEM ??...
?
?
USGANG
WHERE IS THE REST OF THE RAILWAY CARRIAGE ? WHERE ARE THE SEATS ? WHY DID THE ALARMS GO OFF ?
!
NO LIES NOW! TO THE POLICE STATION!
I'M INNOCENT! YOU CAN SEARCH ME!
WHY IS HE PICKING US UP?

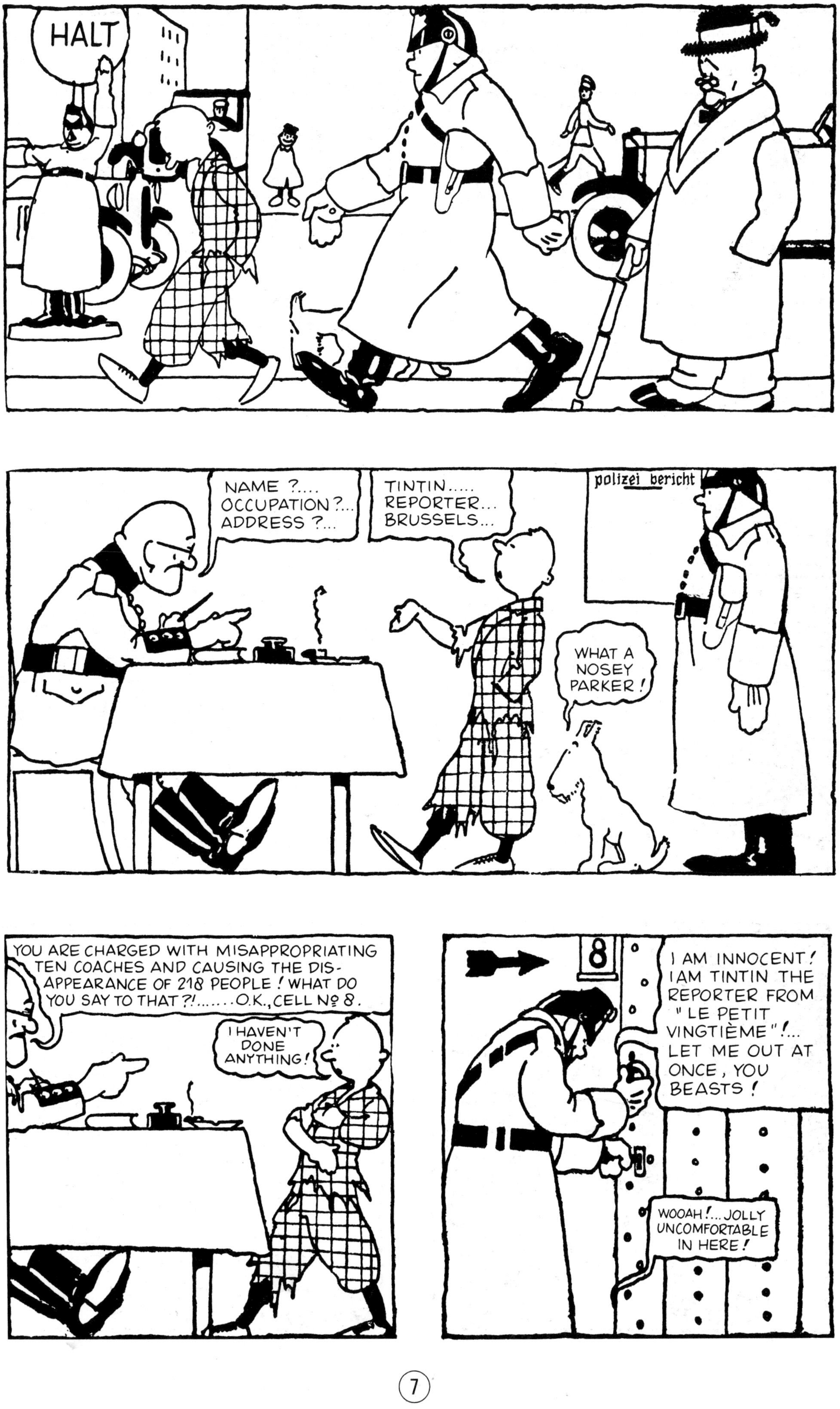
HALT
NAME ?.... OCCUPATION ?... ADDRESS ?...
TINTIN..... REPORTER... BRUSSELS...
polizei bericht
WHAT A NOSEY PARKER !
YOU ARE CHARGED WITH MISAPPROPRIATING TEN COACHES AND CAUSING THE DIS-APPEARANCE OF 218 PEOPLE ! WHAT DO YOU SAY TO THAT ?!.......O.K., CELL Nº 8.
I HAVEN'T DONE ANYTHING !
8
I AM INNOCENT ! I AM TINTIN THE REPORTER FROM " LE PETIT VINGTIÈME " !... LET ME OUT AT ONCE, YOU BEASTS !
WOOAH !... JOLLY UNCOMFORTABLE IN HERE !

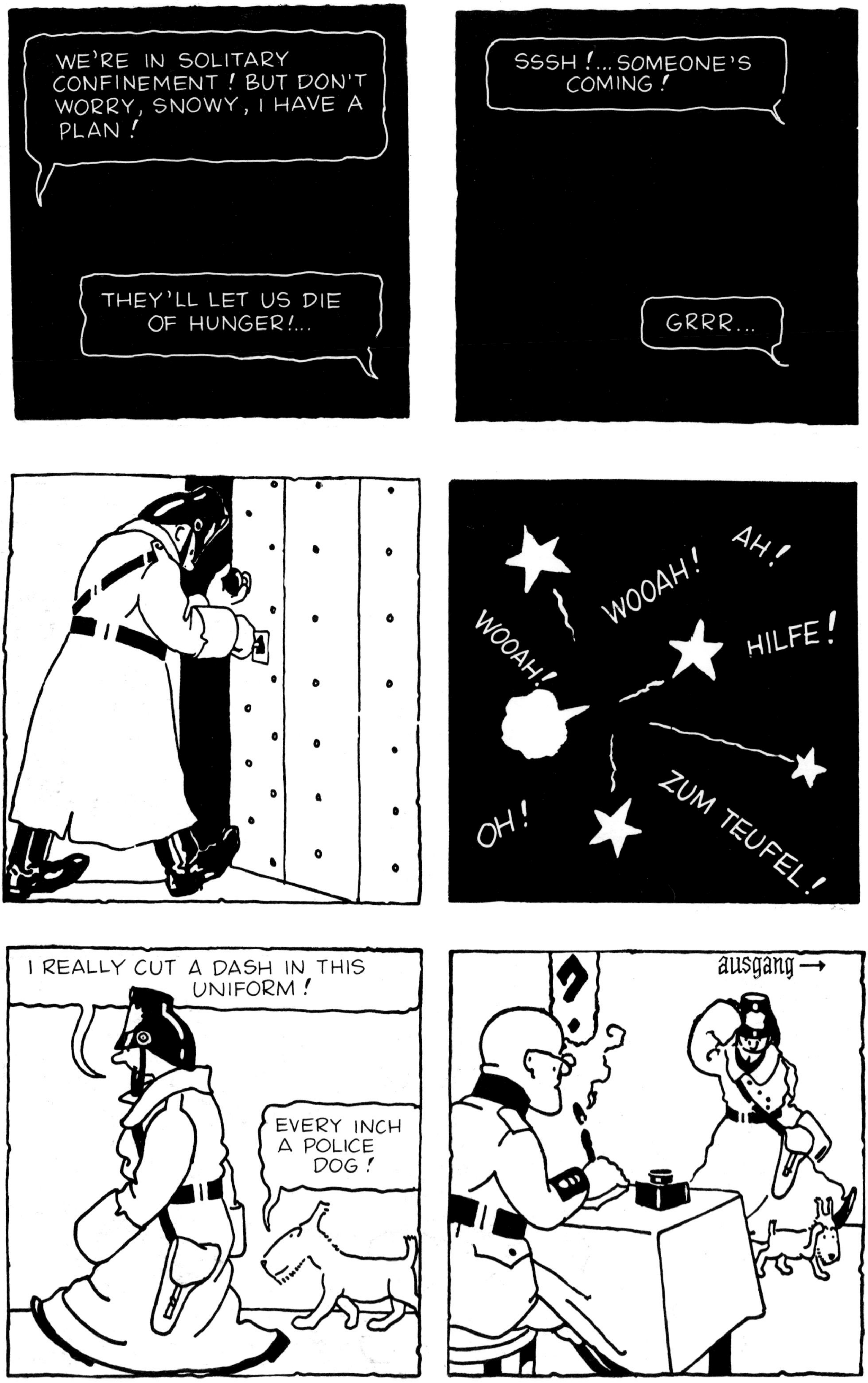

WE'RE IN SOLITARY CONFINEMENT! BUT DON'T WORRY, SNOWY, I HAVE A PLAN!
THEY'LL LET US DIE OF HUNGER!...
SSSH!... SOMEONE'S COMING!
GRRR...
AH!
WOOAH!
WOOAH!
HILFE!
OH!
ZUM TEUFEL!
I REALLY CUT A DASH IN THIS UNIFORM!
EVERY INCH A POLICE DOG!
?
ausgang →

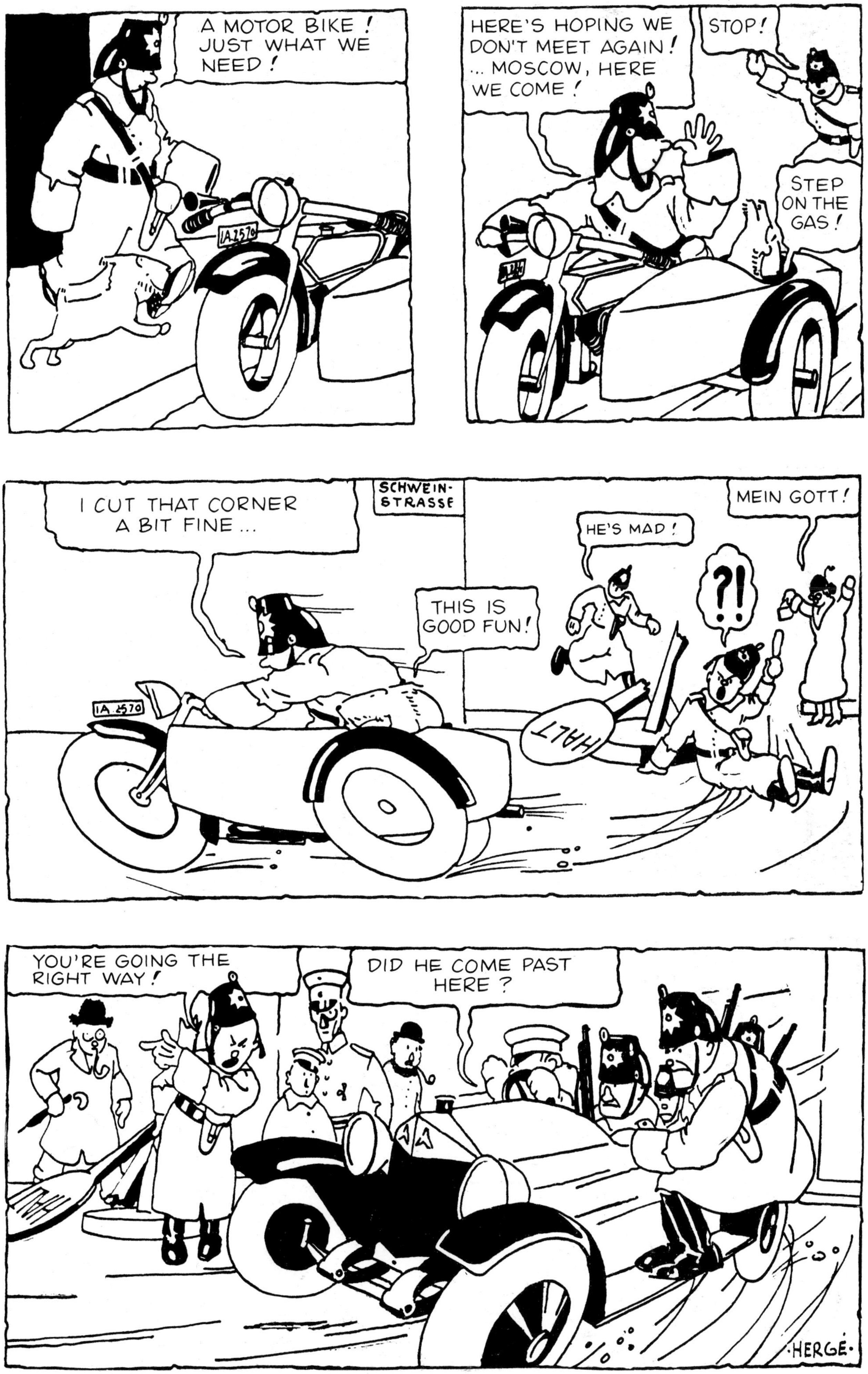
A MOTOR BIKE ! JUST WHAT WE NEED !
HERE'S HOPING WE DON'T MEET AGAIN ! ... MOSCOW, HERE WE COME !
STOP !
STEP ON THE GAS !
I CUT THAT CORNER A BIT FINE ...
SCHWEIN-STRASSE
THIS IS GOOD FUN !
HE'S MAD !
?!
MEIN GOTT !
HALT
YOU'RE GOING THE RIGHT WAY !
DID HE COME PAST HERE ?
HALT
IA 2570
·HERGÉ·

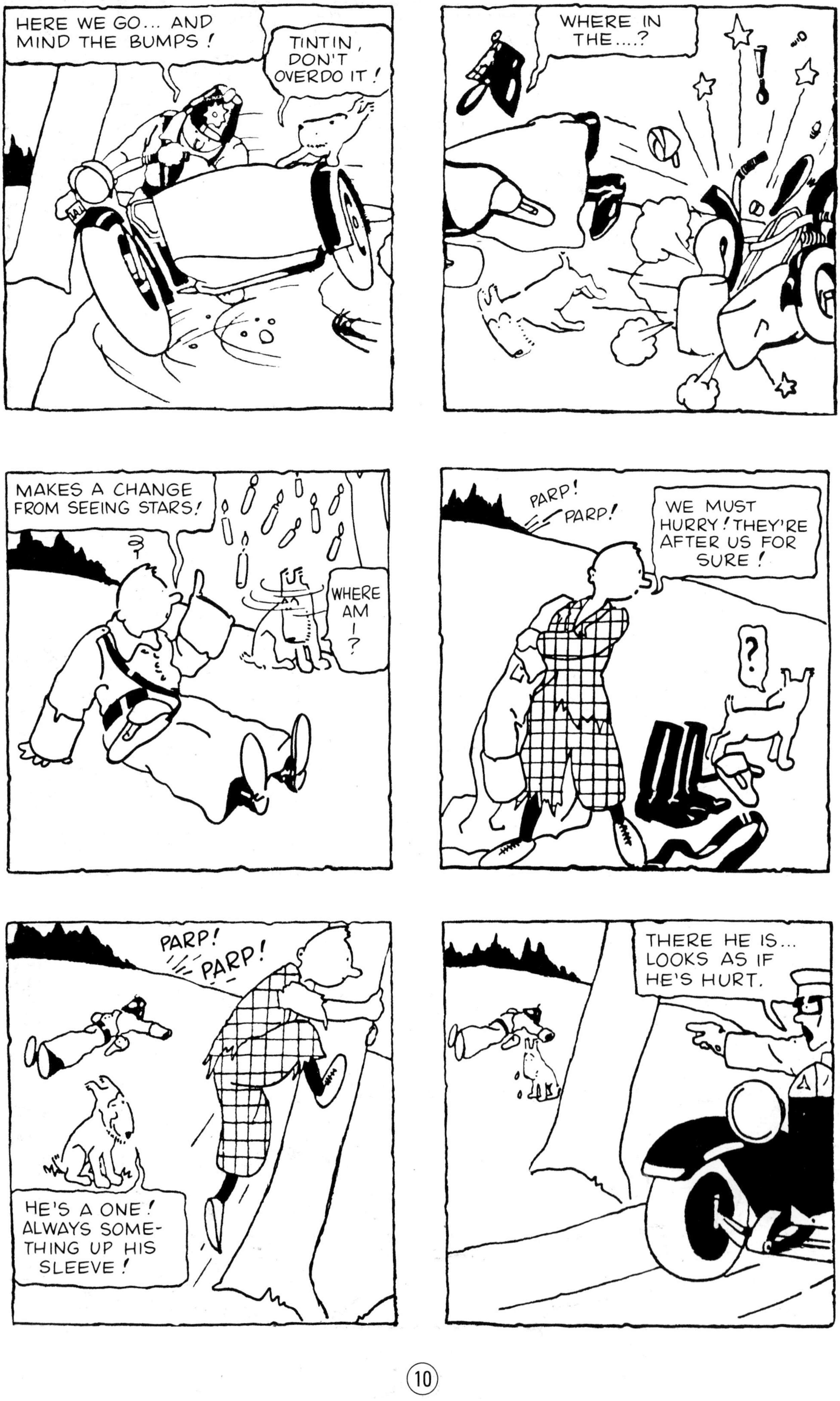
HERE WE GO... AND MIND THE BUMPS!
TINTIN, DON'T OVERDO IT!
WHERE IN THE....?
MAKES A CHANGE FROM SEEING STARS!
WHERE AM I?
PARP! PARP!
WE MUST HURRY! THEY'RE AFTER US FOR SURE!
?
PARP! PARP!
HE'S A ONE! ALWAYS SOMETHING UP HIS SLEEVE!
THERE HE IS... LOOKS AS IF HE'S HURT.

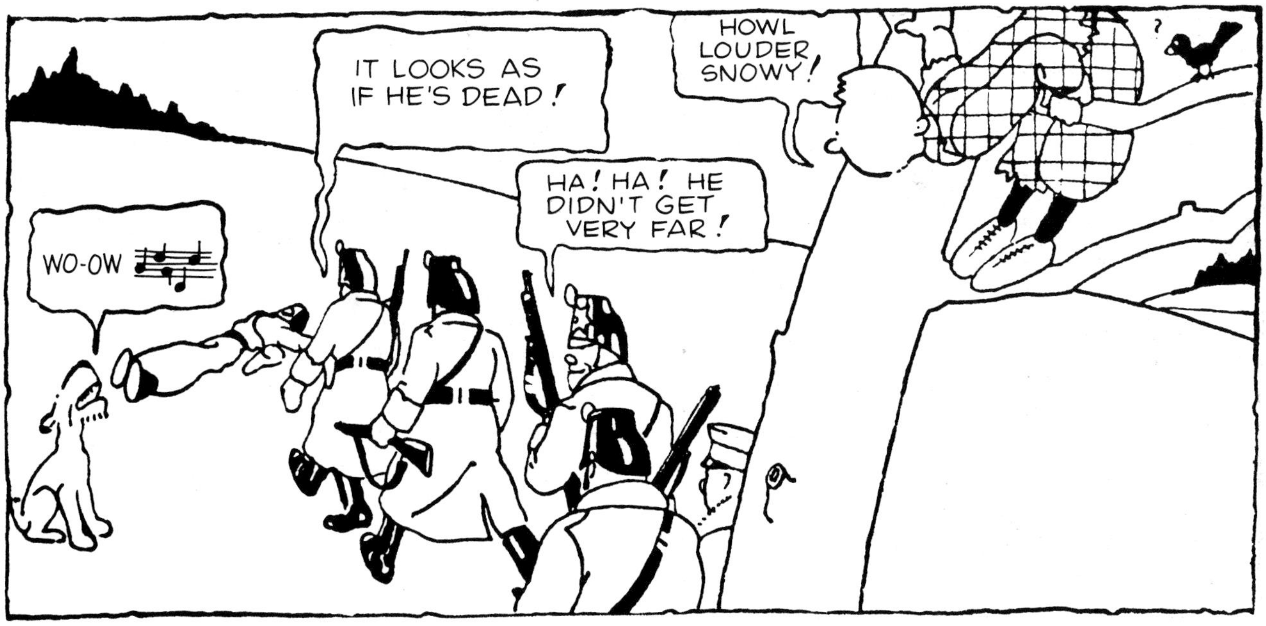
HOWL LOUDER SNOWY!
IT LOOKS AS IF HE'S DEAD!
HA! HA! HE DIDN'T GET VERY FAR!
WO-OW

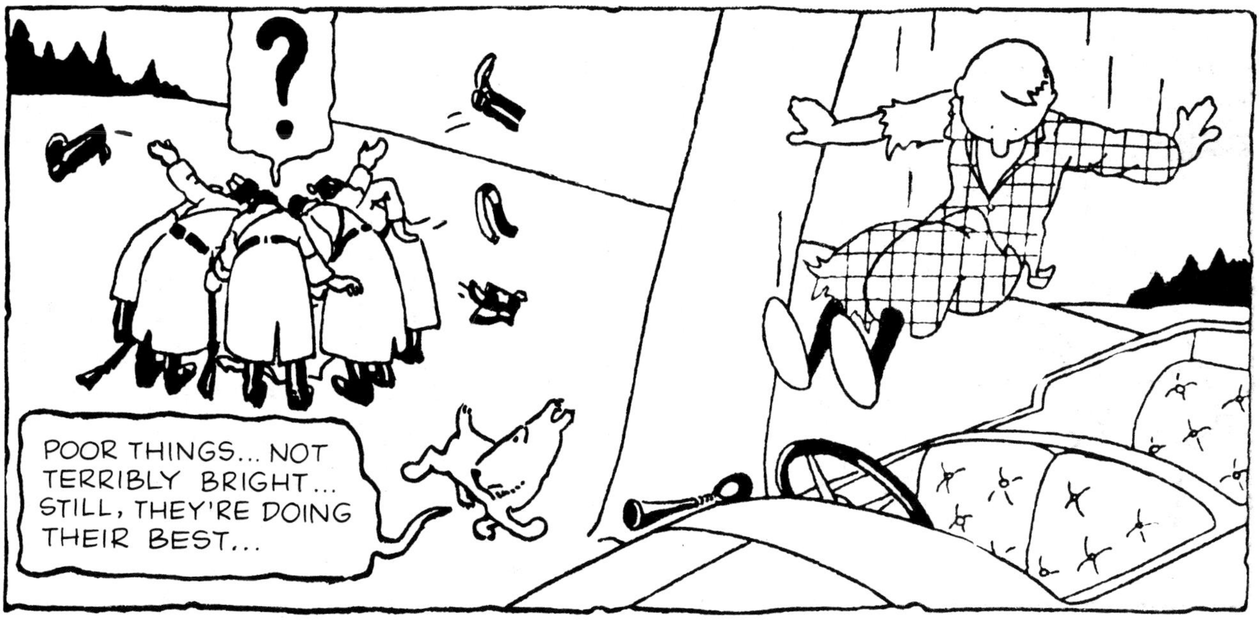
?
POOR THINGS... NOT TERRIBLY BRIGHT... STILL, THEY'RE DOING THEIR BEST...

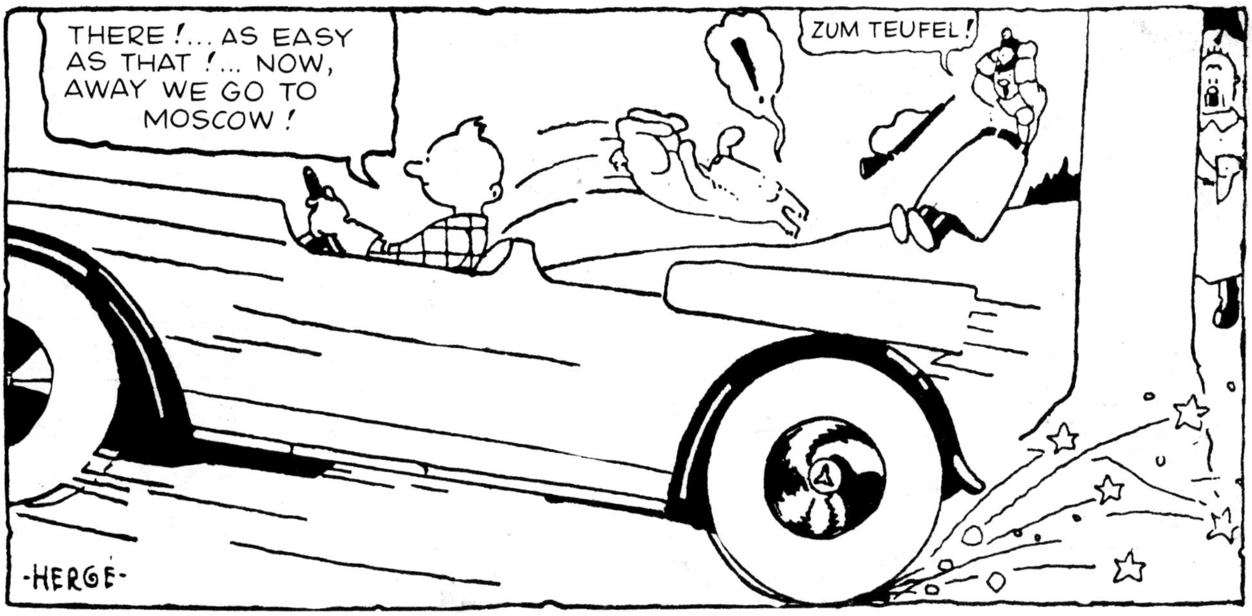
THERE!... AS EASY AS THAT!... NOW, AWAY WE GO TO MOSCOW!
!
ZUM TEUFEL!
-HERGE-

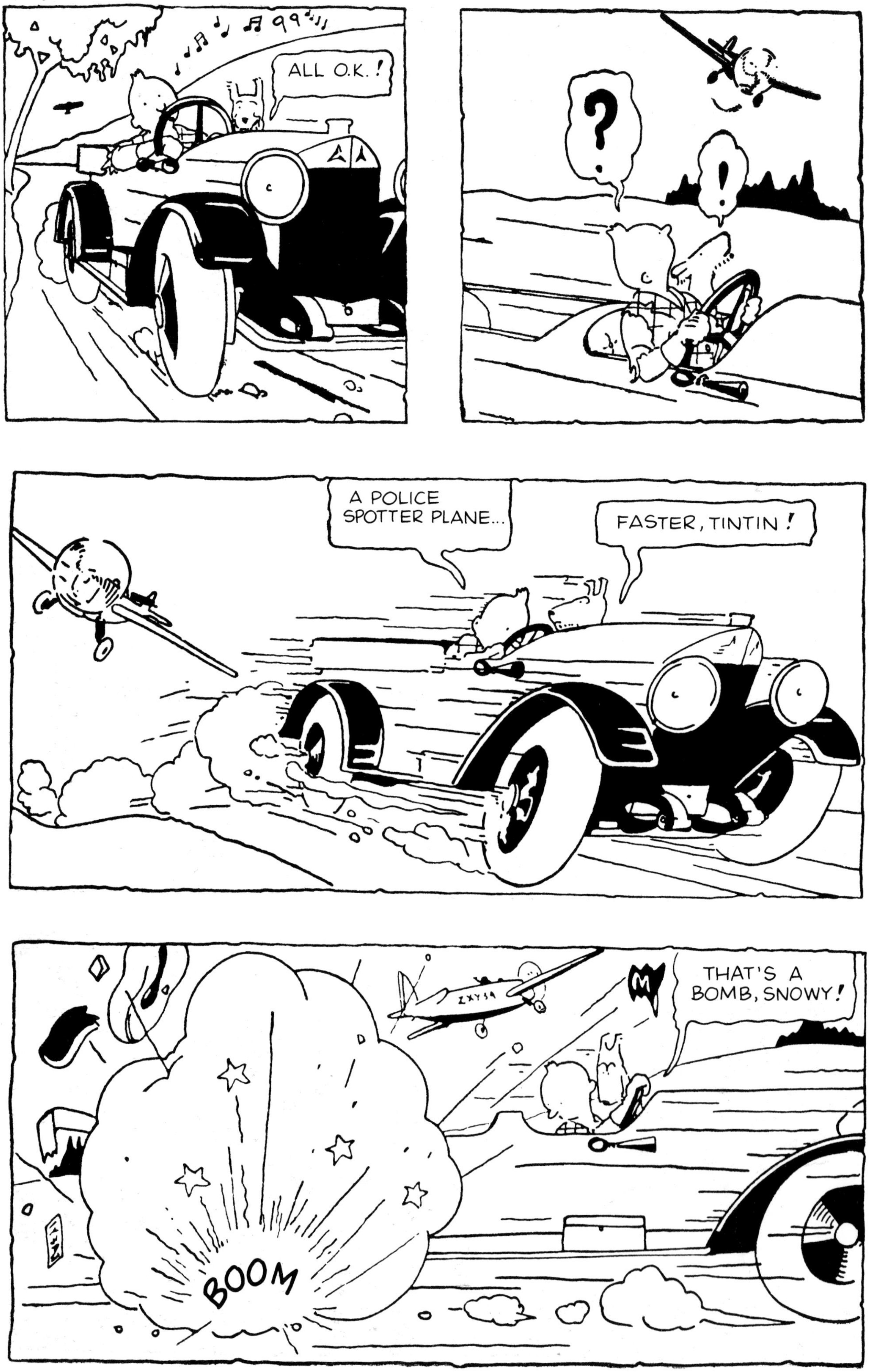
ALL O.K.!
?
!
A POLICE SPOTTER PLANE...
FASTER, TINTIN!
BOOM
THAT'S A BOMB, SNOWY!

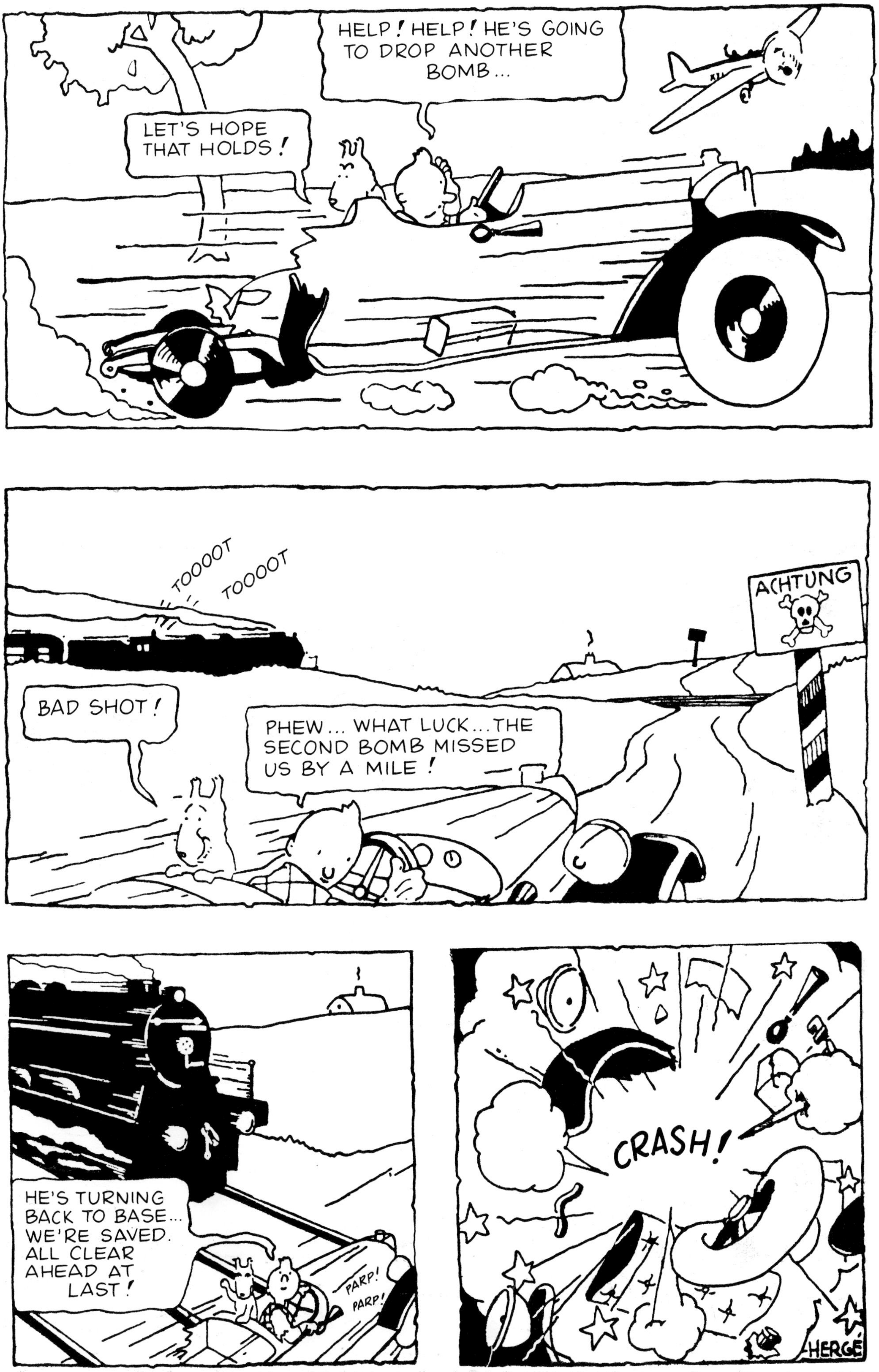
LET'S HOPE THAT HOLDS!
HELP! HELP! HE'S GOING TO DROP ANOTHER BOMB...
TOOOOT
TOOOOT
ACHTUNG
BAD SHOT!
PHEW... WHAT LUCK... THE SECOND BOMB MISSED US BY A MILE!
HE'S TURNING BACK TO BASE... WE'RE SAVED. ALL CLEAR AHEAD AT LAST!
PARP! PARP!
CRASH!
HERGÉ

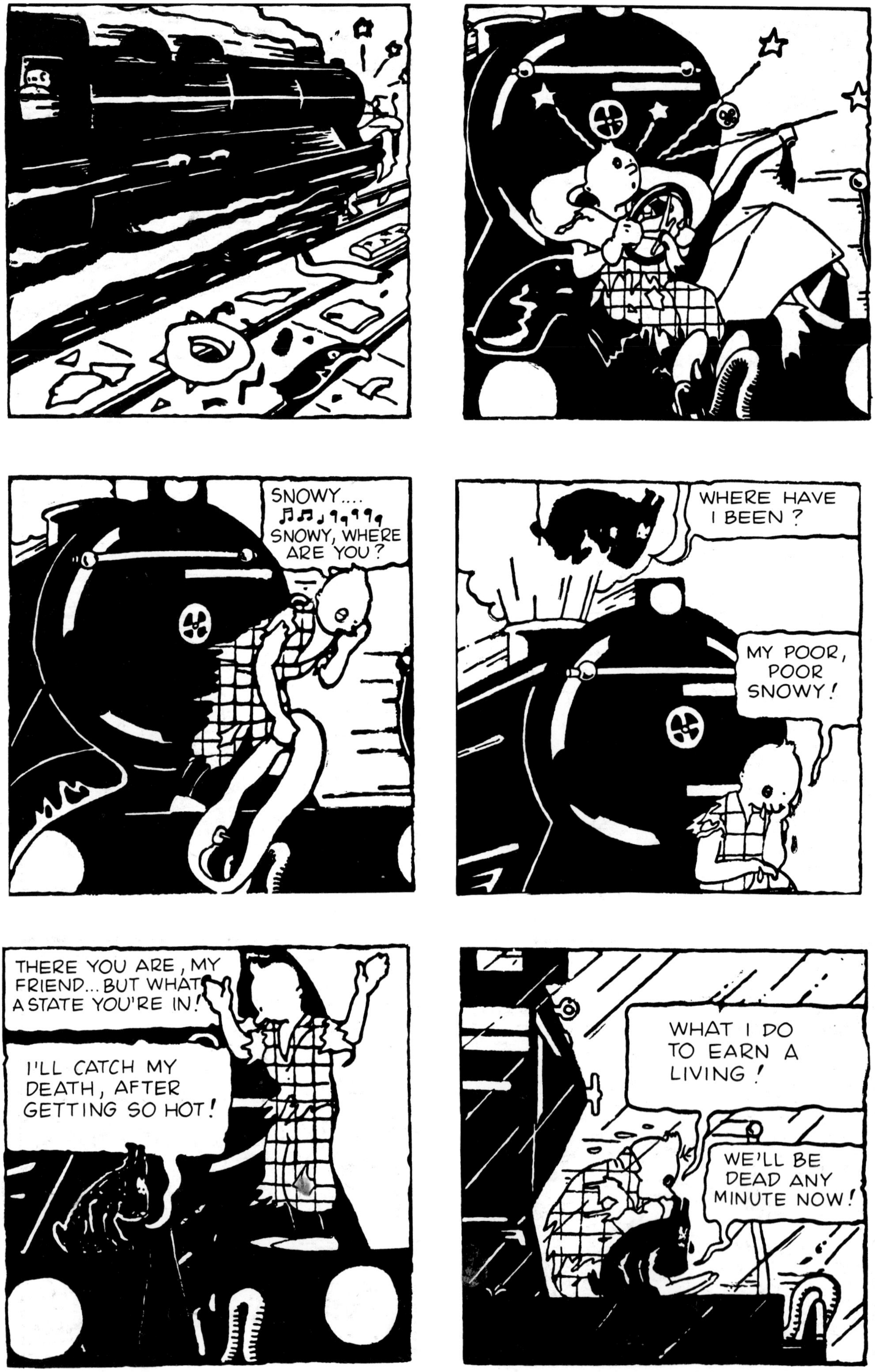
SNOWY.... SNOWY, WHERE ARE YOU?
WHERE HAVE I BEEN?
MY POOR, POOR SNOWY!
THERE YOU ARE, MY FRIEND... BUT WHAT A STATE YOU'RE IN!
I'LL CATCH MY DEATH, AFTER GETTING SO HOT!
WHAT I DO TO EARN A LIVING!
WE'LL BE DEAD ANY MINUTE NOW!

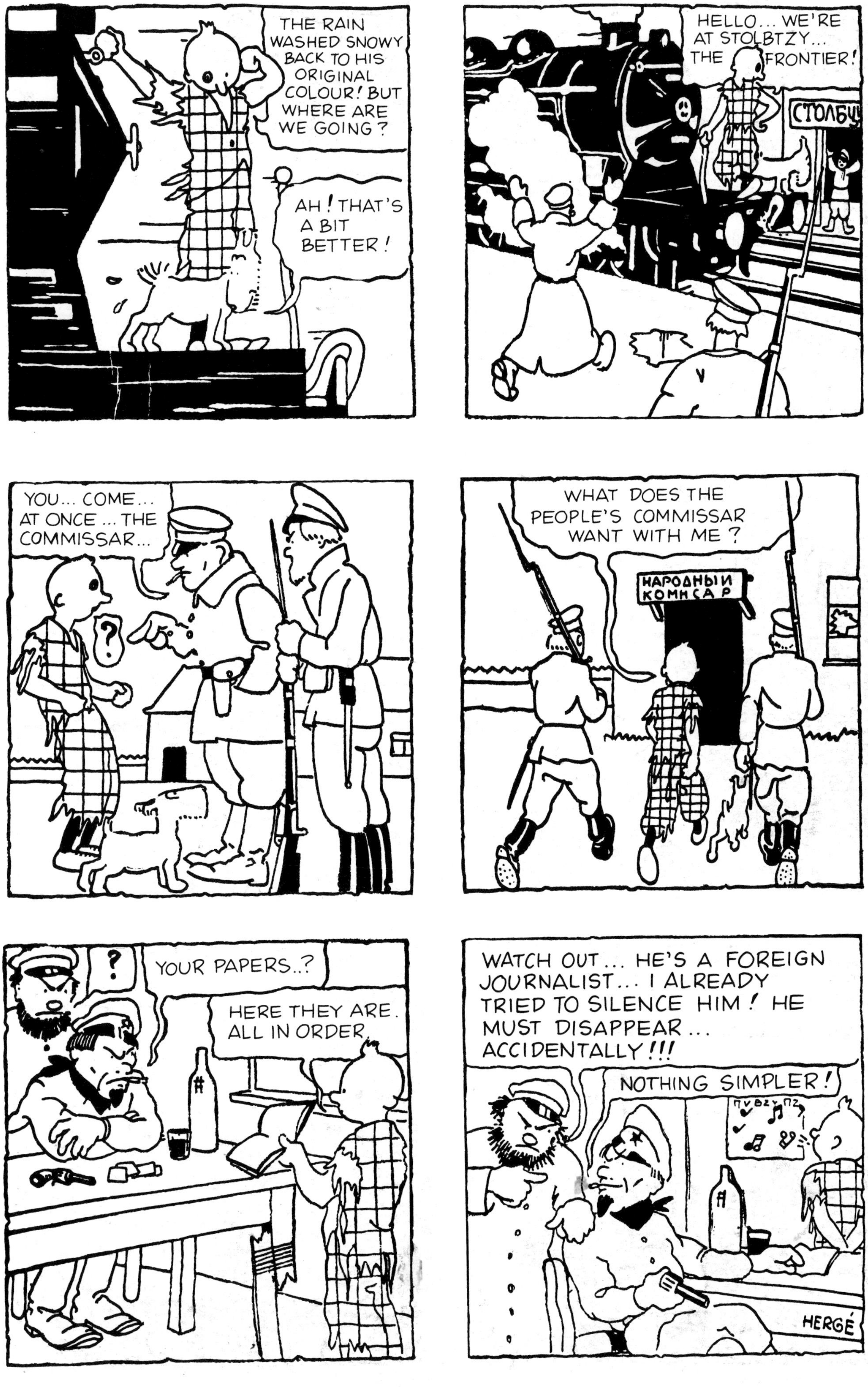
THE RAIN WASHED SNOWY BACK TO HIS ORIGINAL COLOUR! BUT WHERE ARE WE GOING?
AH! THAT'S A BIT BETTER!
HELLO... WE'RE AT STOLBTZY... THE FRONTIER!
СТОЛБЦ
YOU... COME... AT ONCE... THE COMMISSAR...
WHAT DOES THE PEOPLE'S COMMISSAR WANT WITH ME?
НАРОДНЫИ КОМНСАР
YOUR PAPERS..?
HERE THEY ARE. ALL IN ORDER.
WATCH OUT... HE'S A FOREIGN JOURNALIST... I ALREADY TRIED TO SILENCE HIM! HE MUST DISAPPEAR... ACCIDENTALLY!!!
NOTHING SIMPLER!
HERGÉ

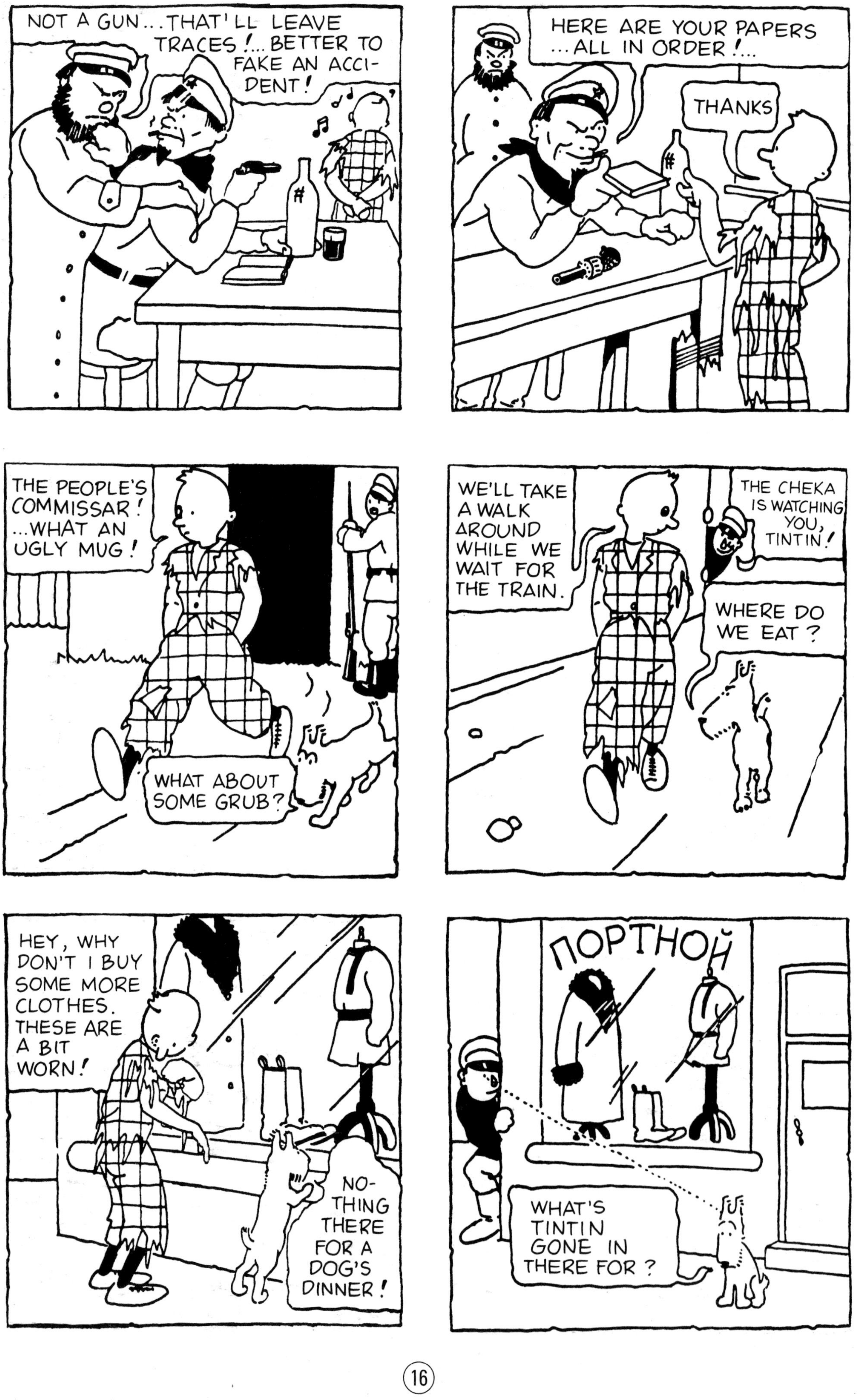
NOT A GUN... THAT'LL LEAVE TRACES!... BETTER TO FAKE AN ACCI-DENT!
HERE ARE YOUR PAPERS ...ALL IN ORDER!...
THANKS
THE PEOPLE'S COMMISSAR! ...WHAT AN UGLY MUG!
WHAT ABOUT SOME GRUB?
WE'LL TAKE A WALK AROUND WHILE WE WAIT FOR THE TRAIN.
THE CHEKA IS WATCHING YOU, TINTIN!
WHERE DO WE EAT?
HEY, WHY DON'T I BUY SOME MORE CLOTHES. THESE ARE A BIT WORN!
NO-THING THERE FOR A DOG'S DINNER!
ПОРТНОЙ
WHAT'S TINTIN GONE IN THERE FOR?

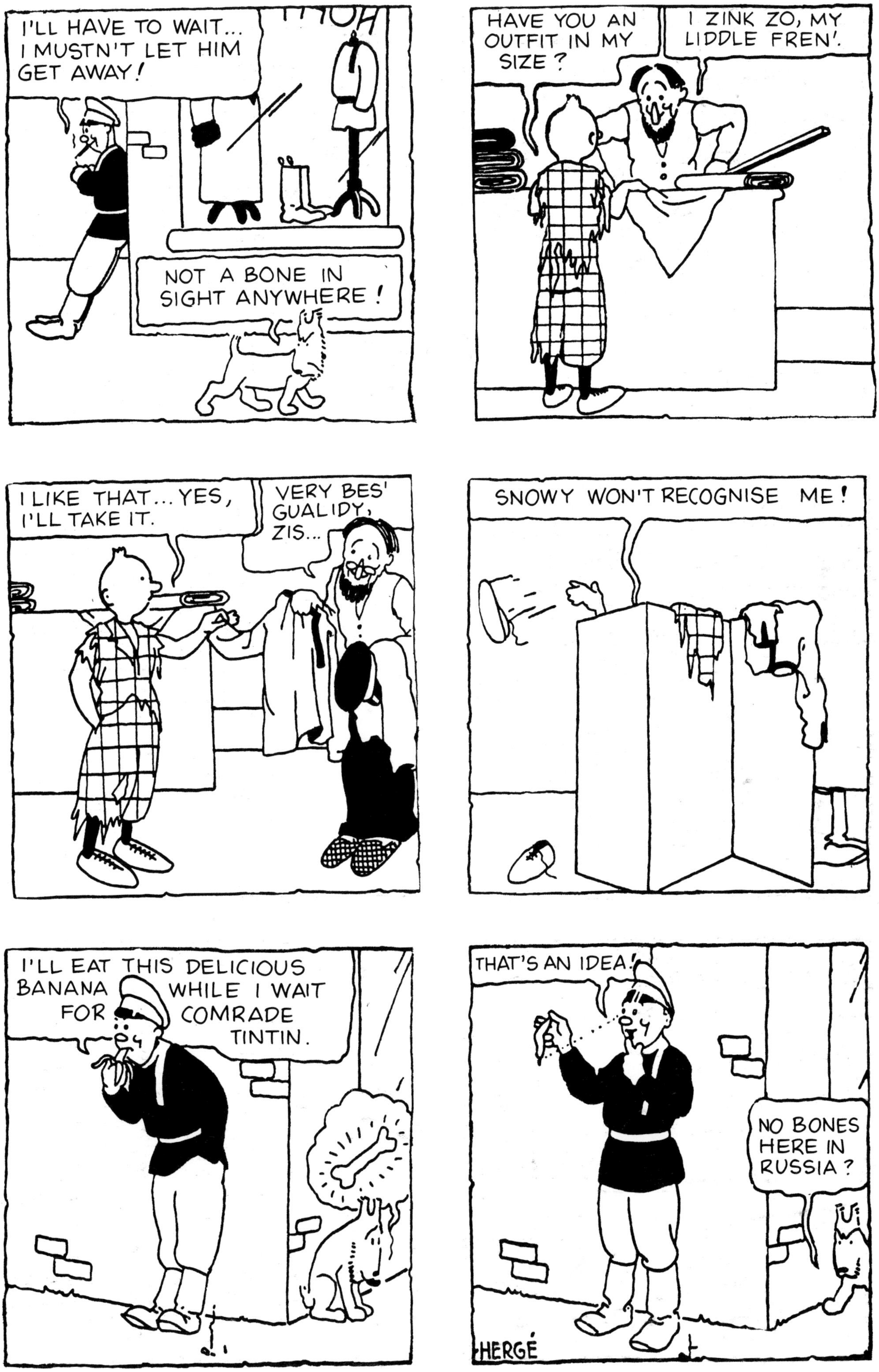
I'LL HAVE TO WAIT... I MUSTN'T LET HIM GET AWAY!
NOT A BONE IN SIGHT ANYWHERE!
HAVE YOU AN OUTFIT IN MY SIZE?
I ZINK ZO, MY LIDDLE FREN'.
I LIKE THAT... YES, I'LL TAKE IT.
VERY BES' GUALIDY, ZIS...
SNOWY WON'T RECOGNISE ME!
I'LL EAT THIS DELICIOUS BANANA WHILE I WAIT FOR COMRADE TINTIN.
THAT'S AN IDEA!
NO BONES HERE IN RUSSIA?
HERGÉ

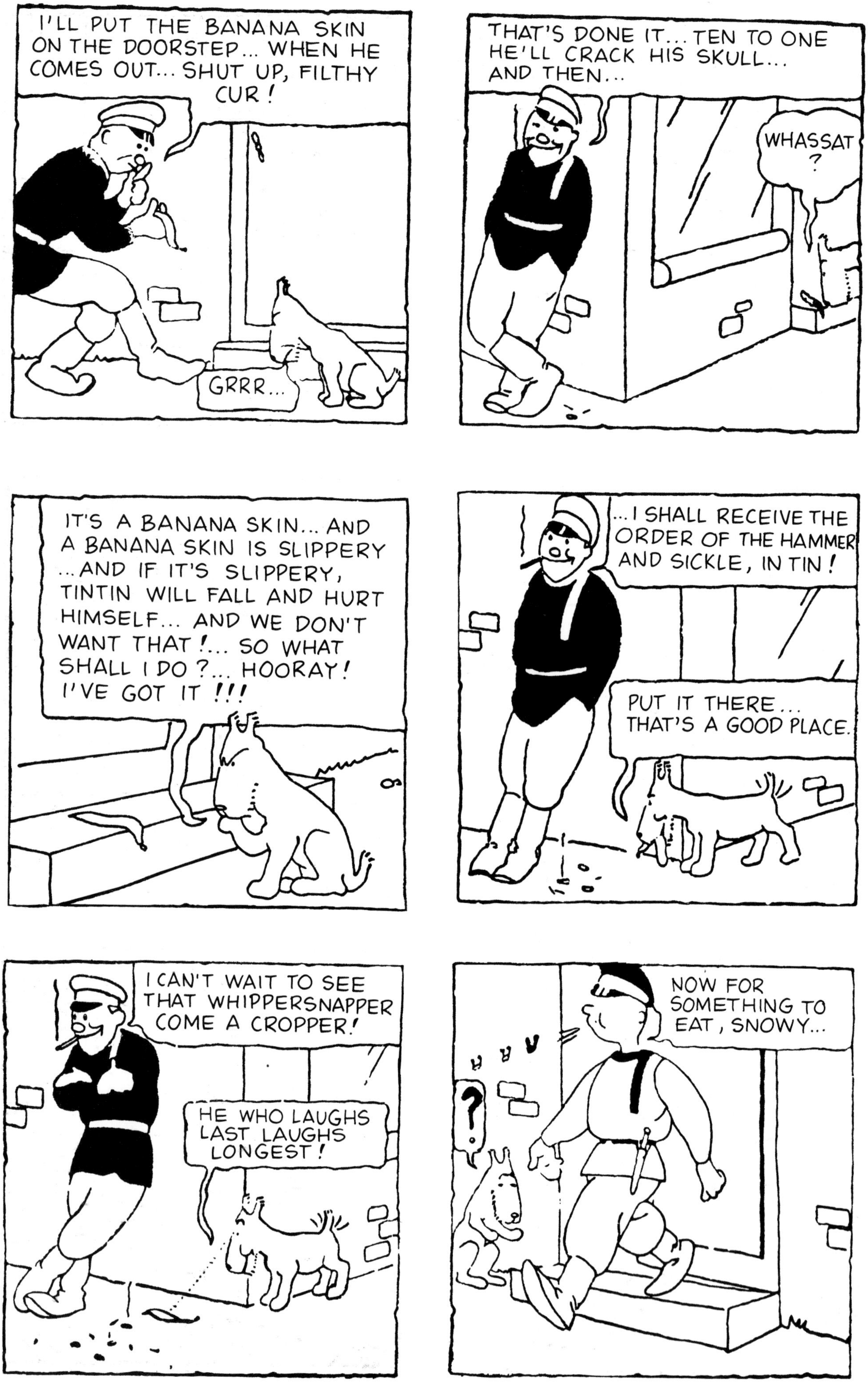
I'LL PUT THE BANANA SKIN ON THE DOORSTEP... WHEN HE COMES OUT... SHUT UP, FILTHY CUR!
GRRR...
THAT'S DONE IT... TEN TO ONE HE'LL CRACK HIS SKULL... AND THEN...
WHASSAT?
IT'S A BANANA SKIN... AND A BANANA SKIN IS SLIPPERY ...AND IF IT'S SLIPPERY, TINTIN WILL FALL AND HURT HIMSELF... AND WE DON'T WANT THAT!... SO WHAT SHALL I DO?... HOORAY! I'VE GOT IT!!!
...I SHALL RECEIVE THE ORDER OF THE HAMMER AND SICKLE, IN TIN!
PUT IT THERE... THAT'S A GOOD PLACE.
I CAN'T WAIT TO SEE THAT WHIPPERSNAPPER COME A CROPPER!
HE WHO LAUGHS LAST LAUGHS LONGEST!
NOW FOR SOMETHING TO EAT, SNOWY...
?

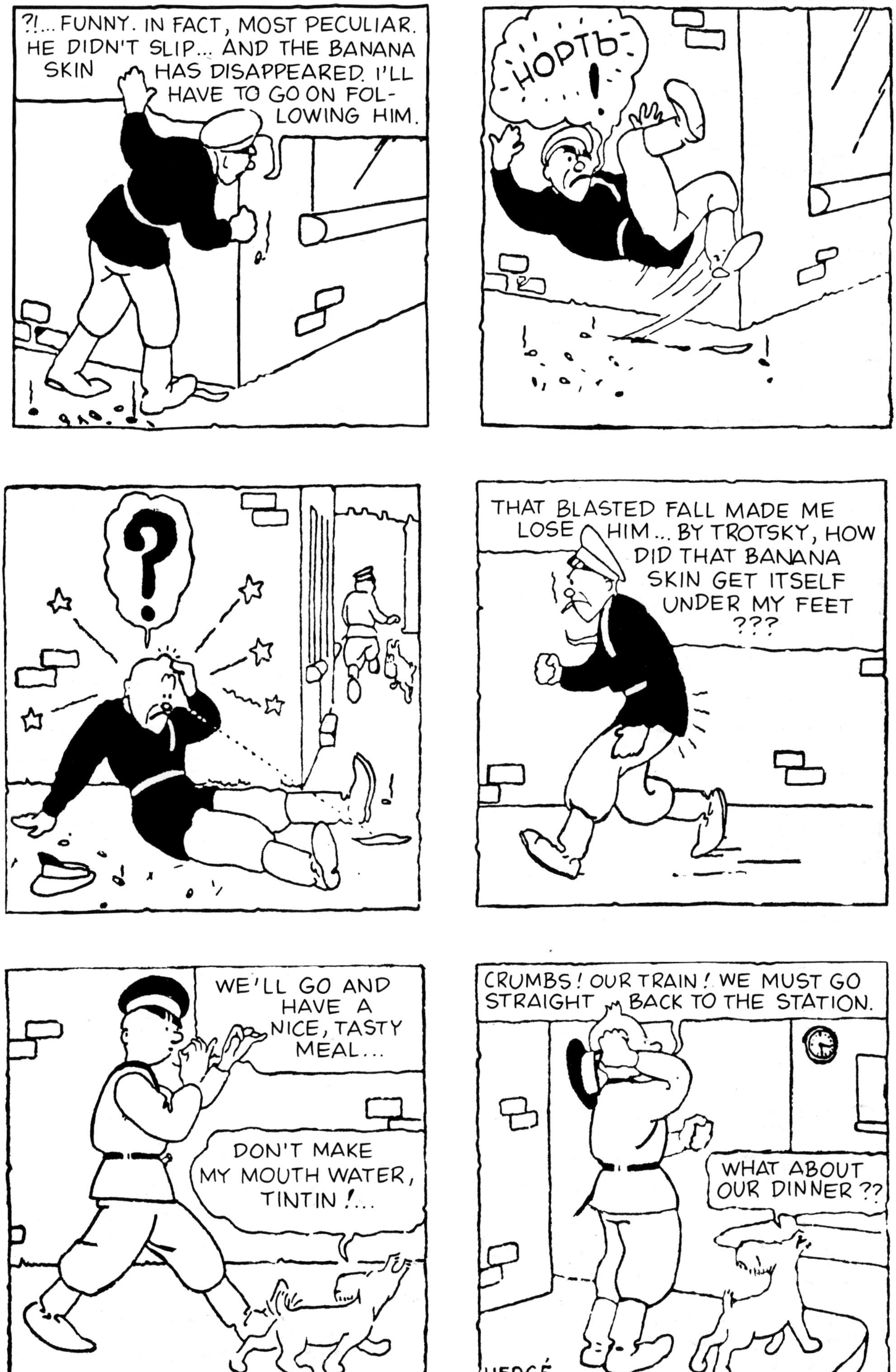
?!... FUNNY. IN FACT, MOST PECULIAR. HE DIDN'T SLIP... AND THE BANANA SKIN HAS DISAPPEARED. I'LL HAVE TO GO ON FOL-LOWING HIM.
НОРТЬ !
?
THAT BLASTED FALL MADE ME LOSE HIM... BY TROTSKY, HOW DID THAT BANANA SKIN GET ITSELF UNDER MY FEET ???
WE'LL GO AND HAVE A NICE, TASTY MEAL...
DON'T MAKE MY MOUTH WATER, TINTIN !...
CRUMBS! OUR TRAIN! WE MUST GO STRAIGHT BACK TO THE STATION.
WHAT ABOUT OUR DINNER ??
HERGÉ

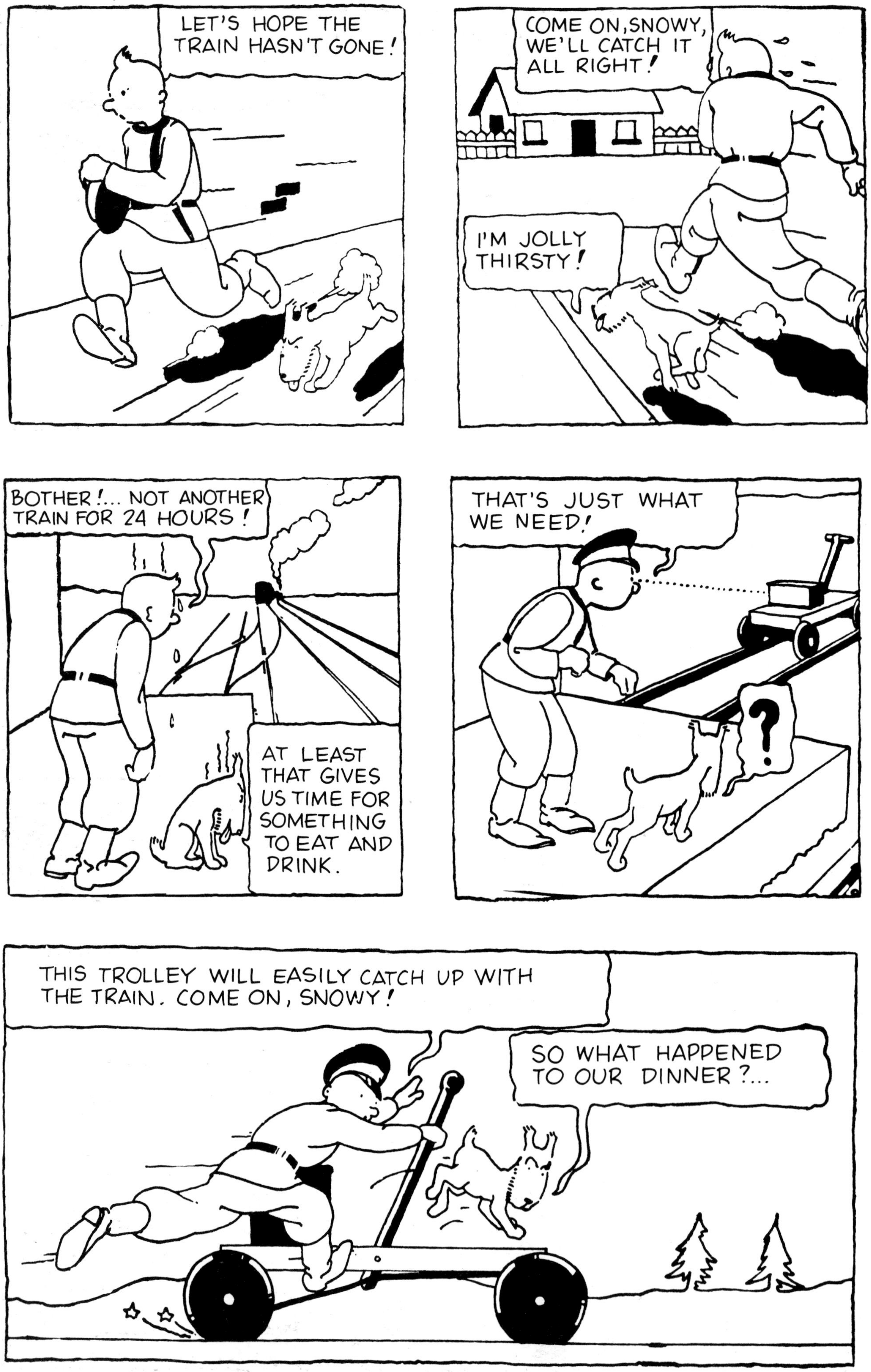
LET'S HOPE THE TRAIN HASN'T GONE!
COME ON, SNOWY, WE'LL CATCH IT ALL RIGHT!
I'M JOLLY THIRSTY!
BOTHER!... NOT ANOTHER TRAIN FOR 24 HOURS!
AT LEAST THAT GIVES US TIME FOR SOMETHING TO EAT AND DRINK.
THAT'S JUST WHAT WE NEED!
?
THIS TROLLEY WILL EASILY CATCH UP WITH THE TRAIN. COME ON, SNOWY!
SO WHAT HAPPENED TO OUR DINNER?...

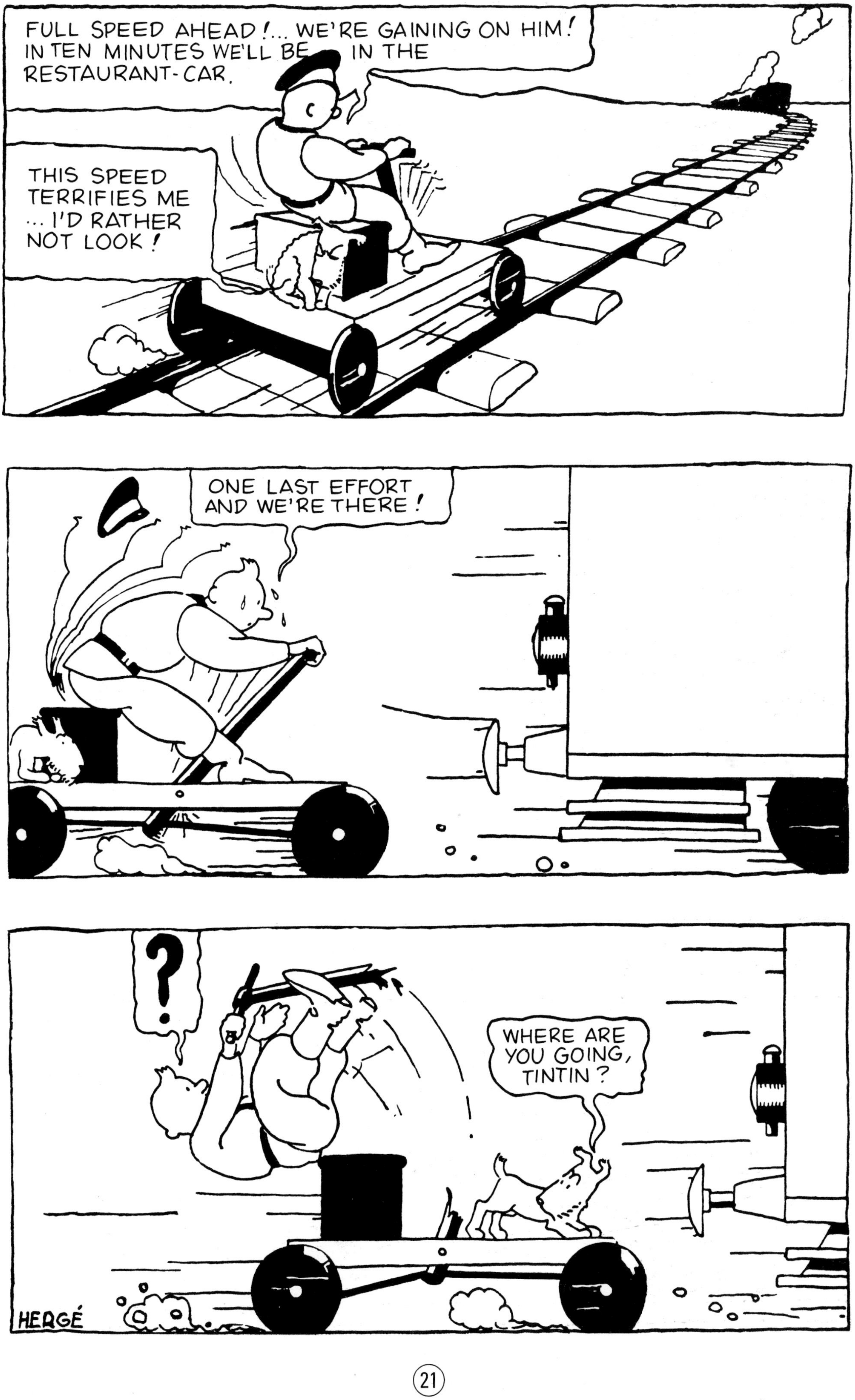
FULL SPEED AHEAD!... WE'RE GAINING ON HIM! IN TEN MINUTES WE'LL BE IN THE RESTAURANT-CAR.
THIS SPEED TERRIFIES ME ... I'D RATHER NOT LOOK!
ONE LAST EFFORT AND WE'RE THERE!
?
WHERE ARE YOU GOING, TINTIN?
HERGÉ

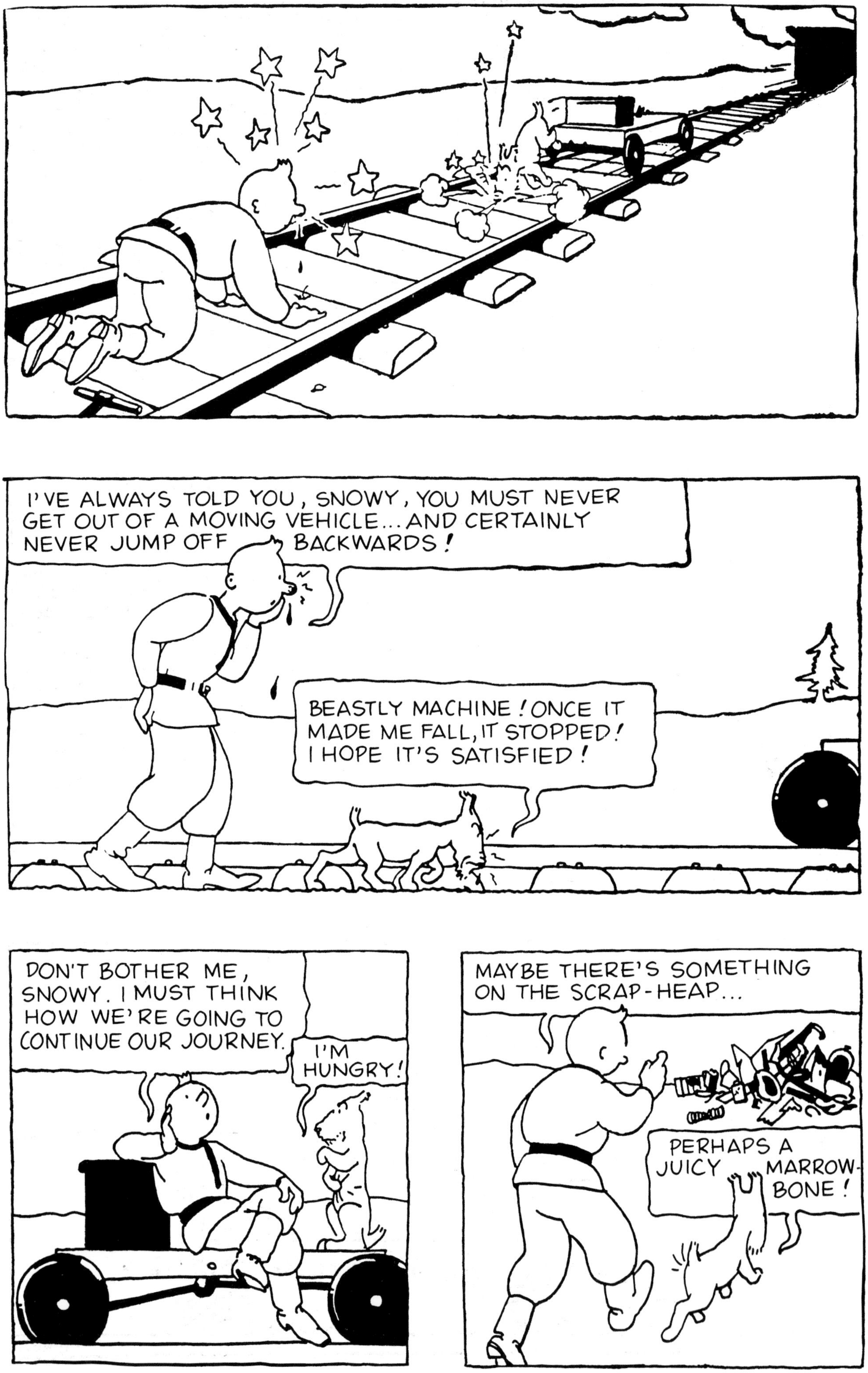
I'VE ALWAYS TOLD YOU, SNOWY, YOU MUST NEVER GET OUT OF A MOVING VEHICLE... AND CERTAINLY NEVER JUMP OFF BACKWARDS!
BEASTLY MACHINE! ONCE IT MADE ME FALL, IT STOPPED! I HOPE IT'S SATISFIED!
DON'T BOTHER ME, SNOWY. I MUST THINK HOW WE'RE GOING TO CONTINUE OUR JOURNEY.
I'M HUNGRY!
MAYBE THERE'S SOMETHING ON THE SCRAP-HEAP...
PERHAPS A JUICY MARROW-BONE!

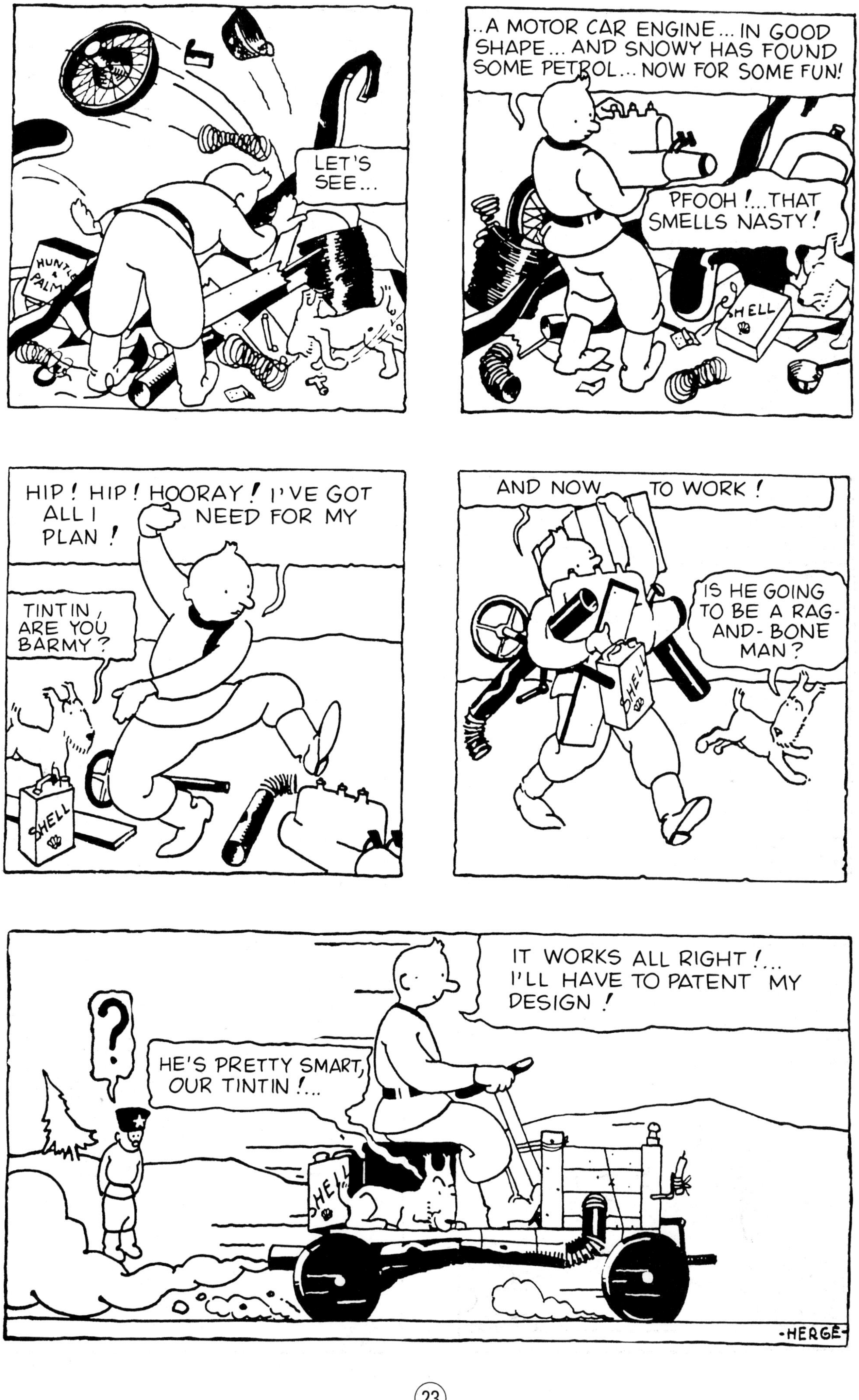
LET'S SEE...
..A MOTOR CAR ENGINE... IN GOOD SHAPE... AND SNOWY HAS FOUND SOME PETROL... NOW FOR SOME FUN!
PFOOH!...THAT SMELLS NASTY!
SHELL
HIP! HIP! HOORAY! I'VE GOT ALL I NEED FOR MY PLAN!
TINTIN, ARE YOU BARMY?
SHELL
AND NOW TO WORK!
IS HE GOING TO BE A RAG-AND-BONE MAN?
SHELL
IT WORKS ALL RIGHT!... I'LL HAVE TO PATENT MY DESIGN!
?
HE'S PRETTY SMART, OUR TINTIN!...
SHELL
-HERGÉ-

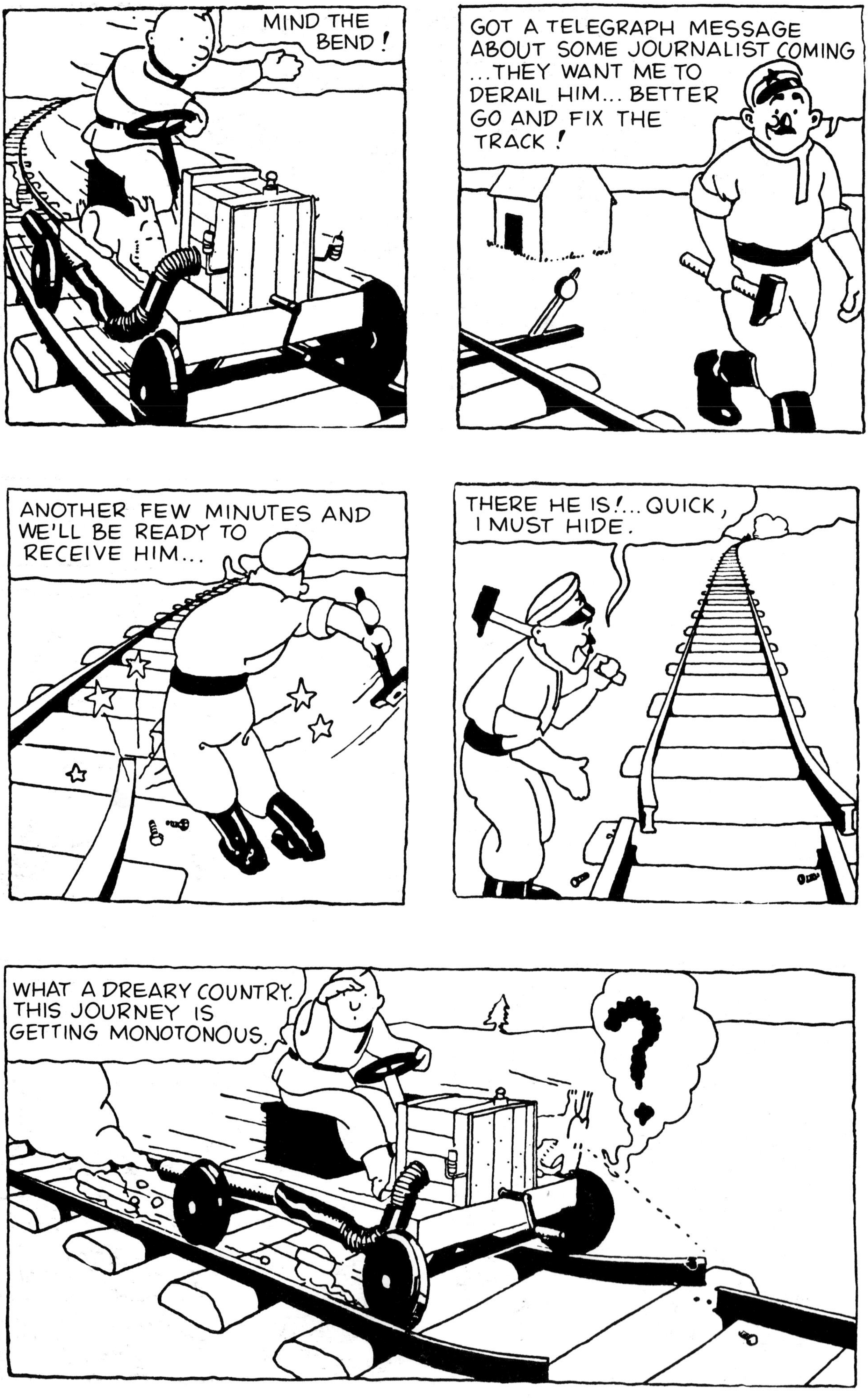
MIND THE BEND!
GOT A TELEGRAPH MESSAGE ABOUT SOME JOURNALIST COMING ...THEY WANT ME TO DERAIL HIM... BETTER GO AND FIX THE TRACK!
ANOTHER FEW MINUTES AND WE'LL BE READY TO RECEIVE HIM...
THERE HE IS!... QUICK, I MUST HIDE.
WHAT A DREARY COUNTRY. THIS JOURNEY IS GETTING MONOTONOUS.
?

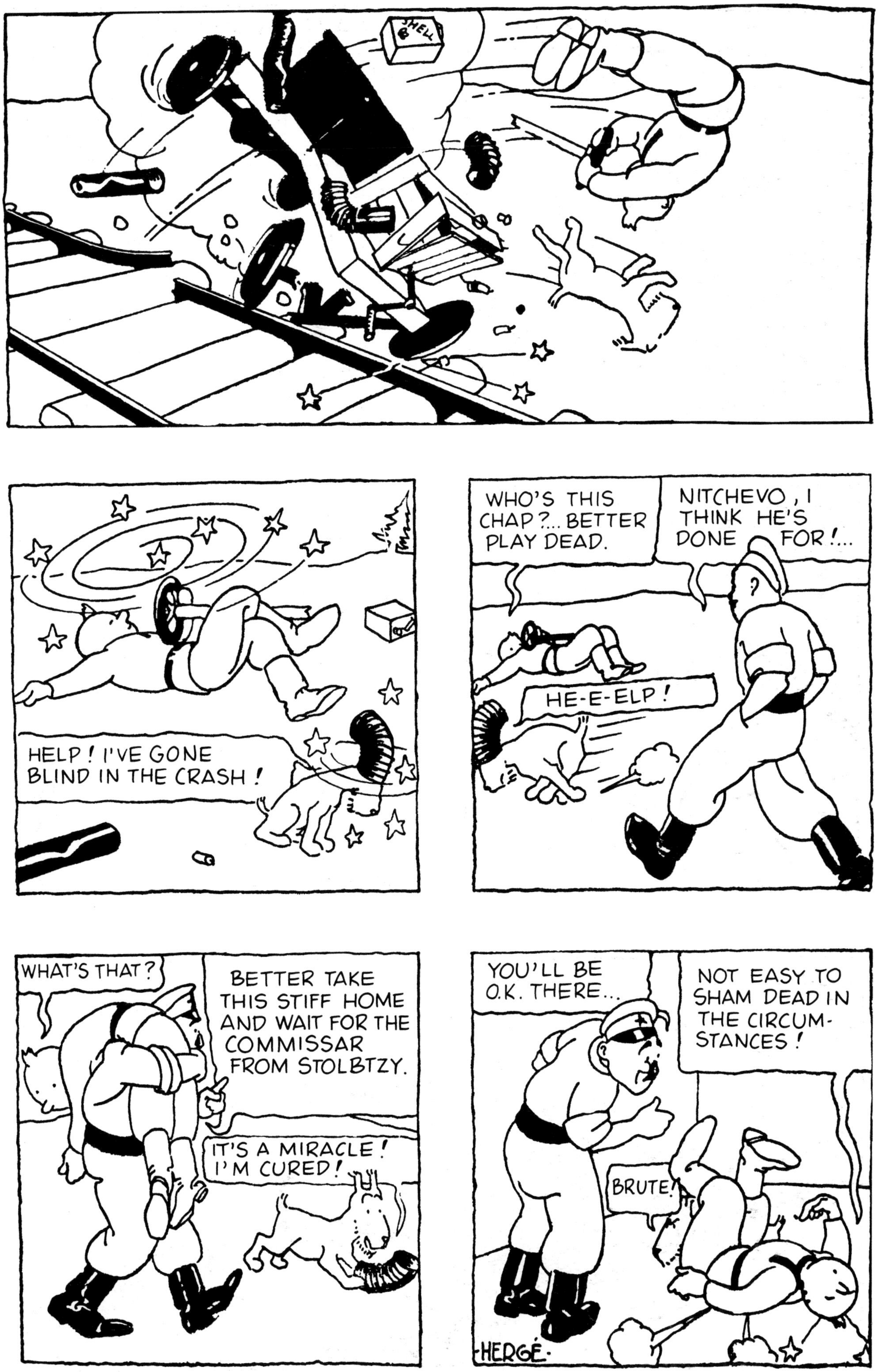
SHELL
HELP! I'VE GONE BLIND IN THE CRASH!
WHO'S THIS CHAP?... BETTER PLAY DEAD.
NITCHEVO, I THINK HE'S DONE FOR!...
HE-E-ELP!
WHAT'S THAT?
BETTER TAKE THIS STIFF HOME AND WAIT FOR THE COMMISSAR FROM STOLBTZY.
IT'S A MIRACLE! I'M CURED!
YOU'LL BE O.K. THERE...
NOT EASY TO SHAM DEAD IN THE CIRCUMSTANCES!
BRUTE!
HERGÉ

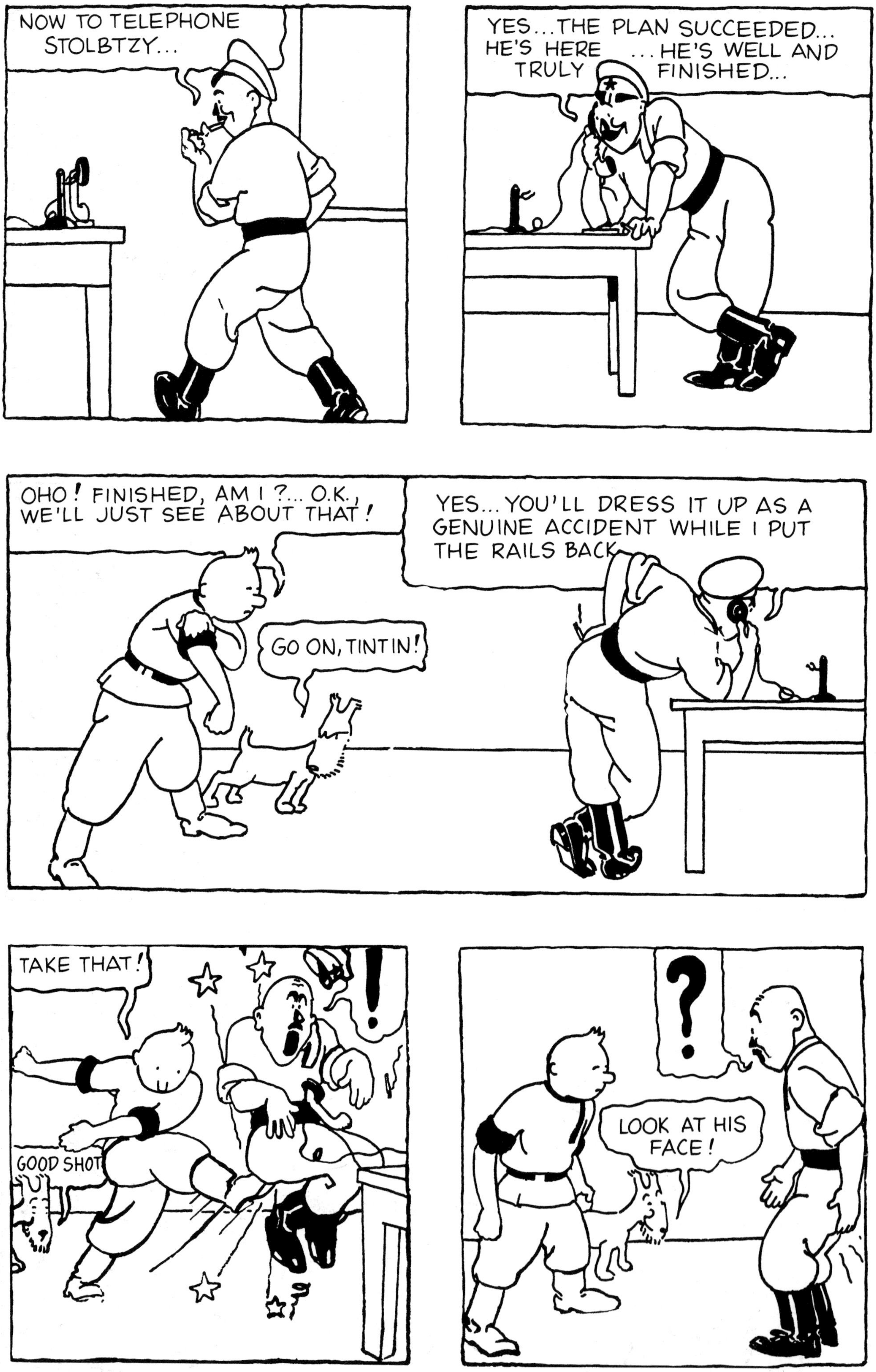

NOW TO TELEPHONE STOLBTZY...
YES...THE PLAN SUCCEEDED... HE'S HERE ...HE'S WELL AND TRULY FINISHED...
OHO! FINISHED, AM I ?... O.K., WE'LL JUST SEE ABOUT THAT!
YES... YOU'LL DRESS IT UP AS A GENUINE ACCIDENT WHILE I PUT THE RAILS BACK
GO ON, TINTIN!
TAKE THAT!
GOOD SHOT
LOOK AT HIS FACE!

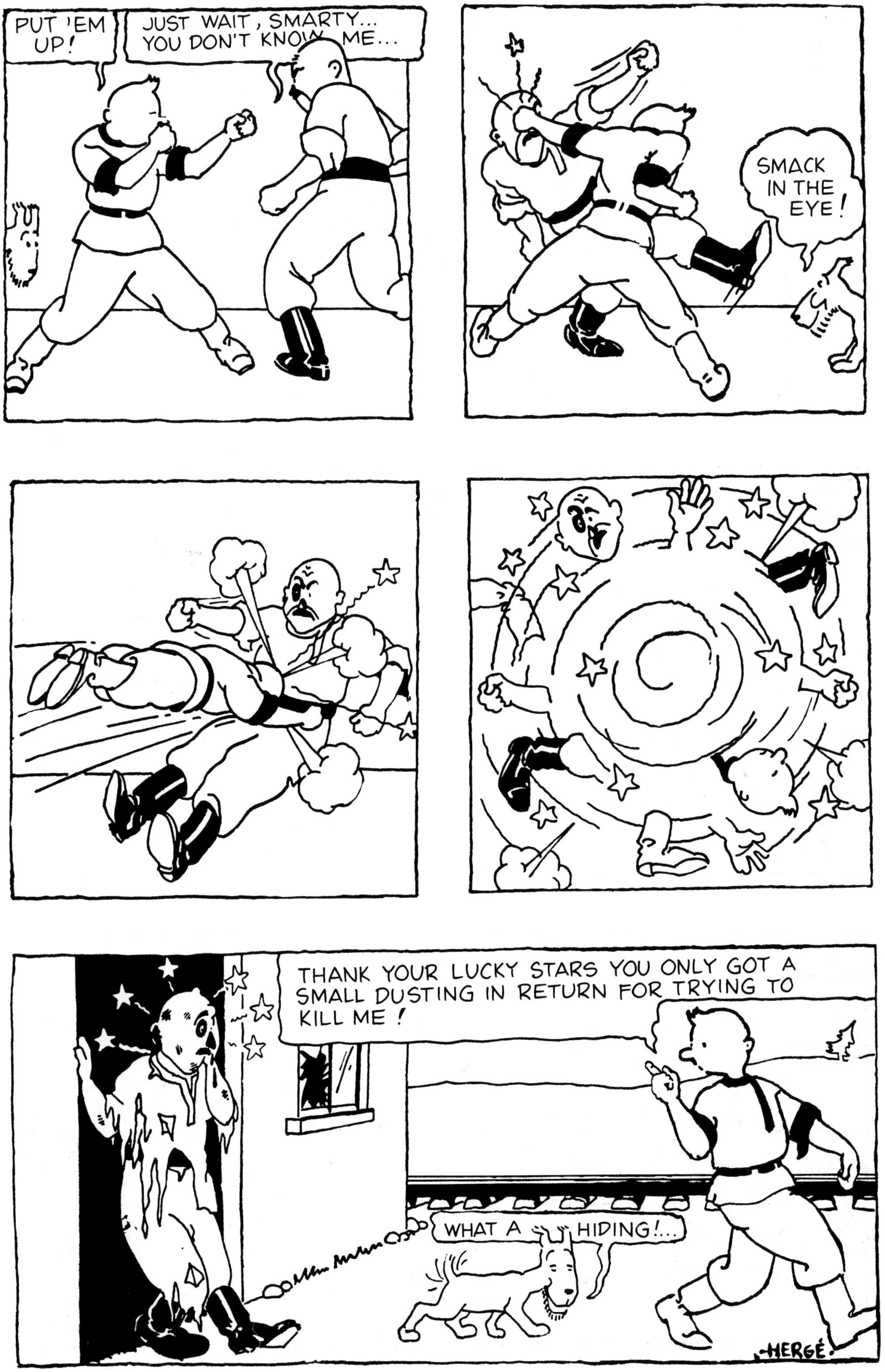

PUT 'EM UP!
JUST WAIT, SMARTY... YOU DON'T KNOW ME...
SMACK IN THE EYE!
THANK YOUR LUCKY STARS YOU ONLY GOT A SMALL DUSTING IN RETURN FOR TRYING TO KILL ME!
WHAT A HIDING!...
HERGÉ

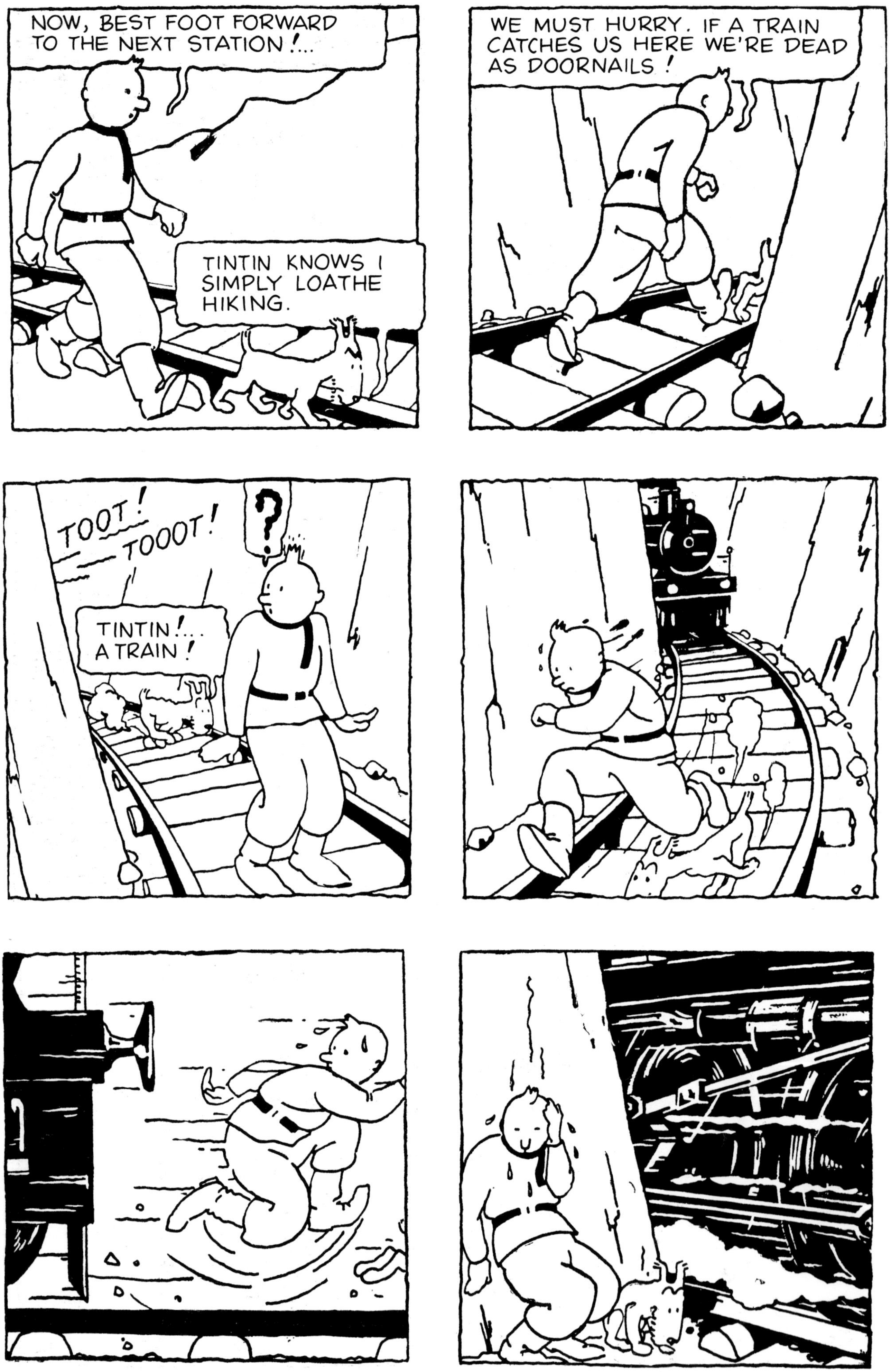
NOW, BEST FOOT FORWARD TO THE NEXT STATION !...
TINTIN KNOWS I SIMPLY LOATHE HIKING.
WE MUST HURRY. IF A TRAIN CATCHES US HERE WE'RE DEAD AS DOORNAILS !
TOOT ! TOOOT !
?
TINTIN !... A TRAIN !

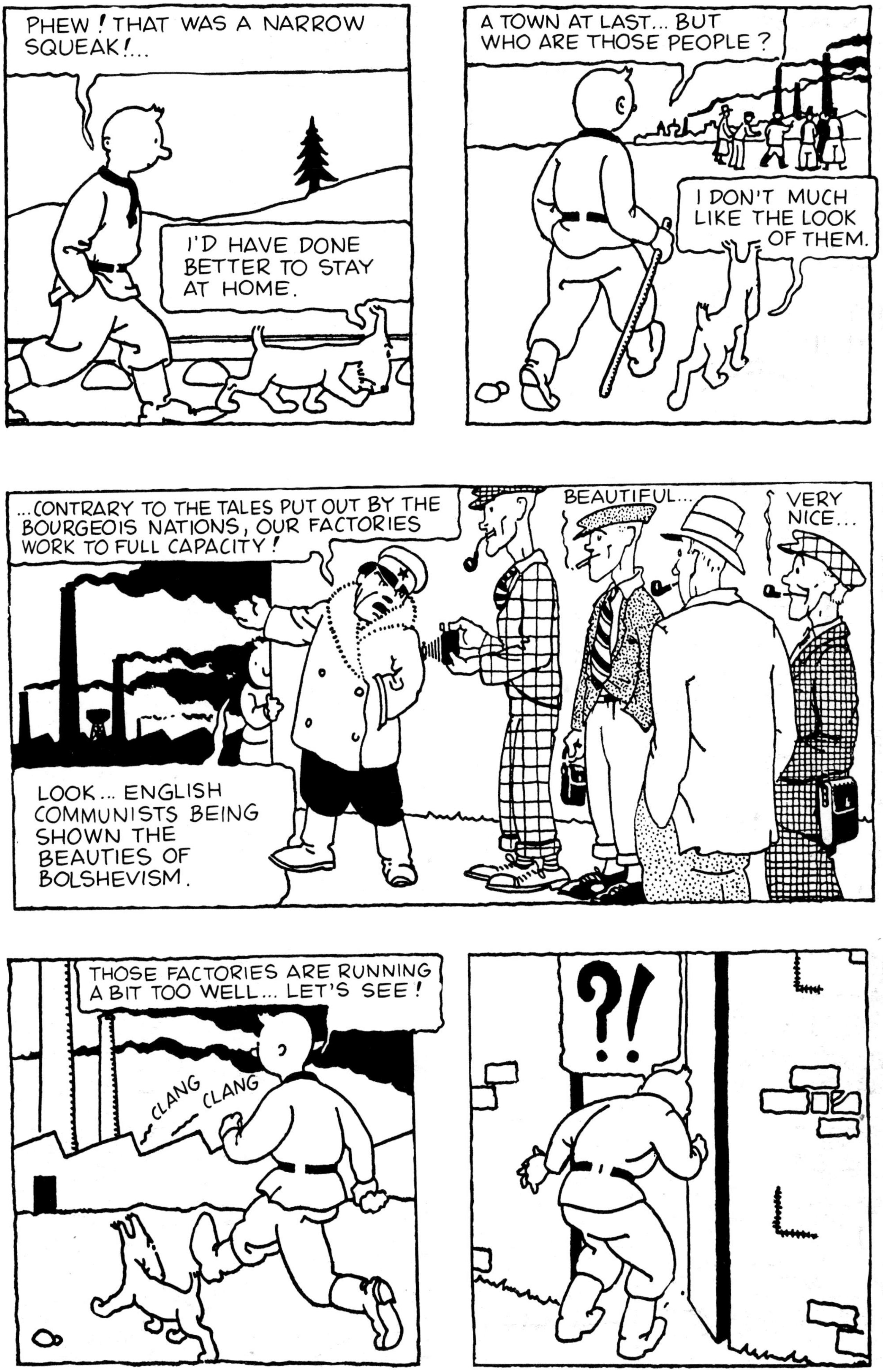
PHEW! THAT WAS A NARROW SQUEAK!...
I'D HAVE DONE BETTER TO STAY AT HOME.
A TOWN AT LAST... BUT WHO ARE THOSE PEOPLE?
I DON'T MUCH LIKE THE LOOK OF THEM.
...CONTRARY TO THE TALES PUT OUT BY THE BOURGEOIS NATIONS, OUR FACTORIES WORK TO FULL CAPACITY!
BEAUTIFUL...
VERY NICE...
LOOK... ENGLISH COMMUNISTS BEING SHOWN THE BEAUTIES OF BOLSHEVISM.
THOSE FACTORIES ARE RUNNING A BIT TOO WELL... LET'S SEE!
CLANG
CLANG
?!

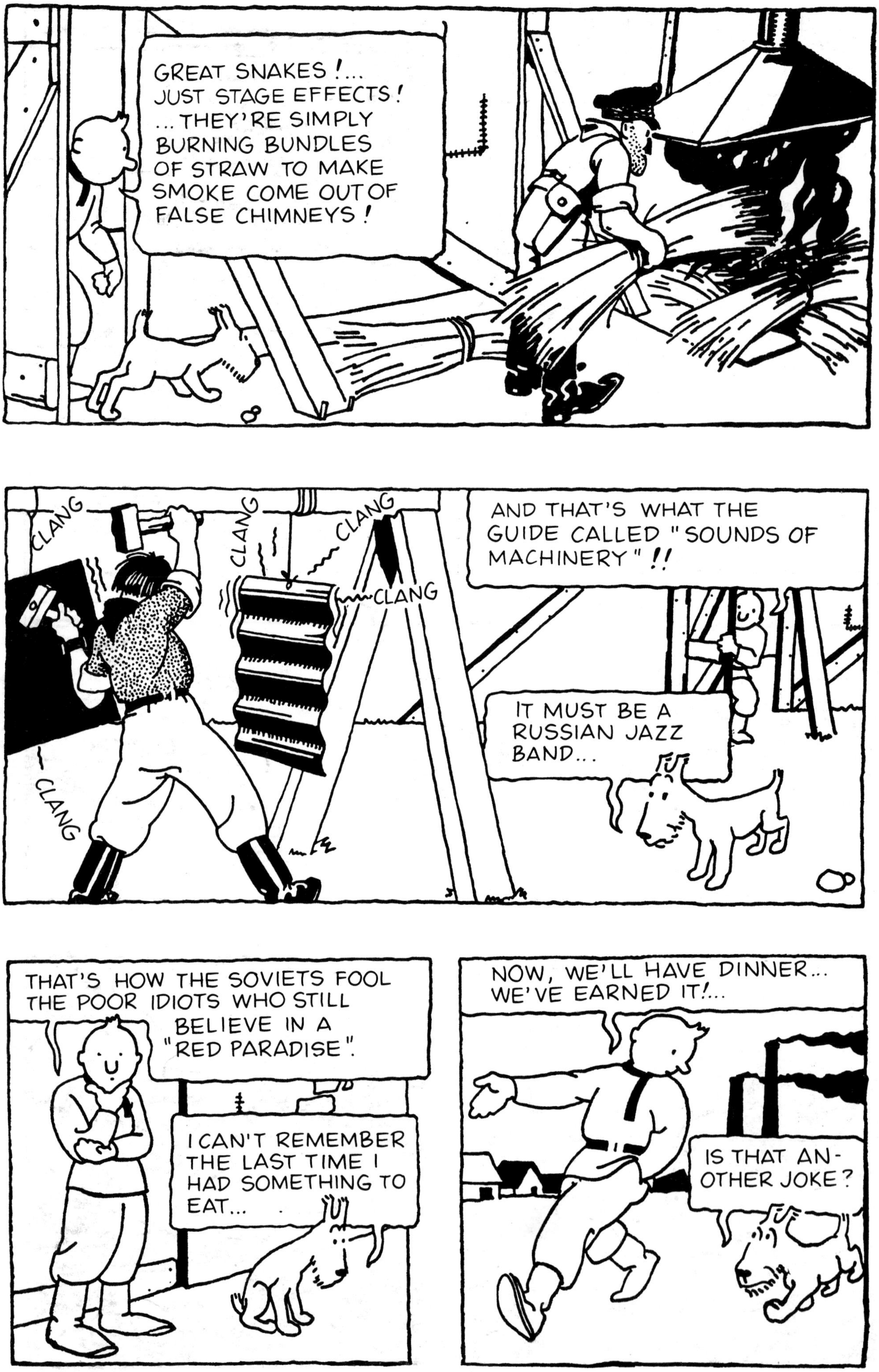
GREAT SNAKES!... JUST STAGE EFFECTS! ...THEY'RE SIMPLY BURNING BUNDLES OF STRAW TO MAKE SMOKE COME OUT OF FALSE CHIMNEYS!
CLANG
CLANG
CLANG
CLANG
CLANG
AND THAT'S WHAT THE GUIDE CALLED "SOUNDS OF MACHINERY"!!
IT MUST BE A RUSSIAN JAZZ BAND...
THAT'S HOW THE SOVIETS FOOL THE POOR IDIOTS WHO STILL BELIEVE IN A "RED PARADISE".
I CAN'T REMEMBER THE LAST TIME I HAD SOMETHING TO EAT...
NOW, WE'LL HAVE DINNER... WE'VE EARNED IT!...
IS THAT AN-OTHER JOKE?

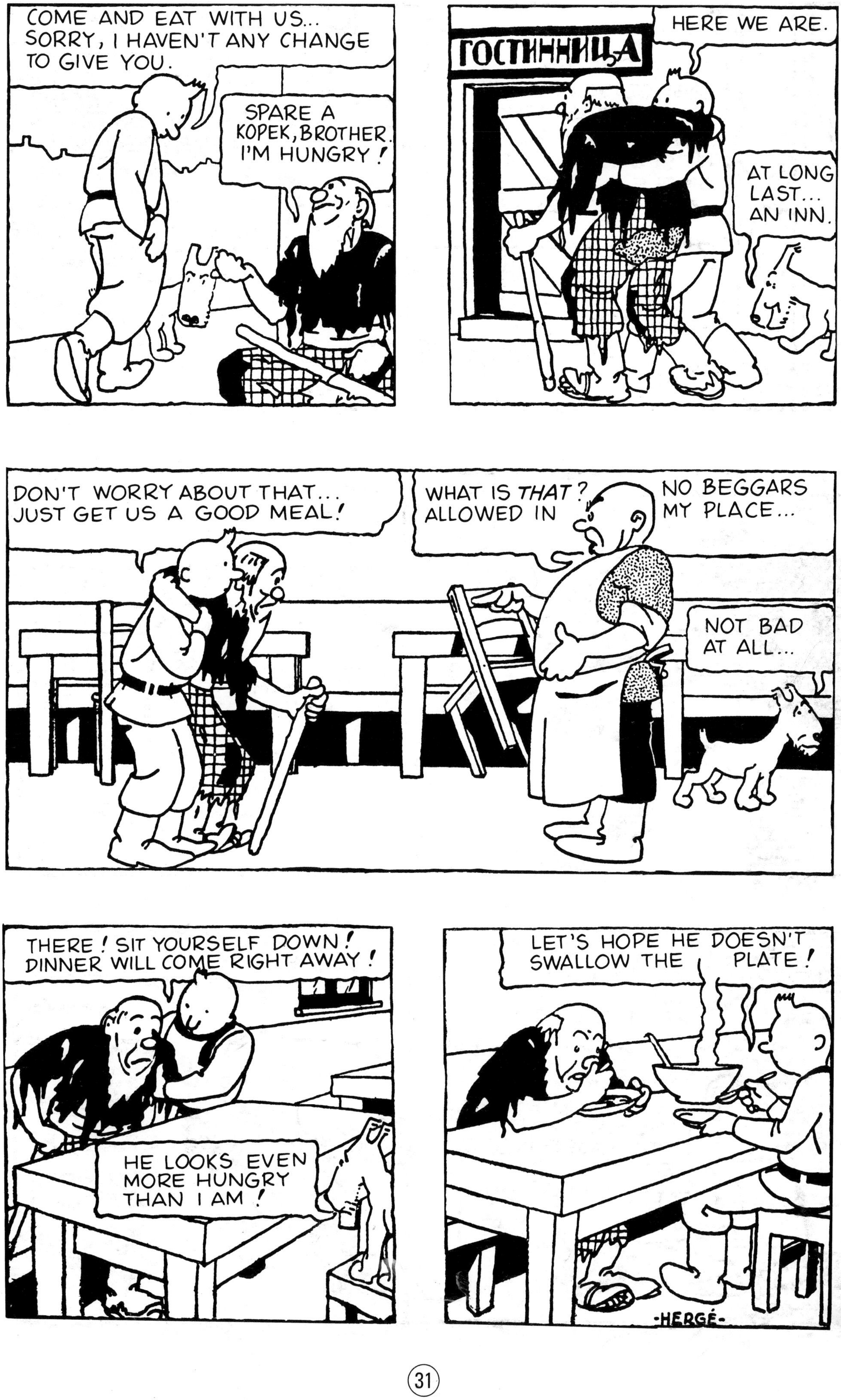
COME AND EAT WITH US... SORRY, I HAVEN'T ANY CHANGE TO GIVE YOU.
SPARE A KOPEK, BROTHER. I'M HUNGRY!
HERE WE ARE.
ГОСТИННИЦА
AT LONG LAST... AN INN.
DON'T WORRY ABOUT THAT... JUST GET US A GOOD MEAL!
WHAT IS *THAT*? NO BEGGARS ALLOWED IN MY PLACE...
NOT BAD AT ALL...
THERE! SIT YOURSELF DOWN! DINNER WILL COME RIGHT AWAY!
HE LOOKS EVEN MORE HUNGRY THAN I AM!
LET'S HOPE HE DOESN'T SWALLOW THE PLATE!
-HERGÉ-

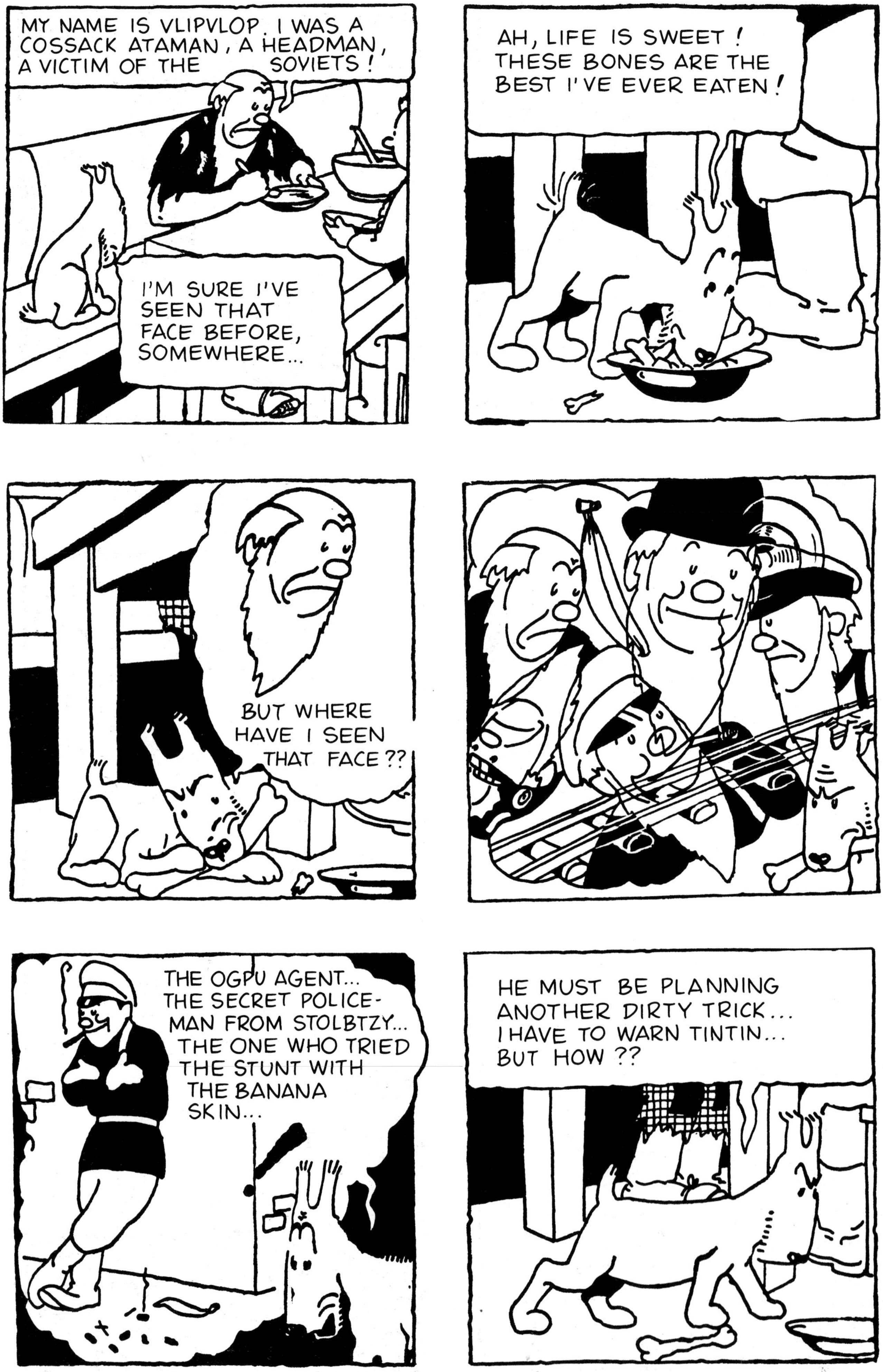
MY NAME IS VLIPVLOP. I WAS A COSSACK ATAMAN, A HEADMAN, A VICTIM OF THE SOVIETS!
I'M SURE I'VE SEEN THAT FACE BEFORE, SOMEWHERE...
AH, LIFE IS SWEET! THESE BONES ARE THE BEST I'VE EVER EATEN!
BUT WHERE HAVE I SEEN THAT FACE??
THE OGPU AGENT... THE SECRET POLICE-MAN FROM STOLBTZY... THE ONE WHO TRIED THE STUNT WITH THE BANANA SKIN...
HE MUST BE PLANNING ANOTHER DIRTY TRICK... I HAVE TO WARN TINTIN... BUT HOW??

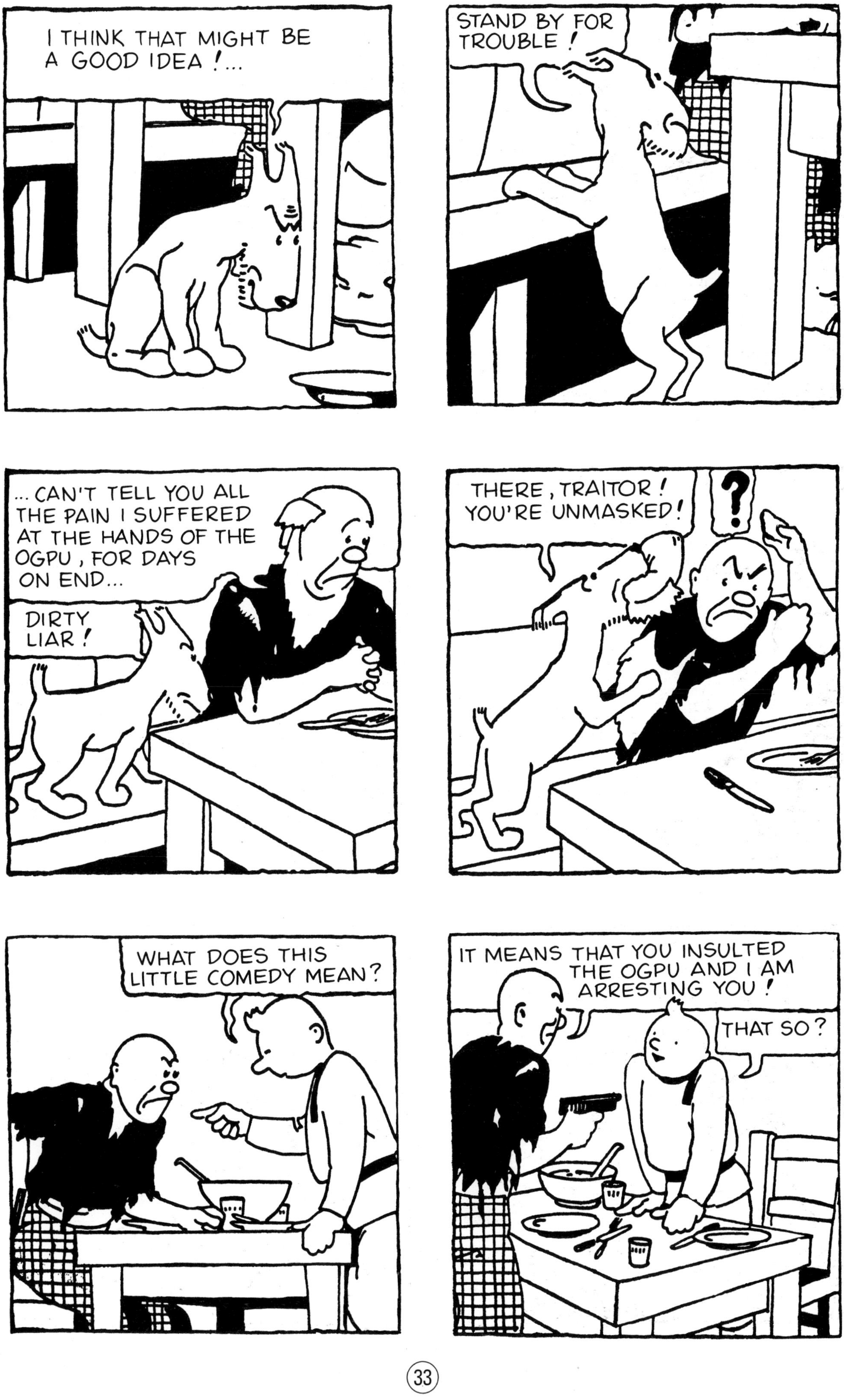
I THINK THAT MIGHT BE A GOOD IDEA !...
STAND BY FOR TROUBLE !
... CAN'T TELL YOU ALL THE PAIN I SUFFERED AT THE HANDS OF THE OGPU , FOR DAYS ON END...
DIRTY LIAR !
THERE , TRAITOR ! YOU'RE UNMASKED !
?
WHAT DOES THIS LITTLE COMEDY MEAN ?
IT MEANS THAT YOU INSULTED THE OGPU AND I AM ARRESTING YOU !
THAT SO ?

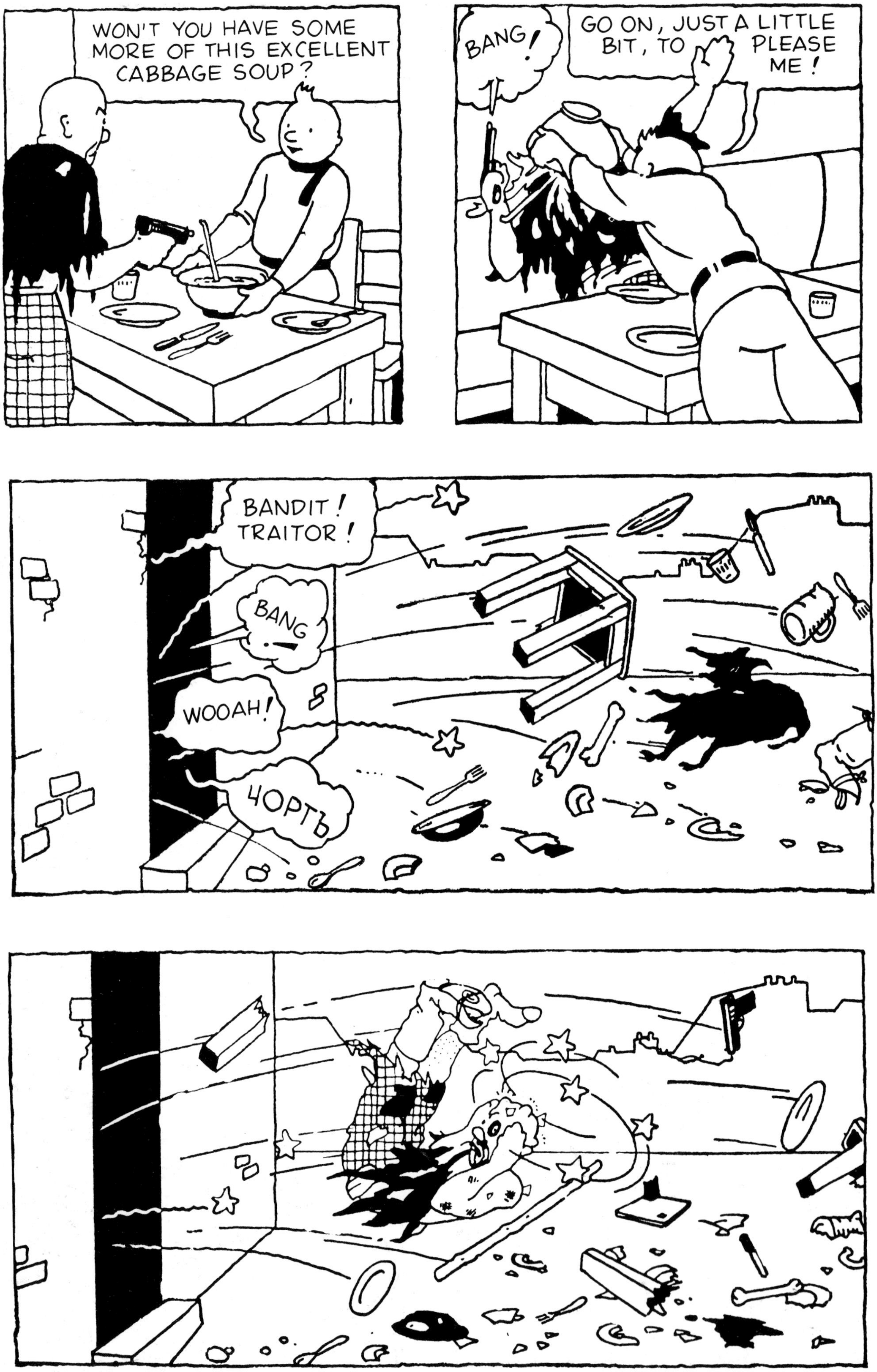
WON'T YOU HAVE SOME MORE OF THIS EXCELLENT CABBAGE SOUP?
BANG!
GO ON, JUST A LITTLE BIT, TO PLEASE ME!
BANDIT! TRAITOR!
BANG
WOOAH!
ЧОРТЪ

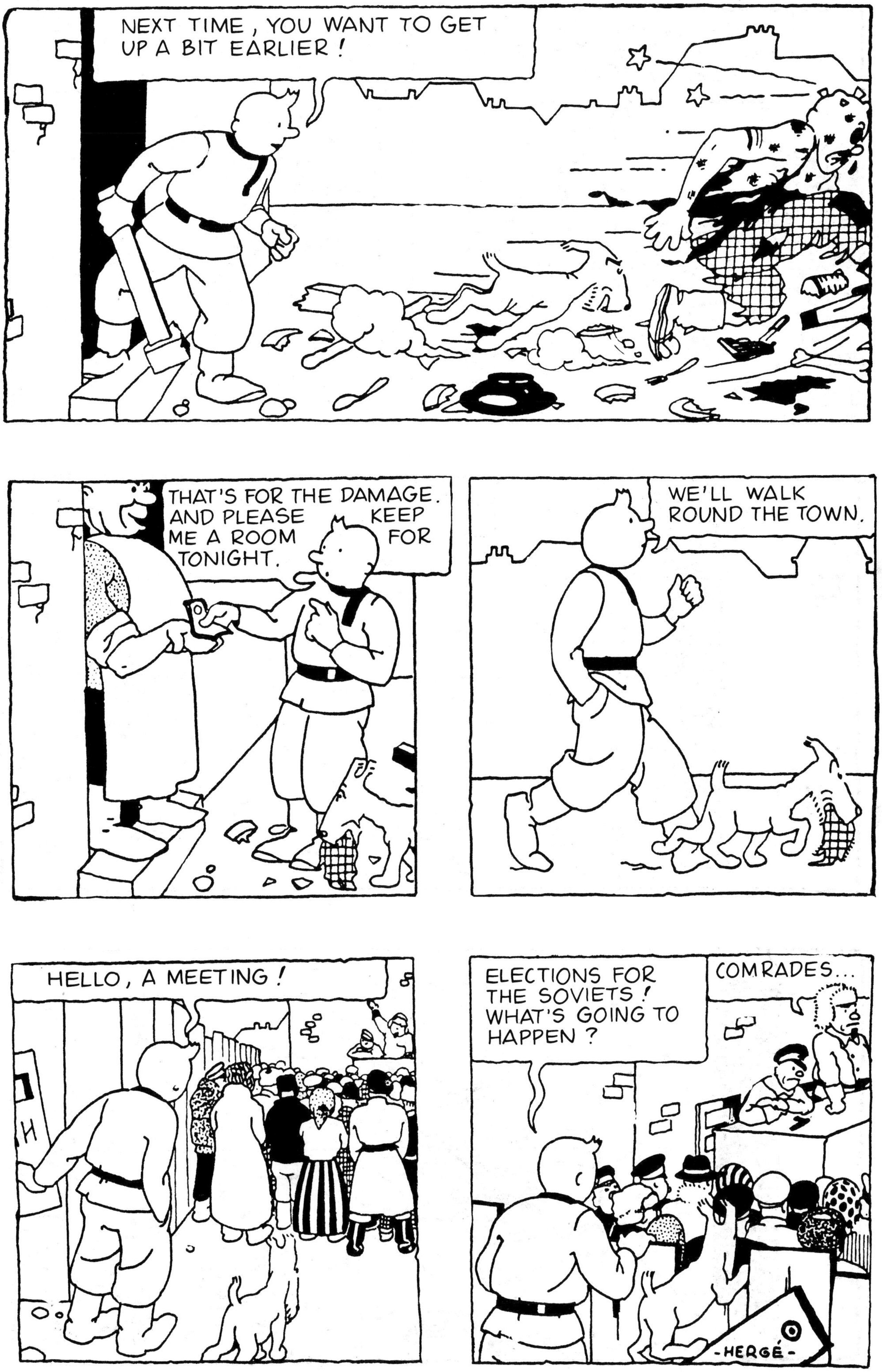
NEXT TIME, YOU WANT TO GET UP A BIT EARLIER!
THAT'S FOR THE DAMAGE. AND PLEASE KEEP ME A ROOM FOR TONIGHT.
WE'LL WALK ROUND THE TOWN.
HELLO, A MEETING!
ELECTIONS FOR THE SOVIETS! WHAT'S GOING TO HAPPEN?
COMRADES...
-HERGÉ-

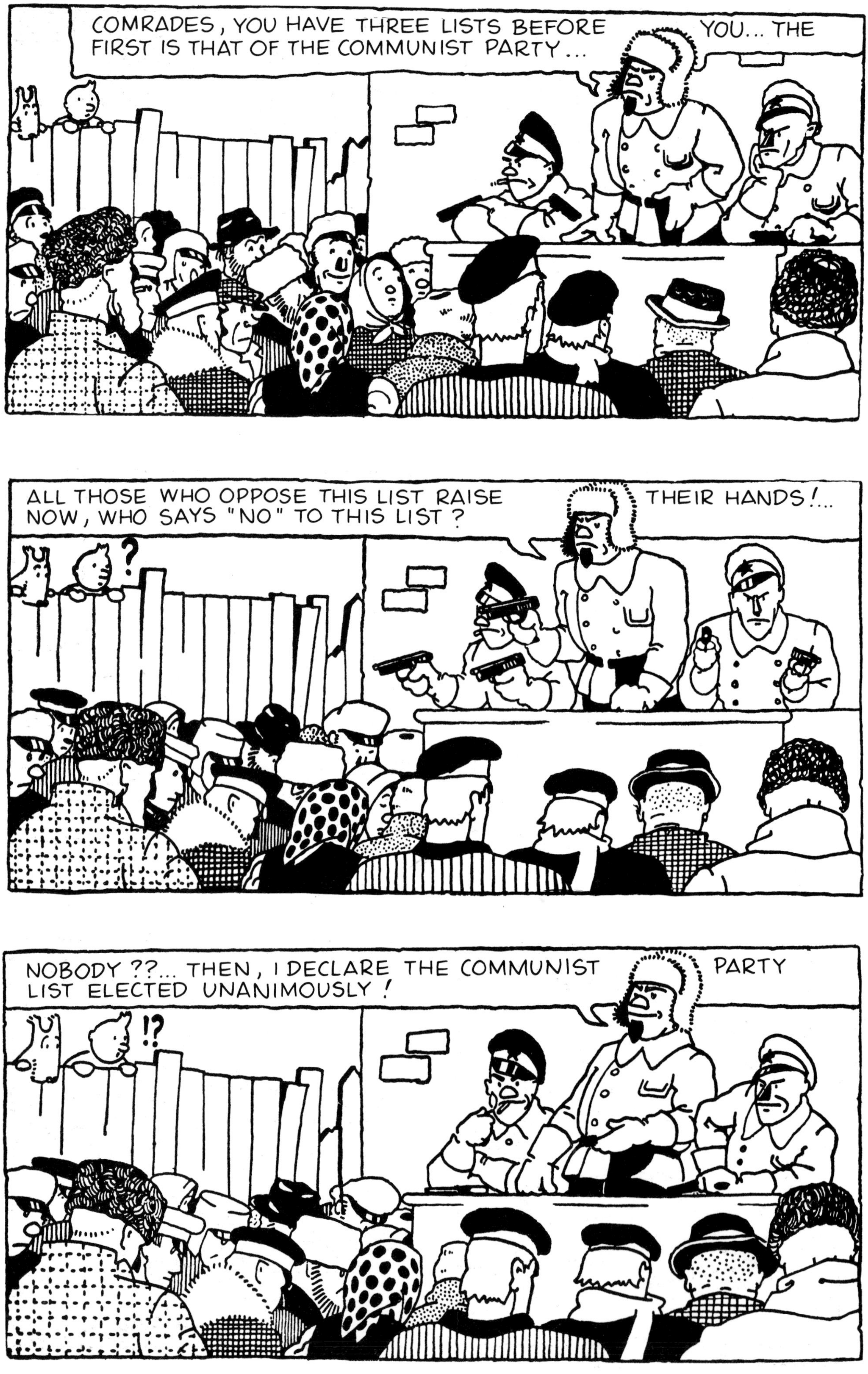
COMRADES, YOU HAVE THREE LISTS BEFORE YOU... THE FIRST IS THAT OF THE COMMUNIST PARTY...
ALL THOSE WHO OPPOSE THIS LIST RAISE THEIR HANDS!... NOW, WHO SAYS "NO" TO THIS LIST?
?
NOBODY ??... THEN, I DECLARE THE COMMUNIST PARTY LIST ELECTED UNANIMOUSLY!
!?

HELLO?
ЧТО ВЫ ТУ ДЕЛАЕТЕ???
WHAT?
ИДИТЕ ЗА МНОЮ!
WHAT'S ALL THIS ABOUT?
YOU ARE A SPY!
JUST WAIT A MOMENT... AND YOU'LL SEE WHAT IT MEANS TO THREATEN TINTIN.
HE DOESN'T SEEM VERY HAPPY!
СВОЛОЧЬ!
КАНАЛЬЯ!
МЕРЗАВЕЦ!
HERGE

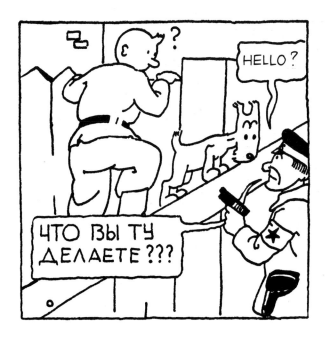

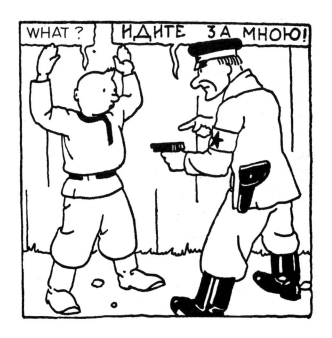

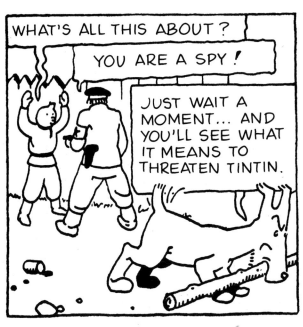

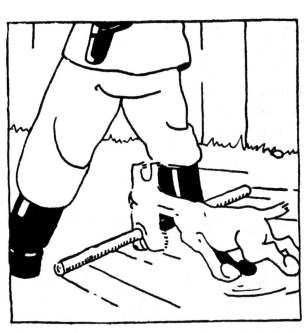

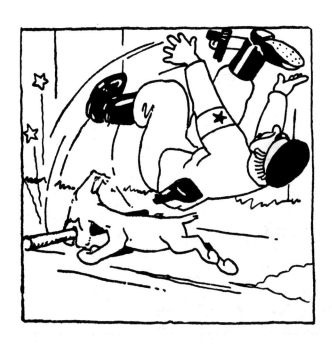

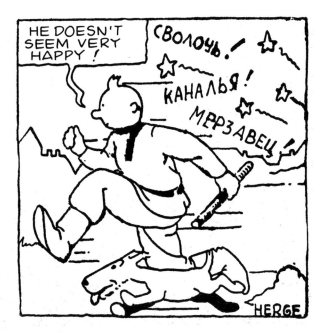

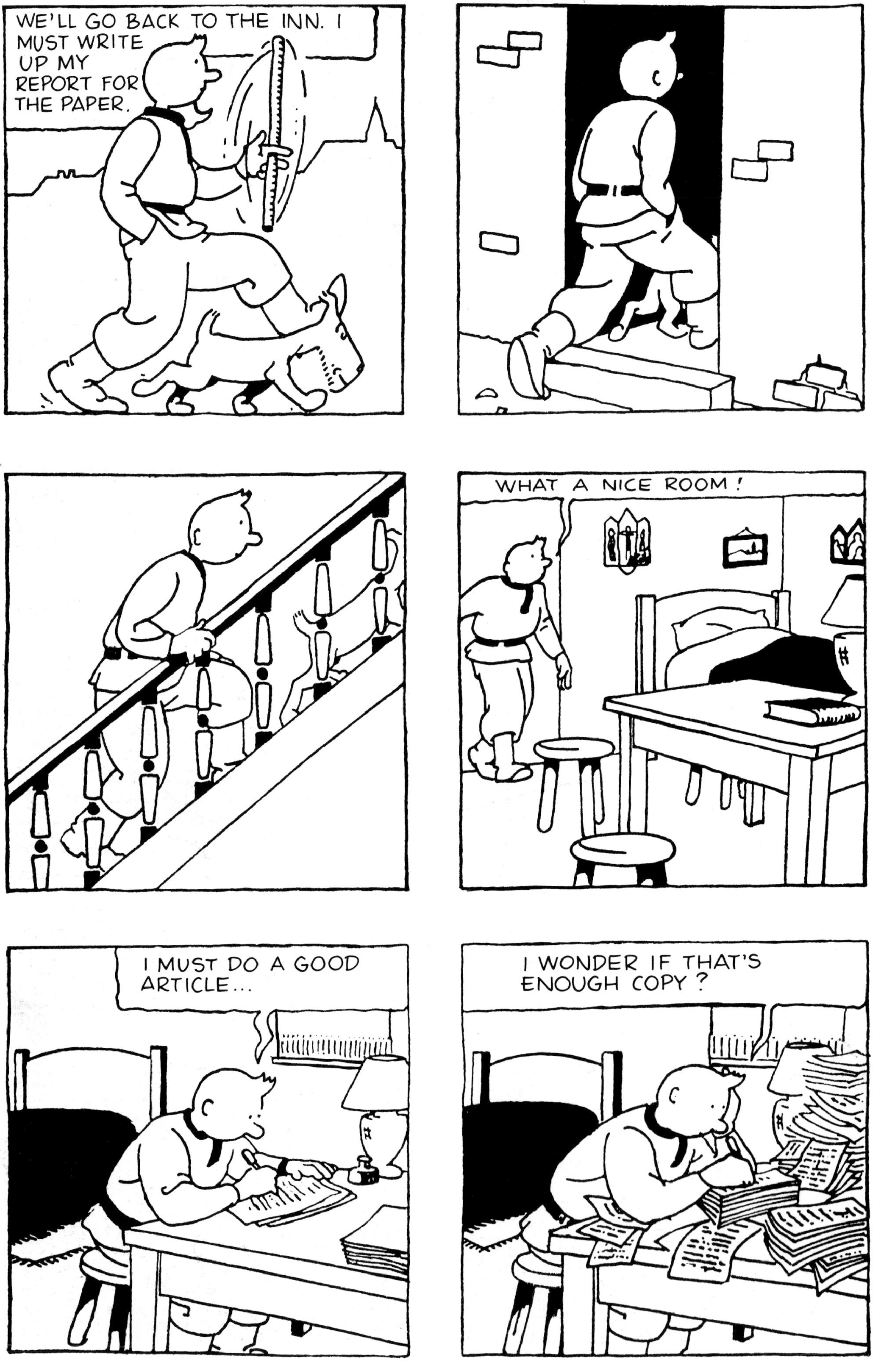
WE'LL GO BACK TO THE INN. I MUST WRITE UP MY REPORT FOR THE PAPER.
WHAT A NICE ROOM!
I MUST DO A GOOD ARTICLE...
I WONDER IF THAT'S ENOUGH COPY?

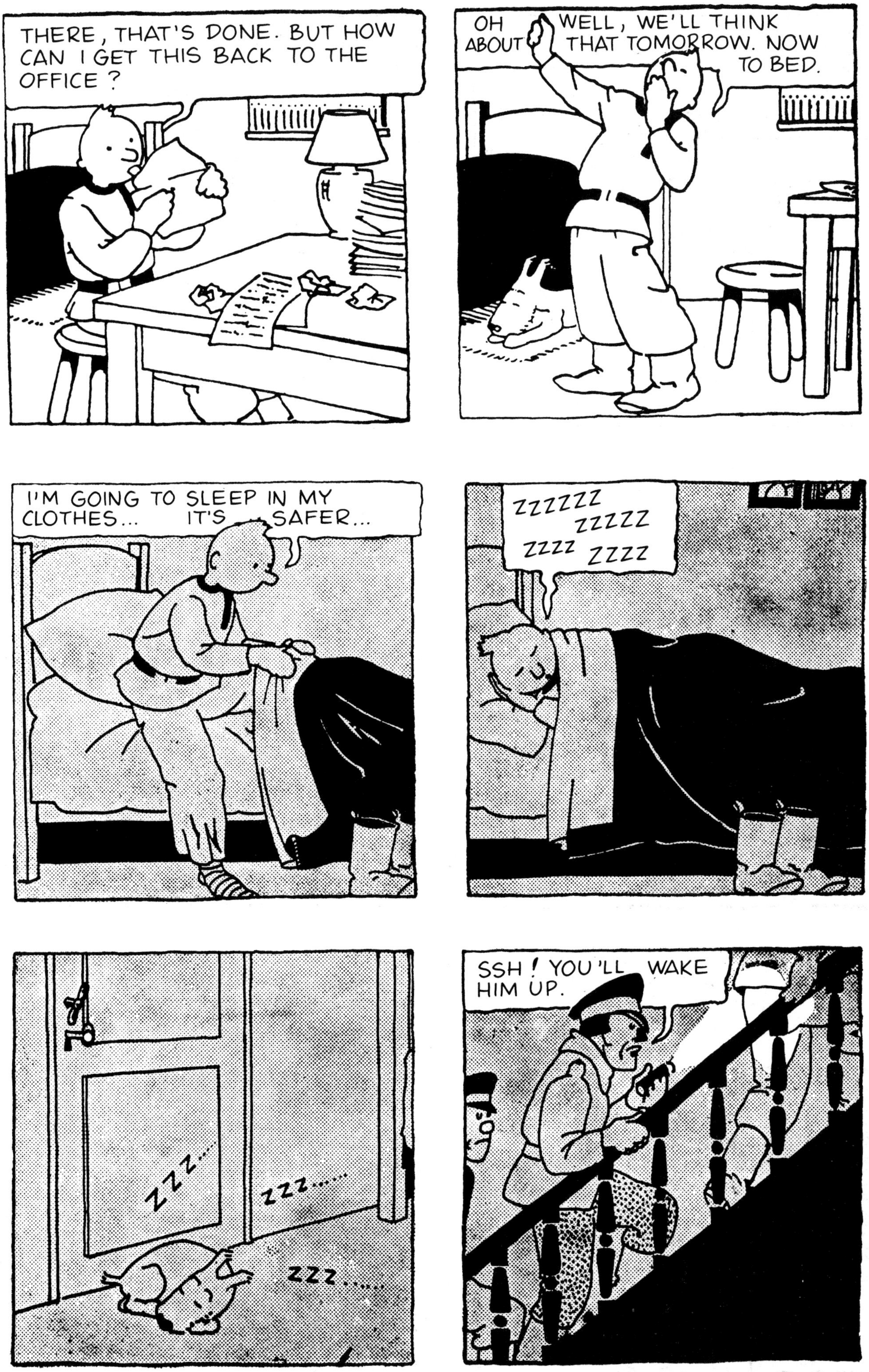
THERE, THAT'S DONE. BUT HOW CAN I GET THIS BACK TO THE OFFICE ?
OH WELL, WE'LL THINK ABOUT THAT TOMORROW. NOW TO BED.
I'M GOING TO SLEEP IN MY CLOTHES... IT'S SAFER...
ZZZZZZ ZZZZZ ZZZZ ZZZZ
ZZZ...
ZZZ.....
ZZZ.....
SSH ! YOU'LL WAKE HIM UP.

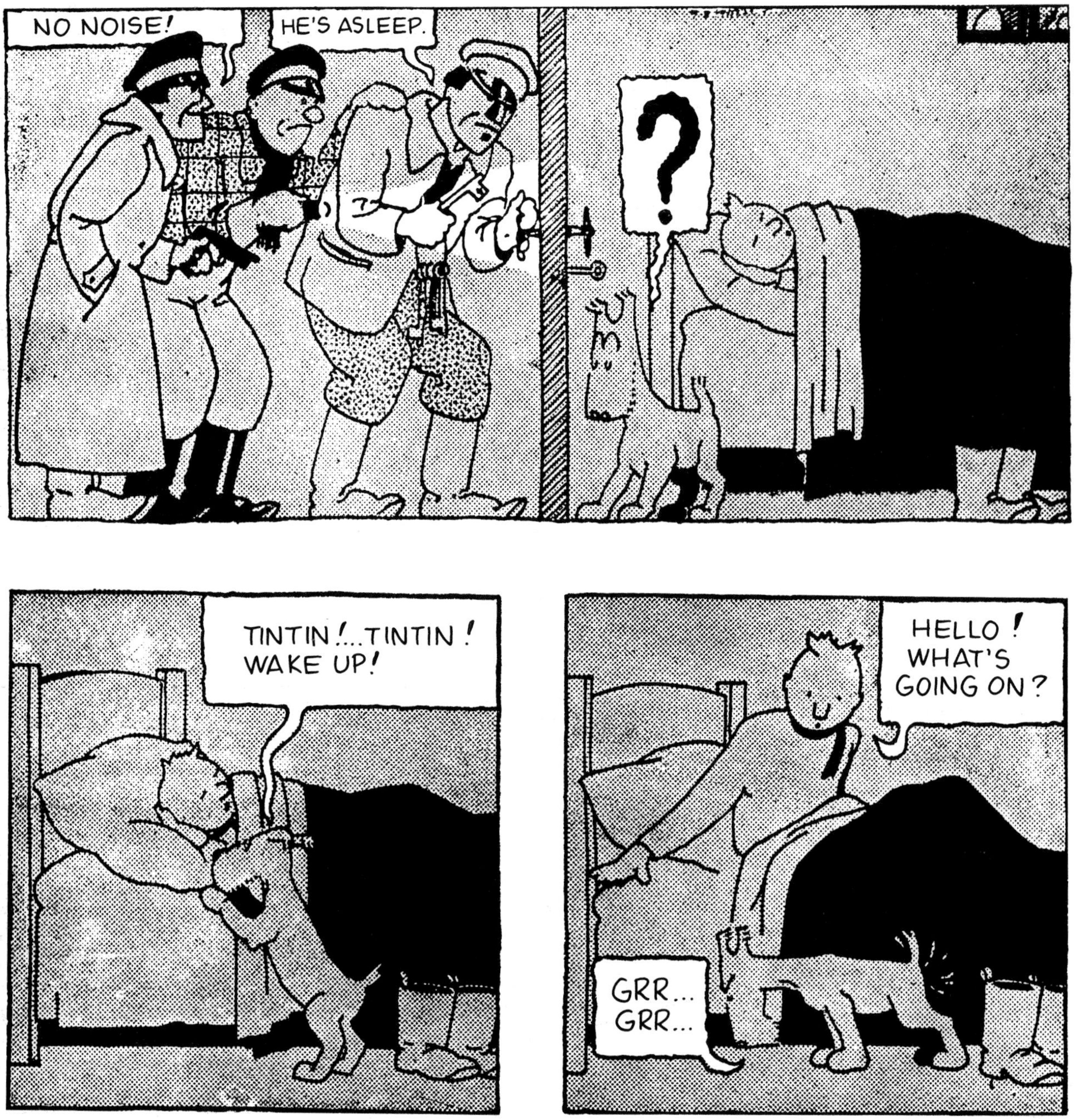
NO NOISE!
HE'S ASLEEP.
?
TINTIN!...TINTIN! WAKE UP!
HELLO! WHAT'S GOING ON?
GRR... GRR...

36

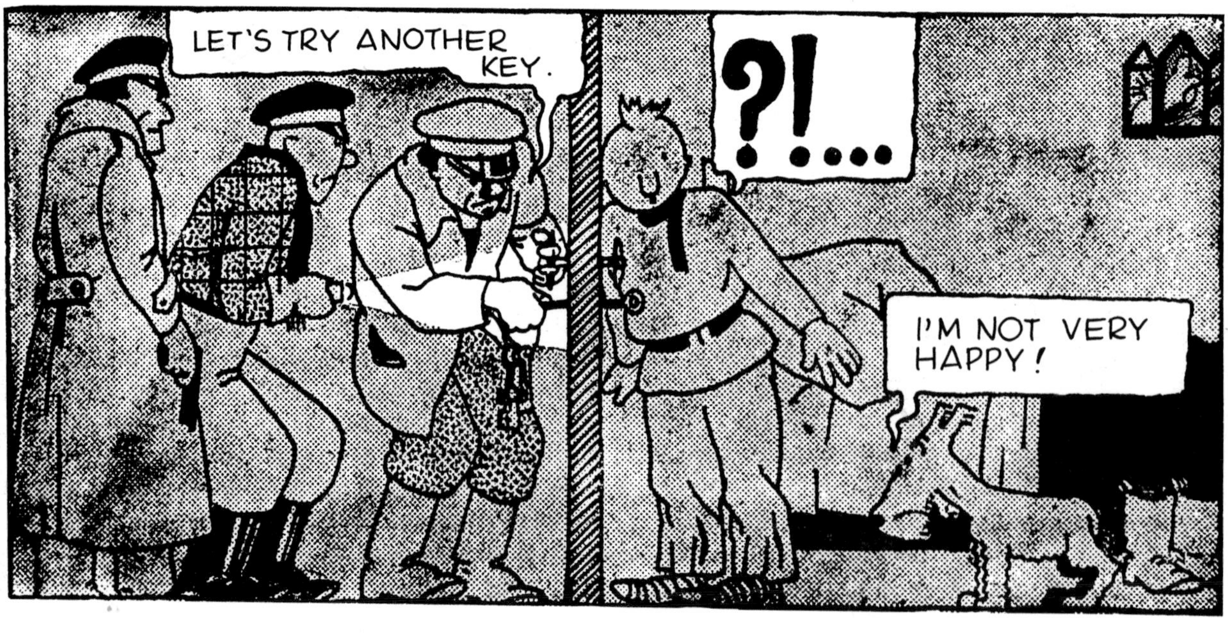
LET'S TRY ANOTHER KEY.
?!...
I'M NOT VERY HAPPY!

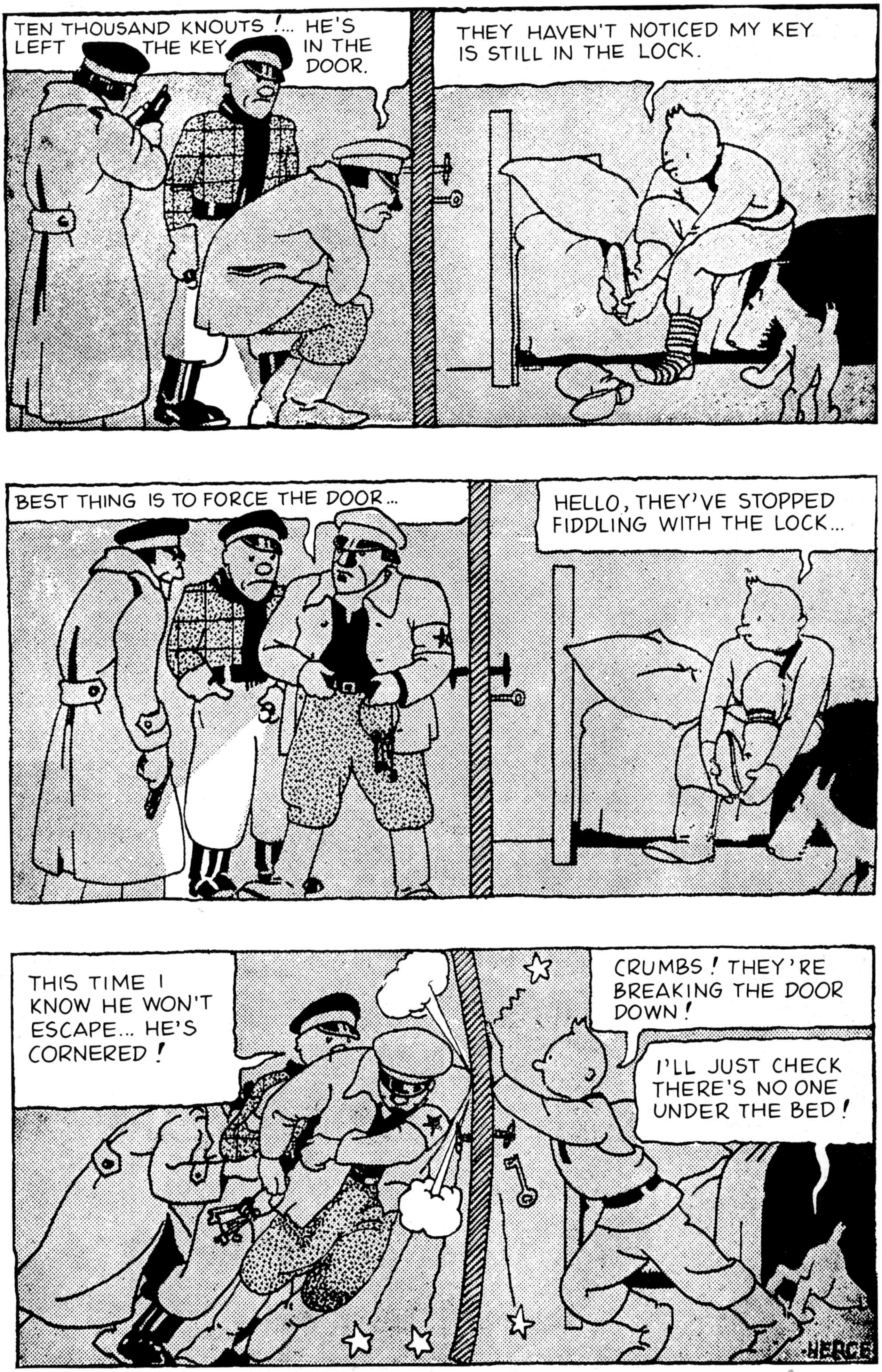
TEN THOUSAND KNOUTS !... HE'S LEFT THE KEY IN THE DOOR.
THEY HAVEN'T NOTICED MY KEY IS STILL IN THE LOCK.
BEST THING IS TO FORCE THE DOOR...
HELLO, THEY'VE STOPPED FIDDLING WITH THE LOCK...
THIS TIME I KNOW HE WON'T ESCAPE... HE'S CORNERED !
CRUMBS ! THEY'RE BREAKING THE DOOR DOWN !
I'LL JUST CHECK THERE'S NO ONE UNDER THE BED !
HERGE

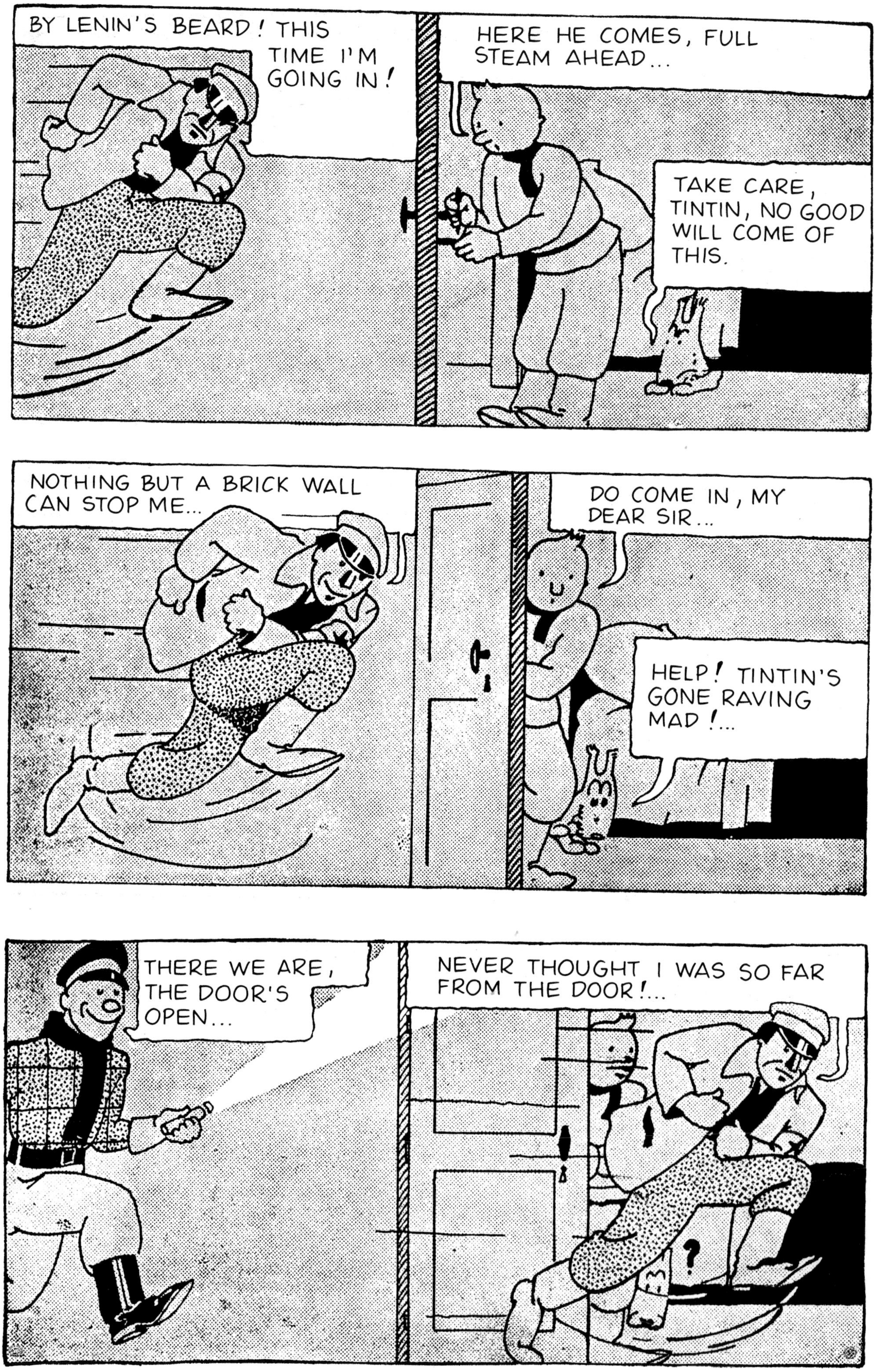
BY LENIN'S BEARD! THIS TIME I'M GOING IN!
HERE HE COMES, FULL STEAM AHEAD...
TAKE CARE, TINTIN, NO GOOD WILL COME OF THIS.
NOTHING BUT A BRICK WALL CAN STOP ME...
DO COME IN, MY DEAR SIR...
HELP! TINTIN'S GONE RAVING MAD!...
THERE WE ARE, THE DOOR'S OPEN...
NEVER THOUGHT I WAS SO FAR FROM THE DOOR!...
?

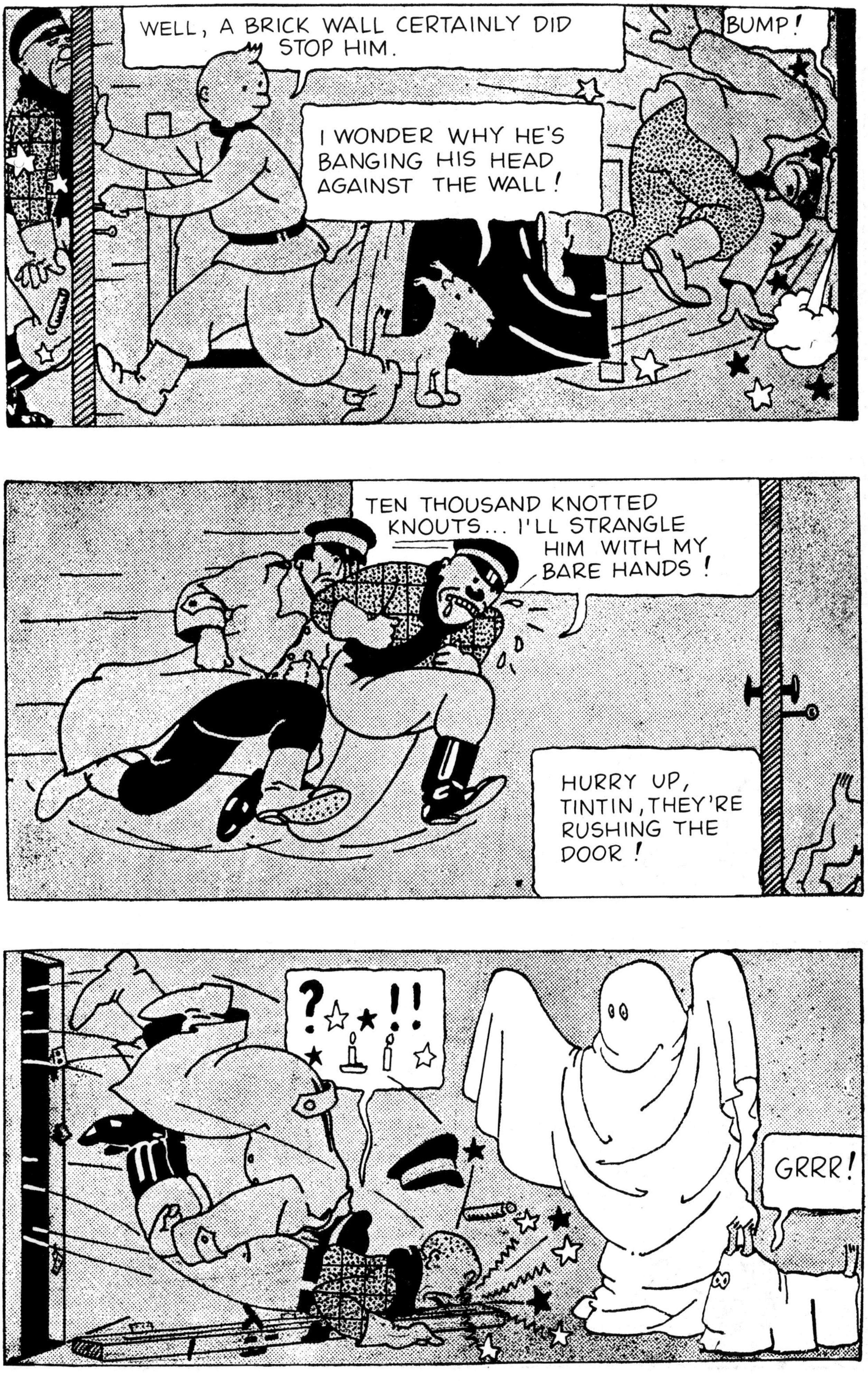
WELL, A BRICK WALL CERTAINLY DID STOP HIM.
BUMP!
I WONDER WHY HE'S BANGING HIS HEAD AGAINST THE WALL!
TEN THOUSAND KNOTTED KNOUTS... I'LL STRANGLE HIM WITH MY BARE HANDS!
HURRY UP, TINTIN, THEY'RE RUSHING THE DOOR!
?!!
GRRR!

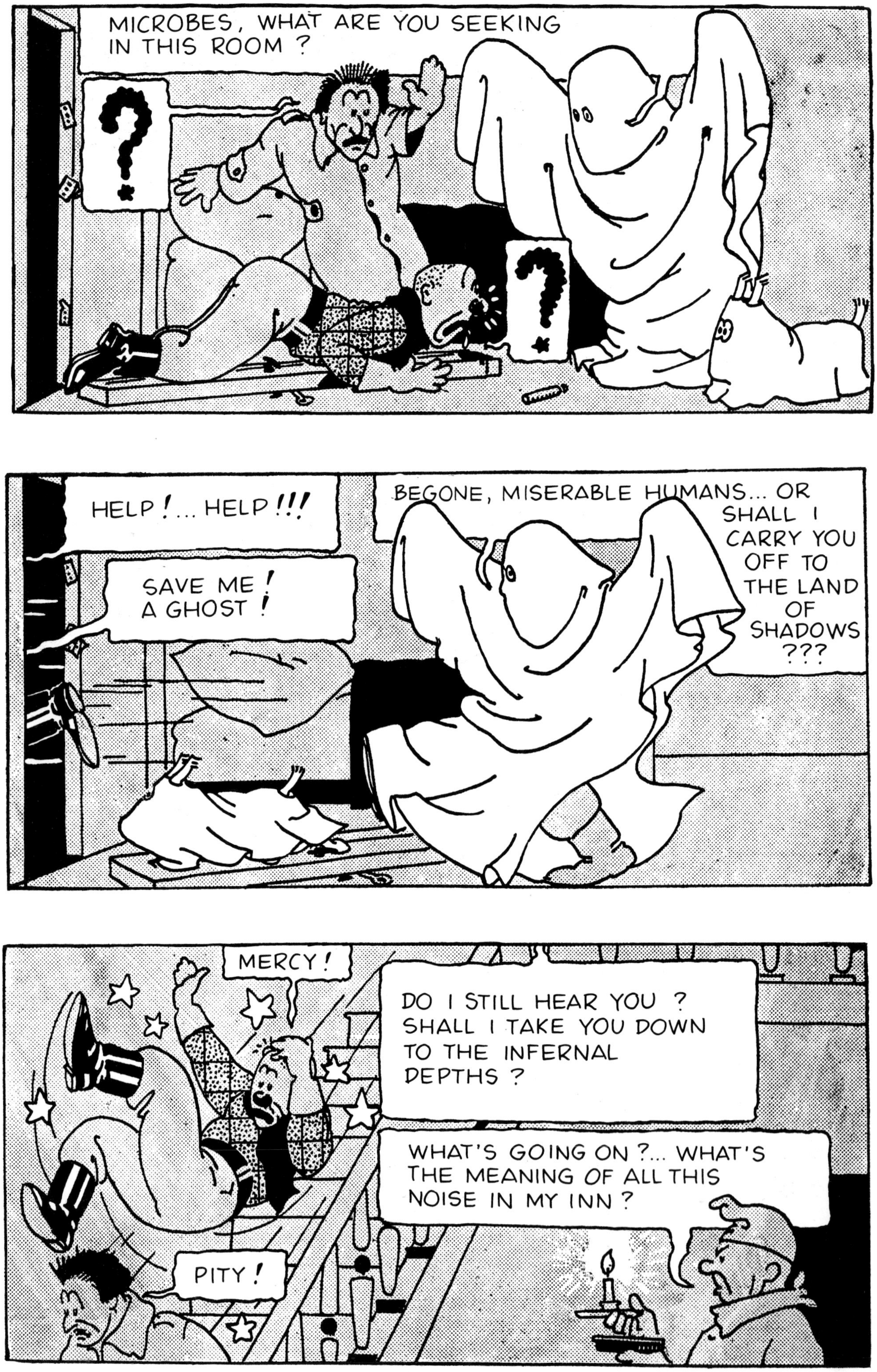

MICROBES, WHAT ARE YOU SEEKING IN THIS ROOM ?
HELP !... HELP !!!
SAVE ME ! A GHOST !
BEGONE, MISERABLE HUMANS... OR SHALL I CARRY YOU OFF TO THE LAND OF SHADOWS ???
MERCY !
DO I STILL HEAR YOU ? SHALL I TAKE YOU DOWN TO THE INFERNAL DEPTHS ?
WHAT'S GOING ON ?... WHAT'S THE MEANING OF ALL THIS NOISE IN MY INN ?
PITY !

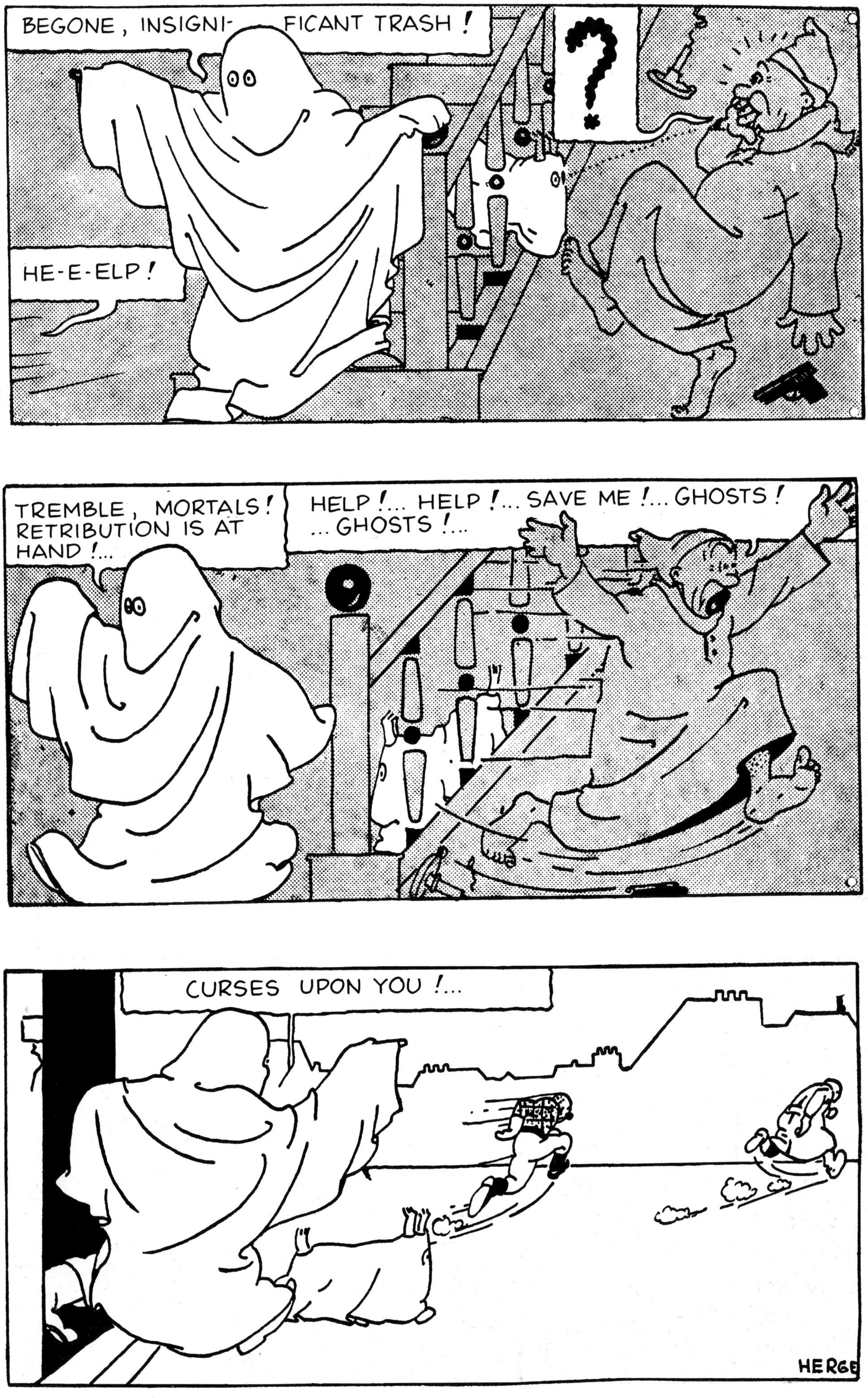

BEGONE, INSIGNI- FICANT TRASH !
HE-E-ELP !
TREMBLE, MORTALS ! RETRIBUTION IS AT HAND !...
HELP !... HELP !... SAVE ME !... GHOSTS ! ... GHOSTS !...
CURSES UPON YOU !...
HERGE

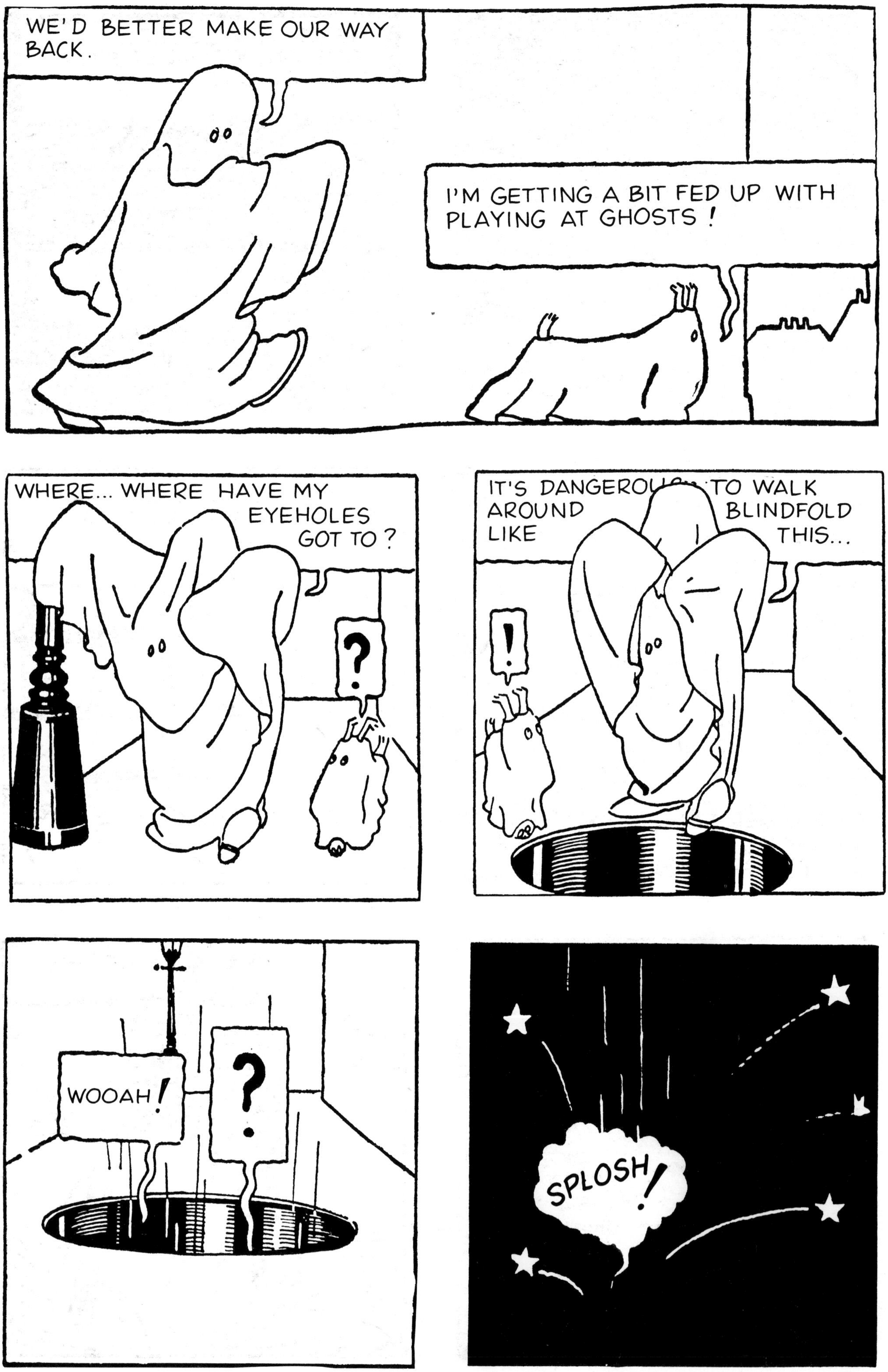
WE'D BETTER MAKE OUR WAY BACK.
I'M GETTING A BIT FED UP WITH PLAYING AT GHOSTS!
WHERE... WHERE HAVE MY EYEHOLES GOT TO?
?
IT'S DANGEROU TO WALK AROUND BLINDFOLD LIKE THIS...
!
WOOAH!
?
SPLOSH!

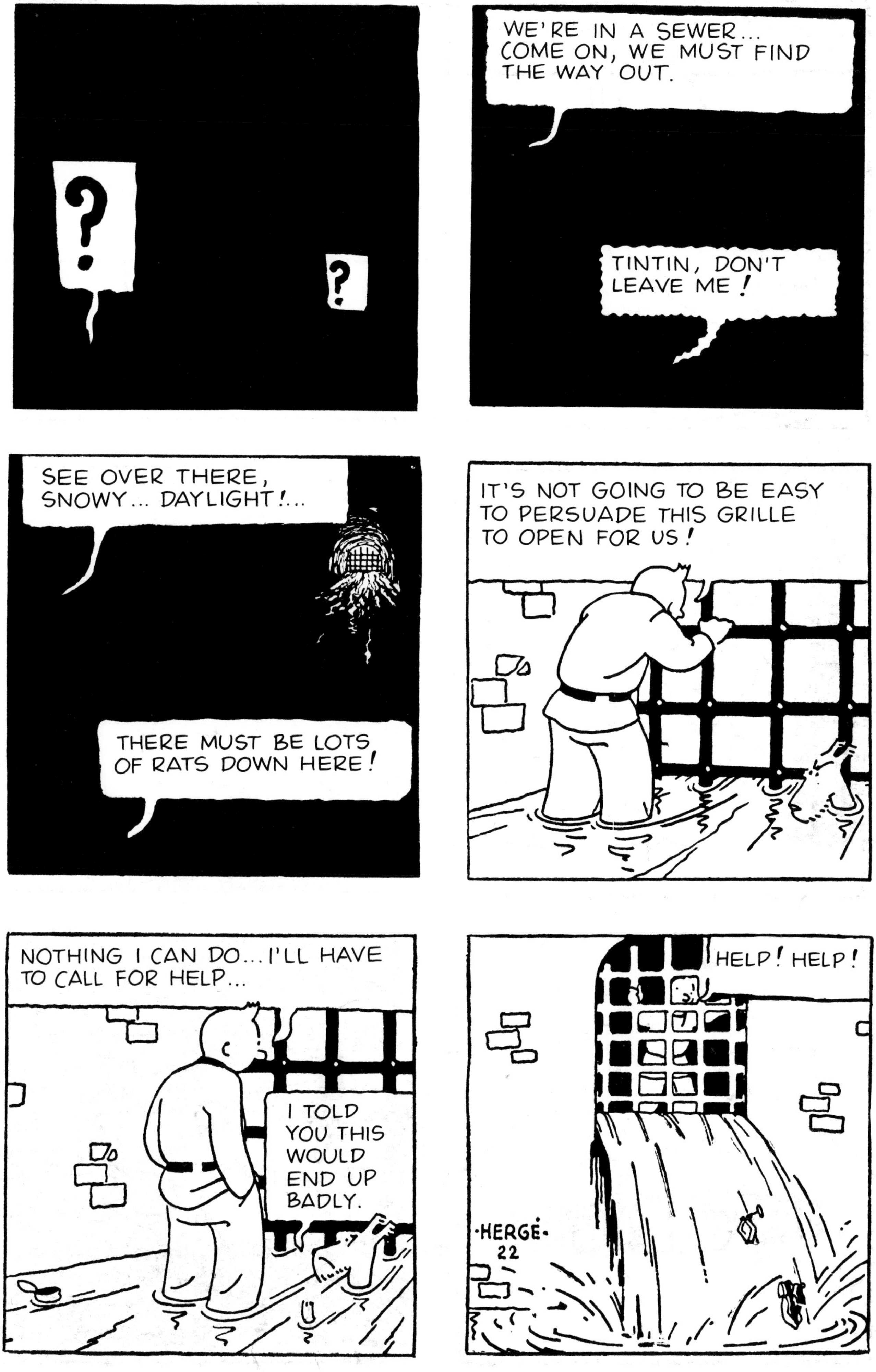
?
?
WE'RE IN A SEWER... COME ON, WE MUST FIND THE WAY OUT.
TINTIN, DON'T LEAVE ME!
SEE OVER THERE, SNOWY... DAYLIGHT!...
THERE MUST BE LOTS OF RATS DOWN HERE!
IT'S NOT GOING TO BE EASY TO PERSUADE THIS GRILLE TO OPEN FOR US!
NOTHING I CAN DO... I'LL HAVE TO CALL FOR HELP...
I TOLD YOU THIS WOULD END UP BADLY.
HELP! HELP!
·HERGÉ· 22

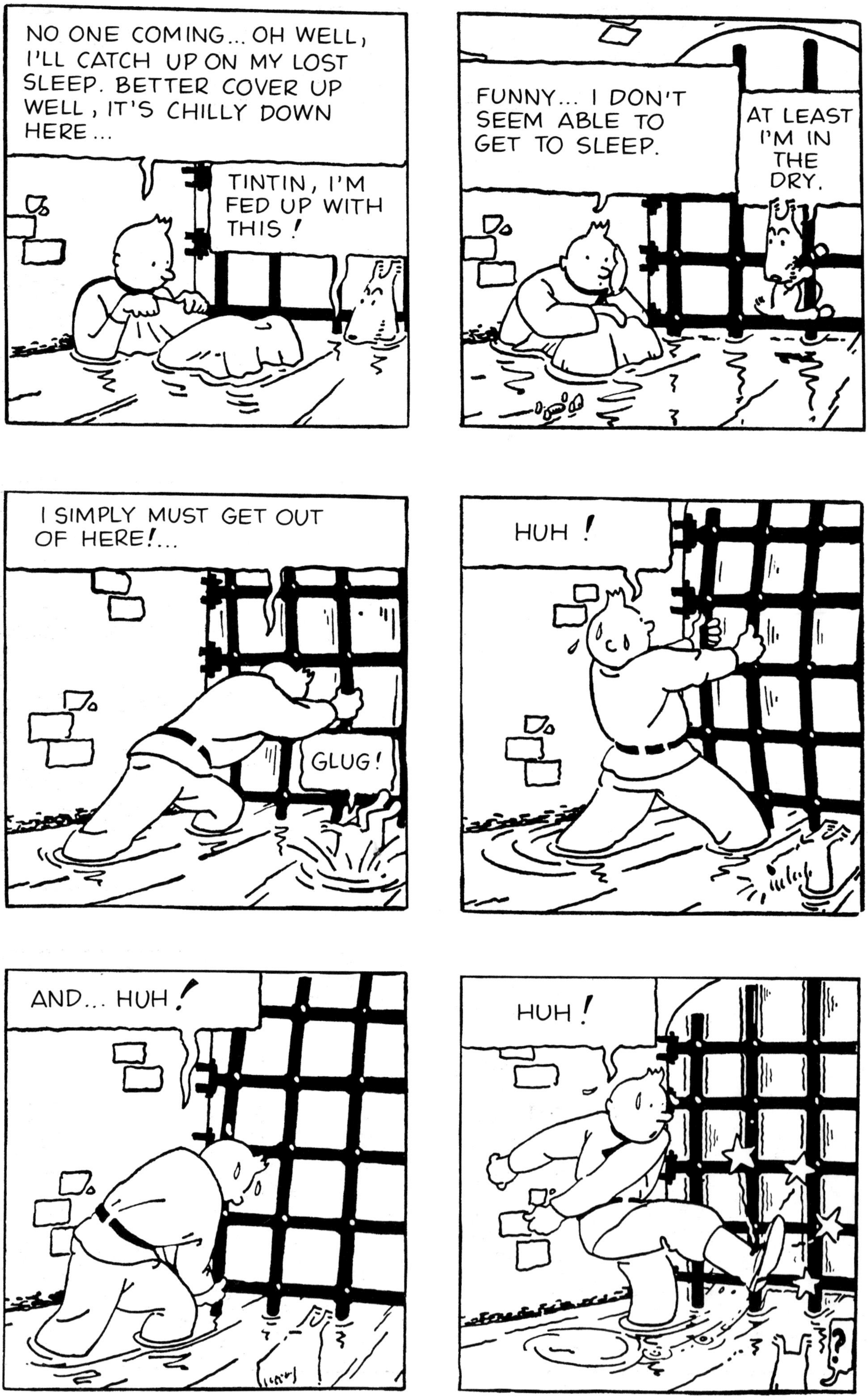
NO ONE COMING... OH WELL, I'LL CATCH UP ON MY LOST SLEEP. BETTER COVER UP WELL, IT'S CHILLY DOWN HERE...
TINTIN, I'M FED UP WITH THIS!
FUNNY... I DON'T SEEM ABLE TO GET TO SLEEP.
AT LEAST I'M IN THE DRY.
I SIMPLY MUST GET OUT OF HERE!...
GLUG!
HUH!
AND... HUH!
HUH!

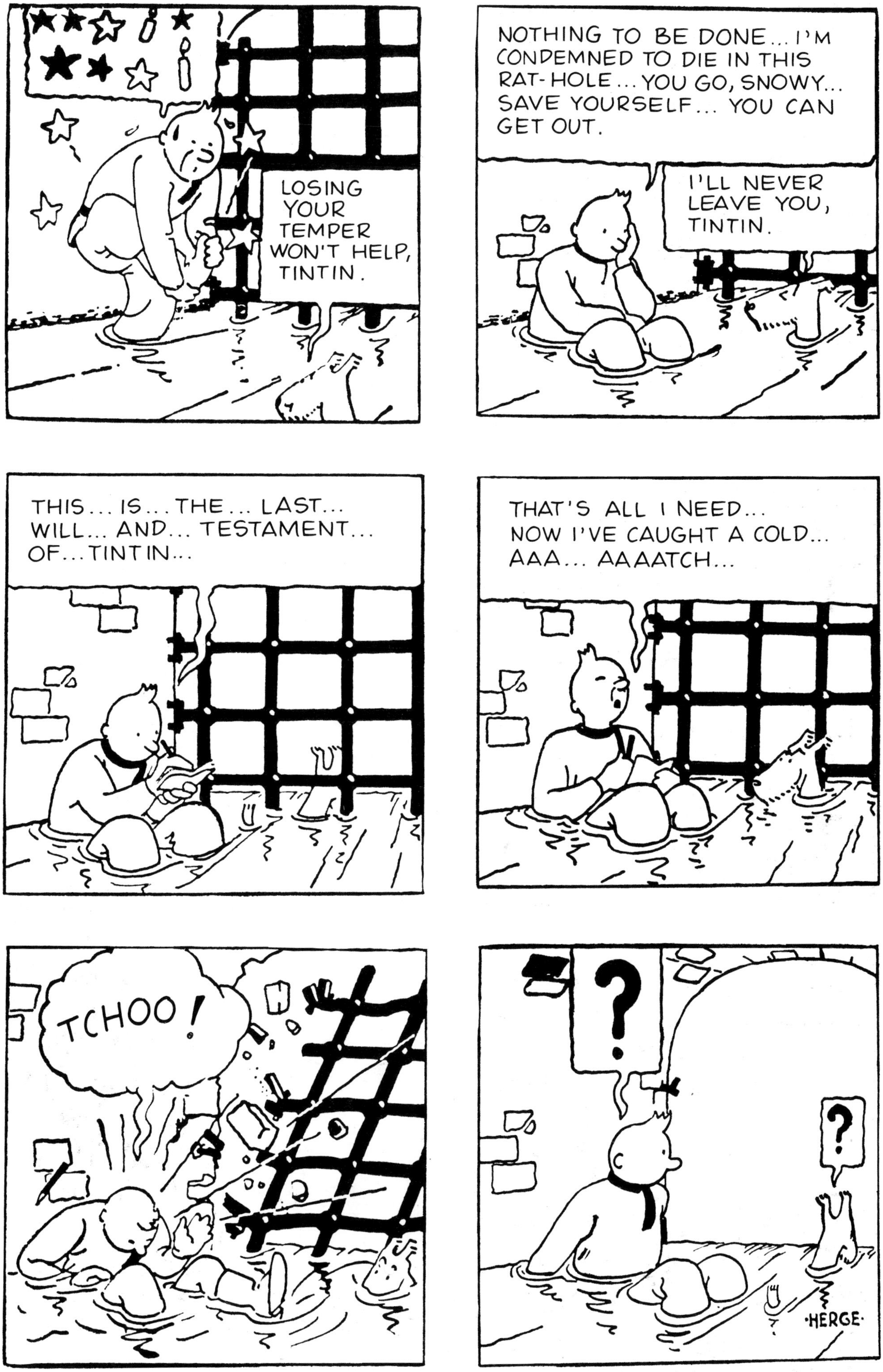
LOSING YOUR TEMPER WON'T HELP, TINTIN.
NOTHING TO BE DONE... I'M CONDEMNED TO DIE IN THIS RAT-HOLE... YOU GO, SNOWY... SAVE YOURSELF... YOU CAN GET OUT.
I'LL NEVER LEAVE YOU, TINTIN.
THIS... IS... THE... LAST... WILL... AND... TESTAMENT... OF... TINTIN...
THAT'S ALL I NEED... NOW I'VE CAUGHT A COLD... AAA... AAAATCH...
TCHOO!
?
?
·HERGE·

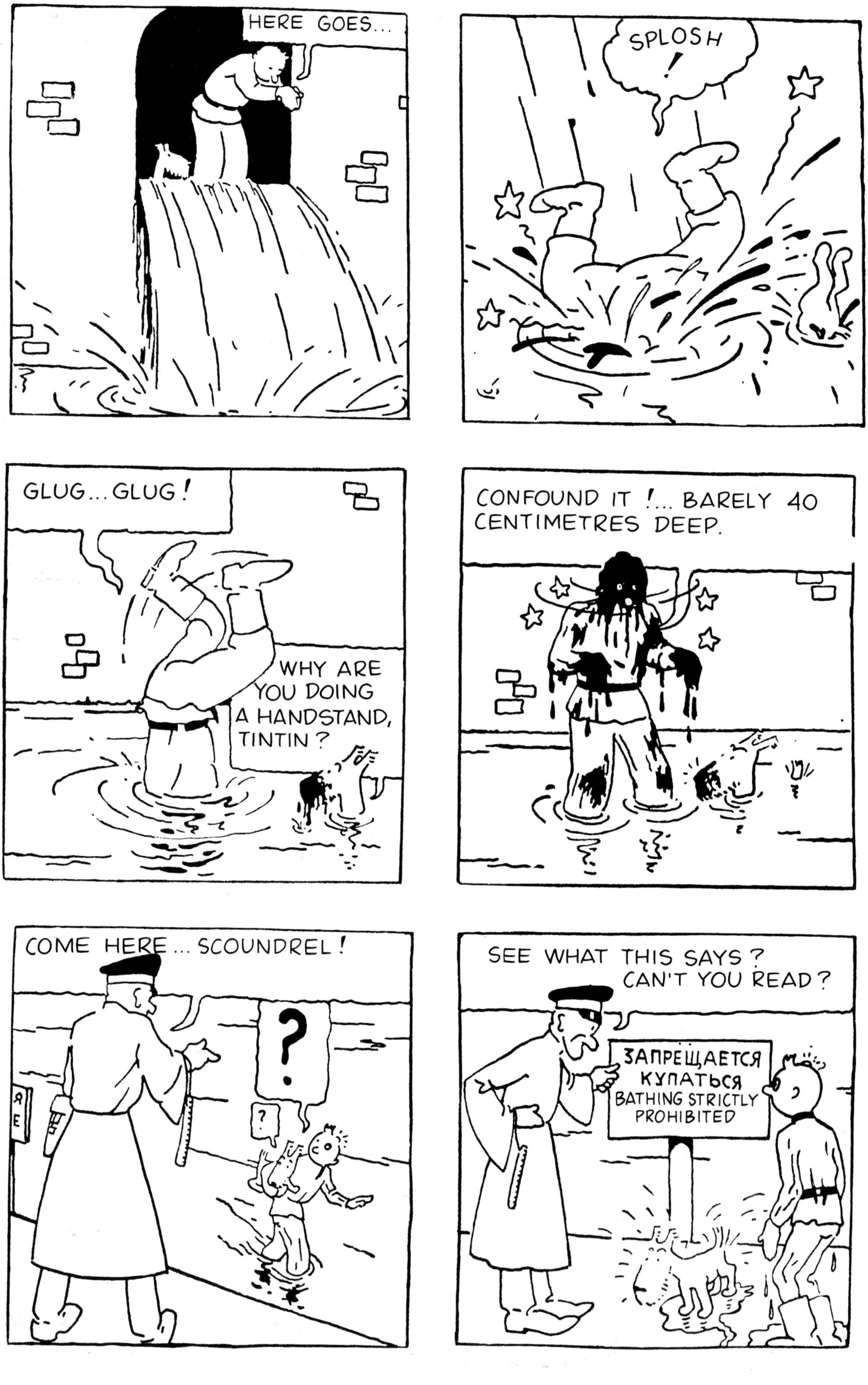
HERE GOES...
SPLOSH !
GLUG...GLUG!
WHY ARE YOU DOING A HANDSTAND, TINTIN ?
CONFOUND IT !... BARELY 40 CENTIMETRES DEEP.
COME HERE... SCOUNDREL!
?
?
SEE WHAT THIS SAYS ? CAN'T YOU READ ?
ЗАПРЕЩАЕТСЯ КУПАТЬСЯ
BATHING STRICTLY PROHIBITED

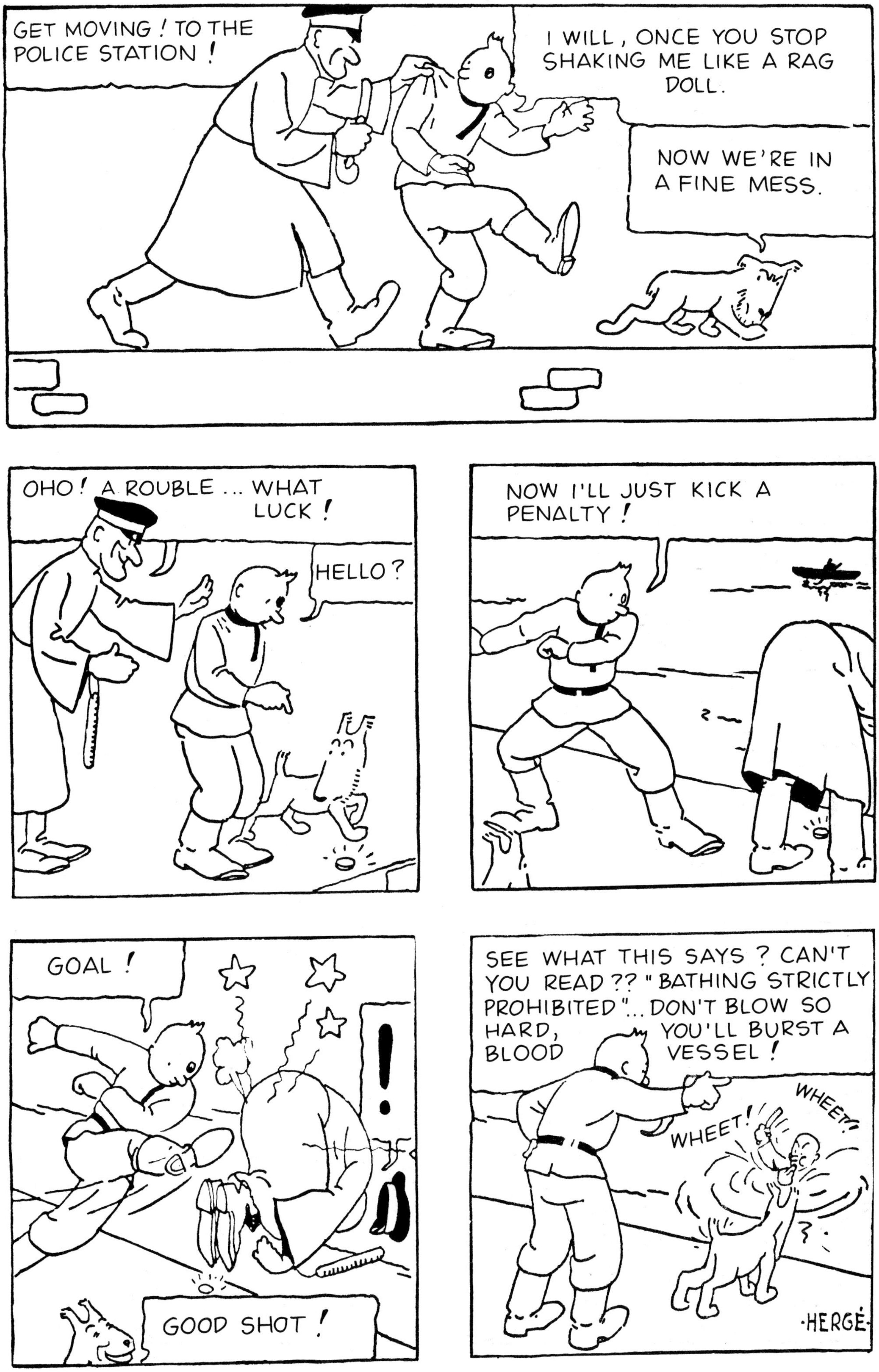
GET MOVING ! TO THE POLICE STATION !
I WILL, ONCE YOU STOP SHAKING ME LIKE A RAG DOLL.
NOW WE'RE IN A FINE MESS.
OHO ! A ROUBLE ... WHAT LUCK !
HELLO ?
NOW I'LL JUST KICK A PENALTY !
GOAL !
GOOD SHOT !
SEE WHAT THIS SAYS ? CAN'T YOU READ ?? "BATHING STRICTLY PROHIBITED"... DON'T BLOW SO HARD, YOU'LL BURST A BLOOD VESSEL !
WHEET !
WHEET !
·HERGÉ·

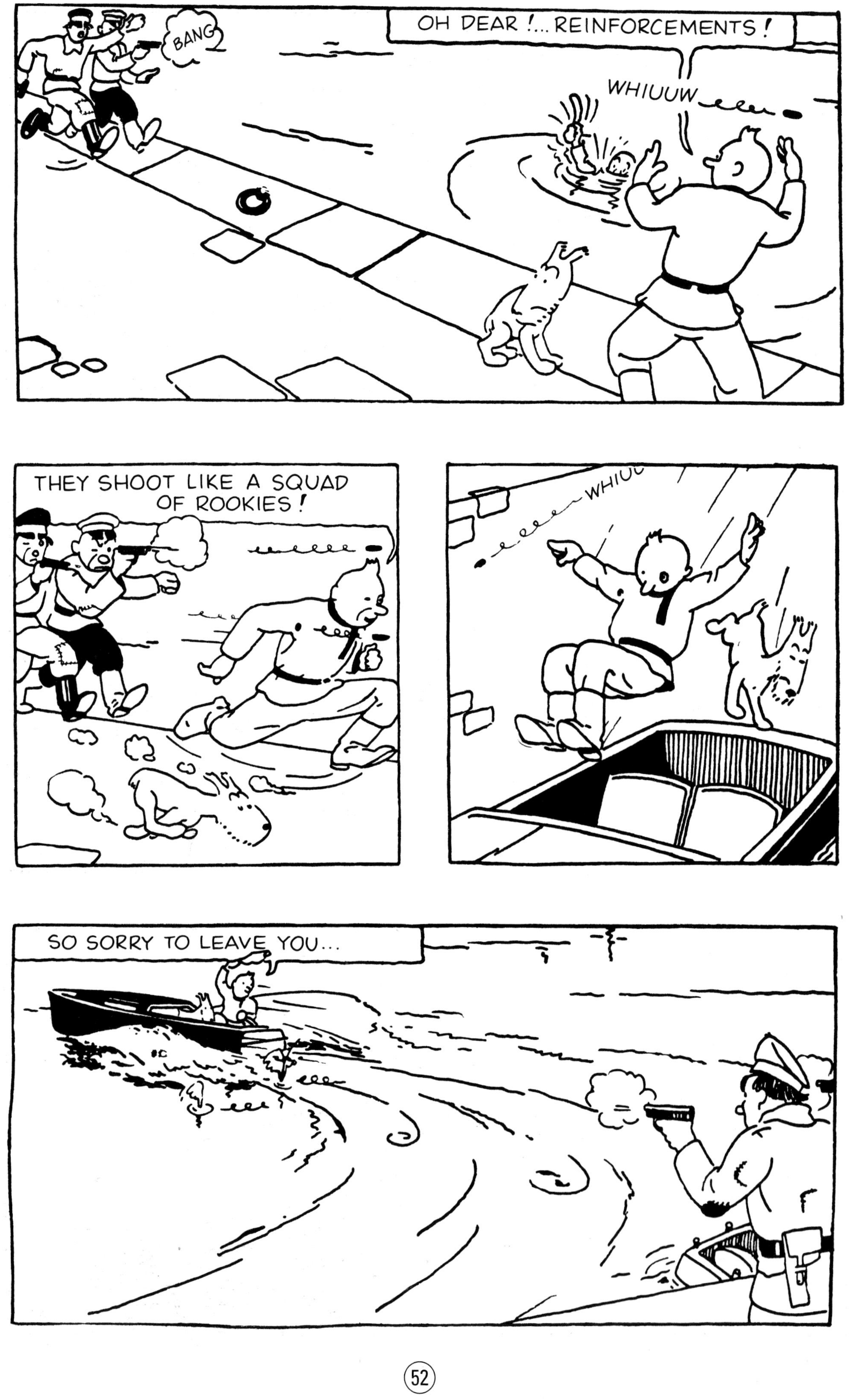
BANG
OH DEAR !... REINFORCEMENTS !
WHIUUW
THEY SHOOT LIKE A SQUAD OF ROOKIES !
SO SORRY TO LEAVE YOU...

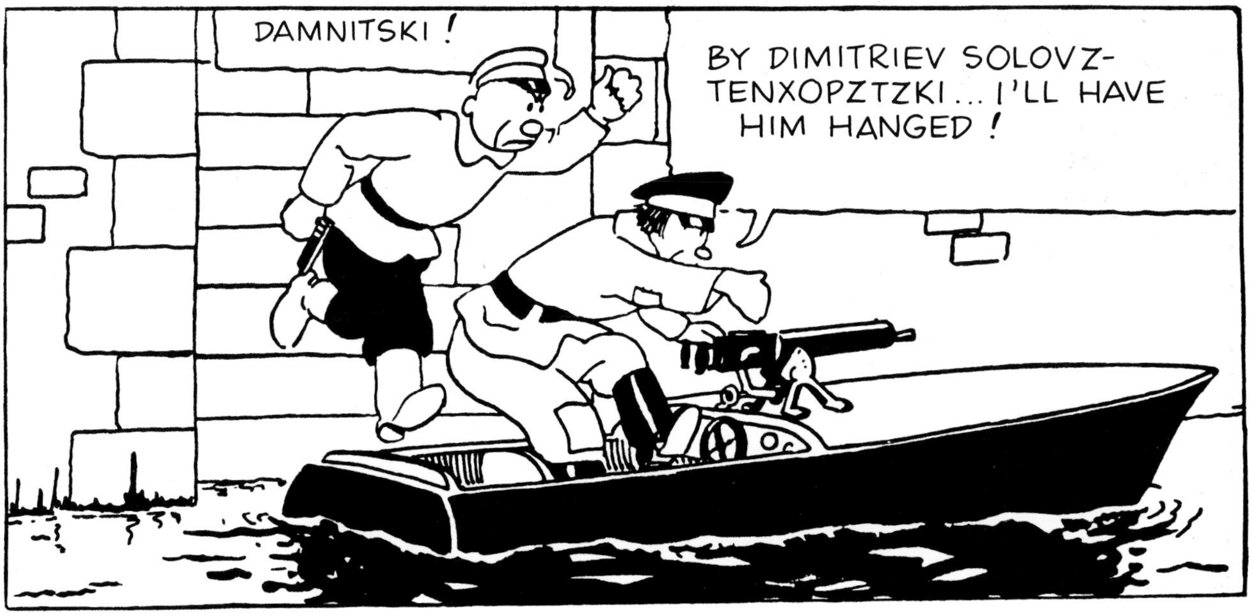
DAMNITSKI !
BY DIMITRIEV SOLOVZ-TENXOPZTZKI... I'LL HAVE HIM HANGED !

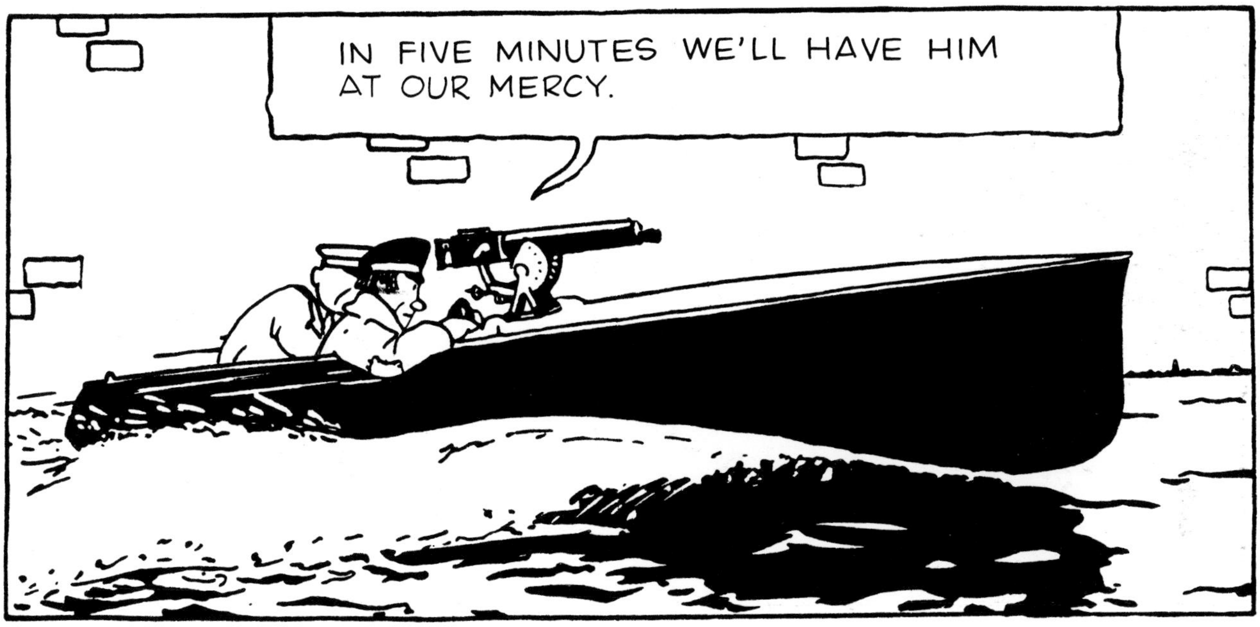
IN FIVE MINUTES WE'LL HAVE HIM AT OUR MERCY.

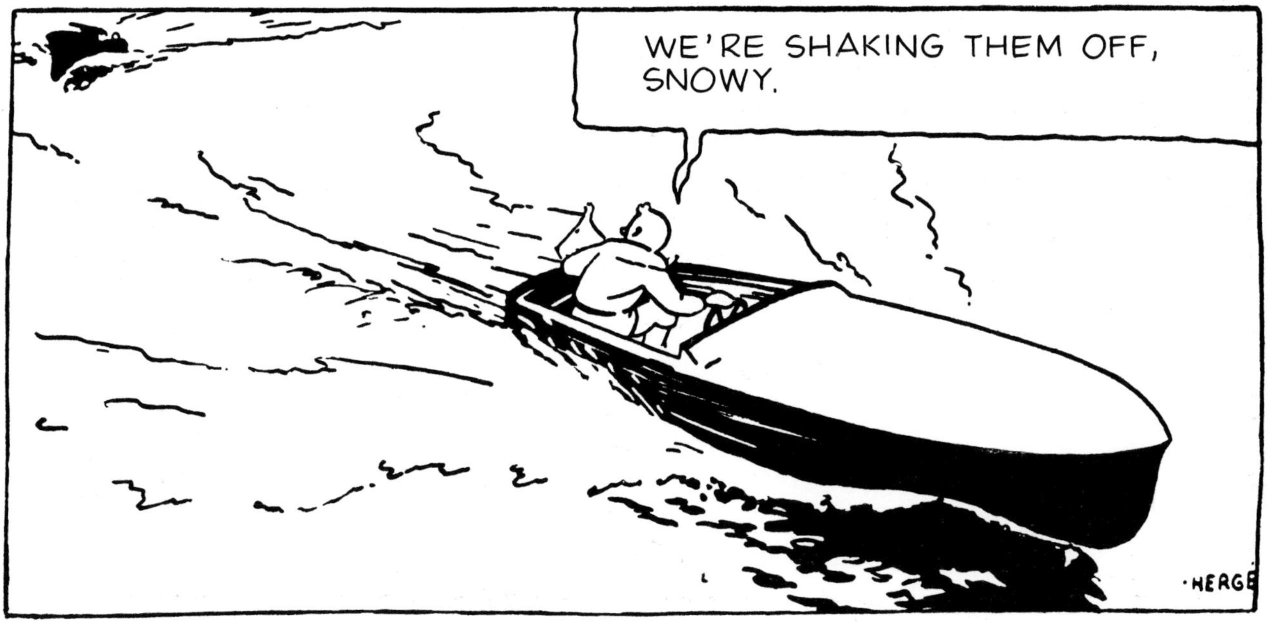
WE'RE SHAKING THEM OFF, SNOWY.
HERGÉ

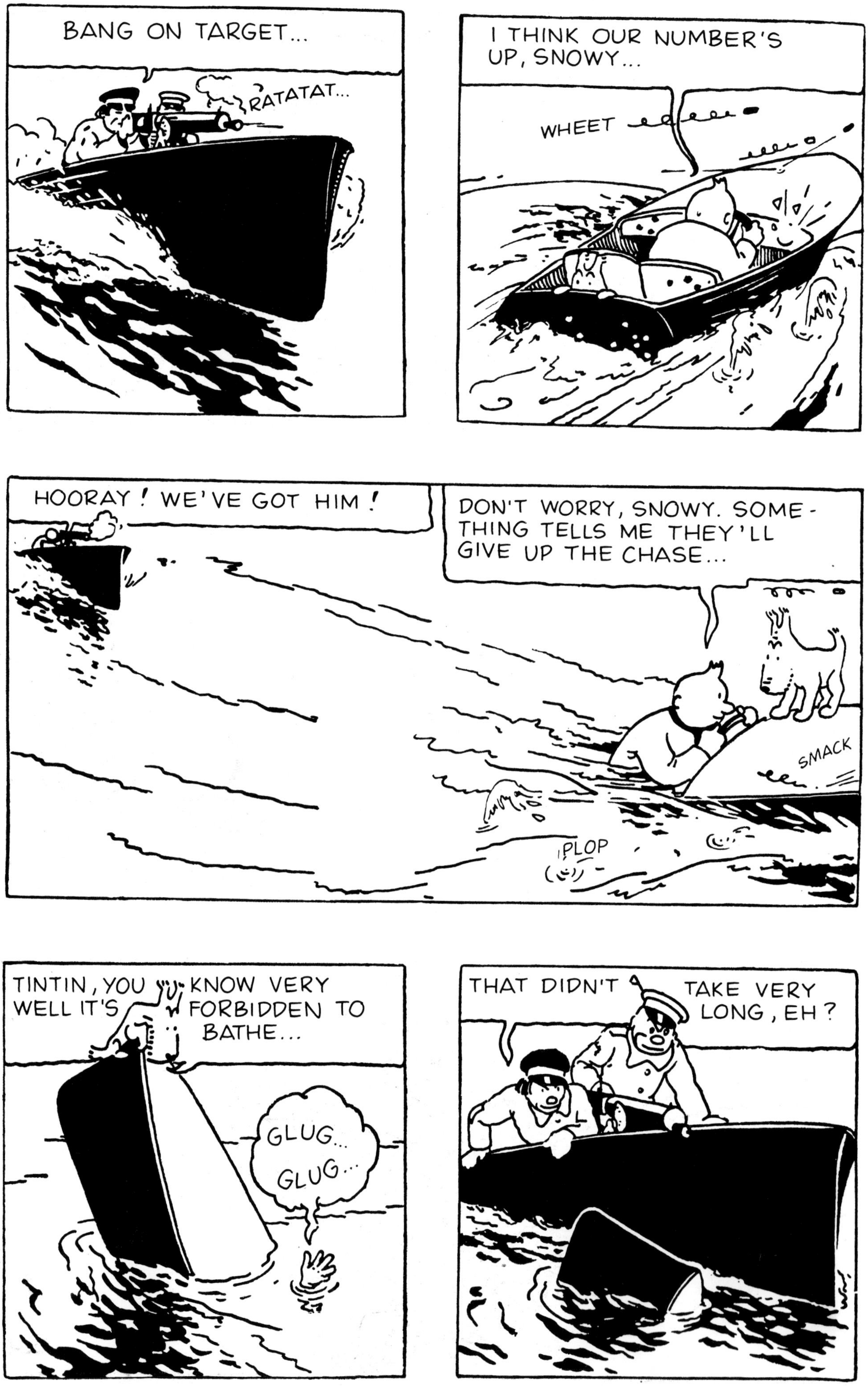
BANG ON TARGET...
RATATAT...
I THINK OUR NUMBER'S UP, SNOWY...
WHEET
HOORAY! WE'VE GOT HIM!
DON'T WORRY, SNOWY. SOME-THING TELLS ME THEY'LL GIVE UP THE CHASE...
SMACK
PLOP
TINTIN, YOU KNOW VERY WELL IT'S FORBIDDEN TO BATHE...
GLUG... GLUG...
THAT DIDN'T TAKE VERY LONG, EH?

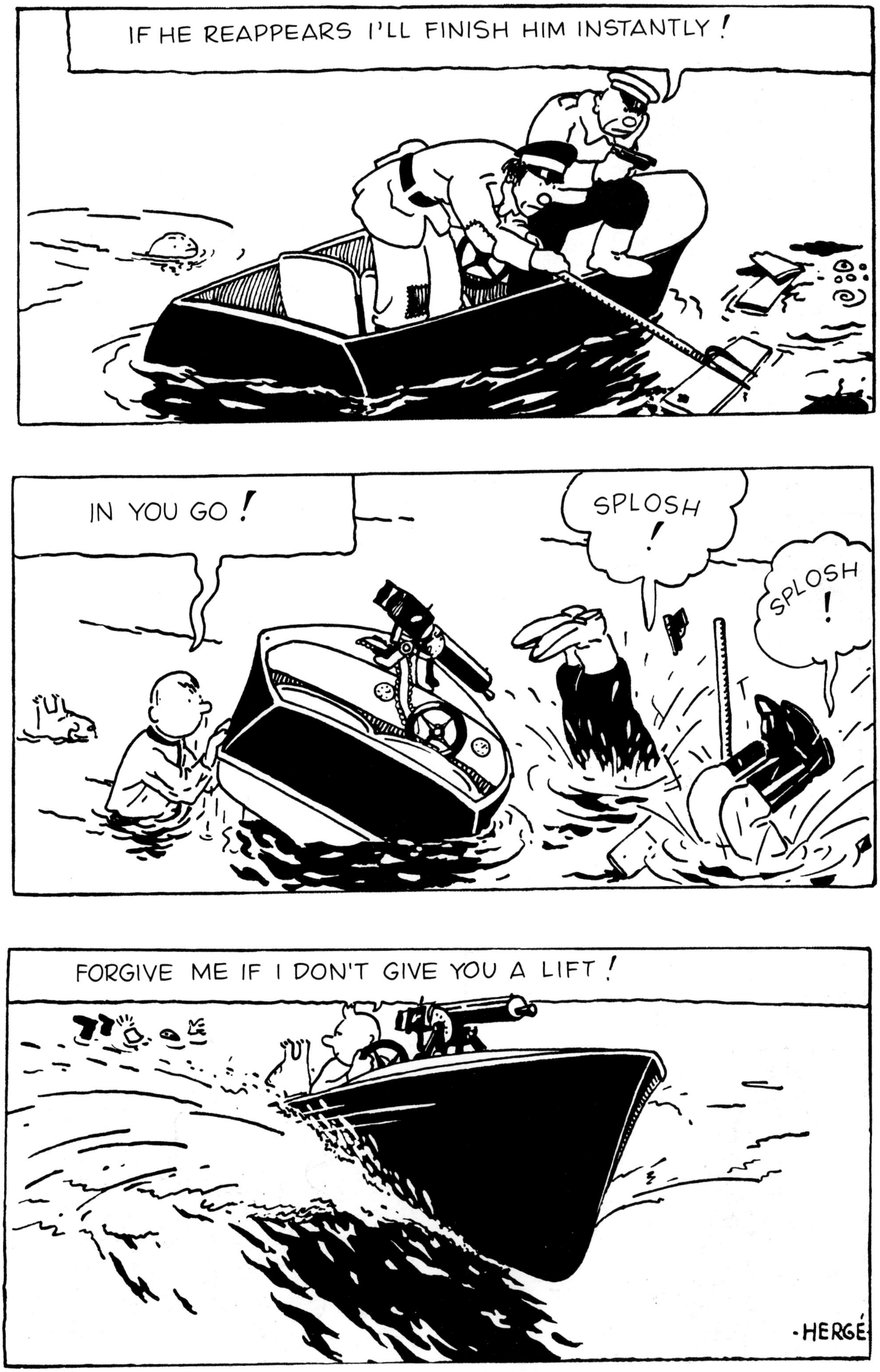
IF HE REAPPEARS I'LL FINISH HIM INSTANTLY !
IN YOU GO !
SPLOSH !
SPLOSH !
FORGIVE ME IF I DON'T GIVE YOU A LIFT !
·HERGÉ

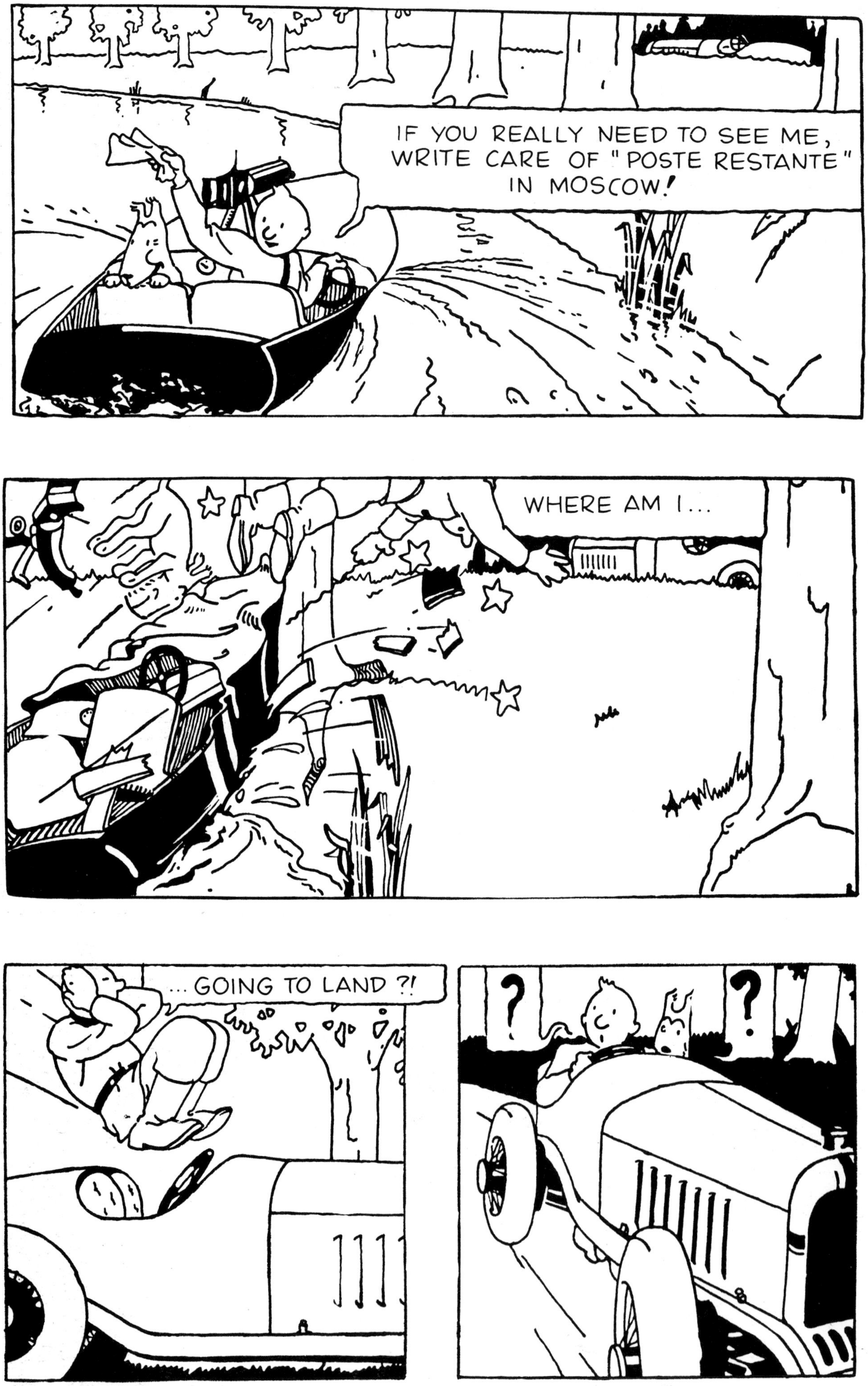
IF YOU REALLY NEED TO SEE ME, WRITE CARE OF "POSTE RESTANTE" IN MOSCOW!
WHERE AM I...
...GOING TO LAND ?!

?
TO PINCH MY CAR FROM UNDER MY VERY NOSE! THAT'S THE LIMIT!
JUST YOU WAIT, MY FRIEND... A MATCH TO THIS TRICKLE OF PETROL...
... AND NOW, BON VOYAGE!
·HERGÉ·

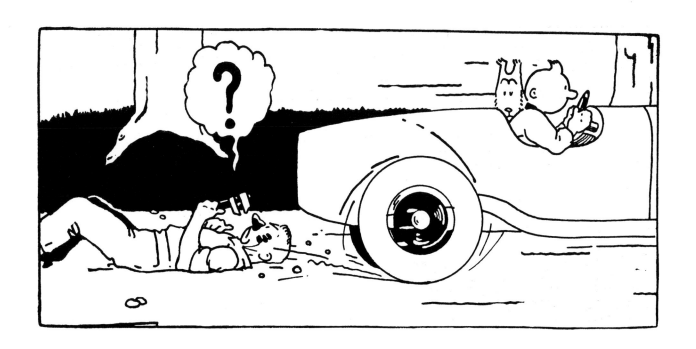

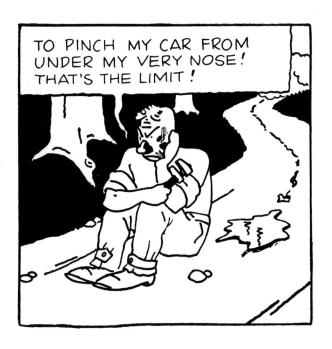

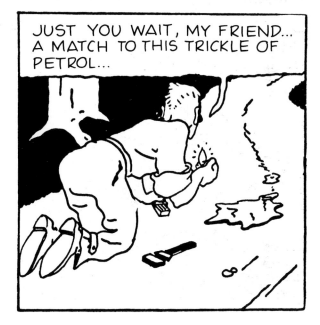

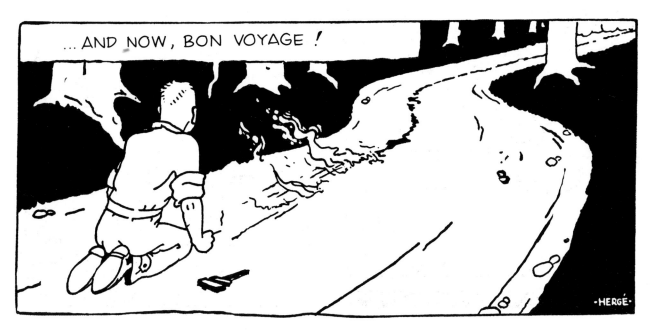

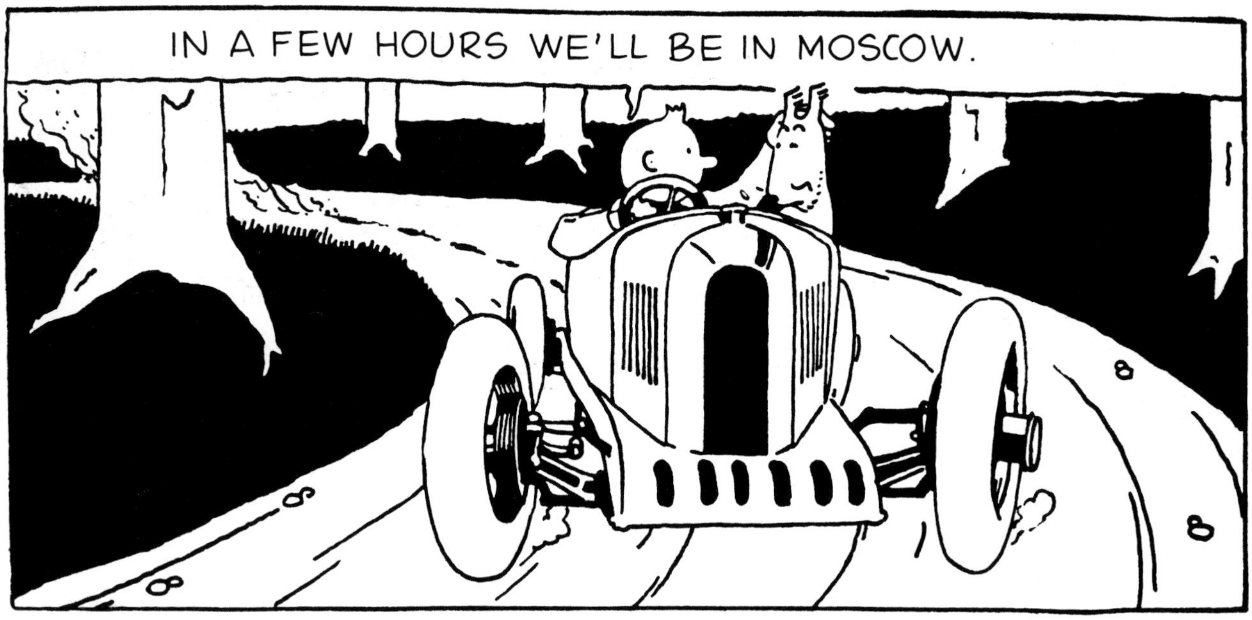
IN A FEW HOURS WE'LL BE IN MOSCOW.

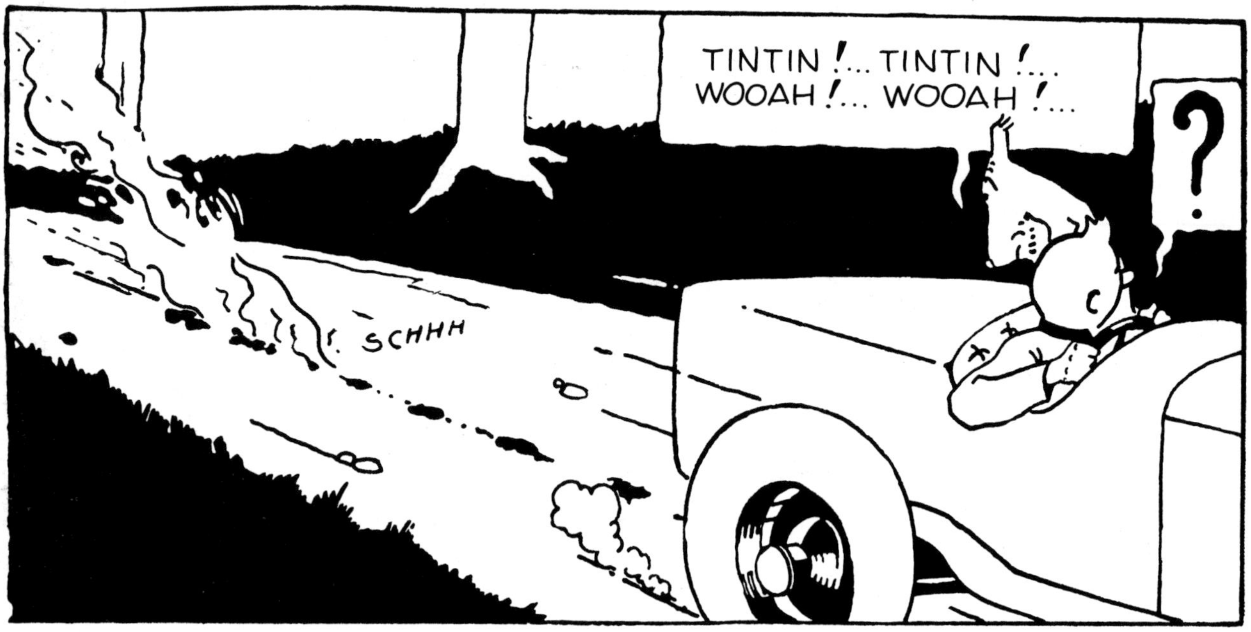
TINTIN !... TINTIN !...
WOOAH !... WOOAH !...
?
SCHHH

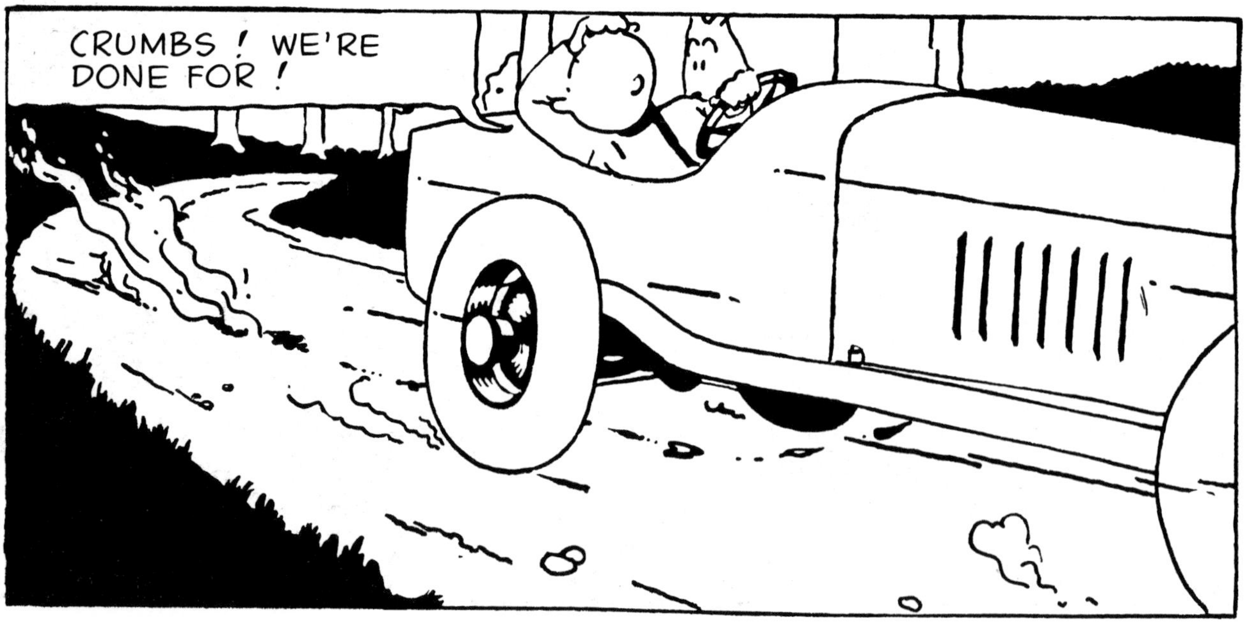
CRUMBS ! WE'RE DONE FOR !

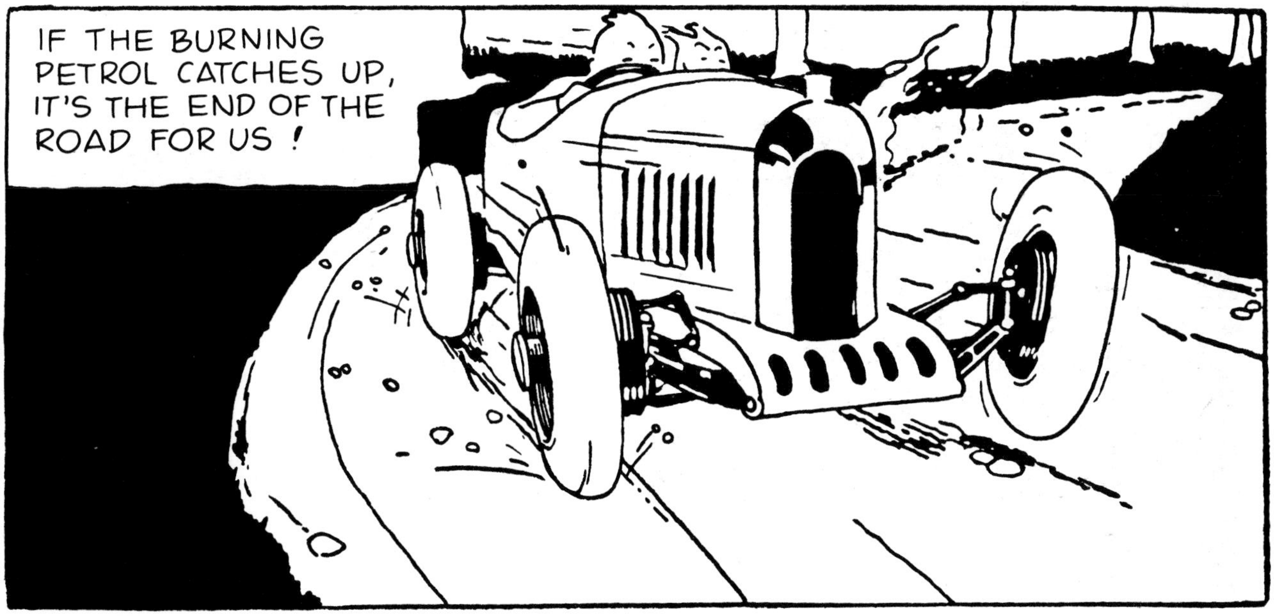
IF THE BURNING PETROL CATCHES UP, IT'S THE END OF THE ROAD FOR US !

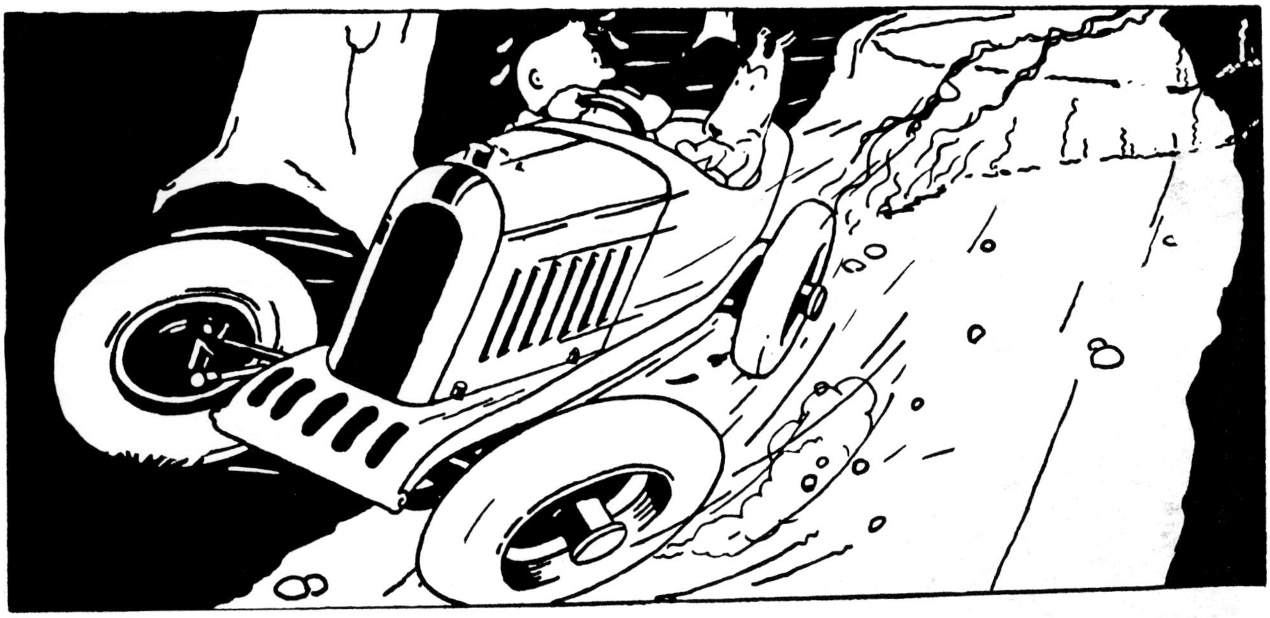

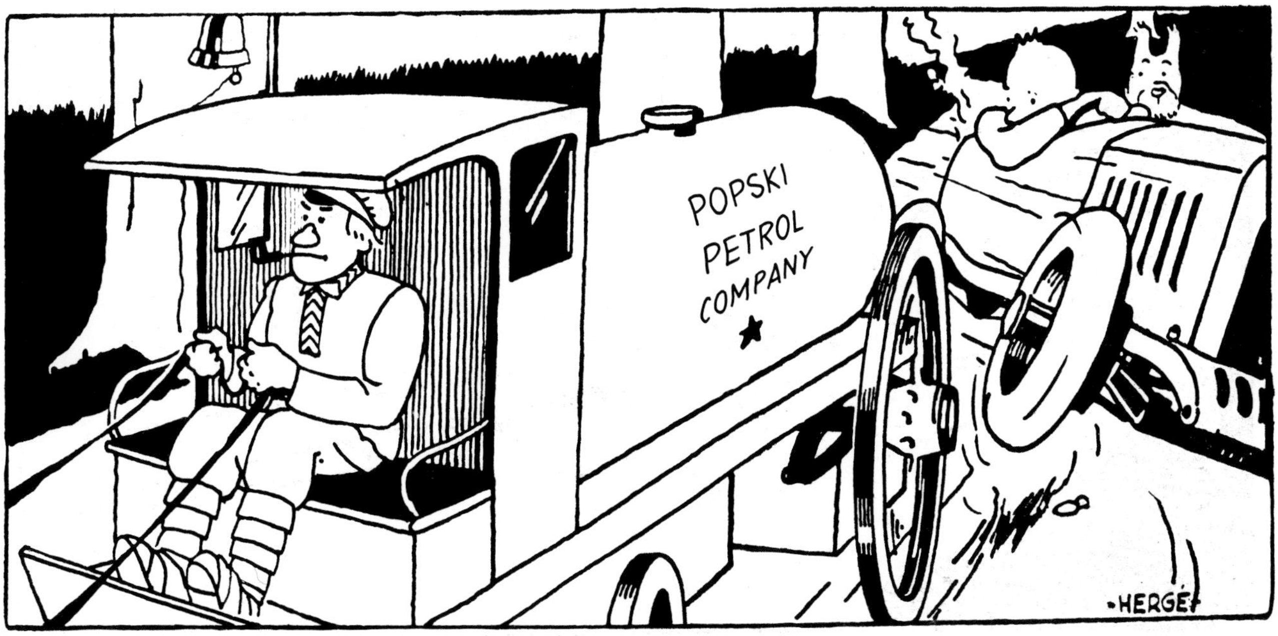
POPSKI PETROL COMPANY
HERGÉ

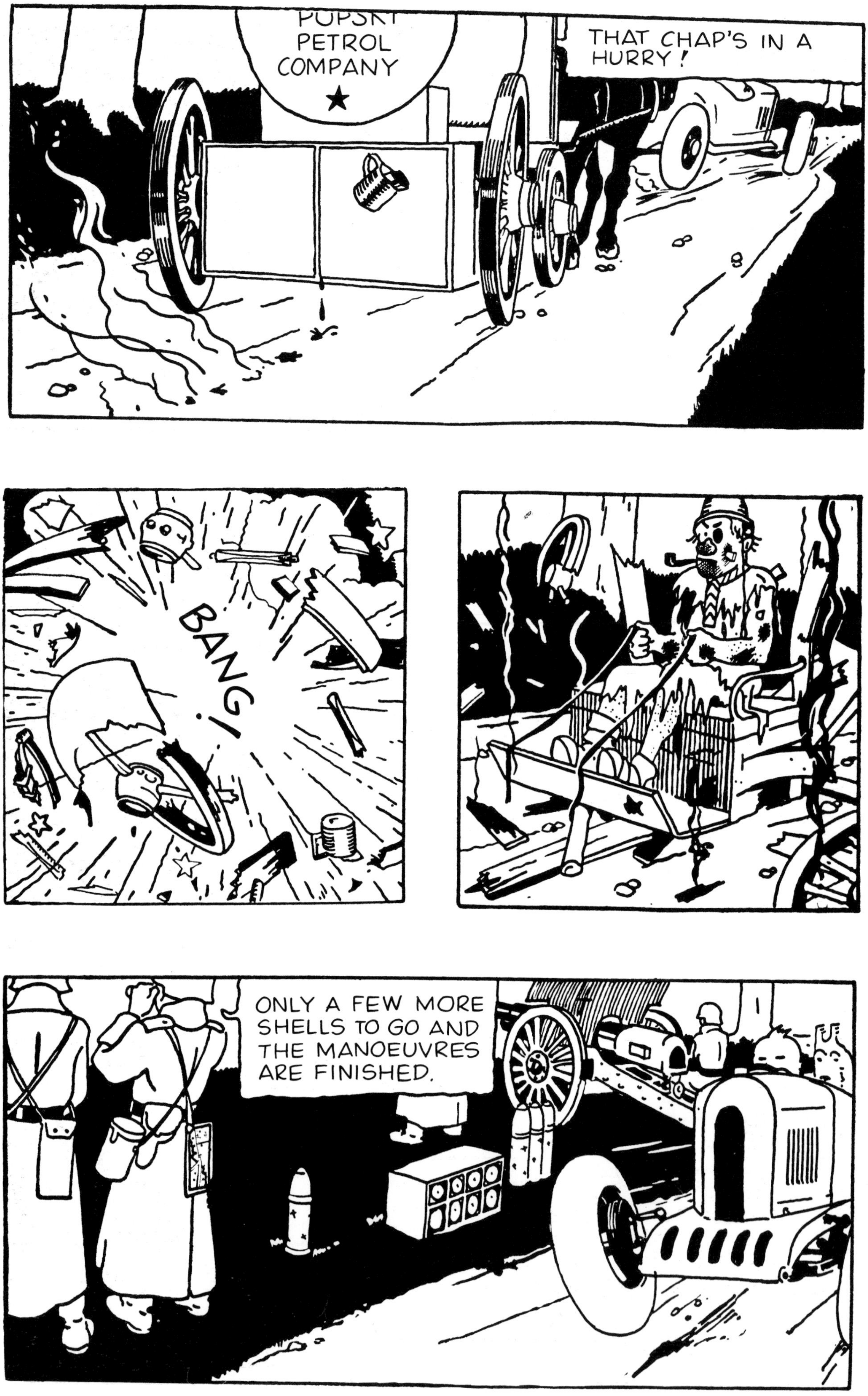
PETROL
COMPANY
THAT CHAP'S IN A HURRY!
BANG!
ONLY A FEW MORE SHELLS TO GO AND THE MANOEUVRES ARE FINISHED.

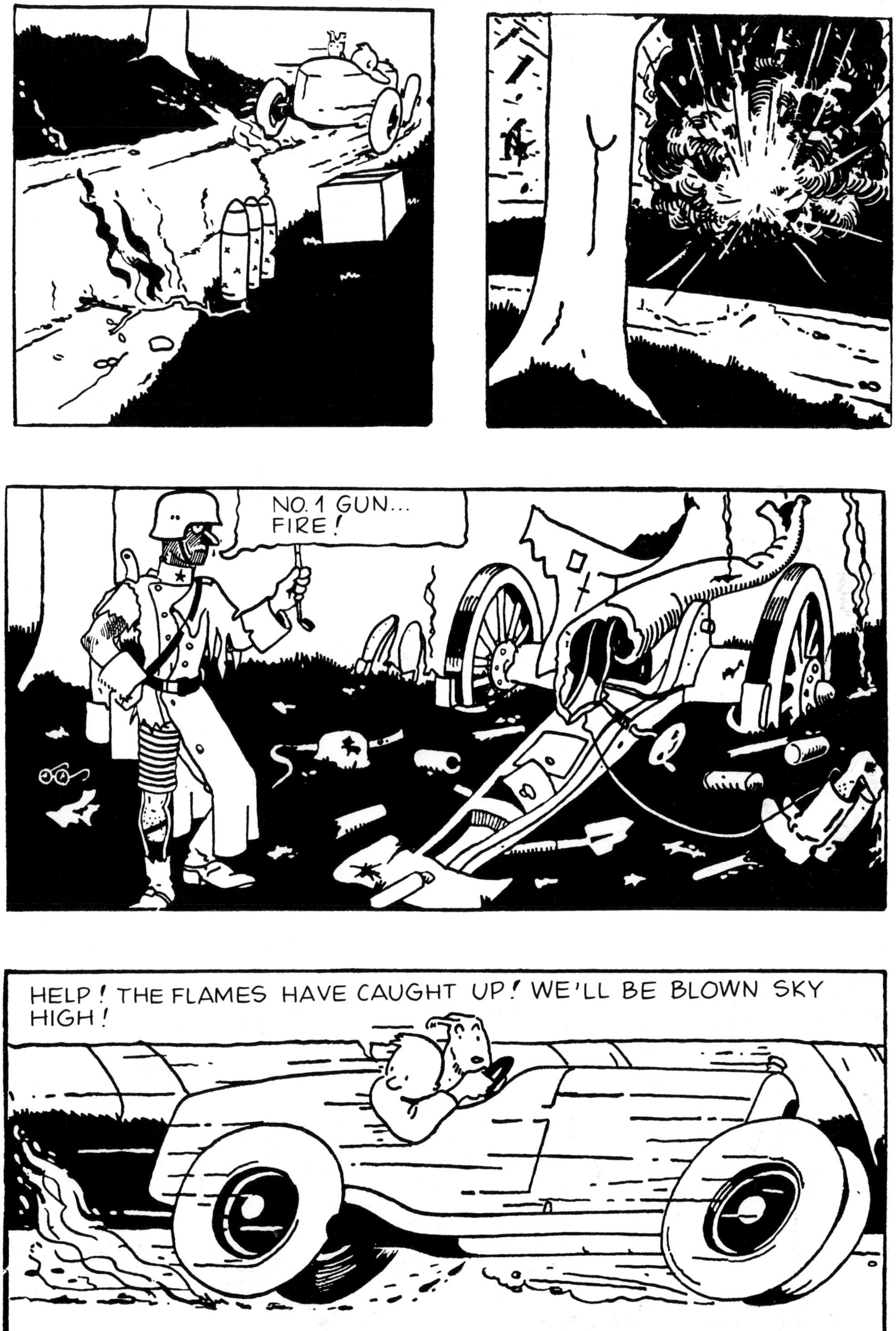
NO. 1 GUN... FIRE!
HELP! THE FLAMES HAVE CAUGHT UP! WE'LL BE BLOWN SKY HIGH!

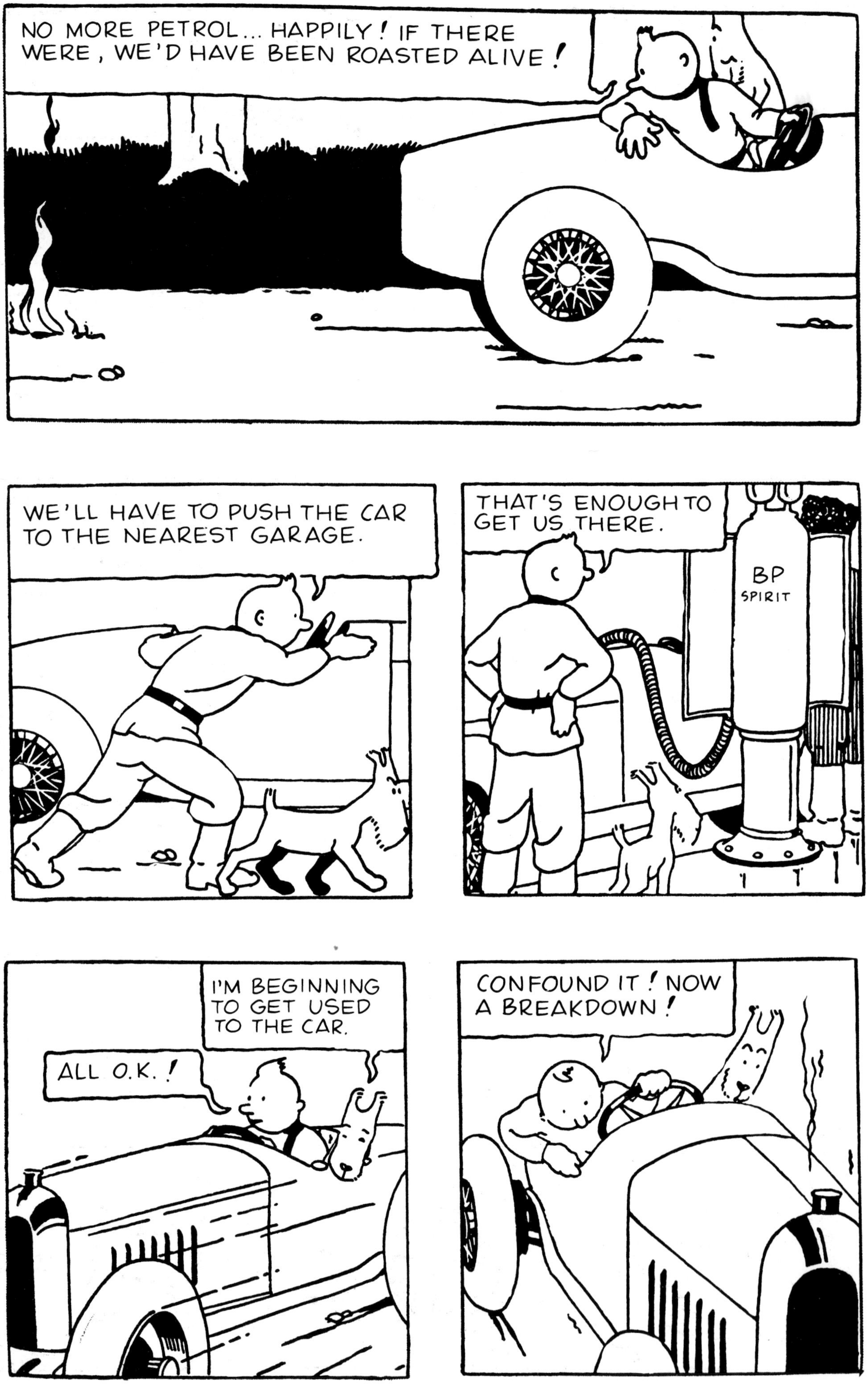
NO MORE PETROL... HAPPILY! IF THERE WERE, WE'D HAVE BEEN ROASTED ALIVE!
WE'LL HAVE TO PUSH THE CAR TO THE NEAREST GARAGE.
THAT'S ENOUGH TO GET US THERE.
BP SPIRIT
I'M BEGINNING TO GET USED TO THE CAR.
ALL O.K.!
CONFOUND IT! NOW A BREAKDOWN!

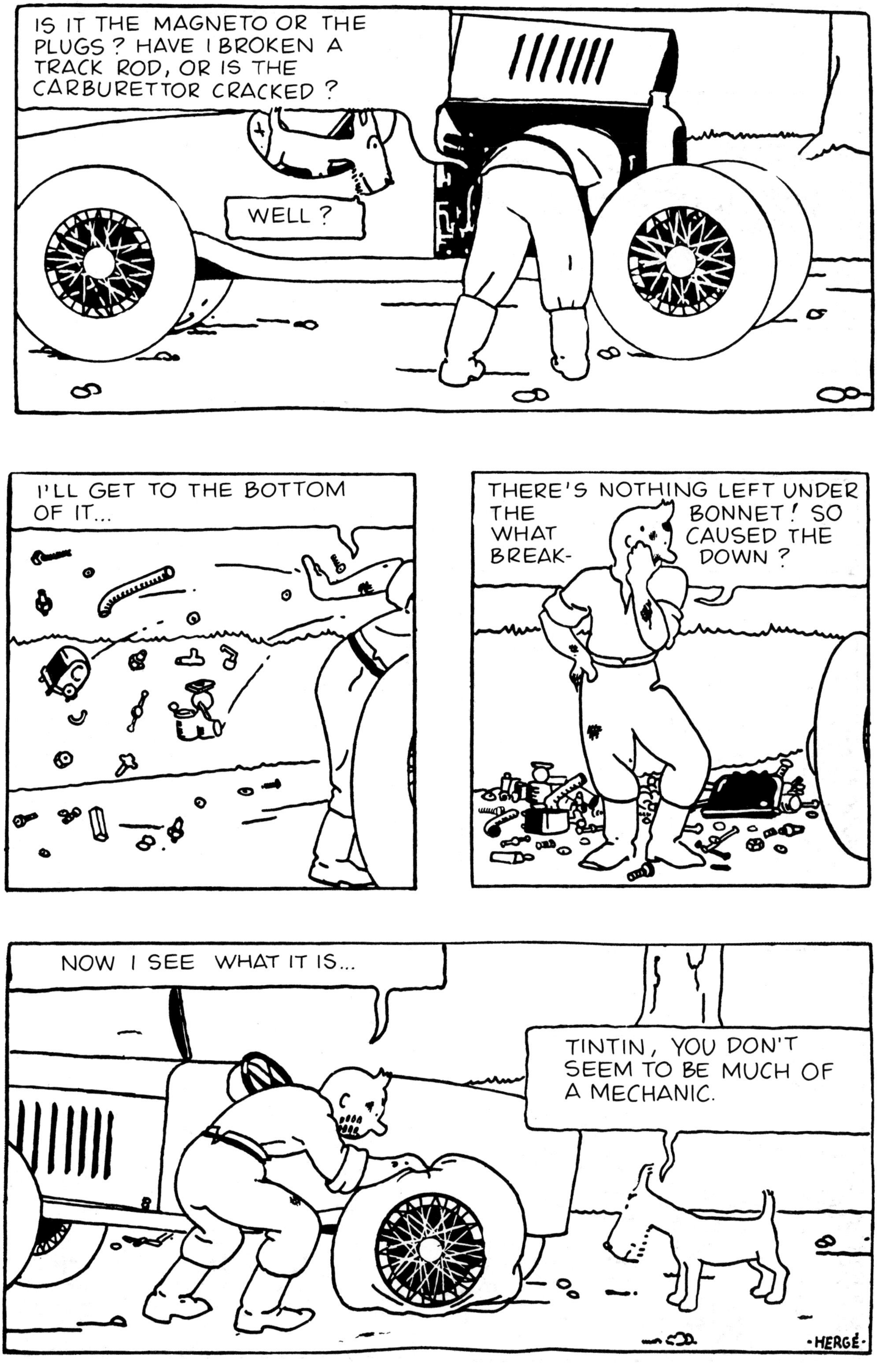
IS IT THE MAGNETO OR THE PLUGS ? HAVE I BROKEN A TRACK ROD, OR IS THE CARBURETTOR CRACKED ?
WELL ?
I'LL GET TO THE BOTTOM OF IT...
THERE'S NOTHING LEFT UNDER THE BONNET ! SO WHAT CAUSED THE BREAK-DOWN ?
NOW I SEE WHAT IT IS...
TINTIN, YOU DON'T SEEM TO BE MUCH OF A MECHANIC.
·HERGÉ·

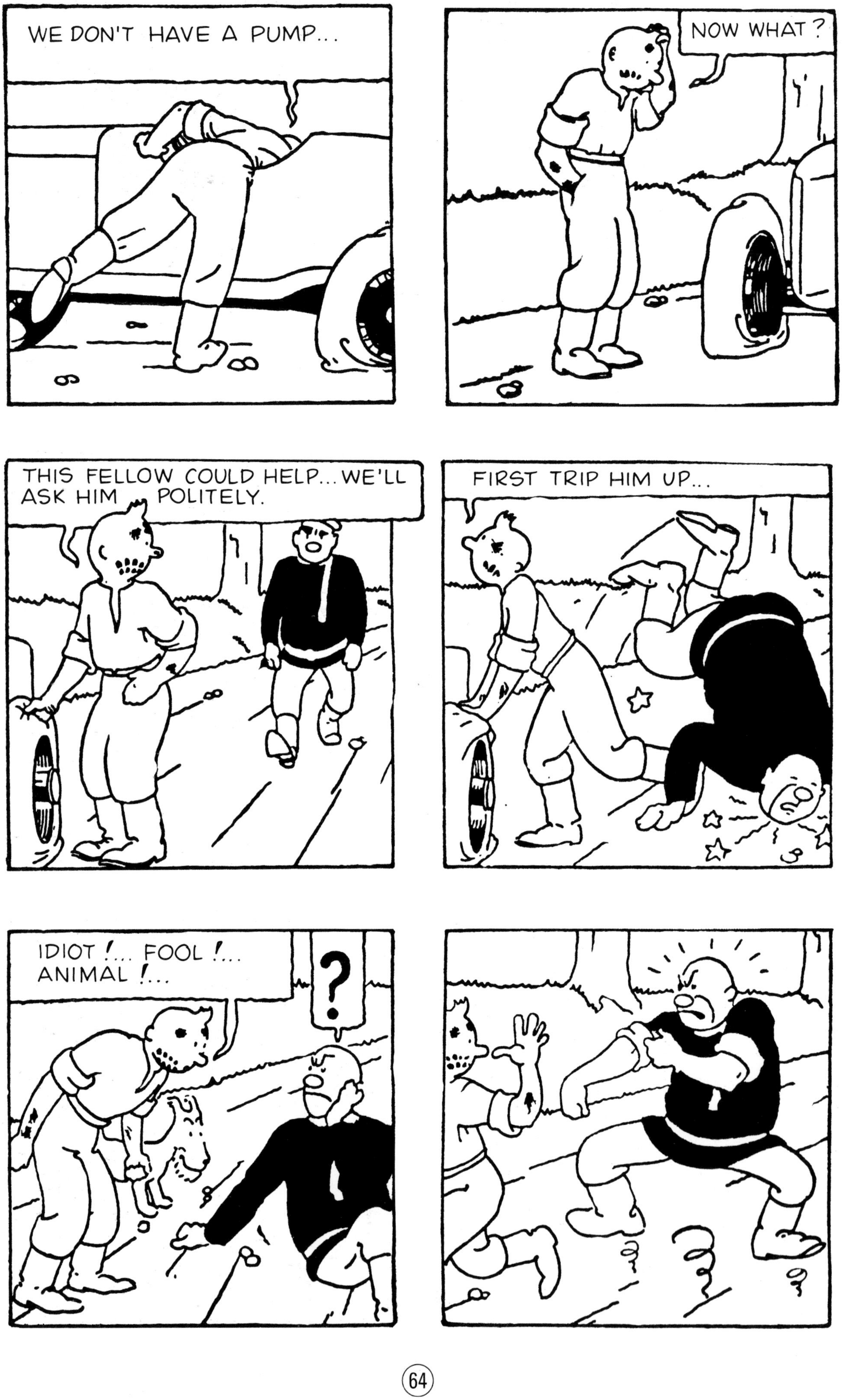
WE DON'T HAVE A PUMP...
NOW WHAT?
THIS FELLOW COULD HELP... WE'LL ASK HIM POLITELY.
FIRST TRIP HIM UP...
IDIOT !... FOOL !... ANIMAL !...
?

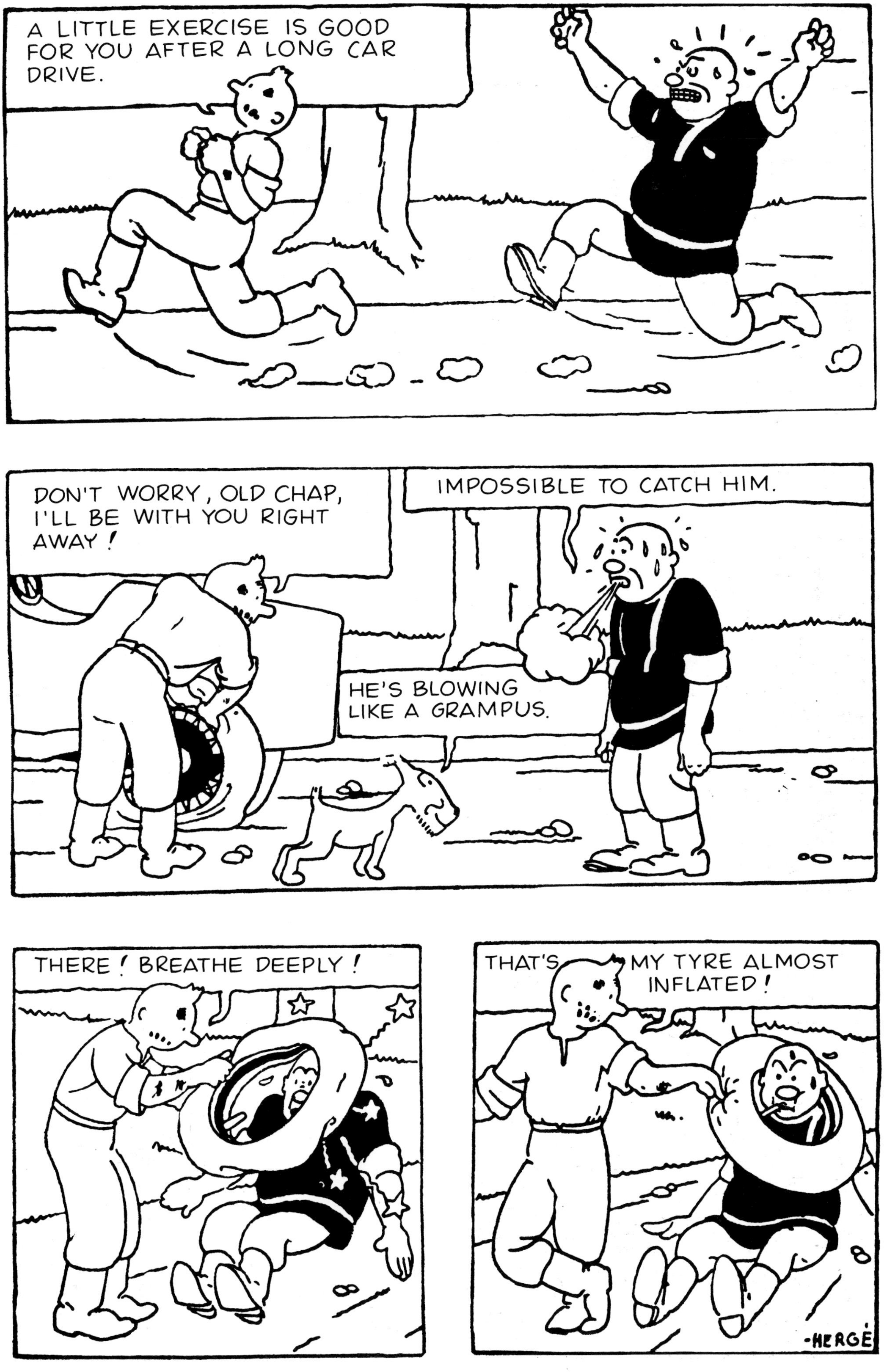
A LITTLE EXERCISE IS GOOD FOR YOU AFTER A LONG CAR DRIVE.
DON'T WORRY, OLD CHAP, I'LL BE WITH YOU RIGHT AWAY!
IMPOSSIBLE TO CATCH HIM.
HE'S BLOWING LIKE A GRAMPUS.
THERE! BREATHE DEEPLY!
THAT'S MY TYRE ALMOST INFLATED!
HERGÉ

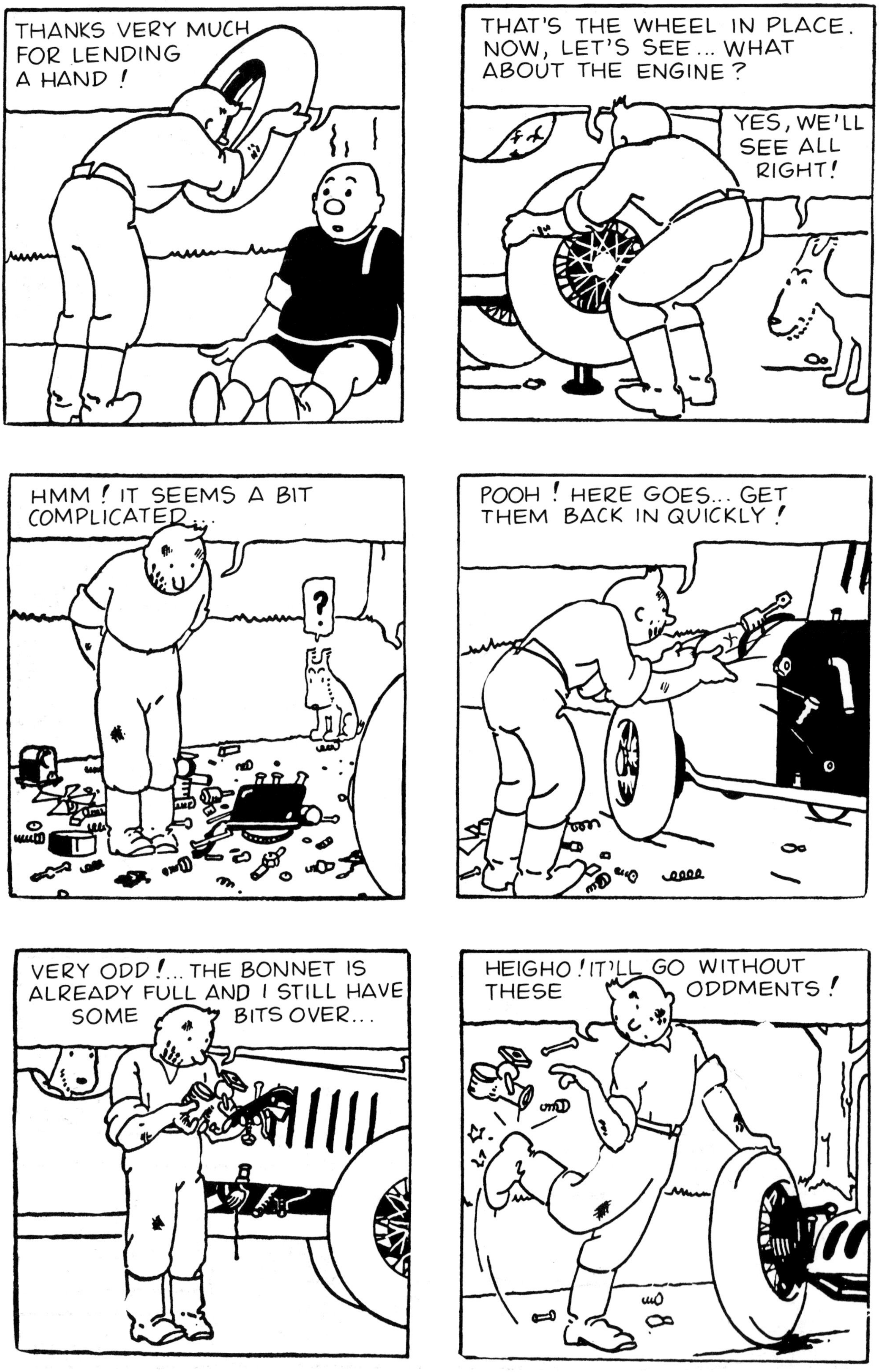
THANKS VERY MUCH FOR LENDING A HAND !
THAT'S THE WHEEL IN PLACE. NOW, LET'S SEE... WHAT ABOUT THE ENGINE ?
YES, WE'LL SEE ALL RIGHT!
HMM ! IT SEEMS A BIT COMPLICATED...
POOH ! HERE GOES... GET THEM BACK IN QUICKLY !
VERY ODD !... THE BONNET IS ALREADY FULL AND I STILL HAVE SOME BITS OVER...
HEIGHO ! IT'LL GO WITHOUT THESE ODDMENTS !

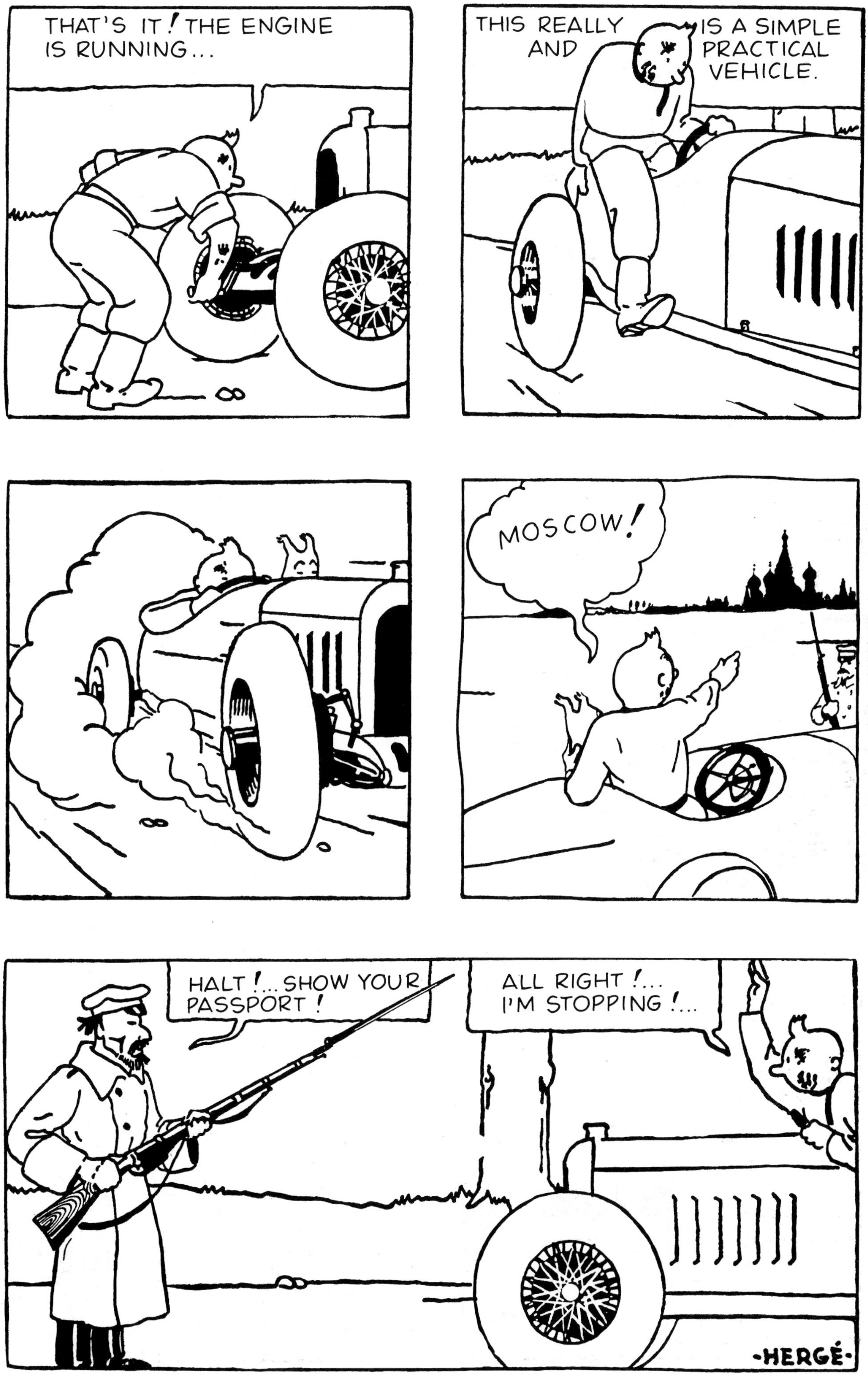
THAT'S IT! THE ENGINE IS RUNNING...
THIS REALLY AND IS A SIMPLE PRACTICAL VEHICLE.
MOSCOW!
HALT!... SHOW YOUR PASSPORT!
ALL RIGHT!... I'M STOPPING!...
-HERGÉ-

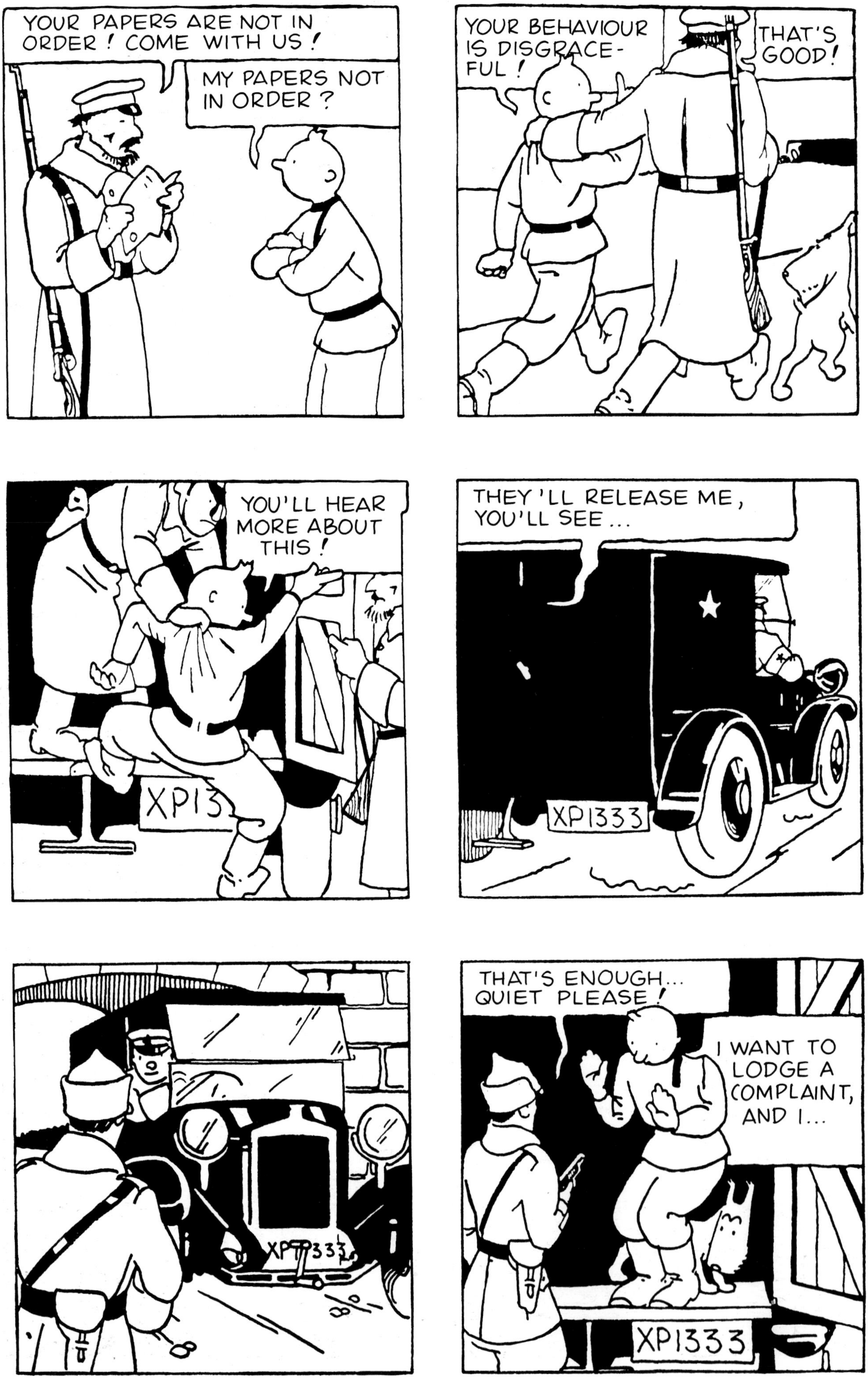
YOUR PAPERS ARE NOT IN ORDER ! COME WITH US !
MY PAPERS NOT IN ORDER ?
YOUR BEHAVIOUR IS DISGRACE-FUL !
THAT'S GOOD !
YOU'LL HEAR MORE ABOUT THIS !
XP13
THEY'LL RELEASE ME, YOU'LL SEE ...
XP1333
THAT'S ENOUGH... QUIET PLEASE !
I WANT TO LODGE A COMPLAINT, AND I...
XP1333

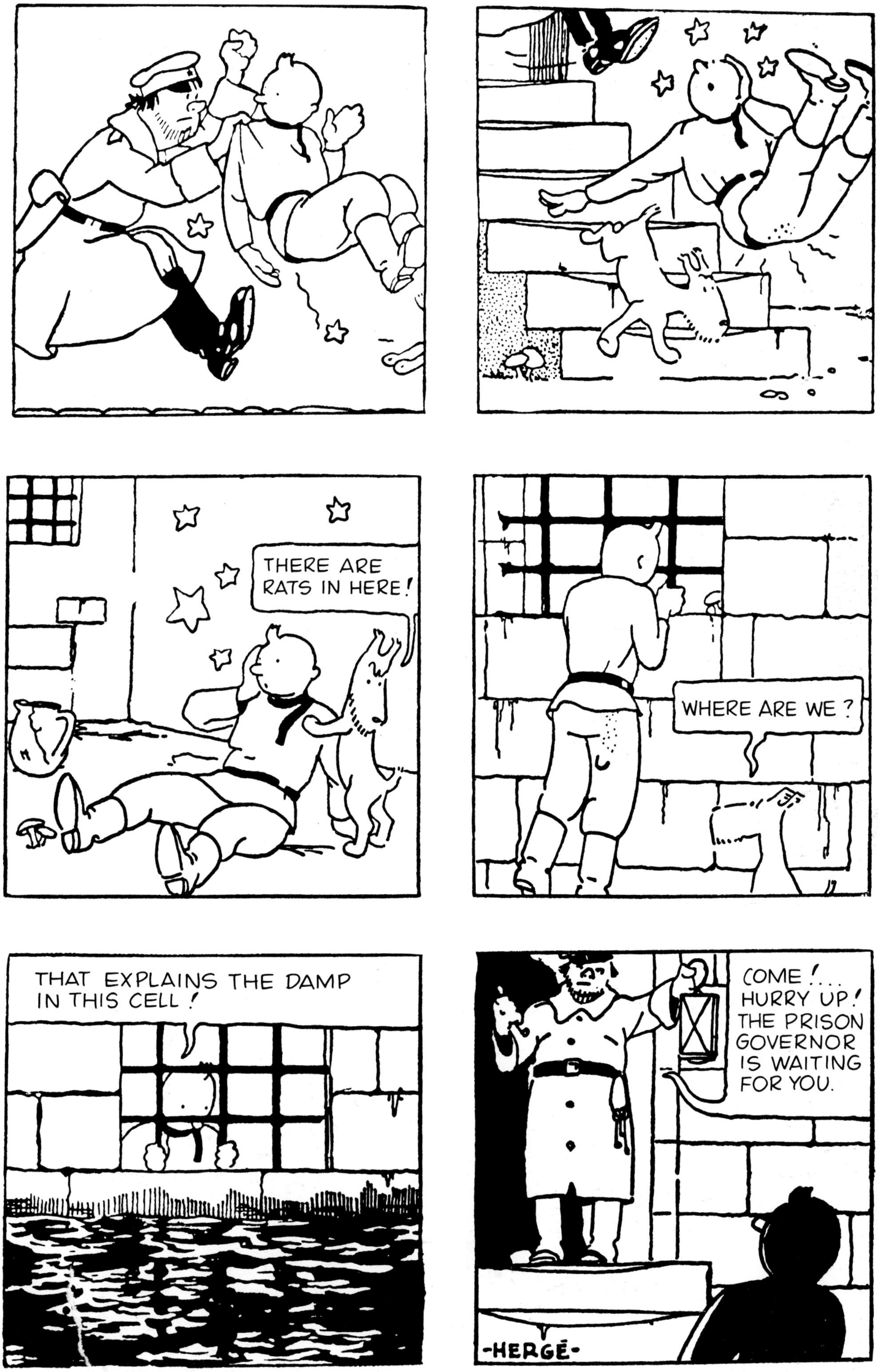

THERE ARE RATS IN HERE!
WHERE ARE WE?
THAT EXPLAINS THE DAMP IN THIS CELL!
COME!... HURRY UP! THE PRISON GOVERNOR IS WAITING FOR YOU.
-HERGÉ-

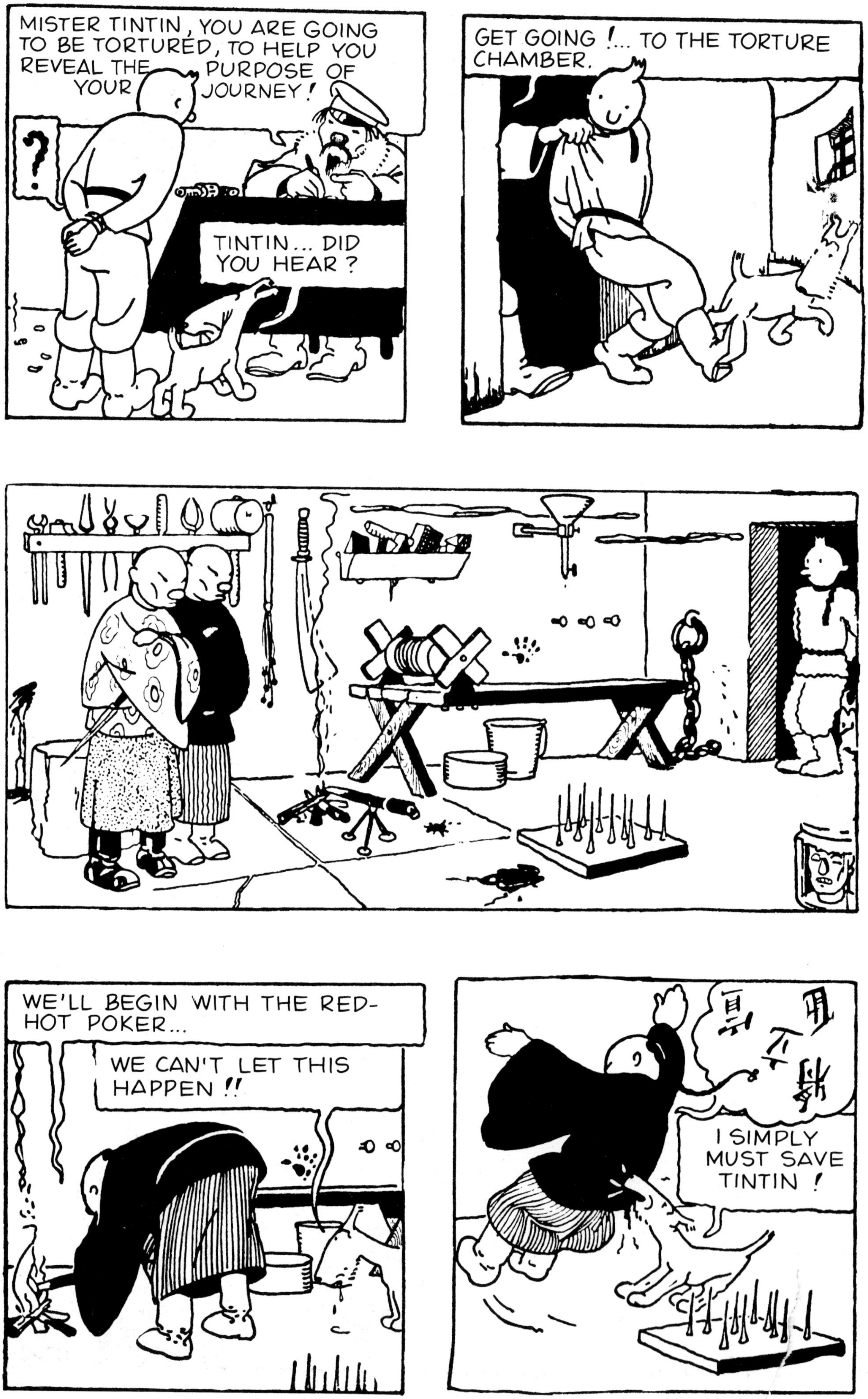
MISTER TINTIN, YOU ARE GOING TO BE TORTURED, TO HELP YOU REVEAL THE PURPOSE OF YOUR JOURNEY!
TINTIN... DID YOU HEAR?
GET GOING!... TO THE TORTURE CHAMBER.
WE'LL BEGIN WITH THE RED-HOT POKER...
WE CAN'T LET THIS HAPPEN!!
I SIMPLY MUST SAVE TINTIN!

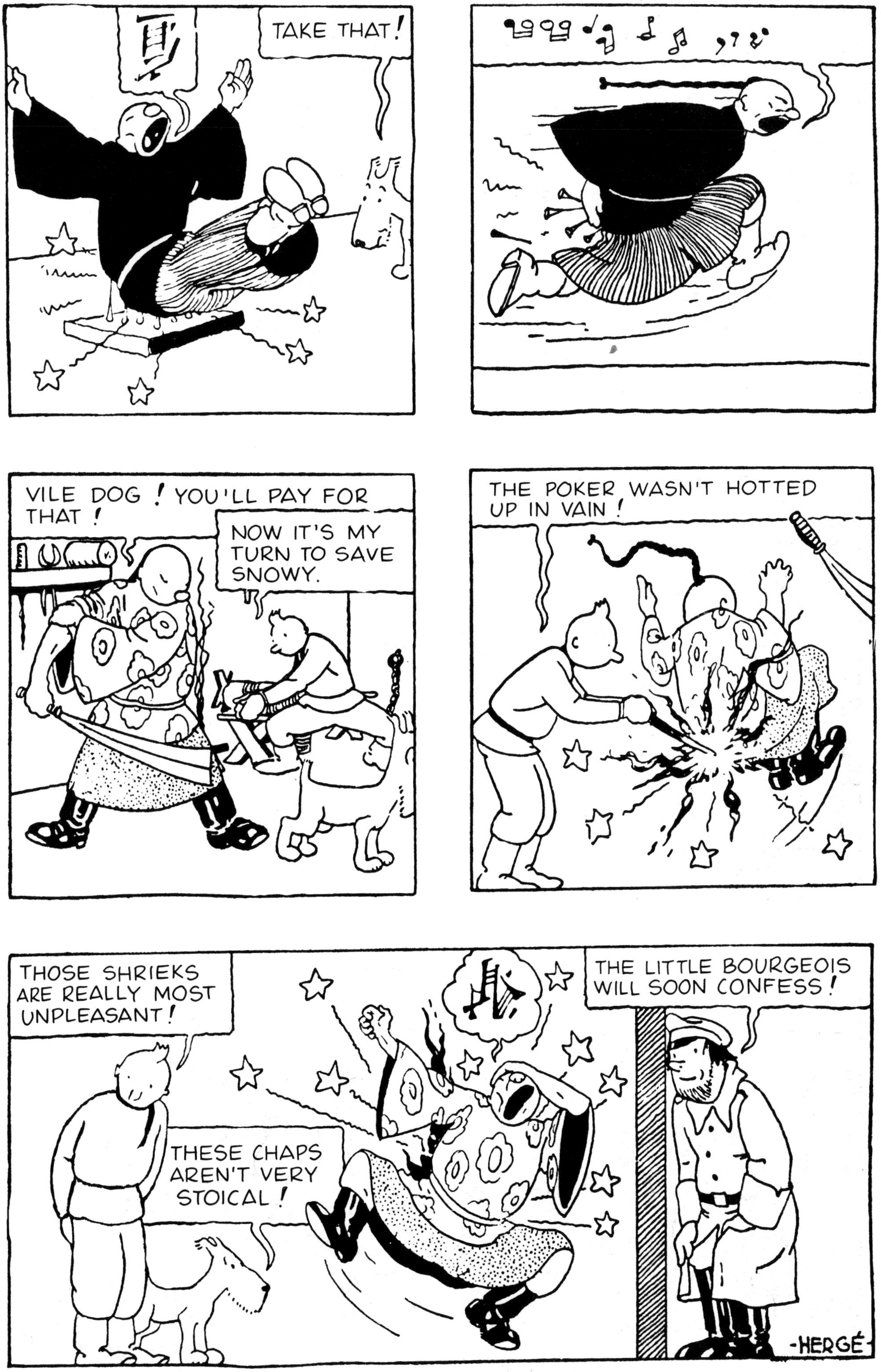

TAKE THAT!
VILE DOG! YOU'LL PAY FOR THAT!
NOW IT'S MY TURN TO SAVE SNOWY.
THE POKER WASN'T HOTTED UP IN VAIN!
THOSE SHRIEKS ARE REALLY MOST UNPLEASANT!
THESE CHAPS AREN'T VERY STOICAL!
THE LITTLE BOURGEOIS WILL SOON CONFESS!
-HERGÉ-

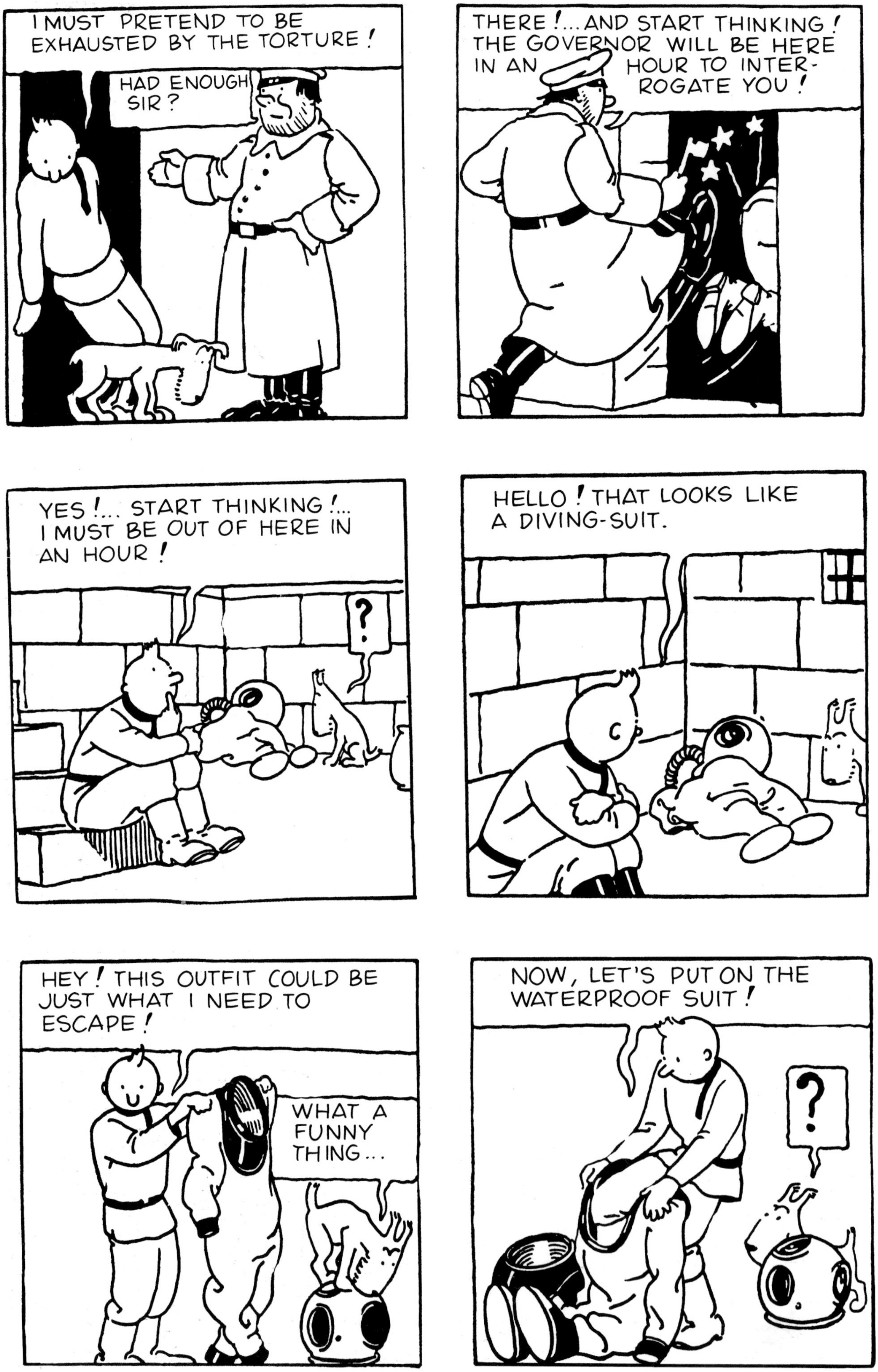

I MUST PRETEND TO BE EXHAUSTED BY THE TORTURE !
HAD ENOUGH SIR ?
THERE !... AND START THINKING ! THE GOVERNOR WILL BE HERE IN AN HOUR TO INTERROGATE YOU !
YES !... START THINKING !... I MUST BE OUT OF HERE IN AN HOUR !
?
HELLO ! THAT LOOKS LIKE A DIVING-SUIT.
HEY ! THIS OUTFIT COULD BE JUST WHAT I NEED TO ESCAPE !
WHAT A FUNNY THING...
NOW, LET'S PUT ON THE WATERPROOF SUIT !
?

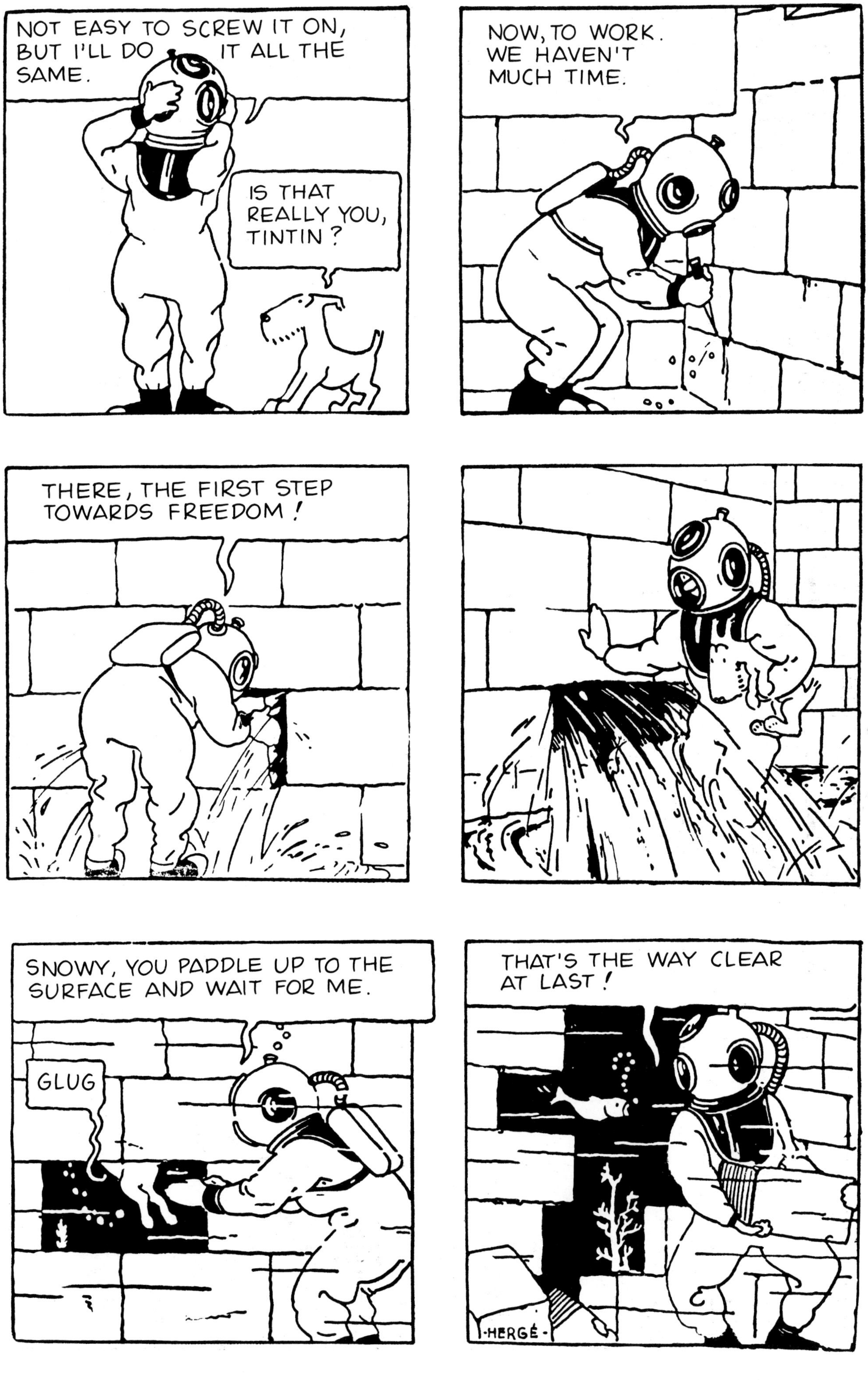
NOT EASY TO SCREW IT ON, BUT I'LL DO IT ALL THE SAME.
IS THAT REALLY YOU, TINTIN?
NOW, TO WORK. WE HAVEN'T MUCH TIME.
THERE, THE FIRST STEP TOWARDS FREEDOM!
SNOWY, YOU PADDLE UP TO THE SURFACE AND WAIT FOR ME.
GLUG
THAT'S THE WAY CLEAR AT LAST!
-HERGÉ-

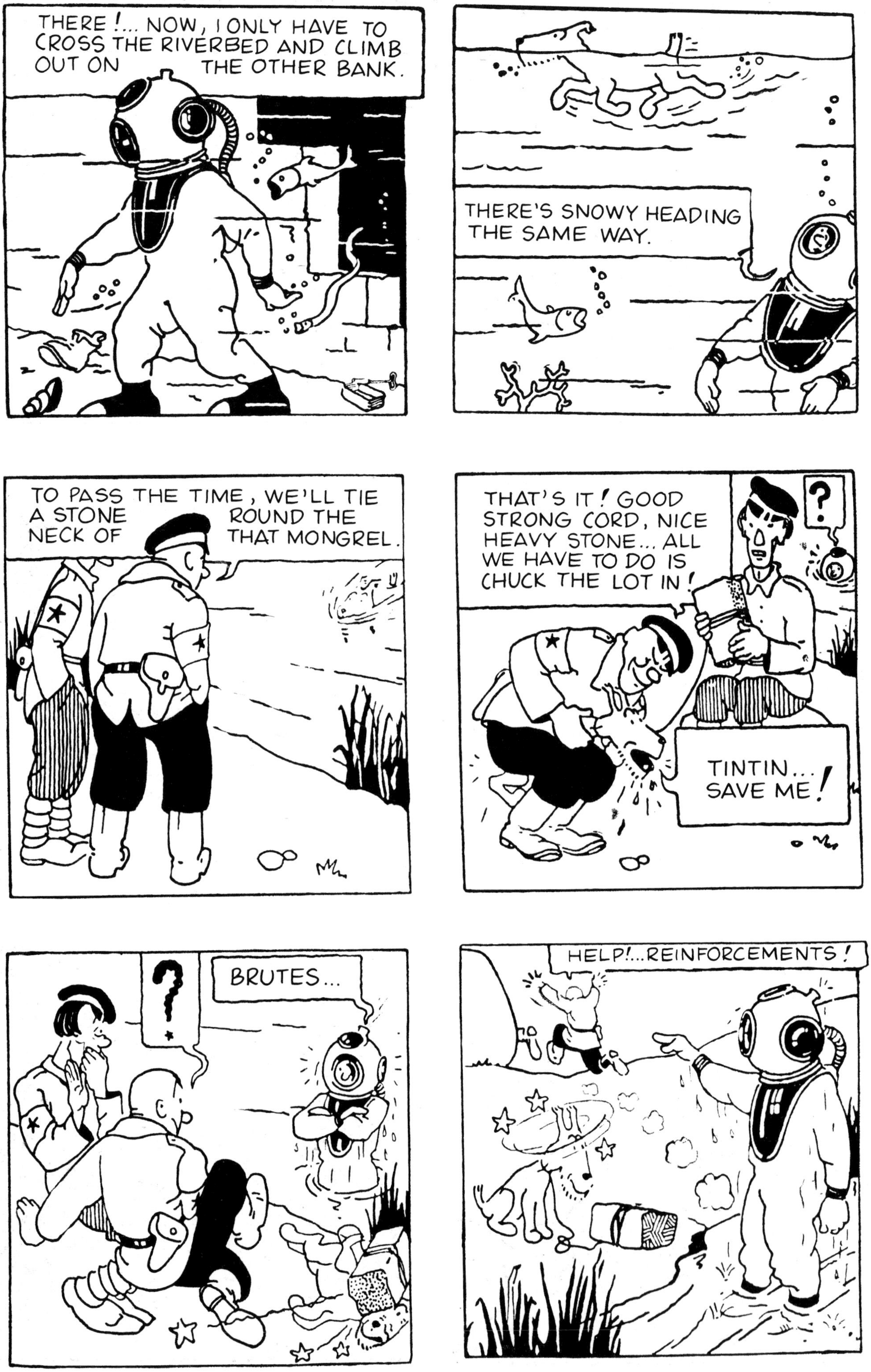
THERE !... NOW, I ONLY HAVE TO CROSS THE RIVERBED AND CLIMB OUT ON THE OTHER BANK.
THERE'S SNOWY HEADING THE SAME WAY.
TO PASS THE TIME, WE'LL TIE A STONE ROUND THE NECK OF THAT MONGREL.
THAT'S IT! GOOD STRONG CORD, NICE HEAVY STONE... ALL WE HAVE TO DO IS CHUCK THE LOT IN!
?
TINTIN... SAVE ME!
?
BRUTES...
HELP!...REINFORCEMENTS!

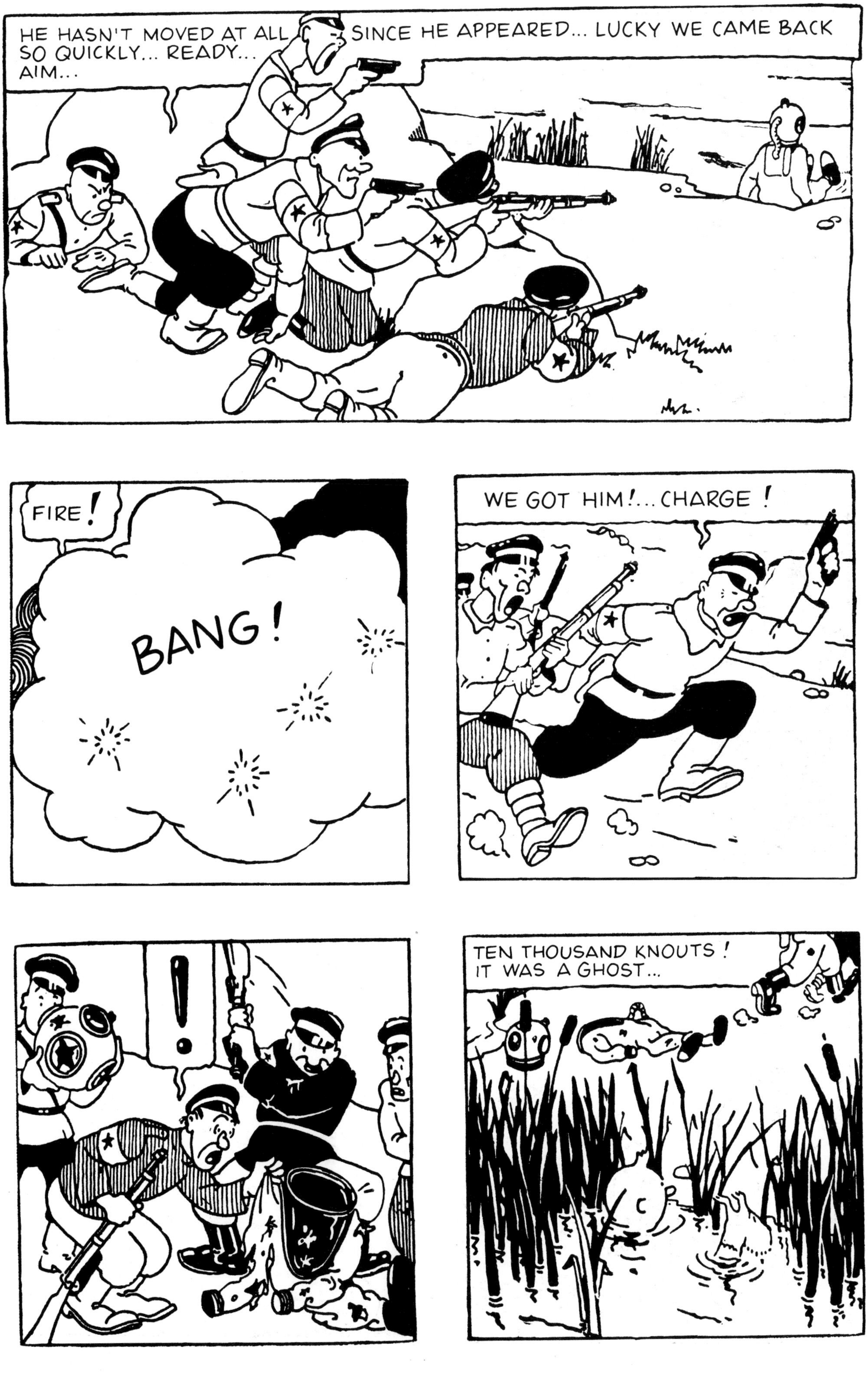
HE HASN'T MOVED AT ALL SINCE HE APPEARED... LUCKY WE CAME BACK SO QUICKLY... READY... AIM...
FIRE!
BANG!
WE GOT HIM!... CHARGE!
!
TEN THOUSAND KNOUTS! IT WAS A GHOST...

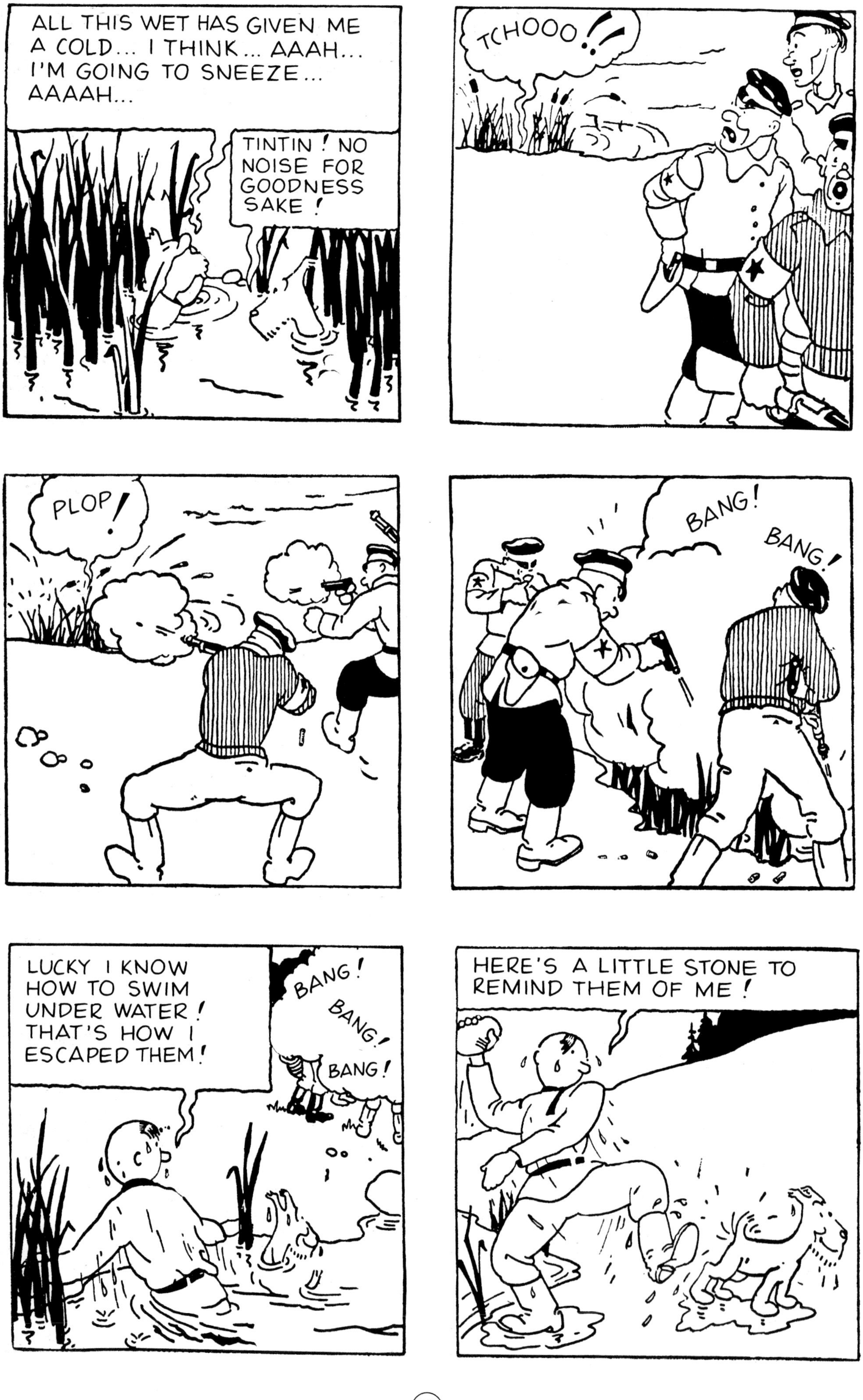
ALL THIS WET HAS GIVEN ME A COLD... I THINK... AAAH... I'M GOING TO SNEEZE... AAAAH...
TINTIN! NO NOISE FOR GOODNESS SAKE!
TCHOOO!!
PLOP!
BANG!
BANG!
LUCKY I KNOW HOW TO SWIM UNDER WATER! THAT'S HOW I ESCAPED THEM!
BANG!
BANG!
BANG!
HERE'S A LITTLE STONE TO REMIND THEM OF ME!

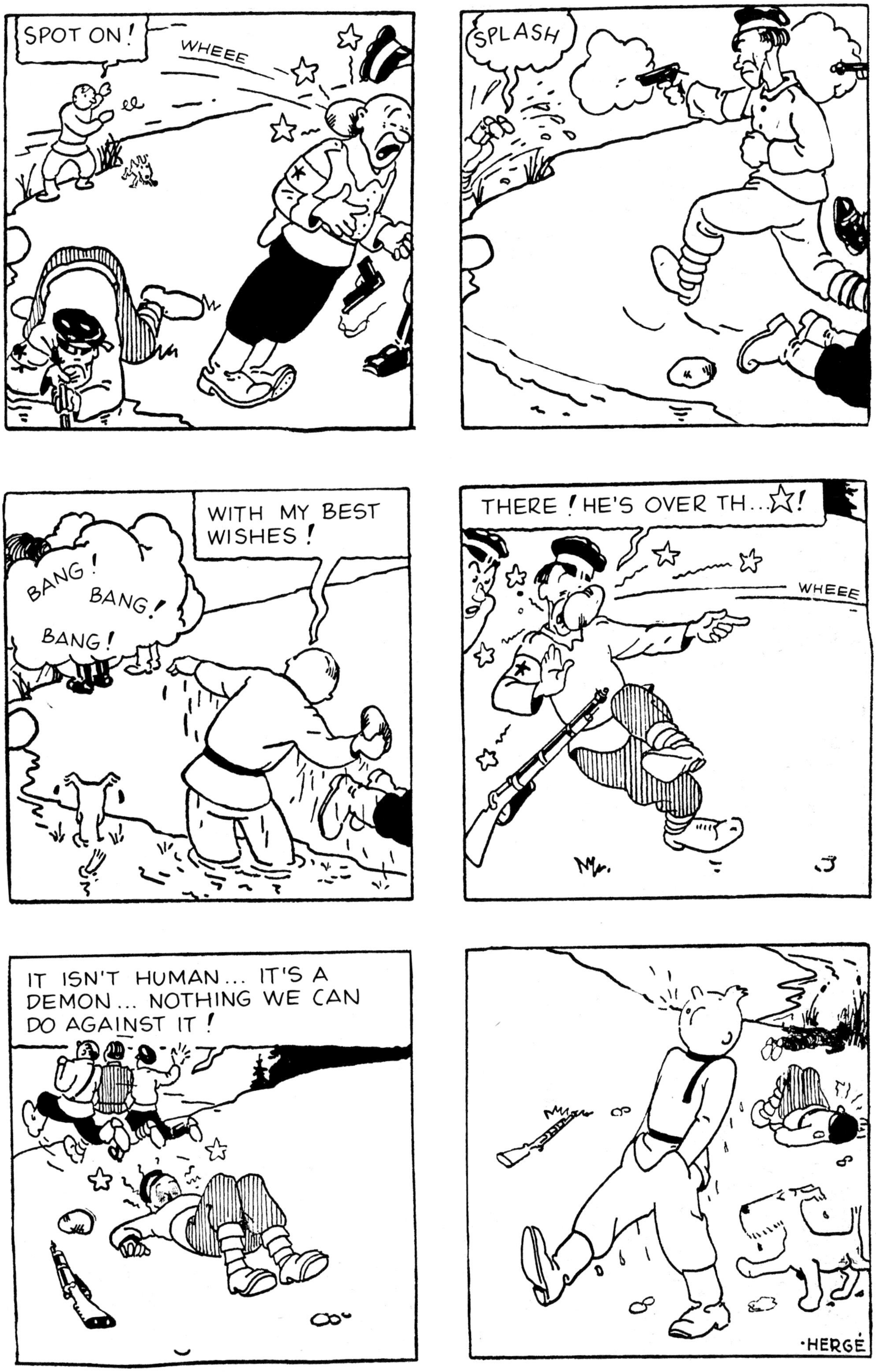

SPOT ON!
WHEEE
SPLASH
WITH MY BEST WISHES!
BANG! BANG! BANG!
THERE! HE'S OVER TH...☆!
WHEEE
IT ISN'T HUMAN... IT'S A DEMON... NOTHING WE CAN DO AGAINST IT!
·HERGÉ

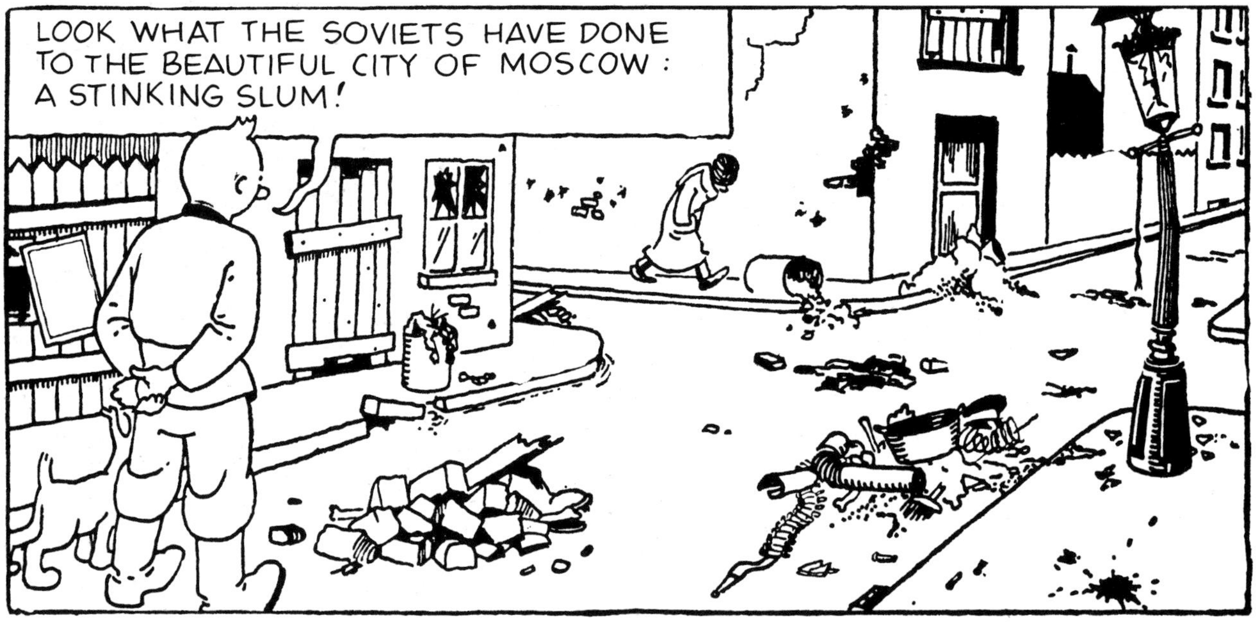
LOOK WHAT THE SOVIETS HAVE DONE TO THE BEAUTIFUL CITY OF MOSCOW : A STINKING SLUM!

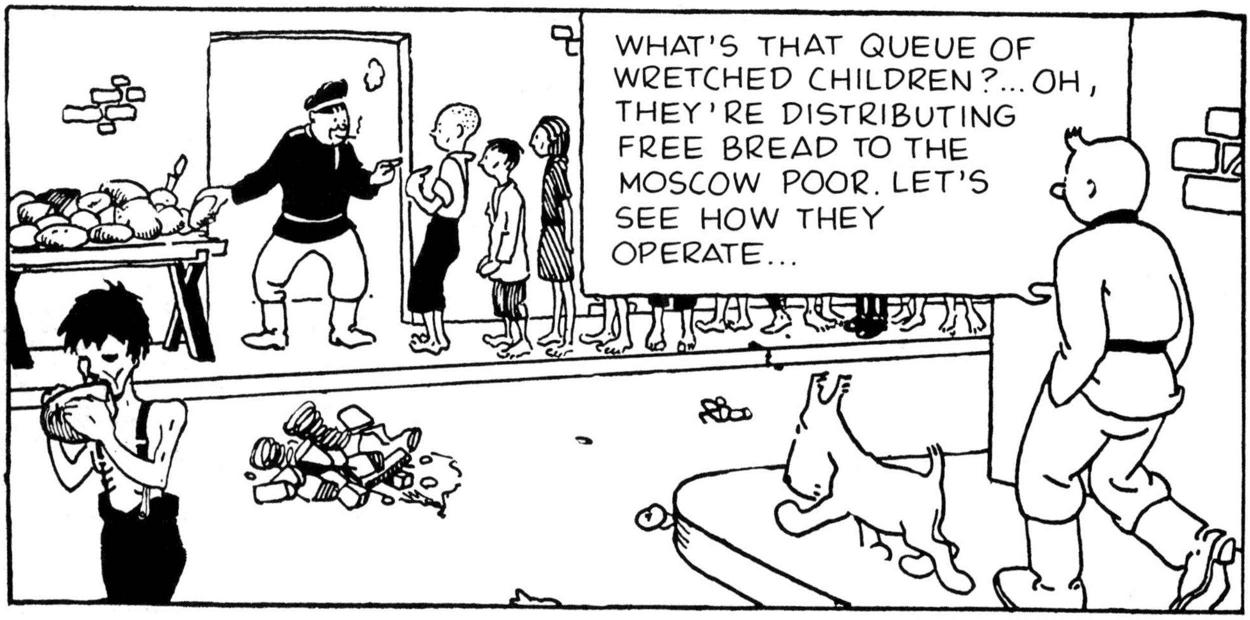
WHAT'S THAT QUEUE OF WRETCHED CHILDREN ?... OH, THEY'RE DISTRIBUTING FREE BREAD TO THE MOSCOW POOR. LET'S SEE HOW THEY OPERATE...

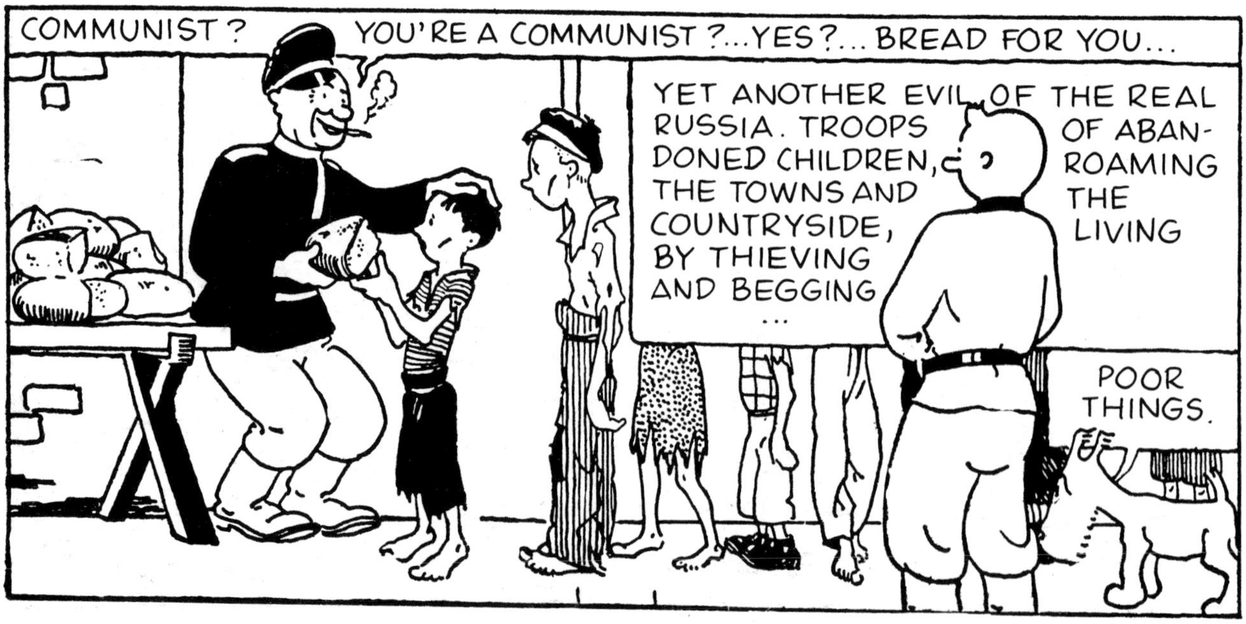
COMMUNIST ?
YOU'RE A COMMUNIST ?... YES ?... BREAD FOR YOU...
YET ANOTHER EVIL OF THE REAL RUSSIA. TROOPS OF ABANDONED CHILDREN, ROAMING THE TOWNS AND COUNTRYSIDE, LIVING BY THIEVING AND BEGGING ...
POOR THINGS.

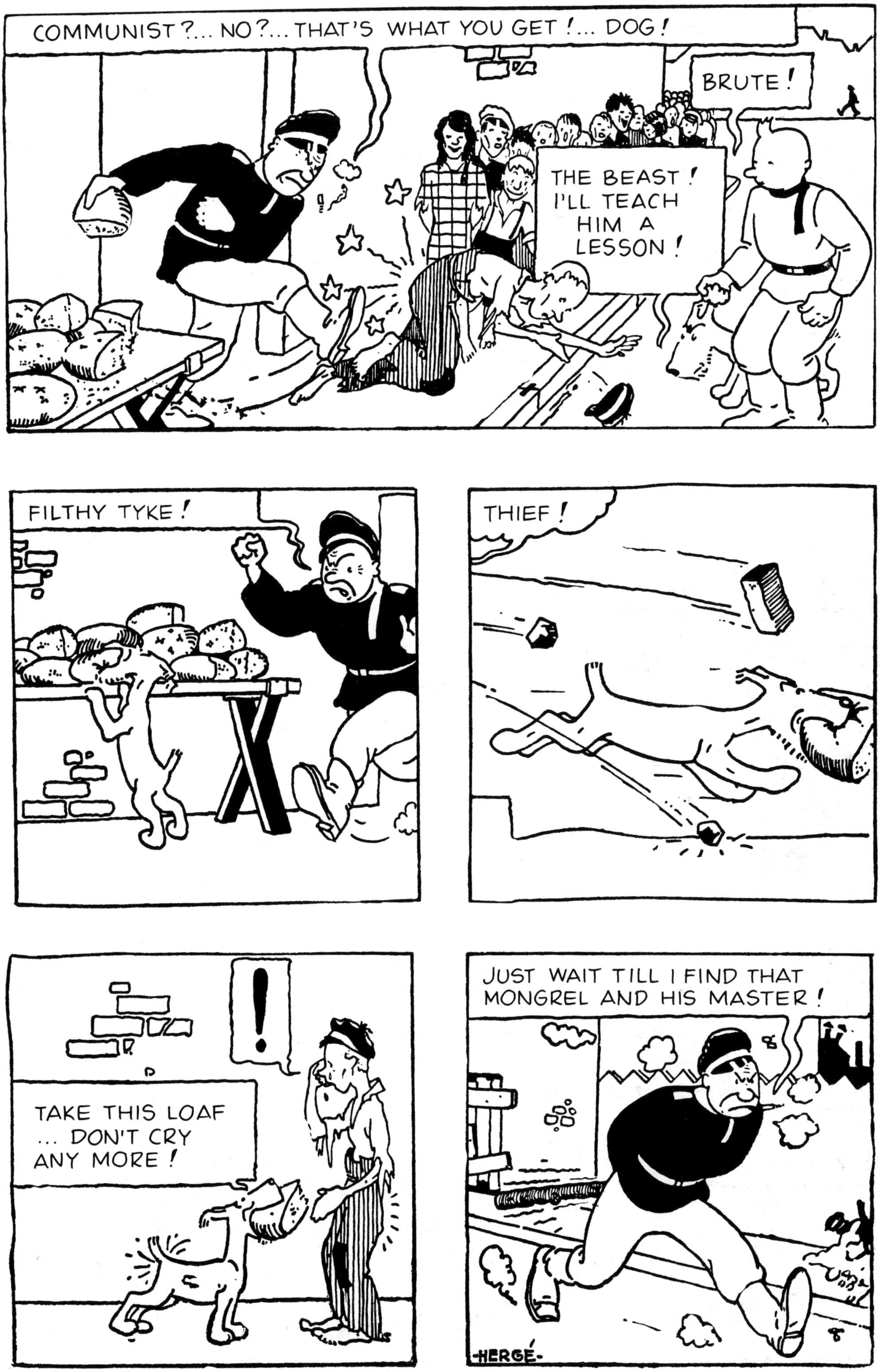
COMMUNIST?... NO?... THAT'S WHAT YOU GET!... DOG!
THE BEAST! I'LL TEACH HIM A LESSON!
BRUTE!
FILTHY TYKE!
THIEF!
!
TAKE THIS LOAF ... DON'T CRY ANY MORE!
JUST WAIT TILL I FIND THAT MONGREL AND HIS MASTER!
HERGÉ

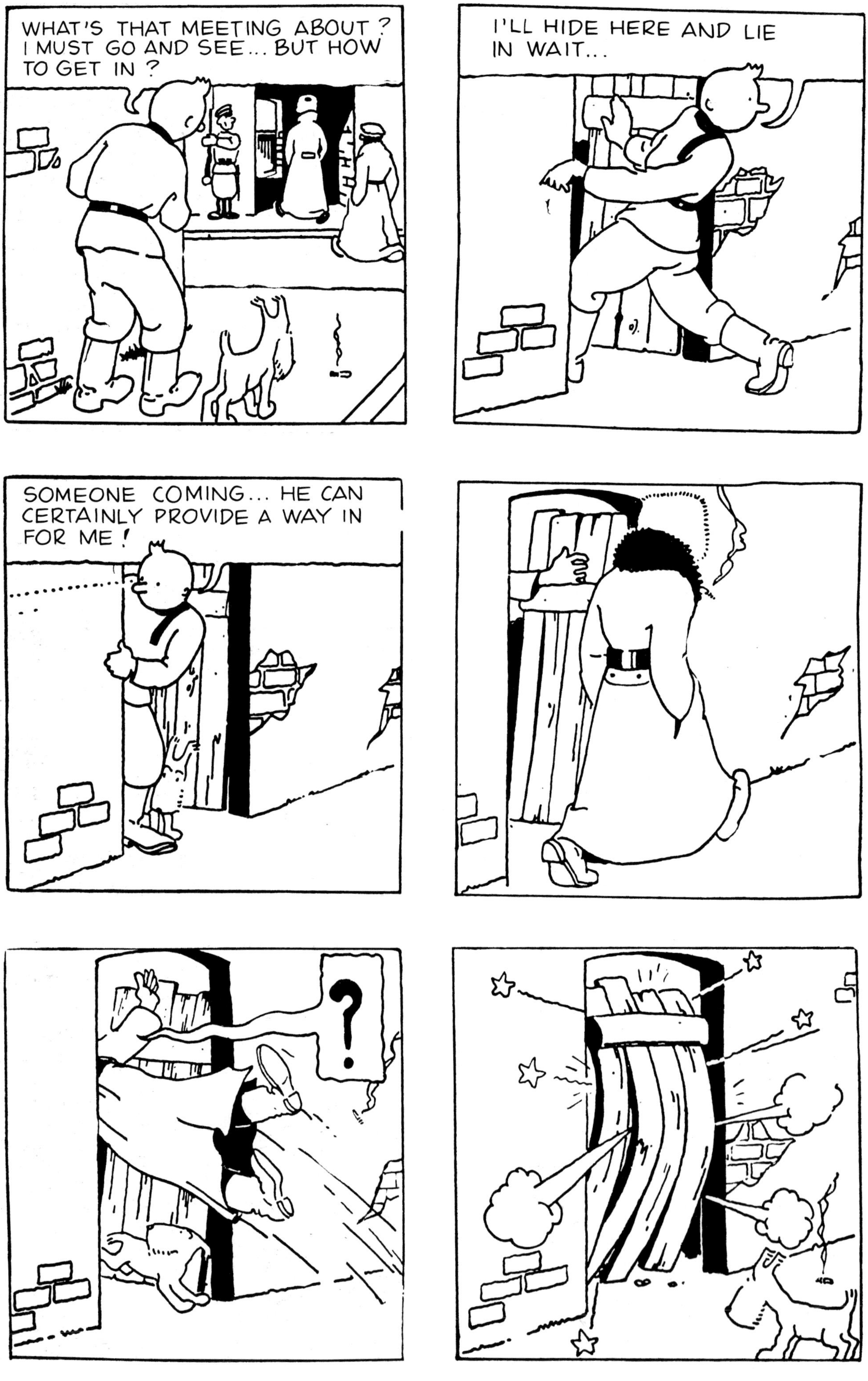
WHAT'S THAT MEETING ABOUT ? I MUST GO AND SEE... BUT HOW TO GET IN ?
I'LL HIDE HERE AND LIE IN WAIT...
SOMEONE COMING... HE CAN CERTAINLY PROVIDE A WAY IN FOR ME !
?

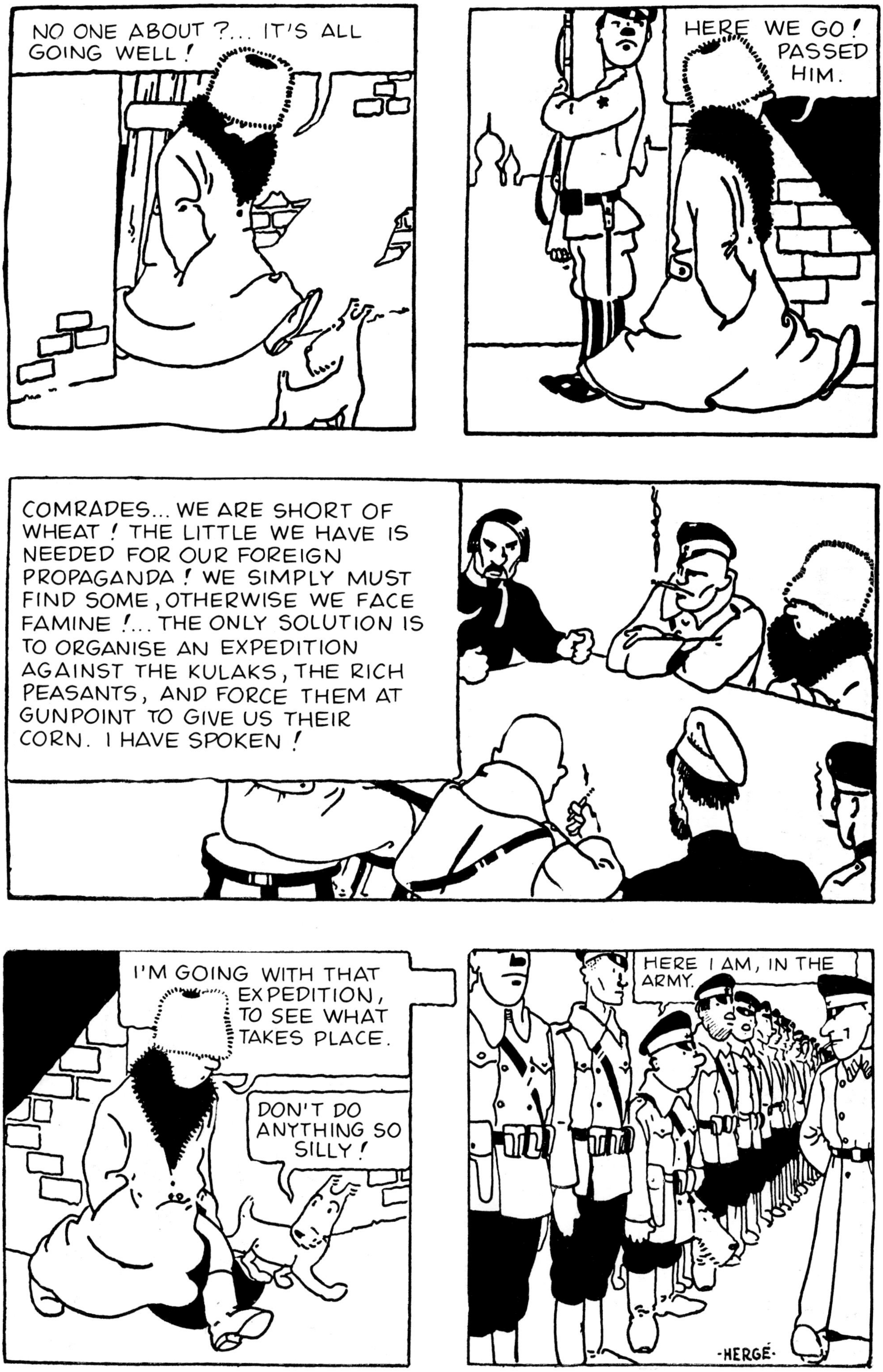
NO ONE ABOUT ?... IT'S ALL GOING WELL !
HERE WE GO ! PASSED HIM.
COMRADES... WE ARE SHORT OF WHEAT ! THE LITTLE WE HAVE IS NEEDED FOR OUR FOREIGN PROPAGANDA ! WE SIMPLY MUST FIND SOME, OTHERWISE WE FACE FAMINE !... THE ONLY SOLUTION IS TO ORGANISE AN EXPEDITION AGAINST THE KULAKS, THE RICH PEASANTS, AND FORCE THEM AT GUNPOINT TO GIVE US THEIR CORN. I HAVE SPOKEN !
I'M GOING WITH THAT EXPEDITION, TO SEE WHAT TAKES PLACE.
DON'T DO ANYTHING SO SILLY !
HERE I AM, IN THE ARMY.
-HERGÉ-

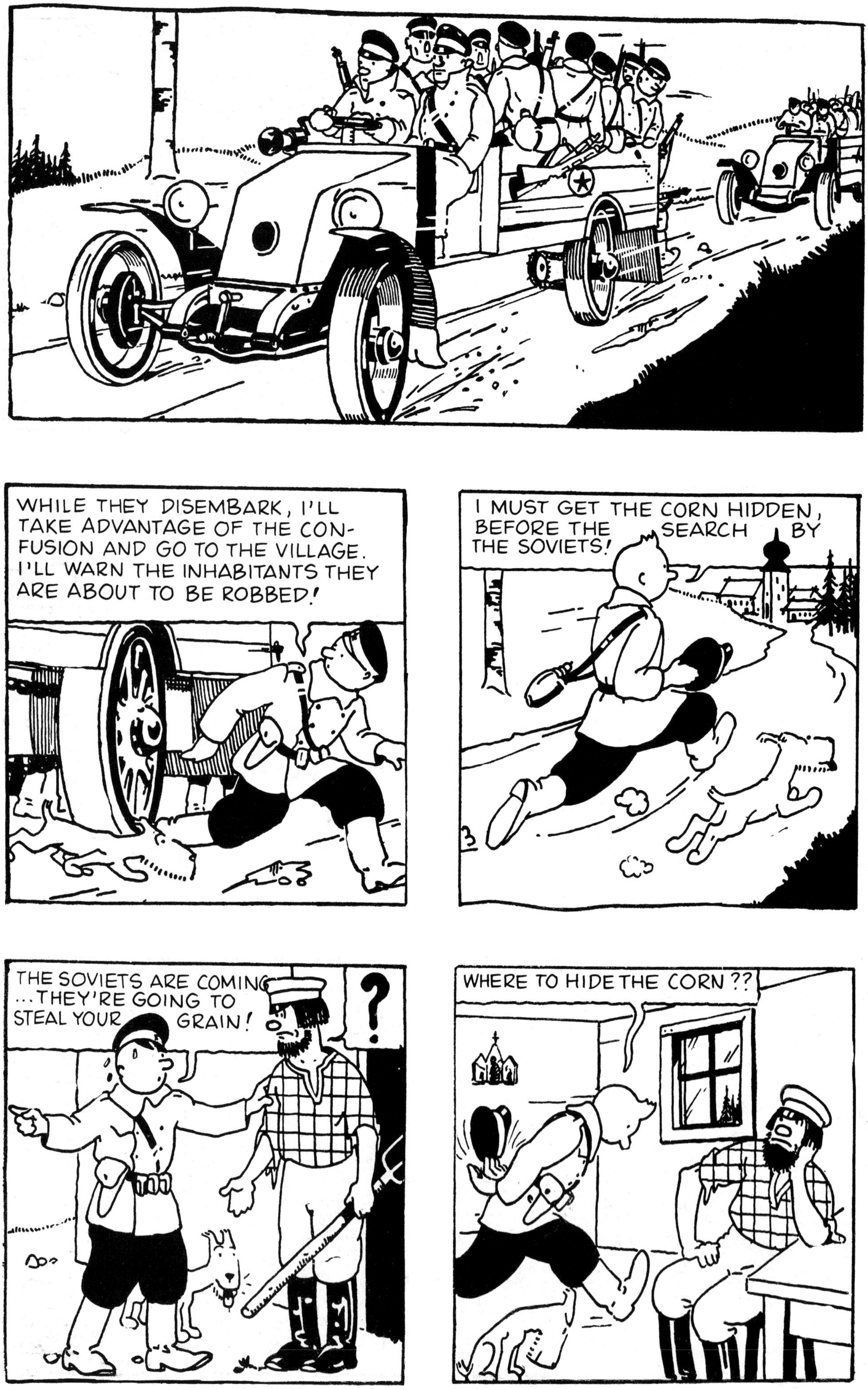
WHILE THEY DISEMBARK, I'LL TAKE ADVANTAGE OF THE CON-FUSION AND GO TO THE VILLAGE. I'LL WARN THE INHABITANTS THEY ARE ABOUT TO BE ROBBED!
I MUST GET THE CORN HIDDEN, BEFORE THE SEARCH BY THE SOVIETS!
THE SOVIETS ARE COMING ...THEY'RE GOING TO STEAL YOUR GRAIN!
?
WHERE TO HIDE THE CORN??

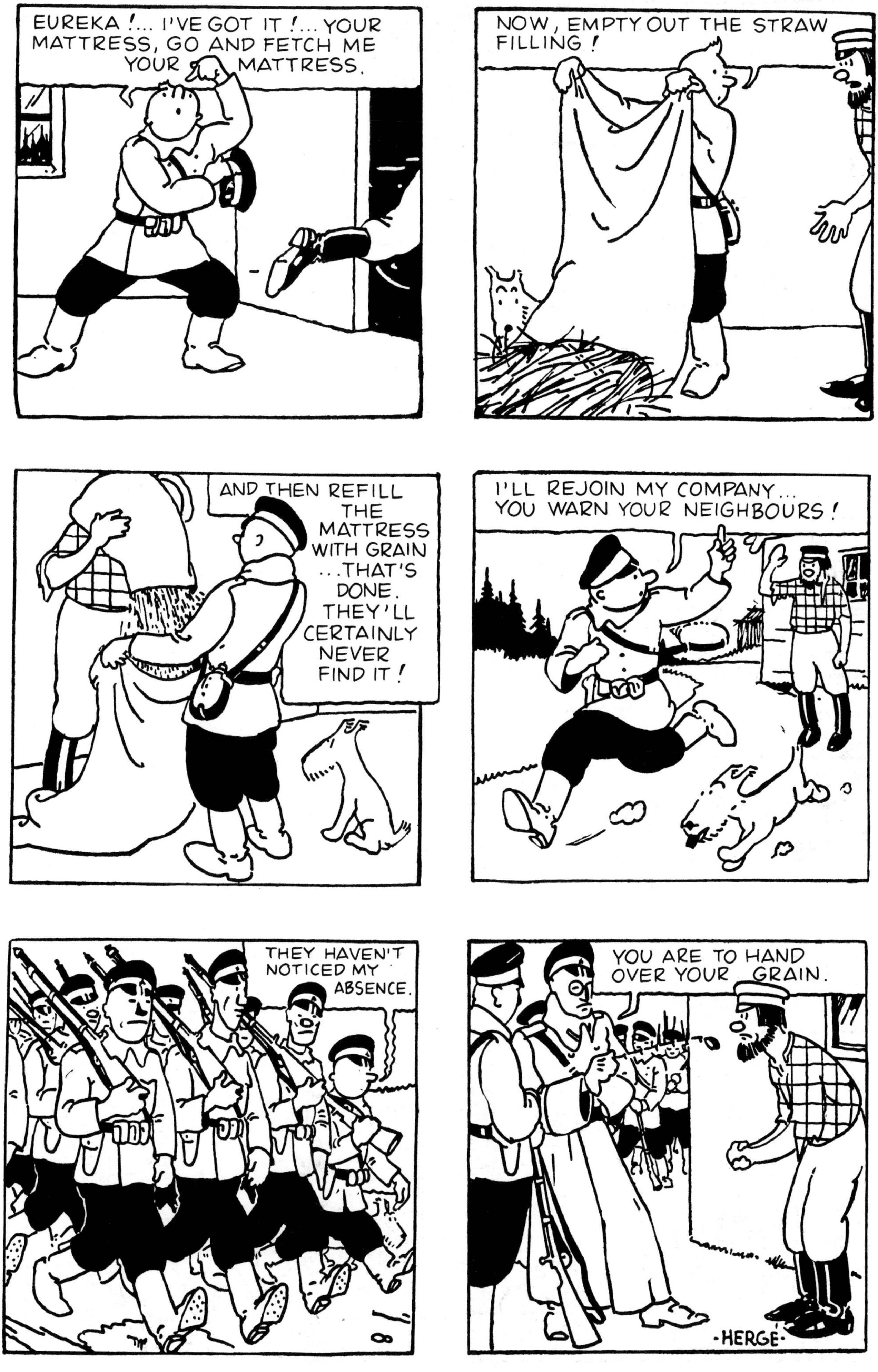
EUREKA !... I'VE GOT IT !... YOUR MATTRESS, GO AND FETCH ME YOUR MATTRESS.
NOW, EMPTY OUT THE STRAW FILLING !
AND THEN REFILL THE MATTRESS WITH GRAIN ...THAT'S DONE. THEY'LL CERTAINLY NEVER FIND IT !
I'LL REJOIN MY COMPANY... YOU WARN YOUR NEIGHBOURS !
THEY HAVEN'T NOTICED MY ABSENCE.
YOU ARE TO HAND OVER YOUR GRAIN.
-HERGÉ-

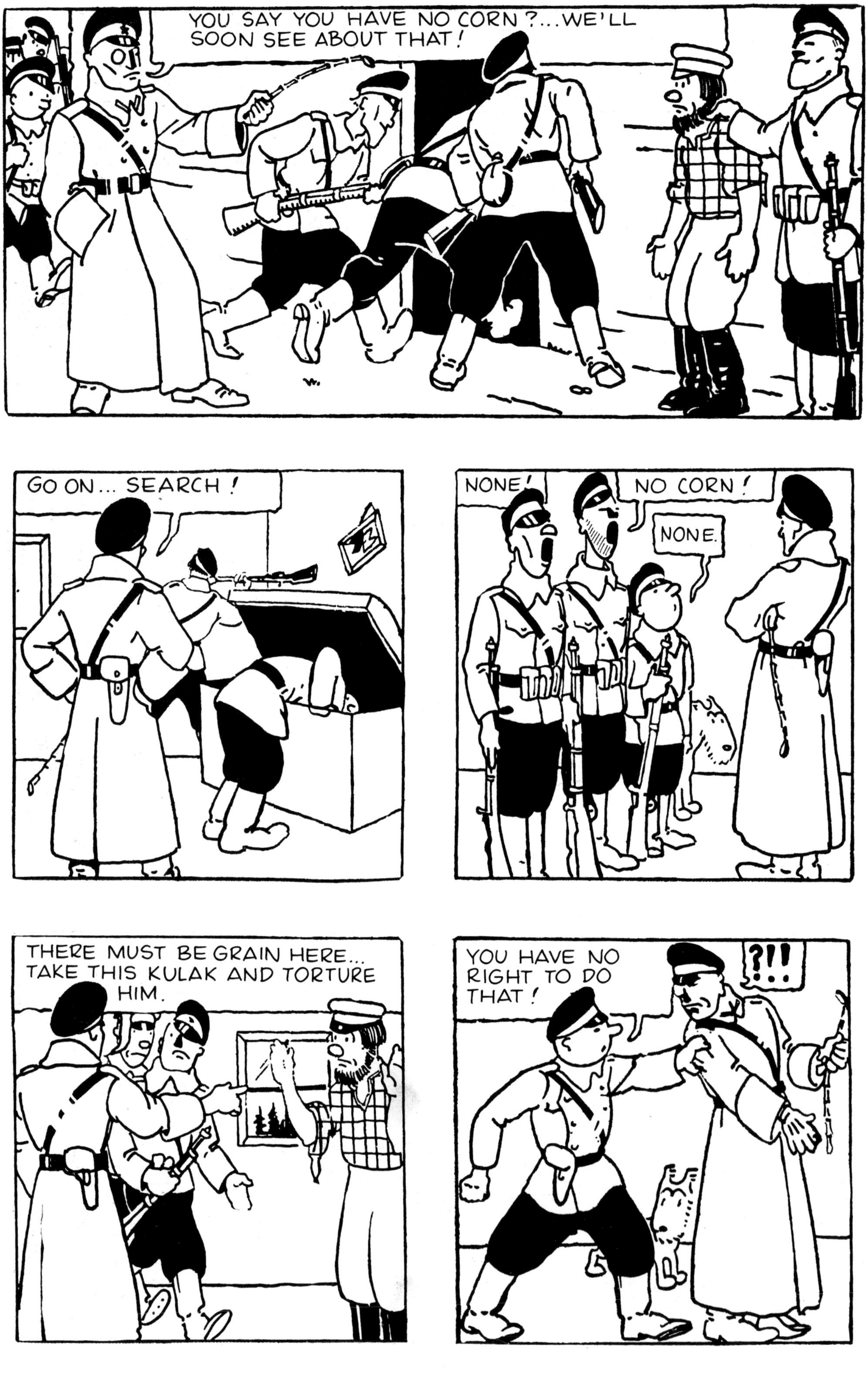
YOU SAY YOU HAVE NO CORN ?... WE'LL SOON SEE ABOUT THAT !
GO ON... SEARCH !
NONE !
NO CORN !
NONE.
THERE MUST BE GRAIN HERE... TAKE THIS KULAK AND TORTURE HIM.
YOU HAVE NO RIGHT TO DO THAT !
?!!

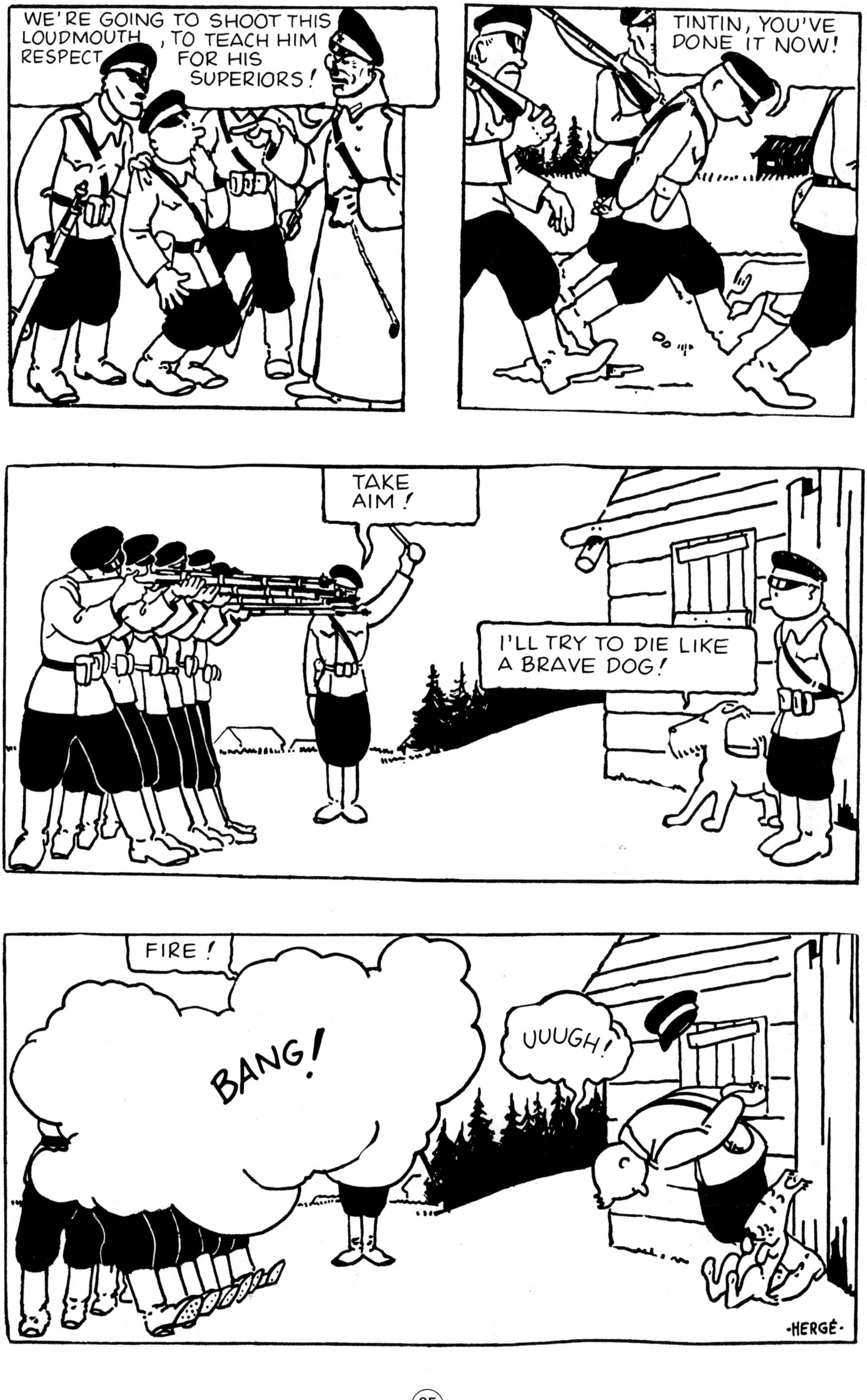
WE'RE GOING TO SHOOT THIS LOUDMOUTH, TO TEACH HIM RESPECT FOR HIS SUPERIORS!
TINTIN, YOU'VE DONE IT NOW!
TAKE AIM!
I'LL TRY TO DIE LIKE A BRAVE DOG!
FIRE!
BANG!
UUUGH!
-HERGÉ-

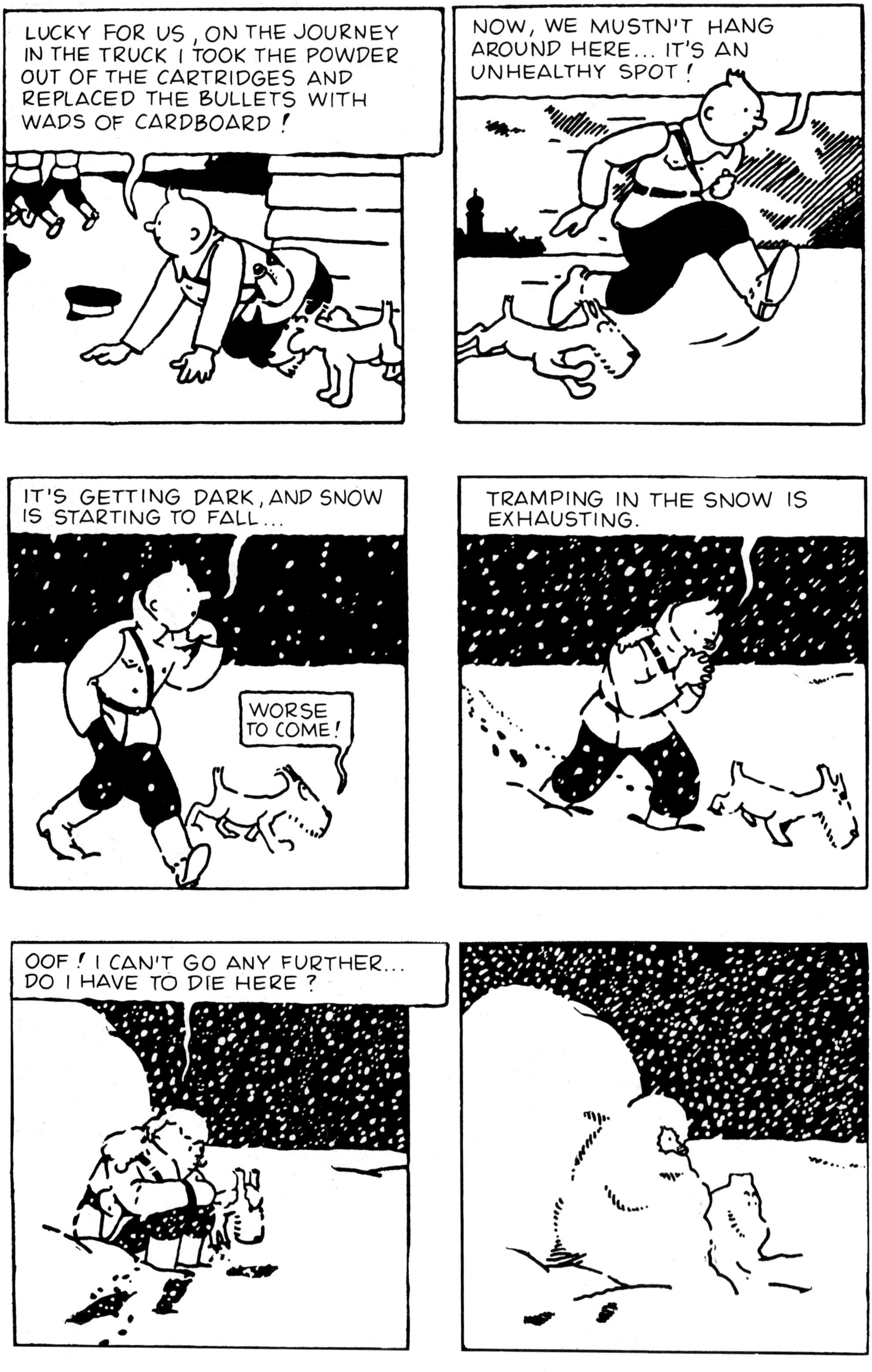
LUCKY FOR US, ON THE JOURNEY IN THE TRUCK I TOOK THE POWDER OUT OF THE CARTRIDGES AND REPLACED THE BULLETS WITH WADS OF CARDBOARD!
NOW, WE MUSTN'T HANG AROUND HERE... IT'S AN UNHEALTHY SPOT!
IT'S GETTING DARK, AND SNOW IS STARTING TO FALL...
WORSE TO COME!
TRAMPING IN THE SNOW IS EXHAUSTING.
OOF! I CAN'T GO ANY FURTHER... DO I HAVE TO DIE HERE?

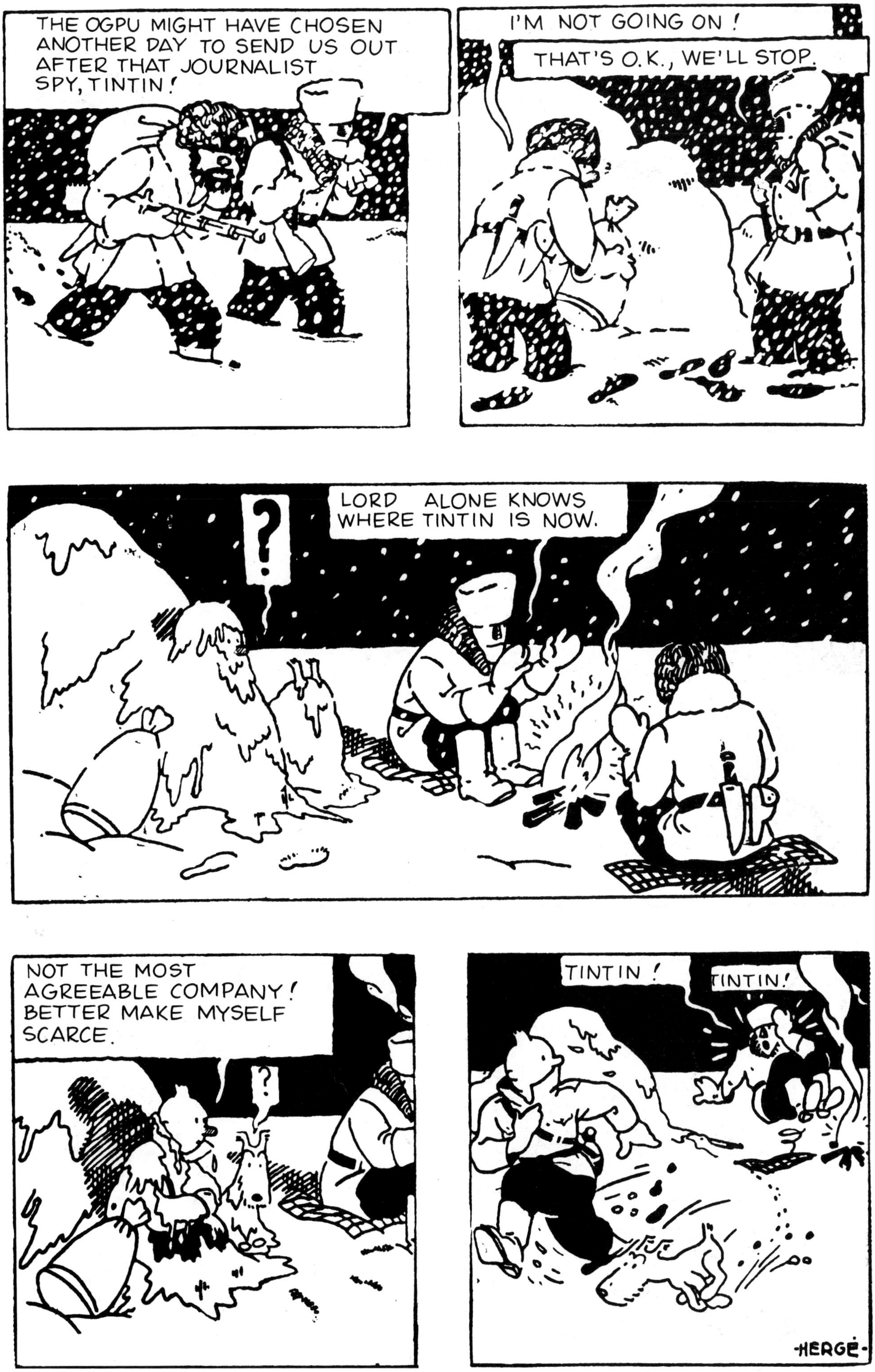
THE OGPU MIGHT HAVE CHOSEN ANOTHER DAY TO SEND US OUT AFTER THAT JOURNALIST SPY, TINTIN!
I'M NOT GOING ON!
THAT'S O.K., WE'LL STOP.
?
LORD ALONE KNOWS WHERE TINTIN IS NOW.
NOT THE MOST AGREEABLE COMPANY! BETTER MAKE MYSELF SCARCE.
?
TINTIN!
TINTIN!
HERGÉ

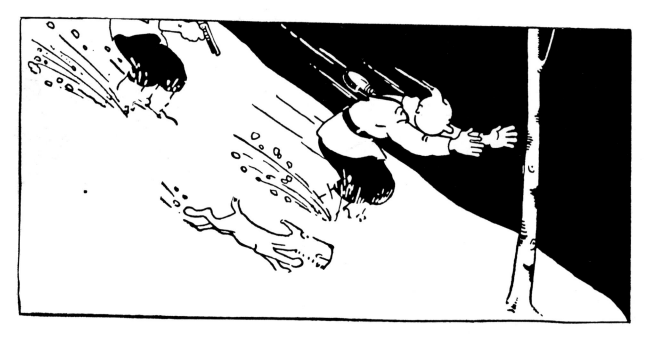

MIND THE BUMP!

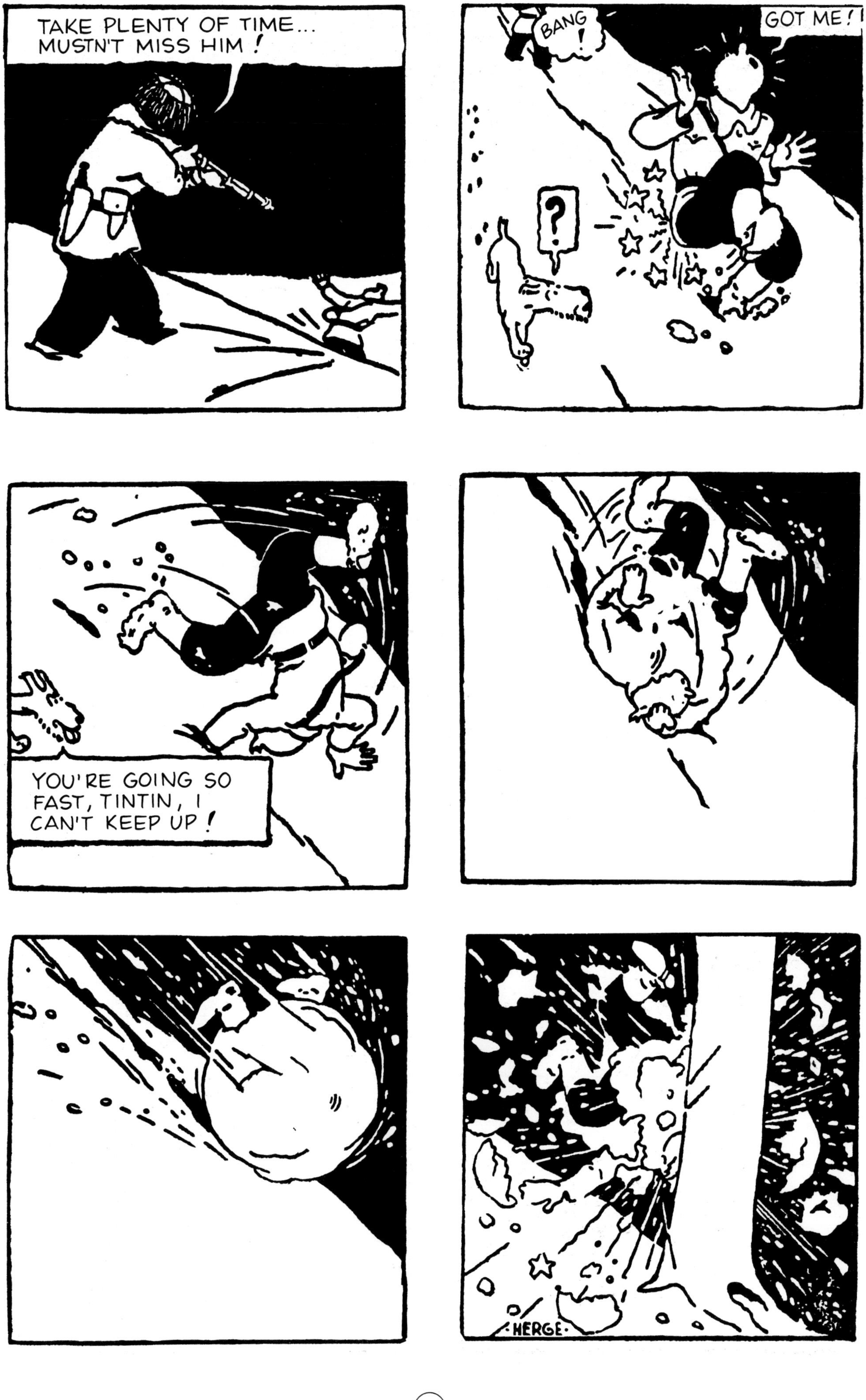

TAKE PLENTY OF TIME... MUSTN'T MISS HIM !
BANG !
GOT ME !
?
YOU'RE GOING SO FAST, TINTIN, I CAN'T KEEP UP !
·HERGE·

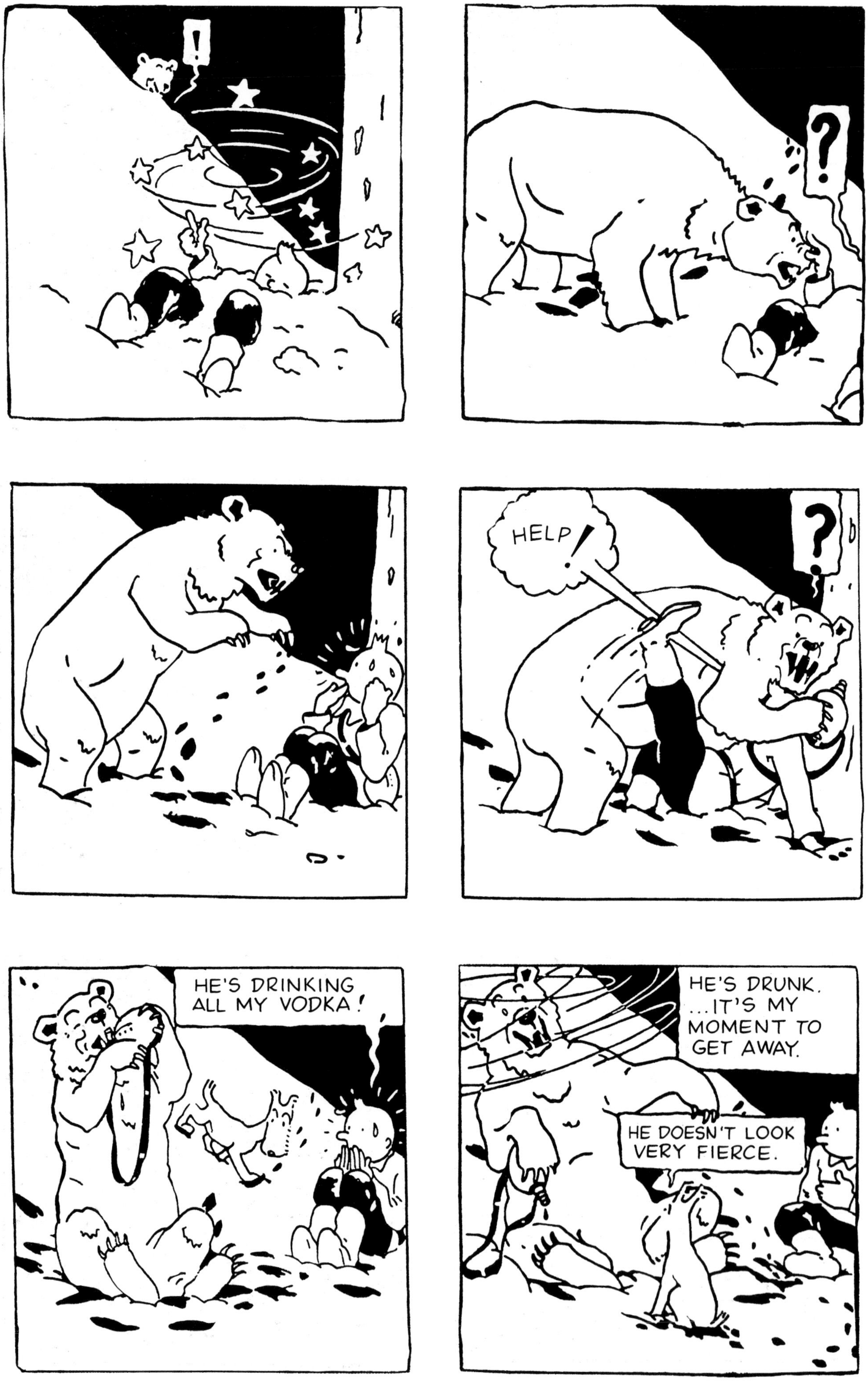
HELP!
HE'S DRINKING ALL MY VODKA!
HE'S DRUNK. ...IT'S MY MOMENT TO GET AWAY.
HE DOESN'T LOOK VERY FIERCE.

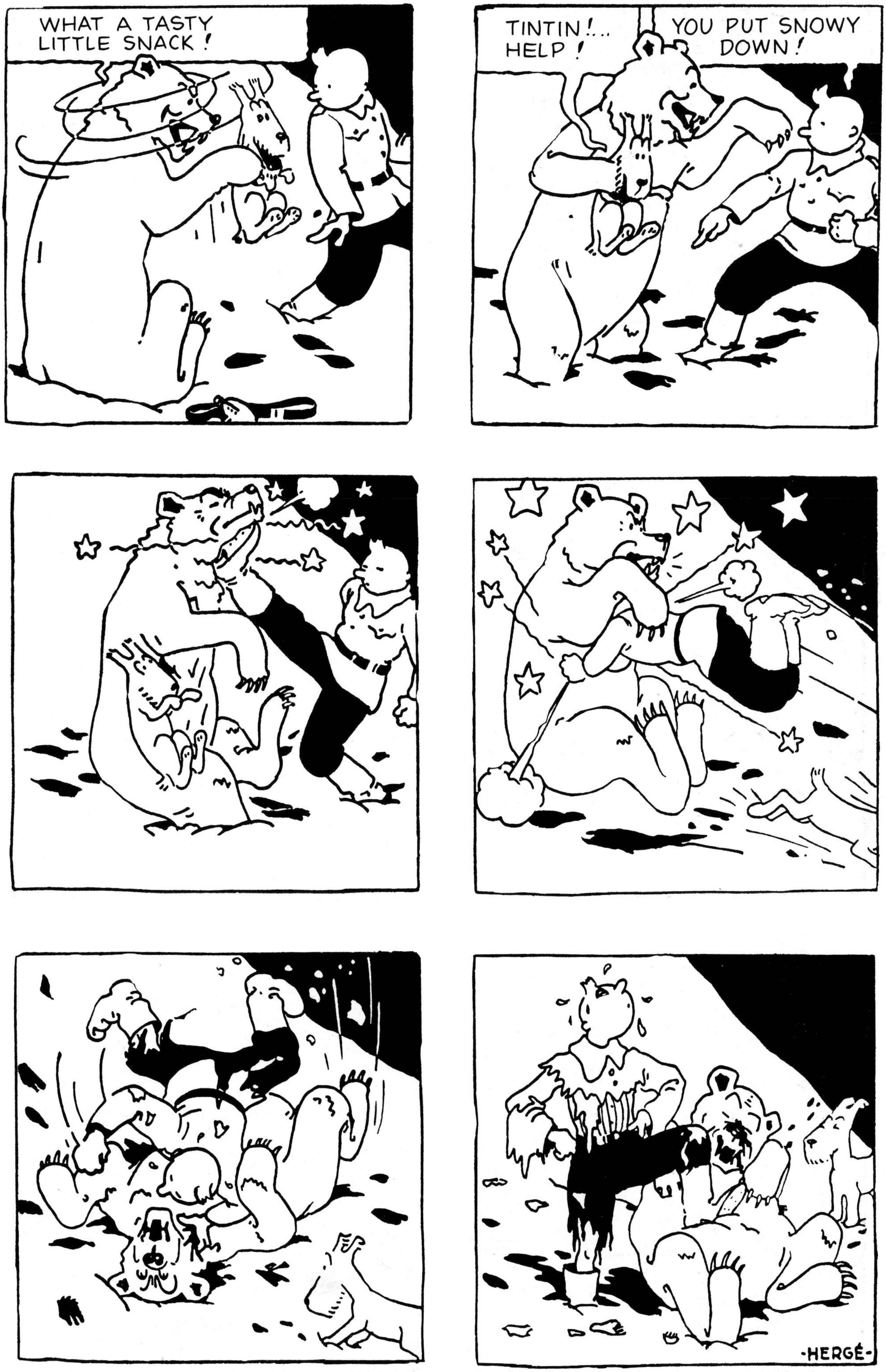
WHAT A TASTY LITTLE SNACK !
TINTIN !... HELP !
YOU PUT SNOWY DOWN !
-HERGÉ-

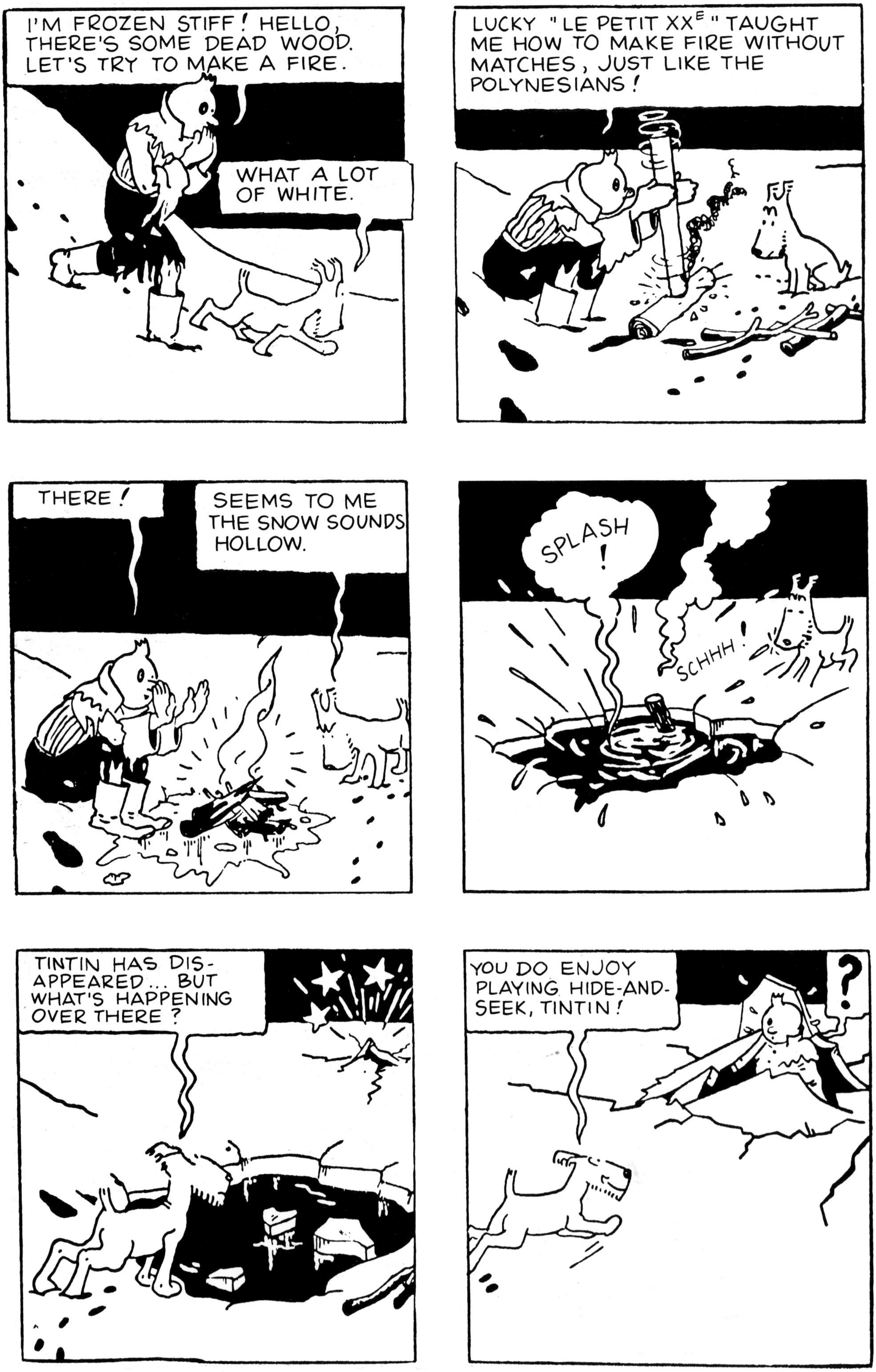
I'M FROZEN STIFF! HELLO, THERE'S SOME DEAD WOOD. LET'S TRY TO MAKE A FIRE.
WHAT A LOT OF WHITE.
LUCKY "LE PETIT XXE" TAUGHT ME HOW TO MAKE FIRE WITHOUT MATCHES, JUST LIKE THE POLYNESIANS!
THERE!
SEEMS TO ME THE SNOW SOUNDS HOLLOW.
SPLASH !
SCHHH!
TINTIN HAS DISAPPEARED... BUT WHAT'S HAPPENING OVER THERE?
YOU DO ENJOY PLAYING HIDE-AND-SEEK, TINTIN!
?

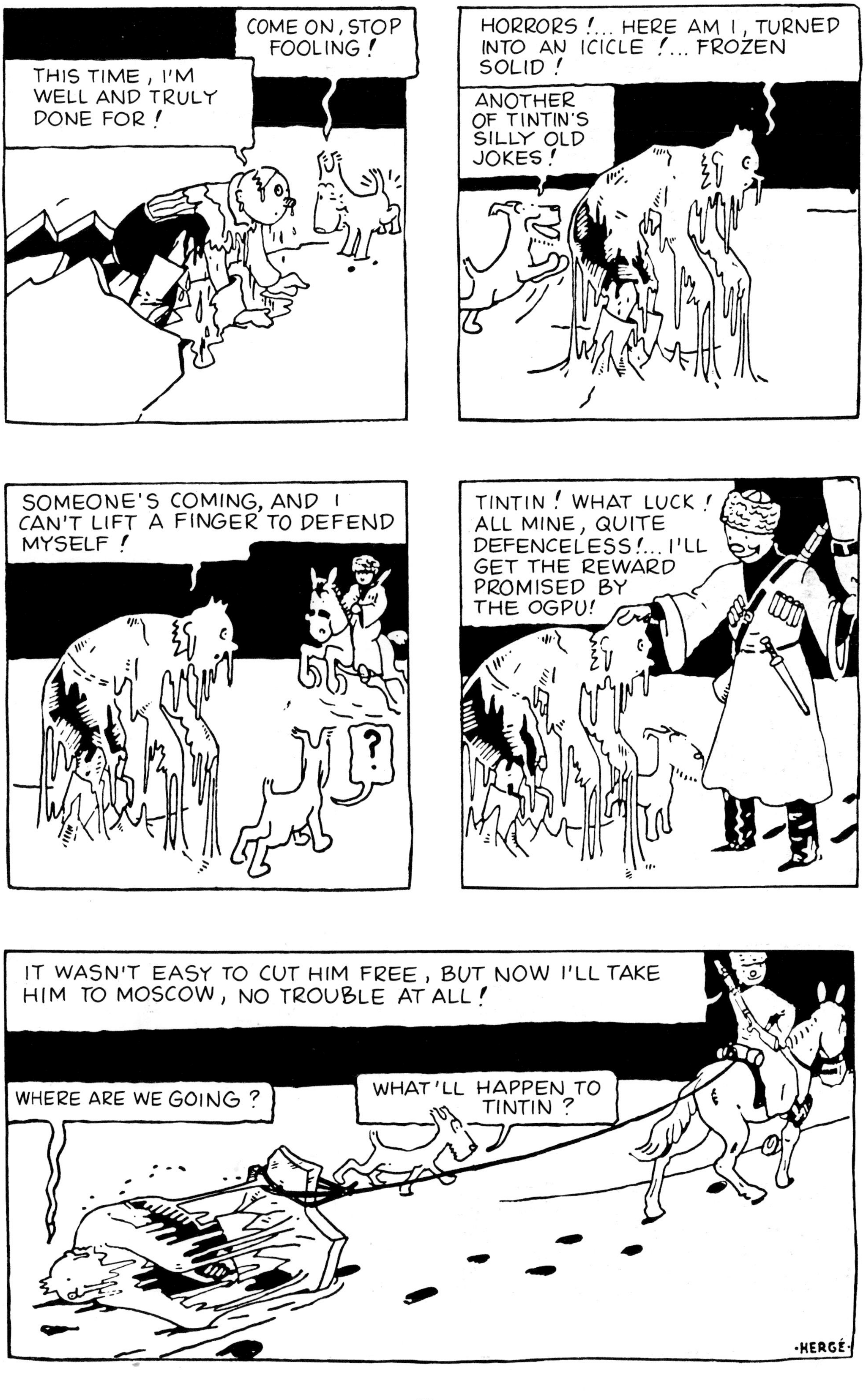
THIS TIME, I'M WELL AND TRULY DONE FOR!
COME ON, STOP FOOLING!
HORRORS!... HERE AM I, TURNED INTO AN ICICLE!... FROZEN SOLID!
ANOTHER OF TINTIN'S SILLY OLD JOKES!
SOMEONE'S COMING, AND I CAN'T LIFT A FINGER TO DEFEND MYSELF!
?
TINTIN! WHAT LUCK! ALL MINE, QUITE DEFENCELESS!... I'LL GET THE REWARD PROMISED BY THE OGPU!
IT WASN'T EASY TO CUT HIM FREE, BUT NOW I'LL TAKE HIM TO MOSCOW, NO TROUBLE AT ALL!
WHERE ARE WE GOING?
WHAT'LL HAPPEN TO TINTIN?
·HERGÉ·

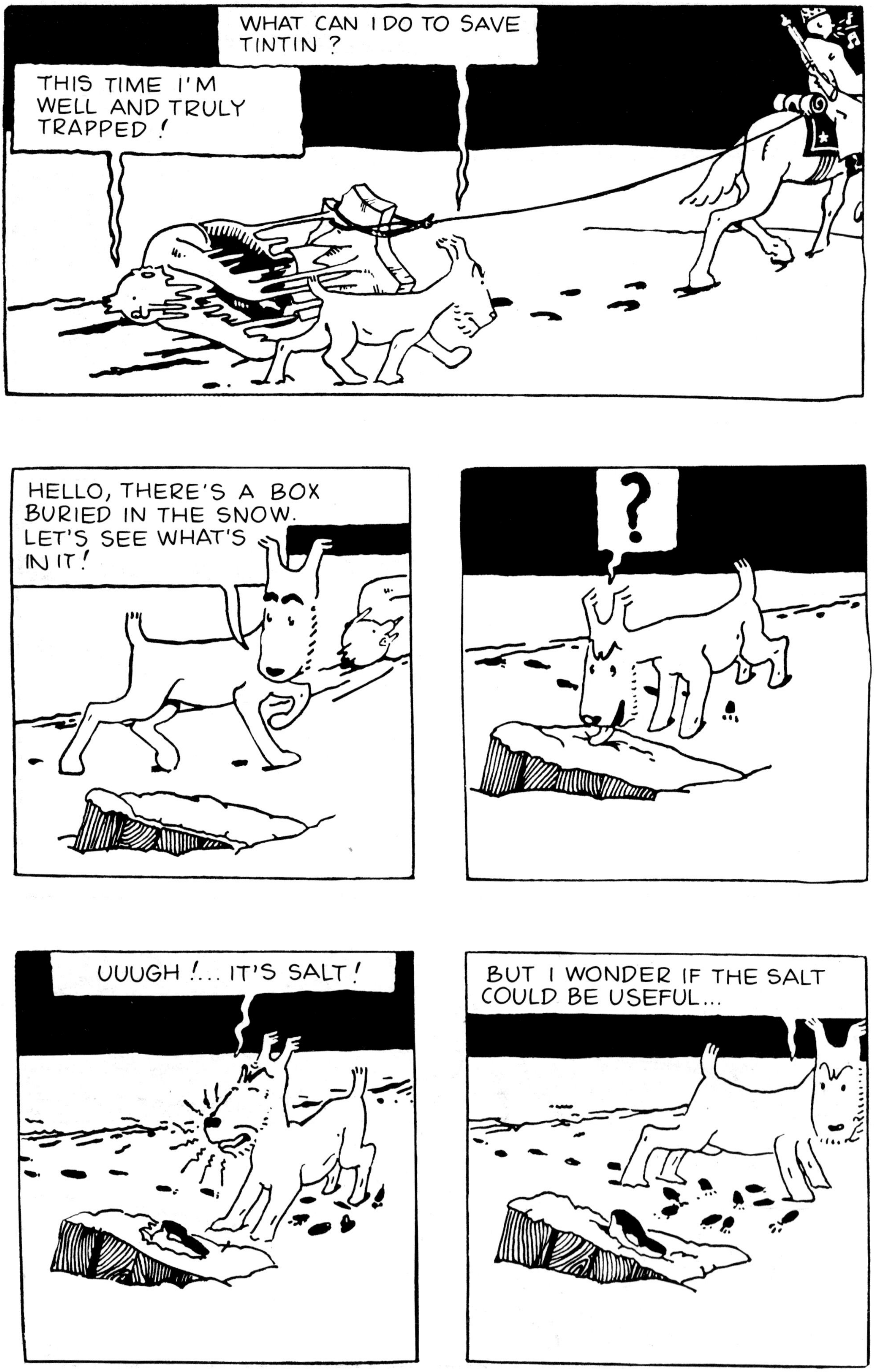
THIS TIME I'M WELL AND TRULY TRAPPED !
WHAT CAN I DO TO SAVE TINTIN ?
HELLO, THERE'S A BOX BURIED IN THE SNOW. LET'S SEE WHAT'S IN IT !
?
UUUGH !... IT'S SALT !
BUT I WONDER IF THE SALT COULD BE USEFUL...

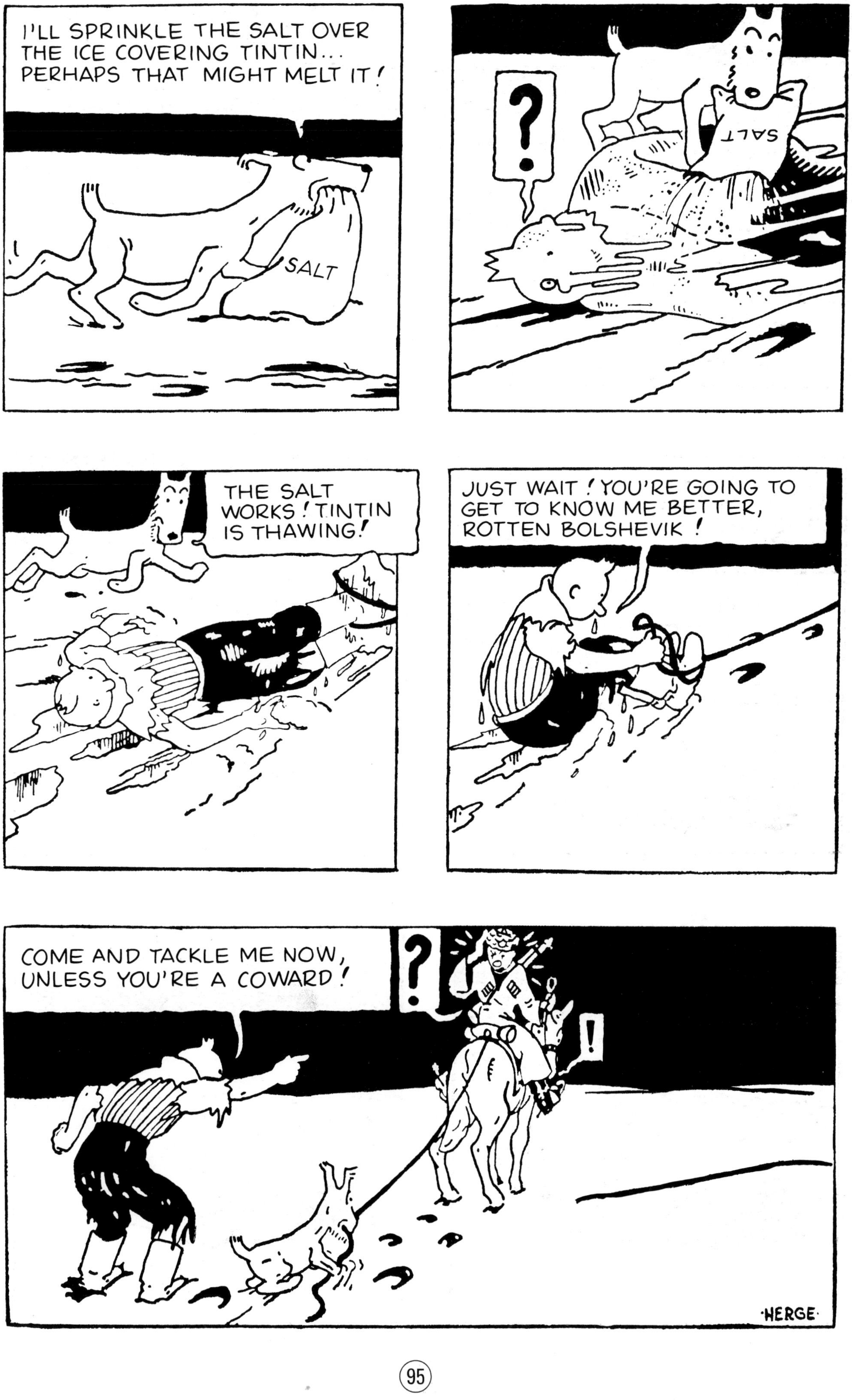
I'LL SPRINKLE THE SALT OVER THE ICE COVERING TINTIN... PERHAPS THAT MIGHT MELT IT!
SALT
?
SALT
THE SALT WORKS! TINTIN IS THAWING!
JUST WAIT! YOU'RE GOING TO GET TO KNOW ME BETTER, ROTTEN BOLSHEVIK!
COME AND TACKLE ME NOW, UNLESS YOU'RE A COWARD!
?
!
HERGE

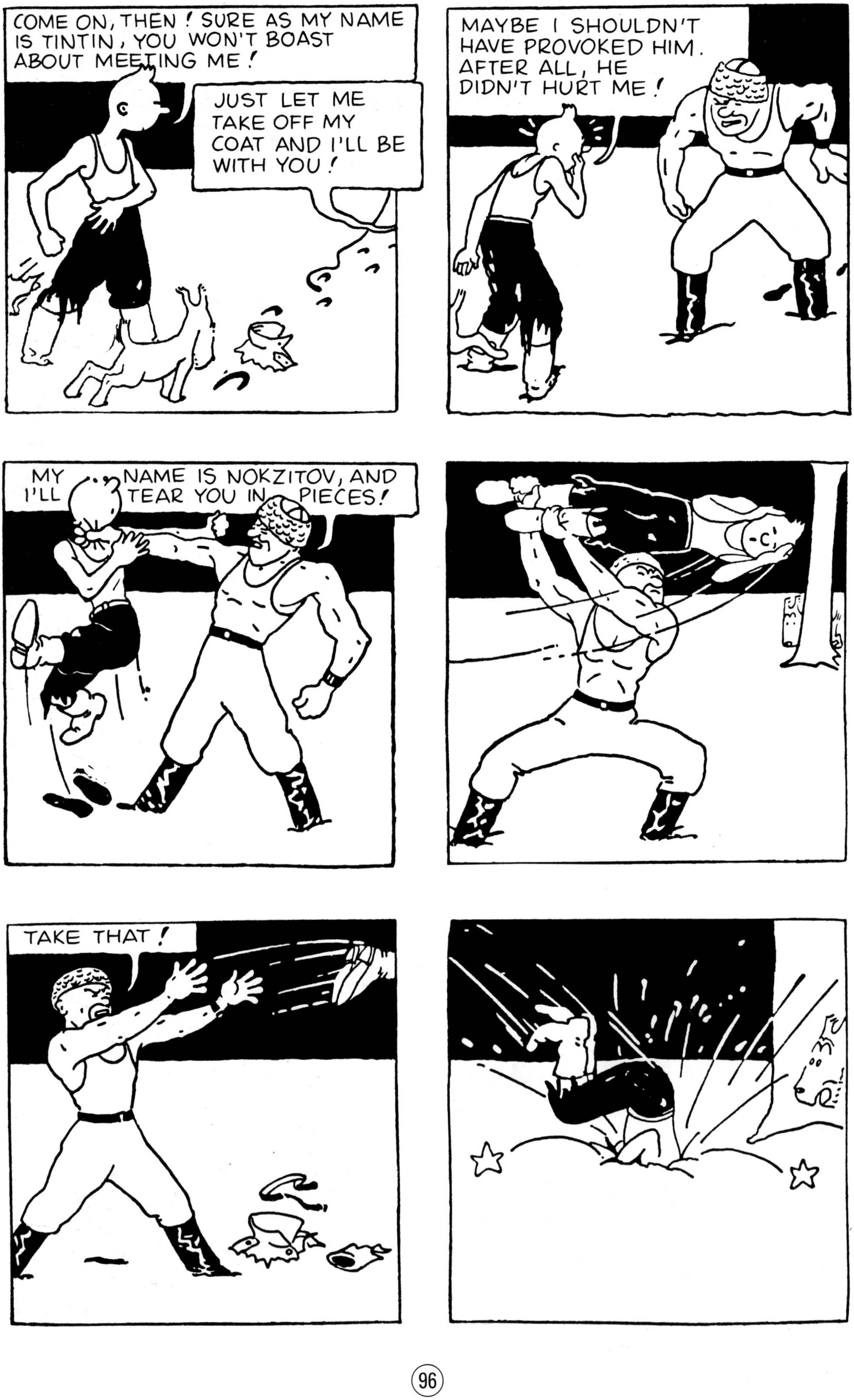
COME ON, THEN ! SURE AS MY NAME IS TINTIN, YOU WON'T BOAST ABOUT MEETING ME !
JUST LET ME TAKE OFF MY COAT AND I'LL BE WITH YOU !
MAYBE I SHOULDN'T HAVE PROVOKED HIM. AFTER ALL, HE DIDN'T HURT ME !
MY NAME IS NOKZITOV, AND I'LL TEAR YOU IN PIECES !
TAKE THAT !

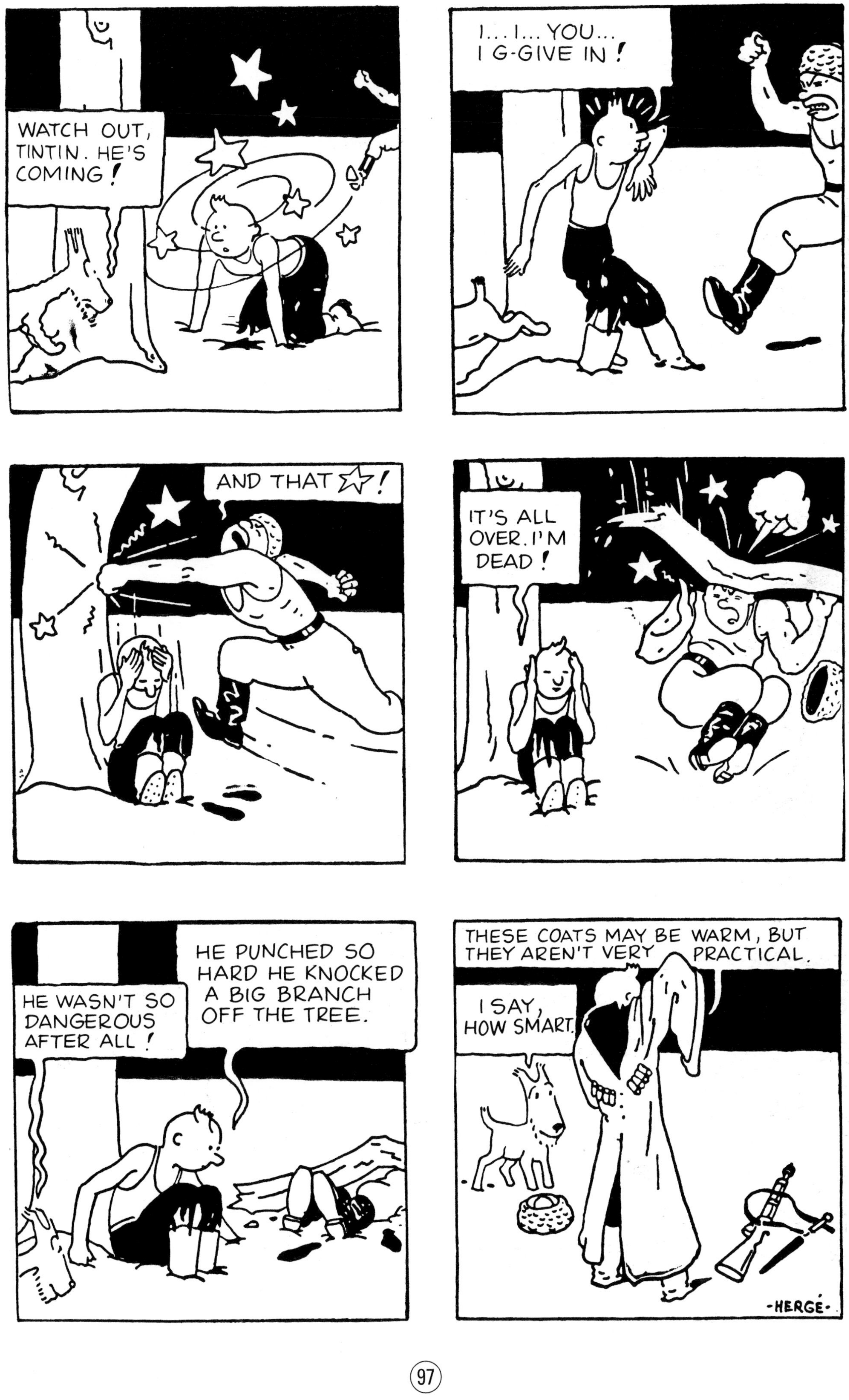
WATCH OUT, TINTIN. HE'S COMING!
I... I... YOU... I G-GIVE IN!
AND THAT!
IT'S ALL OVER. I'M DEAD!
HE WASN'T SO DANGEROUS AFTER ALL!
HE PUNCHED SO HARD HE KNOCKED A BIG BRANCH OFF THE TREE.
THESE COATS MAY BE WARM, BUT THEY AREN'T VERY PRACTICAL.
I SAY, HOW SMART.
-HERGÉ-

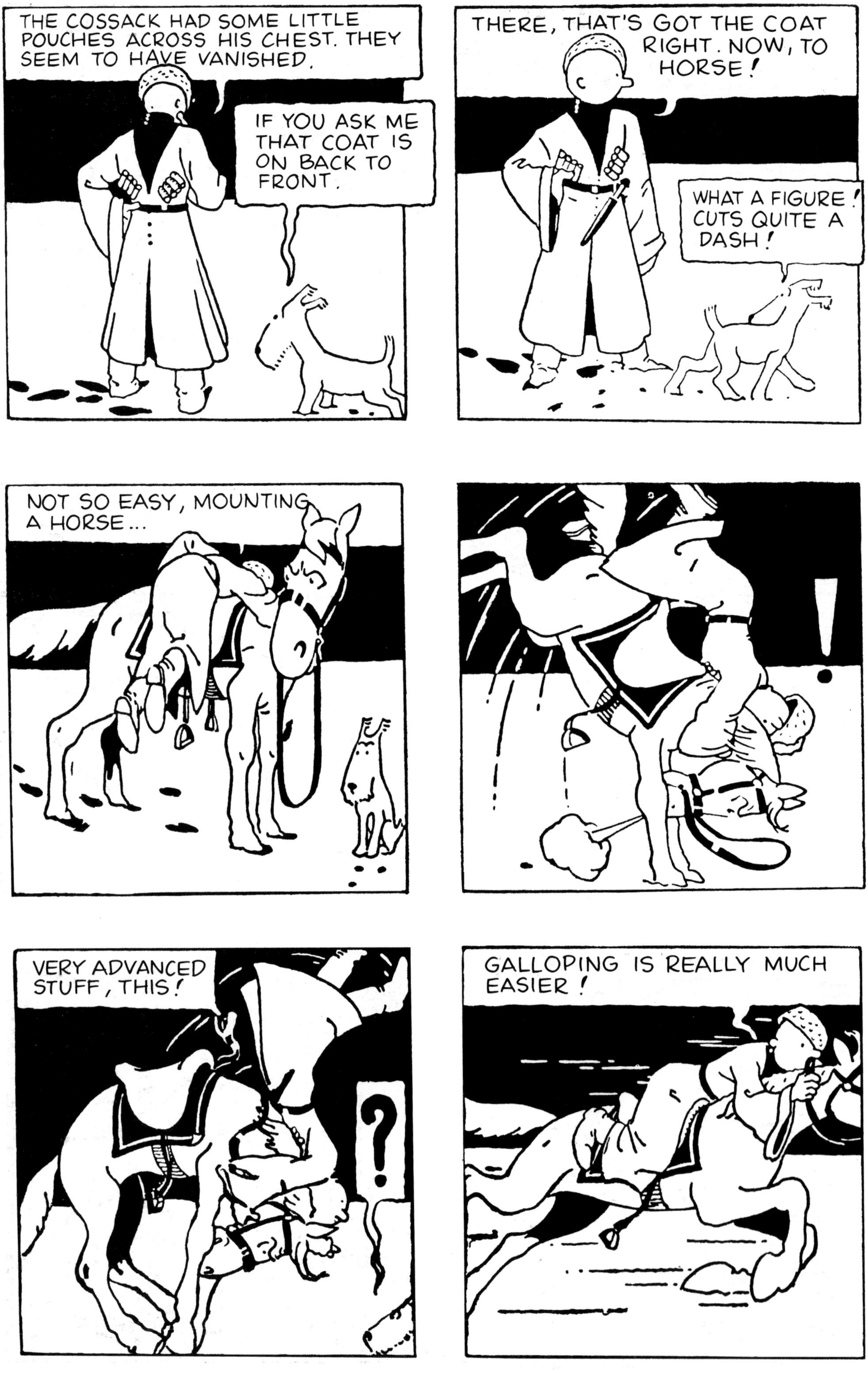
THE COSSACK HAD SOME LITTLE POUCHES ACROSS HIS CHEST. THEY SEEM TO HAVE VANISHED.
IF YOU ASK ME THAT COAT IS ON BACK TO FRONT.
THERE, THAT'S GOT THE COAT RIGHT. NOW, TO HORSE!
WHAT A FIGURE! CUTS QUITE A DASH!
NOT SO EASY, MOUNTING A HORSE...
!
VERY ADVANCED STUFF, THIS!
?
GALLOPING IS REALLY MUCH EASIER!

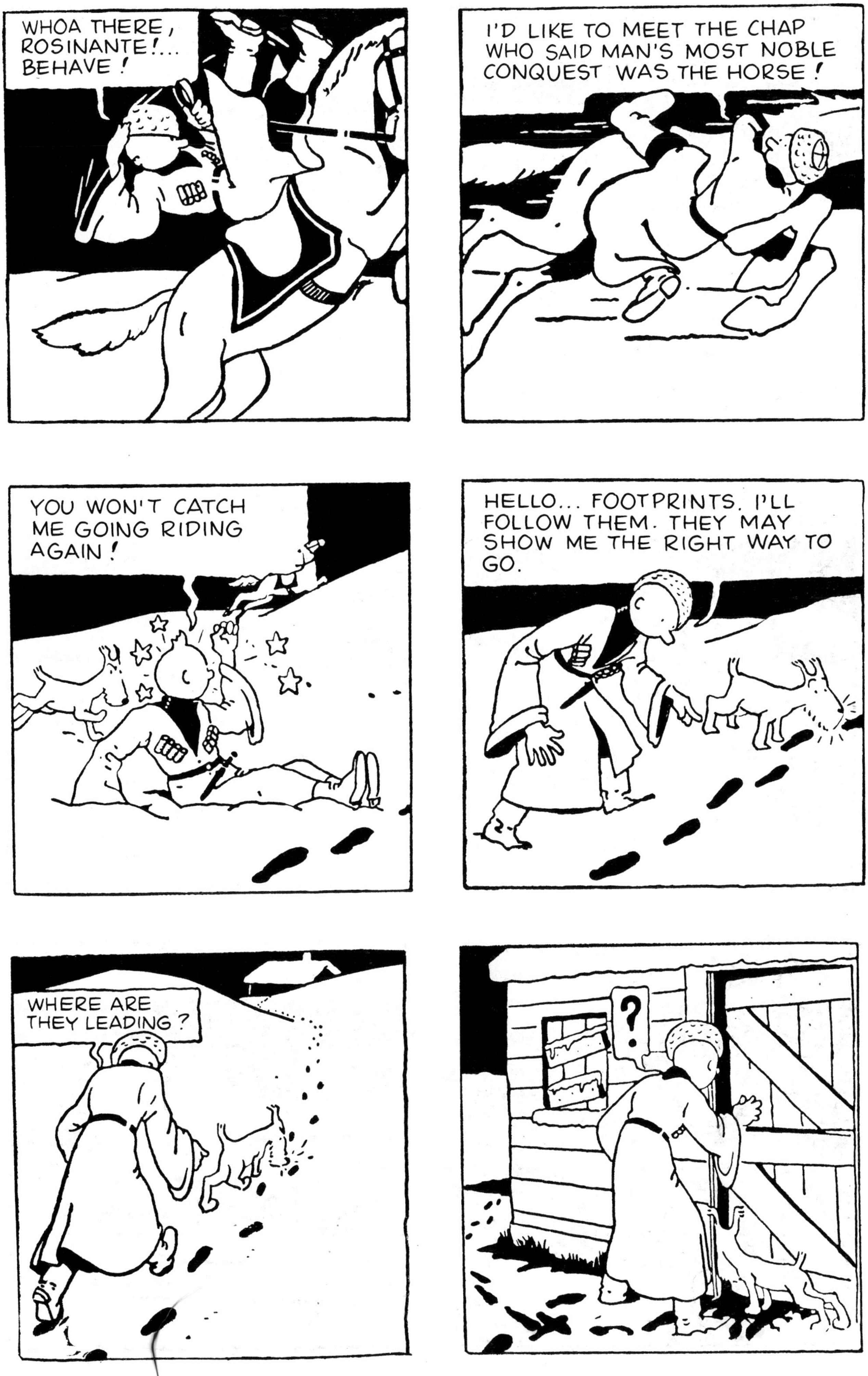
WHOA THERE, ROSINANTE!... BEHAVE!
I'D LIKE TO MEET THE CHAP WHO SAID MAN'S MOST NOBLE CONQUEST WAS THE HORSE!
YOU WON'T CATCH ME GOING RIDING AGAIN!
HELLO... FOOTPRINTS. I'LL FOLLOW THEM. THEY MAY SHOW ME THE RIGHT WAY TO GO.
WHERE ARE THEY LEADING?
?

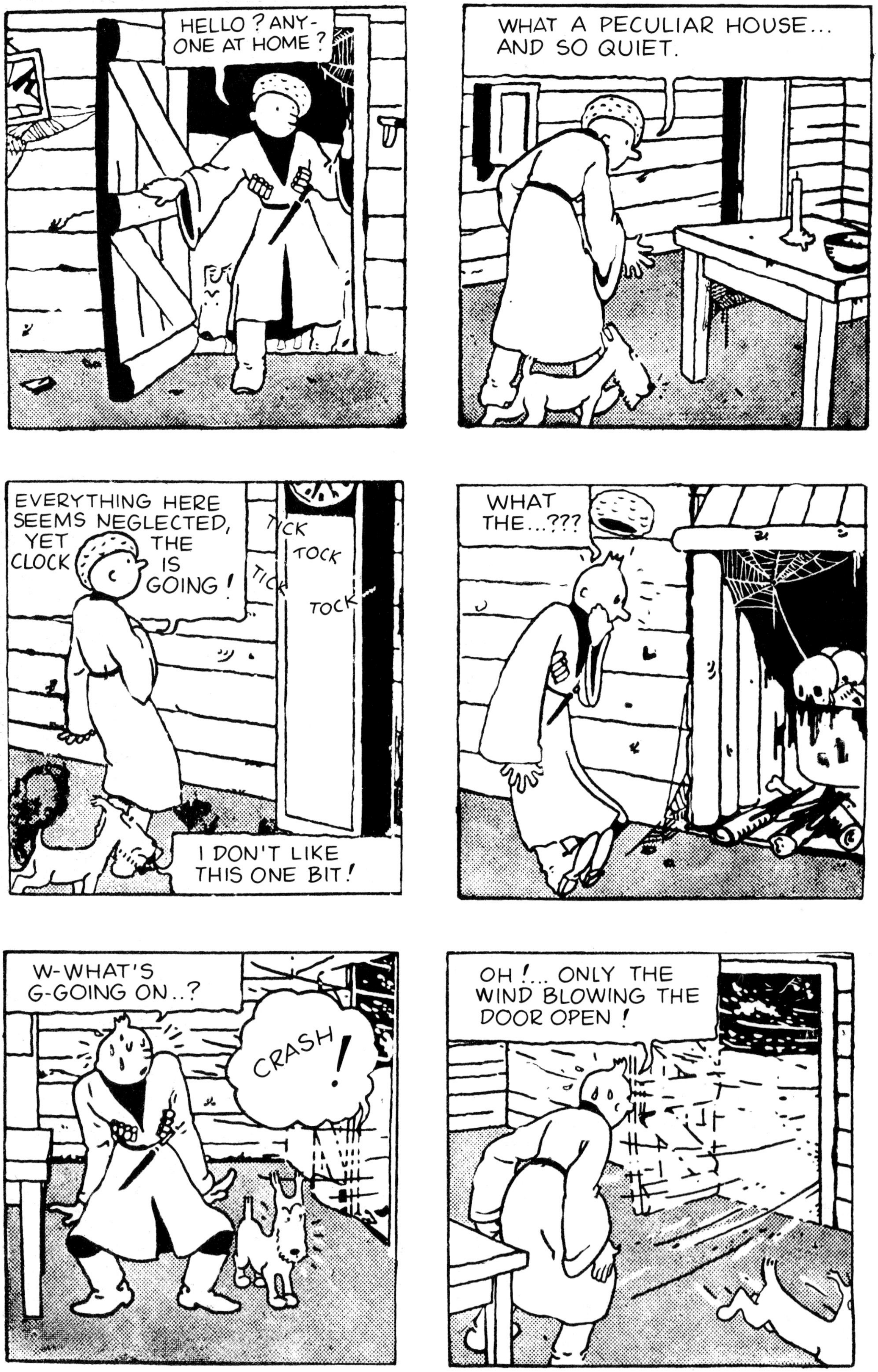
HELLO ? ANY-ONE AT HOME ?
WHAT A PECULIAR HOUSE... AND SO QUIET.
EVERYTHING HERE SEEMS NEGLECTED, YET THE CLOCK IS GOING !
TICK
TOCK
TICK
TOCK
I DON'T LIKE THIS ONE BIT !
WHAT THE...???
W-WHAT'S G-GOING ON..?
CRASH !
OH !... ONLY THE WIND BLOWING THE DOOR OPEN !

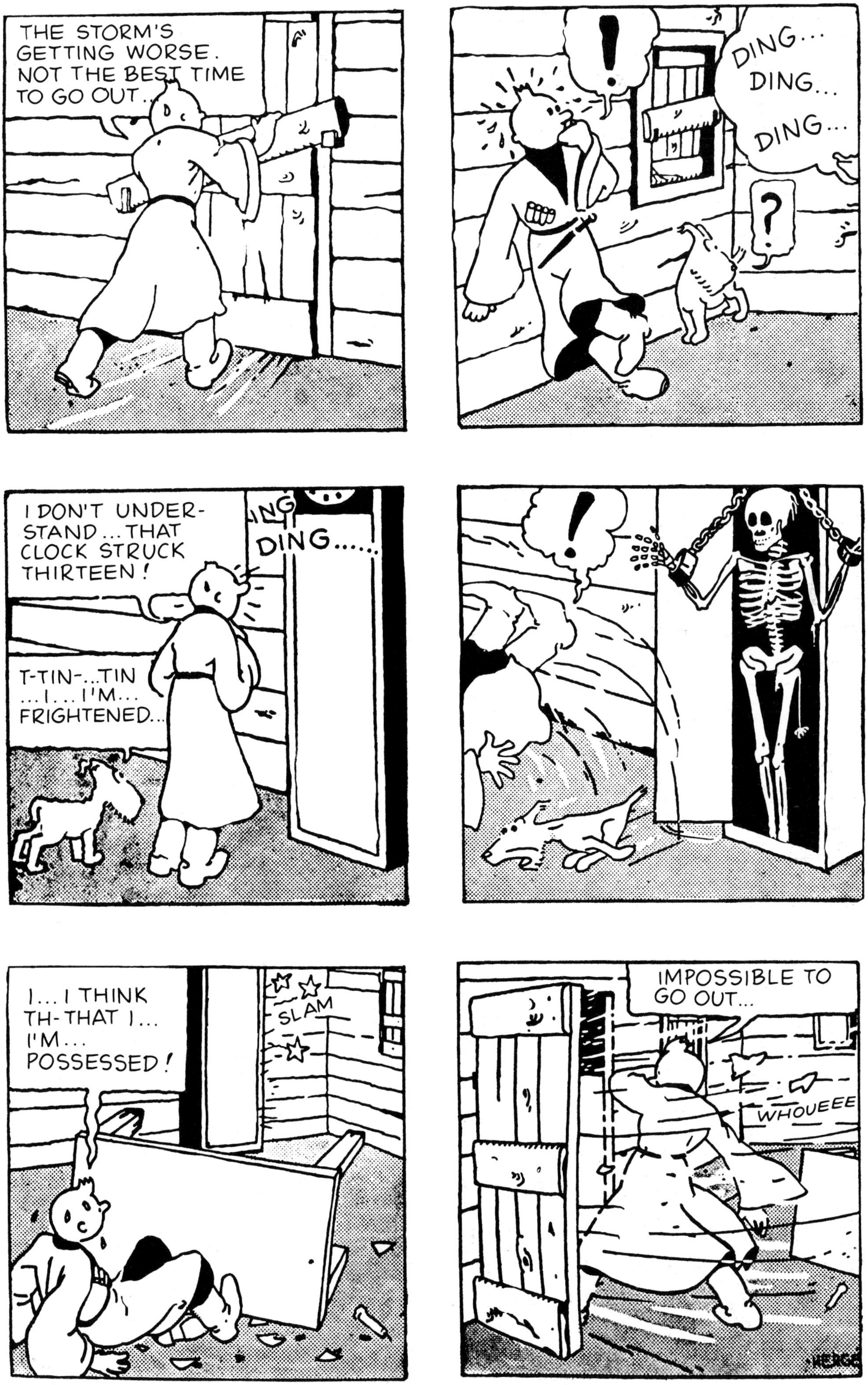
THE STORM'S GETTING WORSE. NOT THE BEST TIME TO GO OUT...
!
DING... DING... DING...
?
I DON'T UNDERSTAND... THAT CLOCK STRUCK THIRTEEN!
DING.....
T-TIN-...TIN ...I...I'M... FRIGHTENED...
!
I... I THINK TH-THAT I... I'M... POSSESSED!
SLAM
IMPOSSIBLE TO GO OUT...
WHOUEEE
HERGÉ

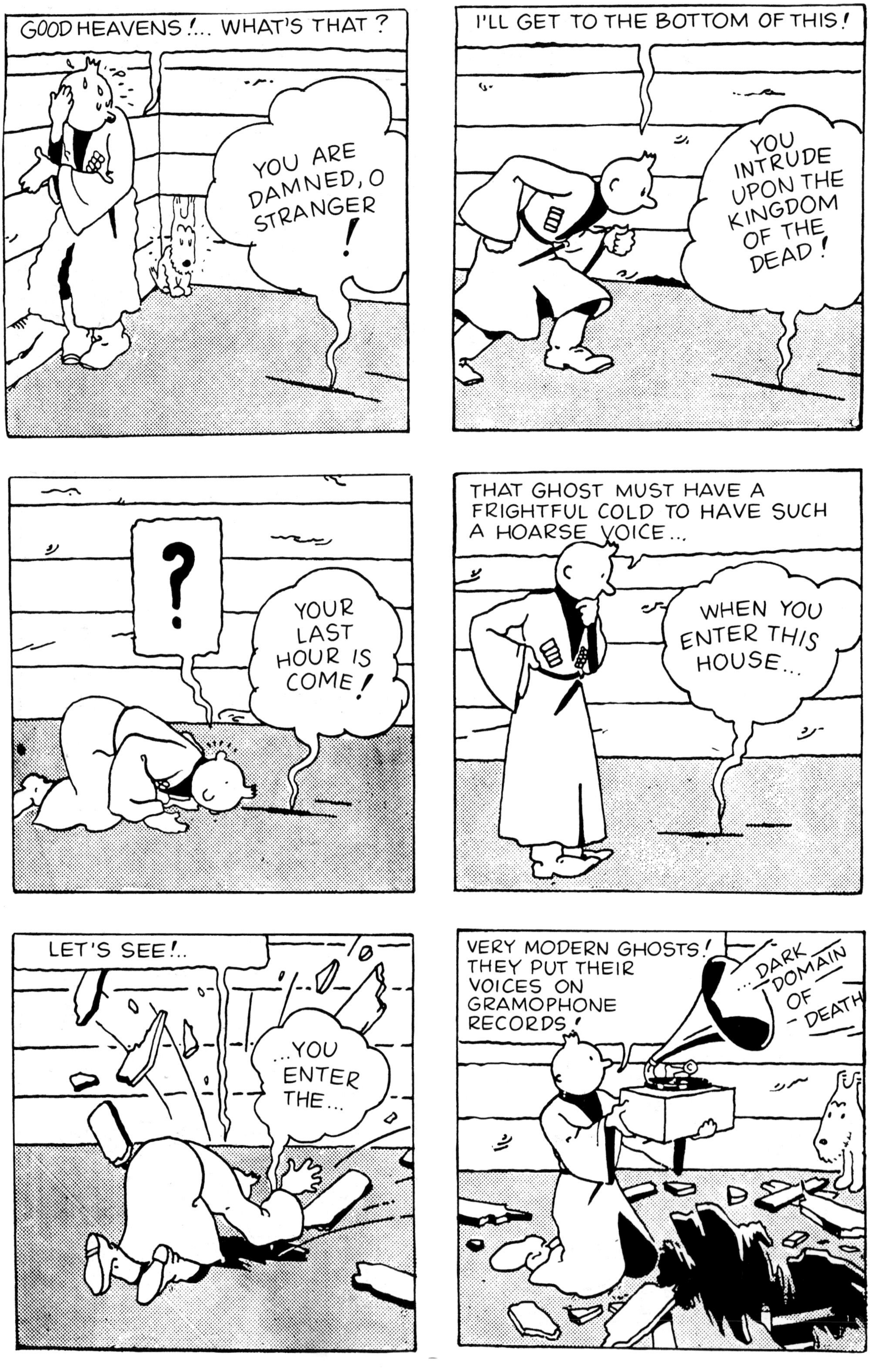
GOOD HEAVENS!... WHAT'S THAT?
YOU ARE DAMNED, O STRANGER!
I'LL GET TO THE BOTTOM OF THIS!
YOU INTRUDE UPON THE KINGDOM OF THE DEAD!
?
YOUR LAST HOUR IS COME!
THAT GHOST MUST HAVE A FRIGHTFUL COLD TO HAVE SUCH A HOARSE VOICE...
WHEN YOU ENTER THIS HOUSE...
LET'S SEE!..
...YOU ENTER THE...
VERY MODERN GHOSTS! THEY PUT THEIR VOICES ON GRAMOPHONE RECORDS!
...DARK DOMAIN OF DEATH

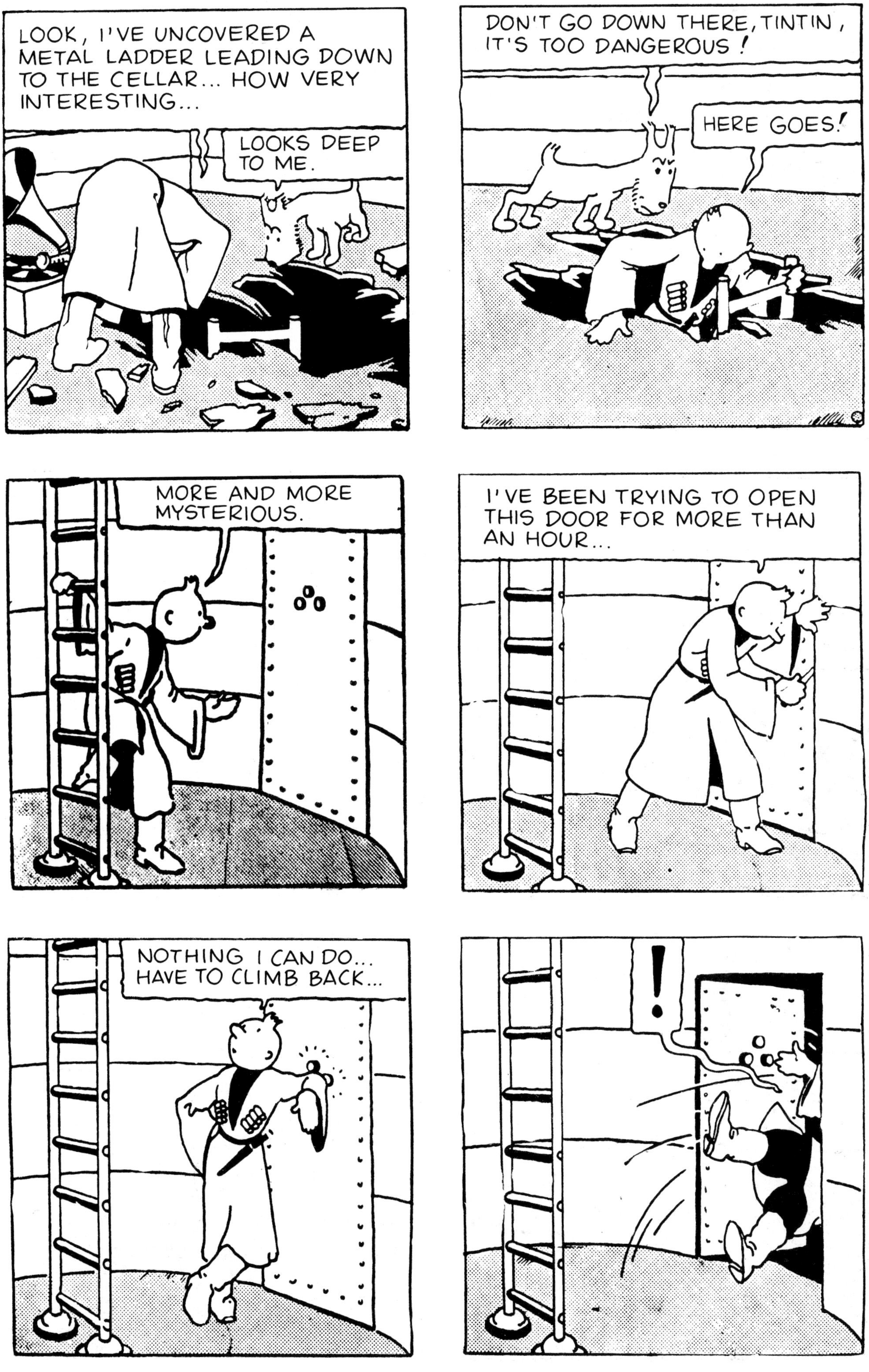
LOOK, I'VE UNCOVERED A METAL LADDER LEADING DOWN TO THE CELLAR... HOW VERY INTERESTING...
LOOKS DEEP TO ME.
DON'T GO DOWN THERE, TINTIN, IT'S TOO DANGEROUS!
HERE GOES!
MORE AND MORE MYSTERIOUS.
I'VE BEEN TRYING TO OPEN THIS DOOR FOR MORE THAN AN HOUR...
NOTHING I CAN DO... HAVE TO CLIMB BACK...
!

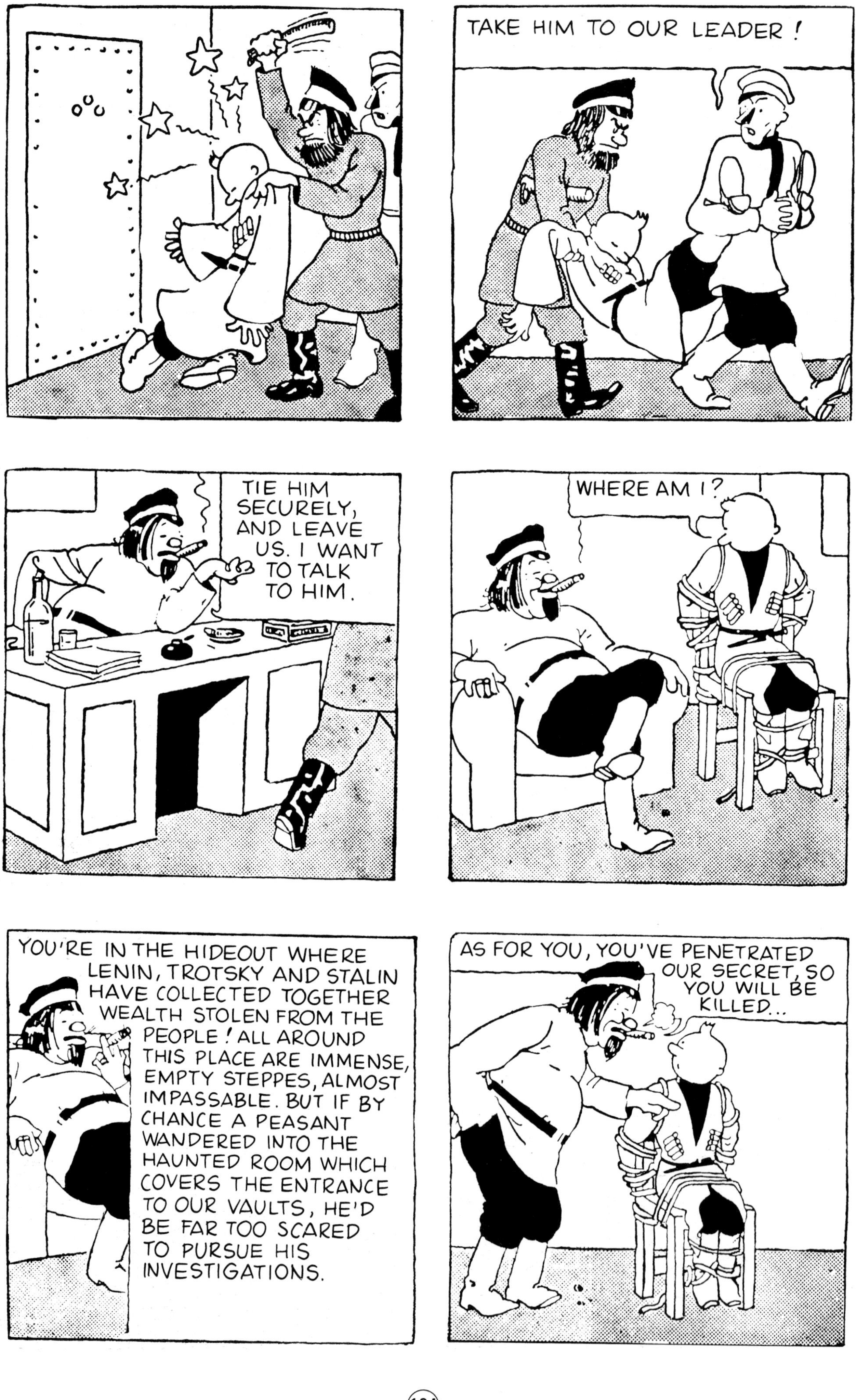
TAKE HIM TO OUR LEADER !
TIE HIM SECURELY, AND LEAVE US. I WANT TO TALK TO HIM.
WHERE AM I ?
YOU'RE IN THE HIDEOUT WHERE LENIN, TROTSKY AND STALIN HAVE COLLECTED TOGETHER WEALTH STOLEN FROM THE PEOPLE ! ALL AROUND THIS PLACE ARE IMMENSE, EMPTY STEPPES, ALMOST IMPASSABLE. BUT IF BY CHANCE A PEASANT WANDERED INTO THE HAUNTED ROOM WHICH COVERS THE ENTRANCE TO OUR VAULTS, HE'D BE FAR TOO SCARED TO PURSUE HIS INVESTIGATIONS.
AS FOR YOU, YOU'VE PENETRATED OUR SECRET, SO YOU WILL BE KILLED...

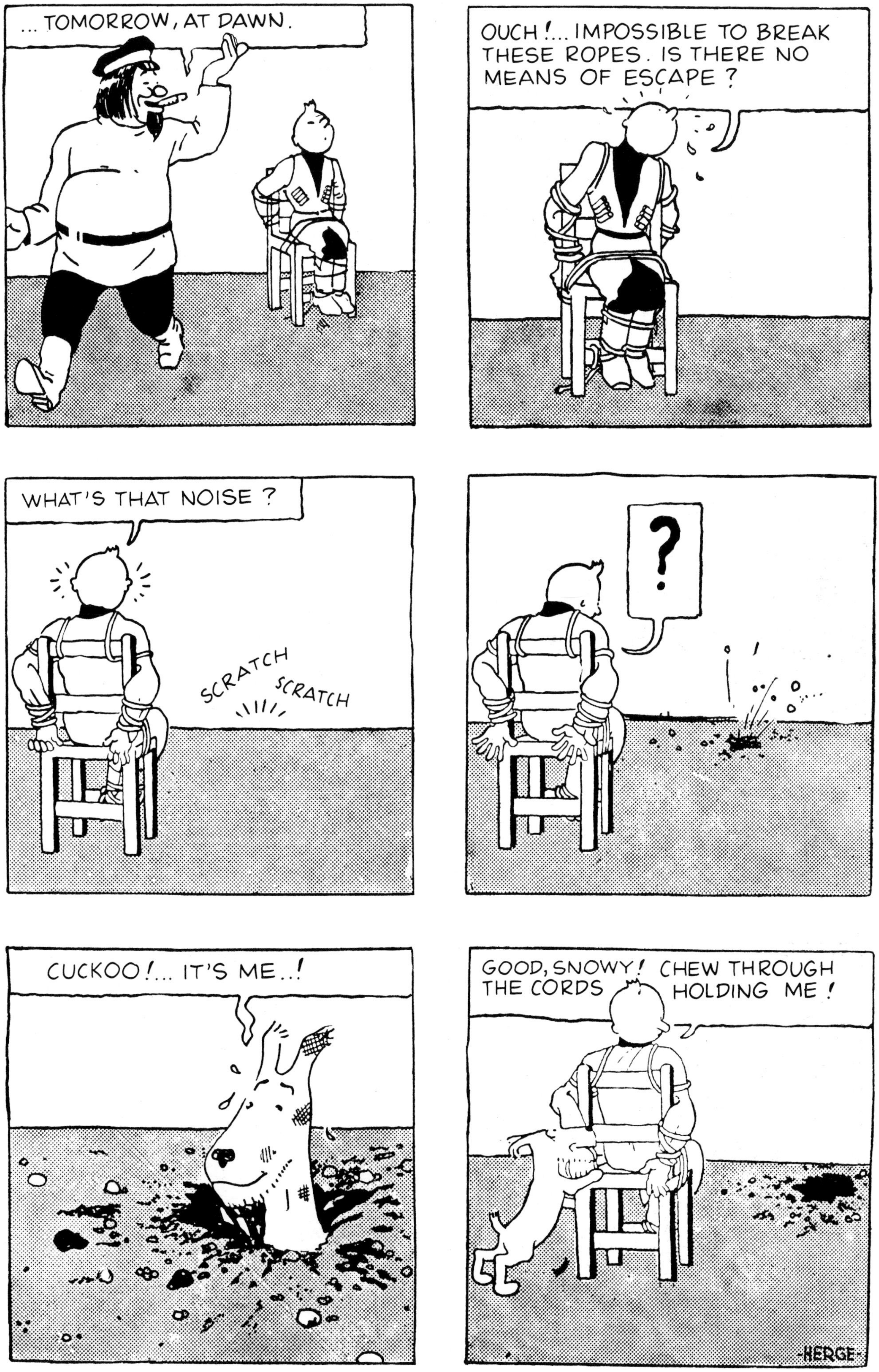
... TOMORROW, AT DAWN.
OUCH!... IMPOSSIBLE TO BREAK THESE ROPES. IS THERE NO MEANS OF ESCAPE?
WHAT'S THAT NOISE?
SCRATCH SCRATCH
?
CUCKOO!... IT'S ME..!
GOOD, SNOWY! CHEW THROUGH THE CORDS HOLDING ME!
HERGE

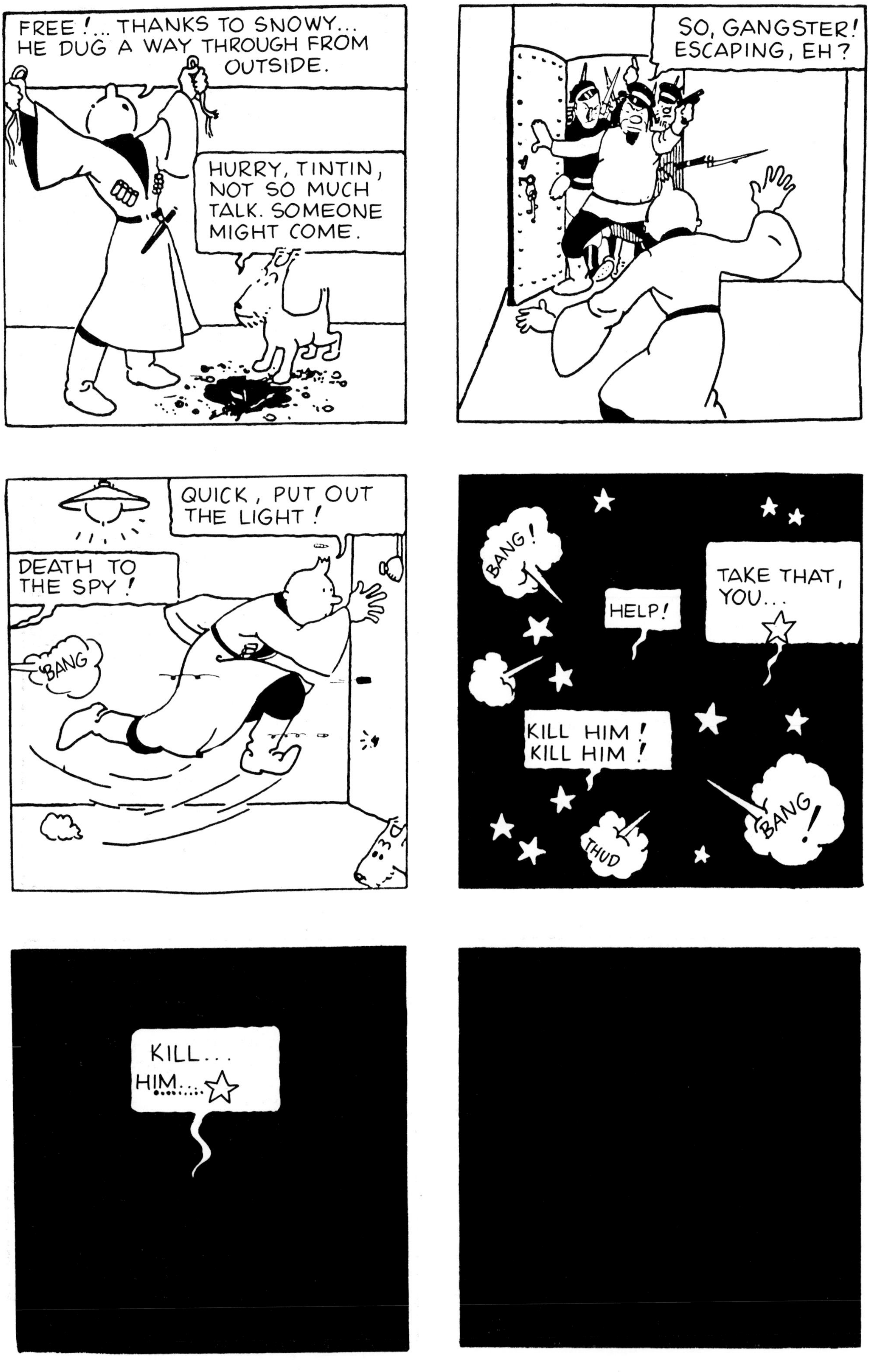
FREE !... THANKS TO SNOWY... HE DUG A WAY THROUGH FROM OUTSIDE.
HURRY, TINTIN, NOT SO MUCH TALK. SOMEONE MIGHT COME.
SO, GANGSTER! ESCAPING, EH?
QUICK, PUT OUT THE LIGHT!
DEATH TO THE SPY!
BANG
BANG!
HELP!
TAKE THAT, YOU...
KILL HIM! KILL HIM!
THUD
BANG!
KILL... HIM......

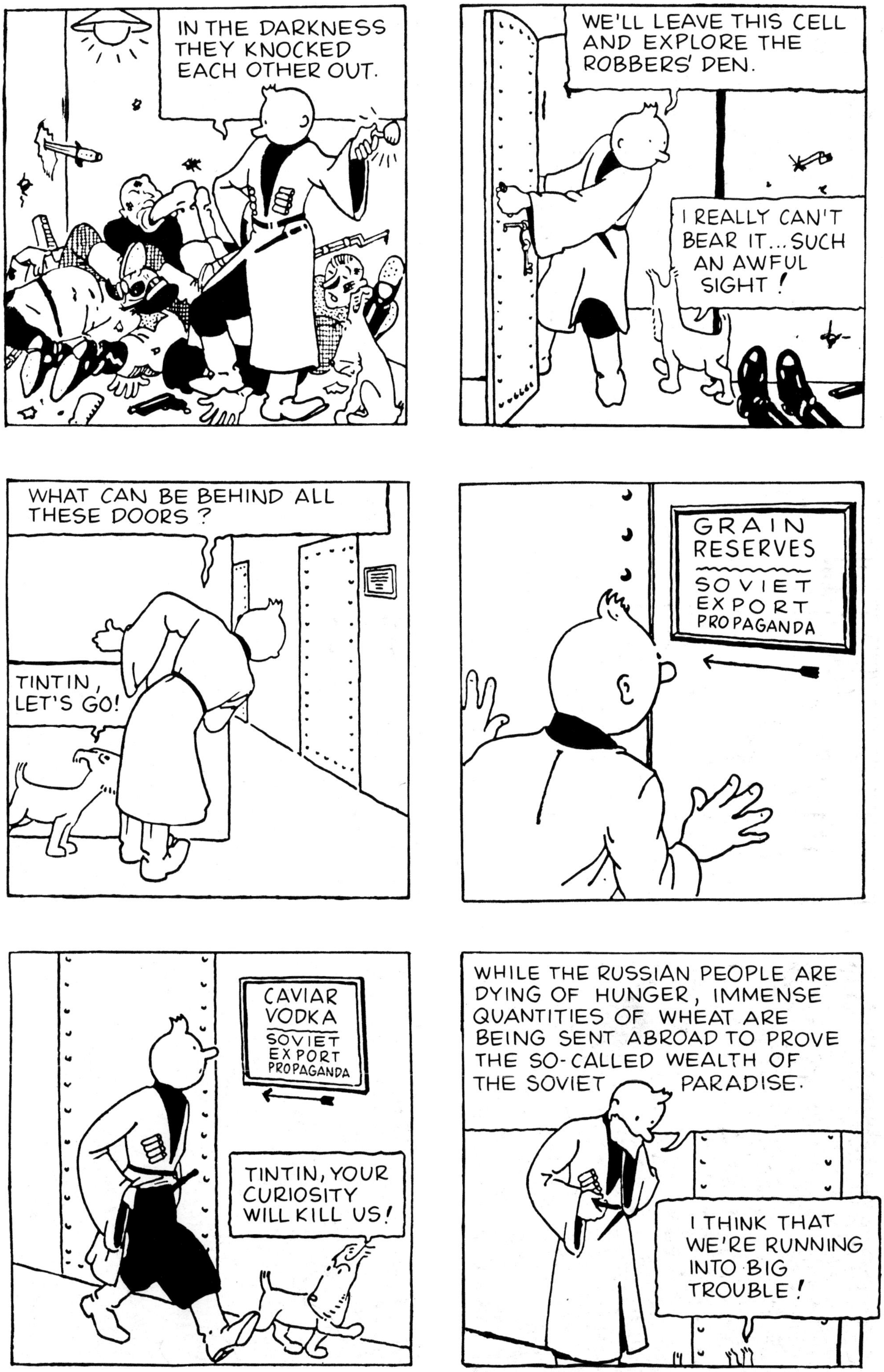
IN THE DARKNESS THEY KNOCKED EACH OTHER OUT.
WE'LL LEAVE THIS CELL AND EXPLORE THE ROBBERS' DEN.
I REALLY CAN'T BEAR IT... SUCH AN AWFUL SIGHT!
WHAT CAN BE BEHIND ALL THESE DOORS?
TINTIN, LET'S GO!
GRAIN RESERVES
SOVIET EXPORT PROPAGANDA
CAVIAR VODKA
SOVIET EXPORT PROPAGANDA
TINTIN, YOUR CURIOSITY WILL KILL US!
WHILE THE RUSSIAN PEOPLE ARE DYING OF HUNGER, IMMENSE QUANTITIES OF WHEAT ARE BEING SENT ABROAD TO PROVE THE SO-CALLED WEALTH OF THE SOVIET PARADISE.
I THINK THAT WE'RE RUNNING INTO BIG TROUBLE!

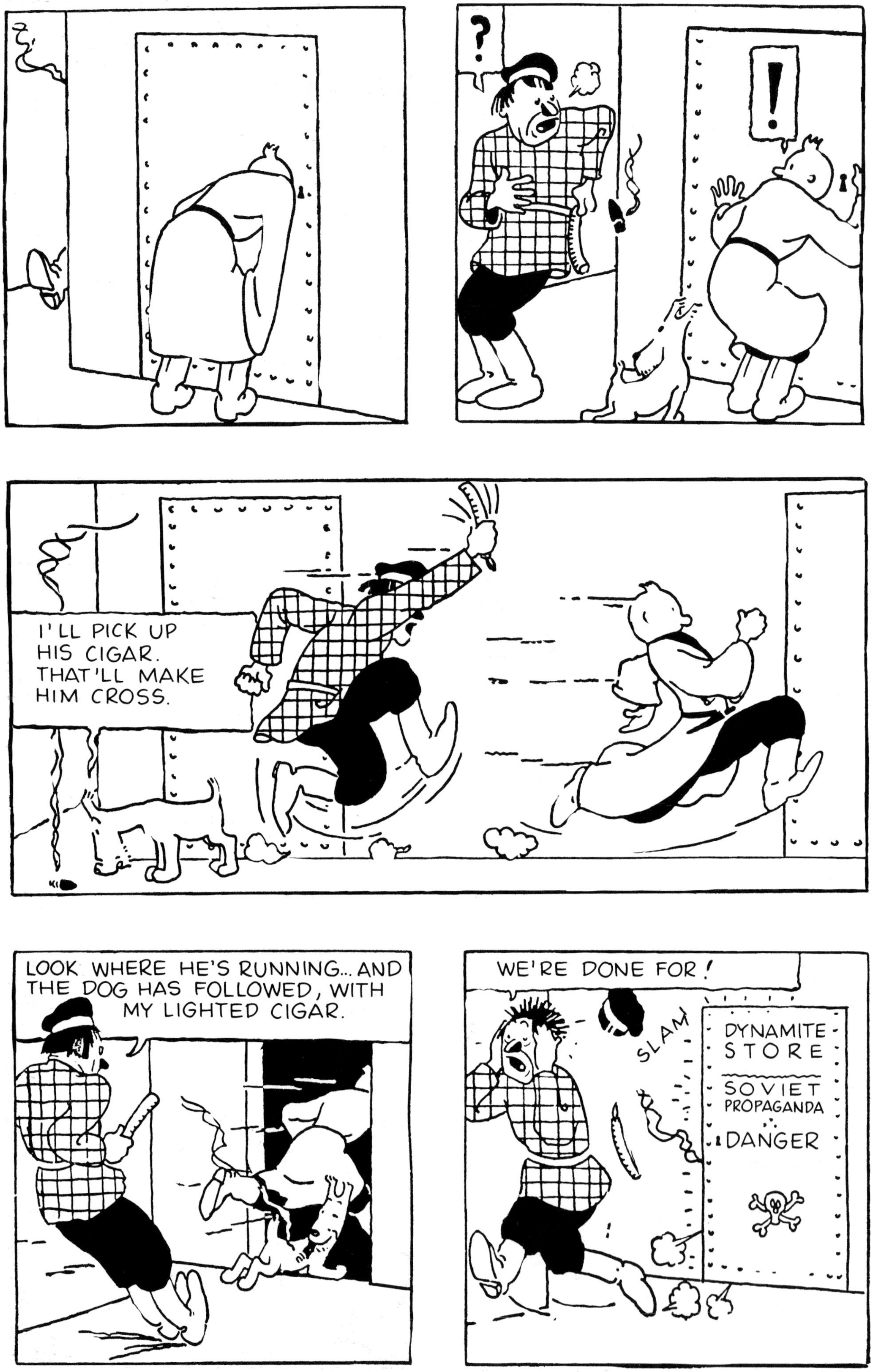
?
!
I'LL PICK UP HIS CIGAR. THAT'LL MAKE HIM CROSS.
LOOK WHERE HE'S RUNNING... AND THE DOG HAS FOLLOWED, WITH MY LIGHTED CIGAR.
WE'RE DONE FOR!
SLAM
DYNAMITE STORE
SOVIET PROPAGANDA
DANGER

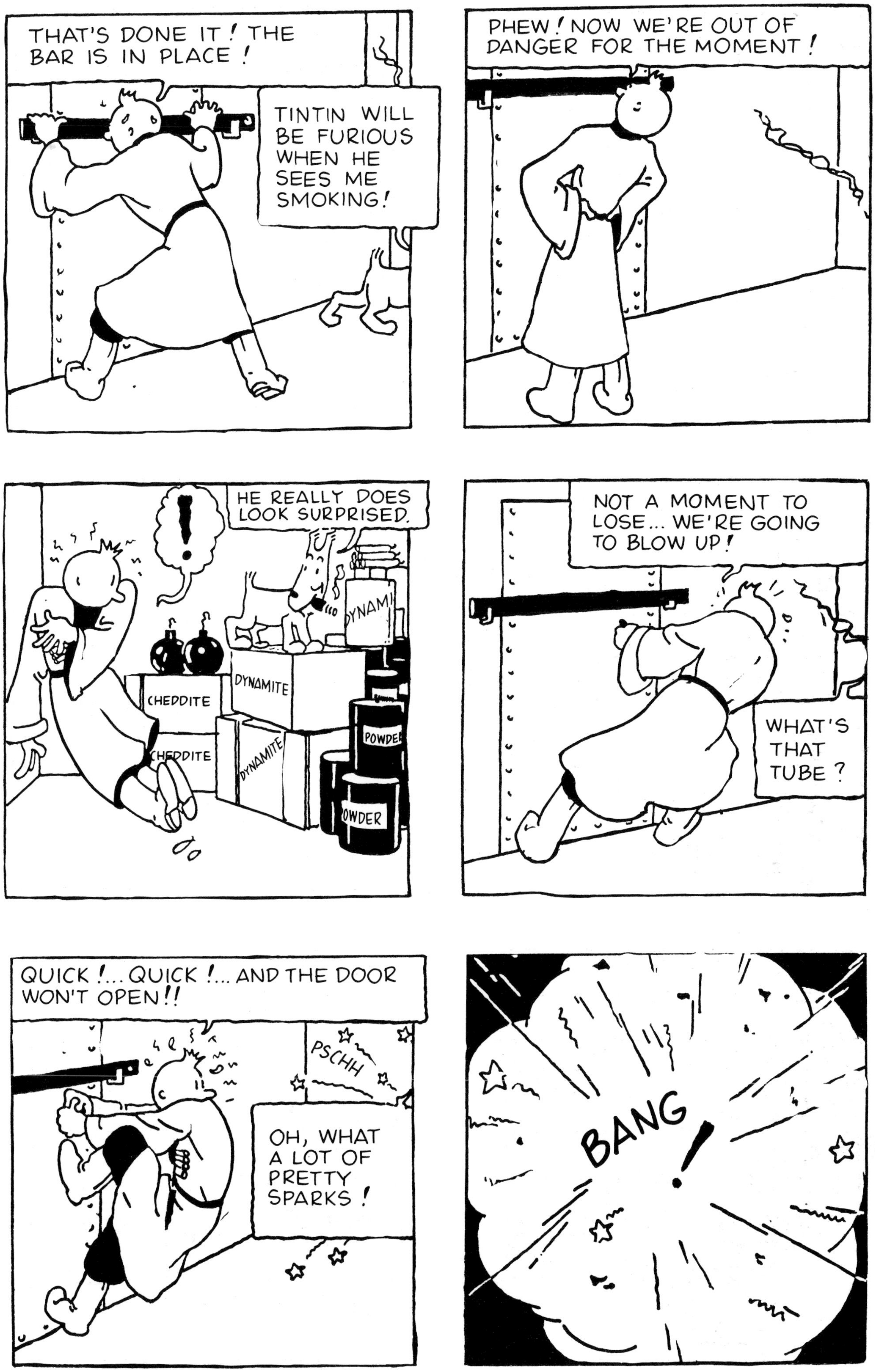

THAT'S DONE IT! THE BAR IS IN PLACE!
TINTIN WILL BE FURIOUS WHEN HE SEES ME SMOKING!
PHEW! NOW WE'RE OUT OF DANGER FOR THE MOMENT!
HE REALLY DOES LOOK SURPRISED.
!
CHEDDITE
DYNAMITE
CHEDDITE
DYNAMITE
POWDER
POWDER
NOT A MOMENT TO LOSE... WE'RE GOING TO BLOW UP!
WHAT'S THAT TUBE?
QUICK!... QUICK!... AND THE DOOR WON'T OPEN!!
PSCHH
OH, WHAT A LOT OF PRETTY SPARKS!
BANG!

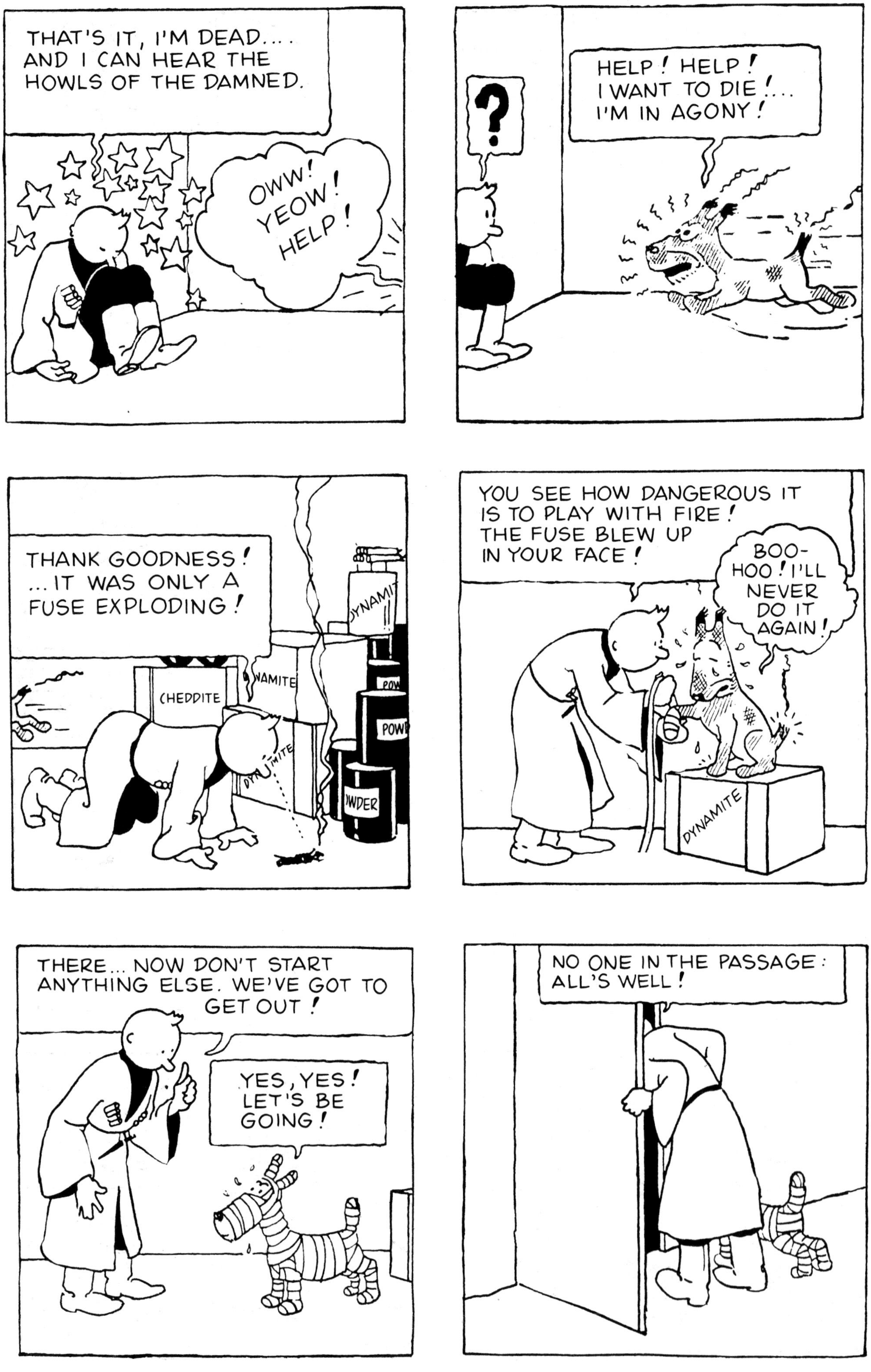
THAT'S IT, I'M DEAD.... AND I CAN HEAR THE HOWLS OF THE DAMNED.
OWW! YEOW! HELP!
?
HELP! HELP! I WANT TO DIE!... I'M IN AGONY!
THANK GOODNESS! ...IT WAS ONLY A FUSE EXPLODING!
CHEDDITE
DYNAMITE
POWDER
YOU SEE HOW DANGEROUS IT IS TO PLAY WITH FIRE! THE FUSE BLEW UP IN YOUR FACE!
BOO-HOO! I'LL NEVER DO IT AGAIN!
DYNAMITE
THERE... NOW DON'T START ANYTHING ELSE. WE'VE GOT TO GET OUT!
YES, YES! LET'S BE GOING!
NO ONE IN THE PASSAGE: ALL'S WELL!

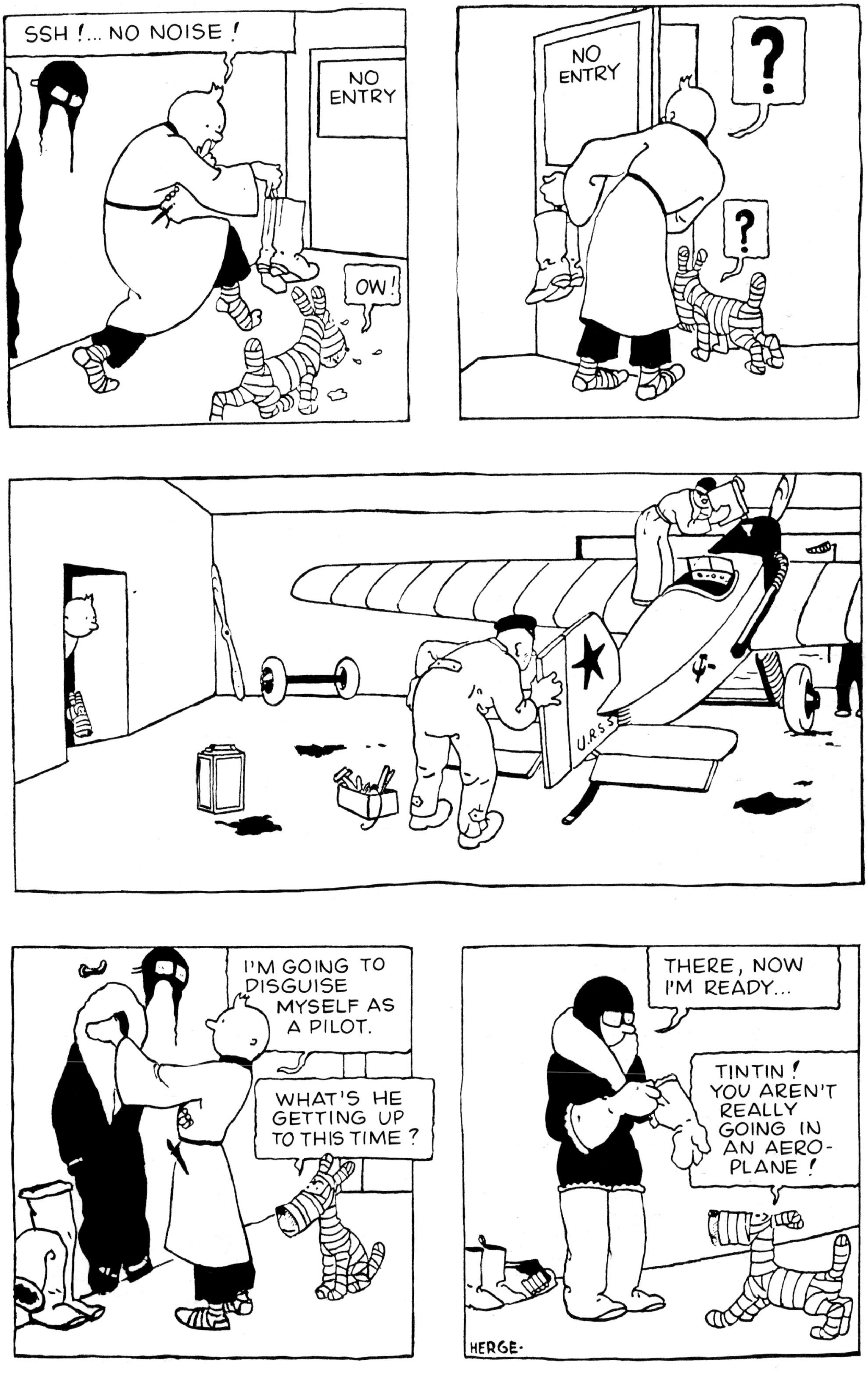
SSH !... NO NOISE !
NO ENTRY
OW !
NO ENTRY
?
?
I'M GOING TO DISGUISE MYSELF AS A PILOT.
WHAT'S HE GETTING UP TO THIS TIME ?
THERE, NOW I'M READY...
TINTIN ! YOU AREN'T REALLY GOING IN AN AERO-PLANE !
U.R.S.S
HERGE

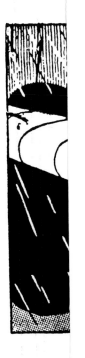

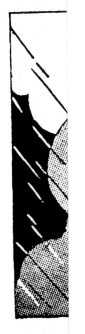

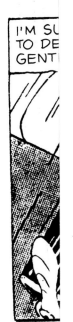

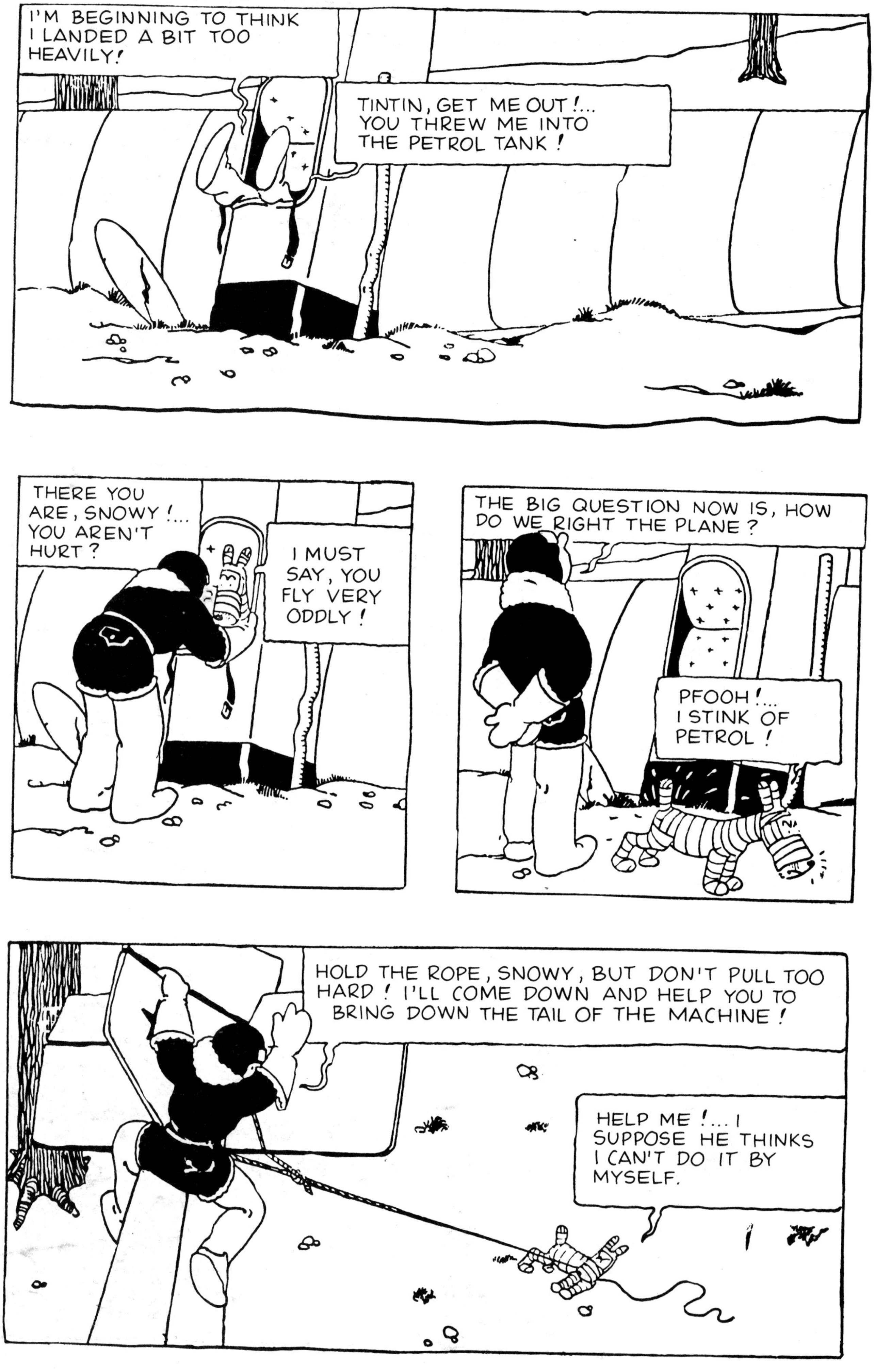
I'M BEGINNING TO THINK I LANDED A BIT TOO HEAVILY!
TINTIN, GET ME OUT!... YOU THREW ME INTO THE PETROL TANK!
THERE YOU ARE, SNOWY!... YOU AREN'T HURT?
I MUST SAY, YOU FLY VERY ODDLY!
THE BIG QUESTION NOW IS, HOW DO WE RIGHT THE PLANE?
PFOOH!... I STINK OF PETROL!
HOLD THE ROPE, SNOWY, BUT DON'T PULL TOO HARD! I'LL COME DOWN AND HELP YOU TO BRING DOWN THE TAIL OF THE MACHINE!
HELP ME!... I SUPPOSE HE THINKS I CAN'T DO IT BY MYSELF.

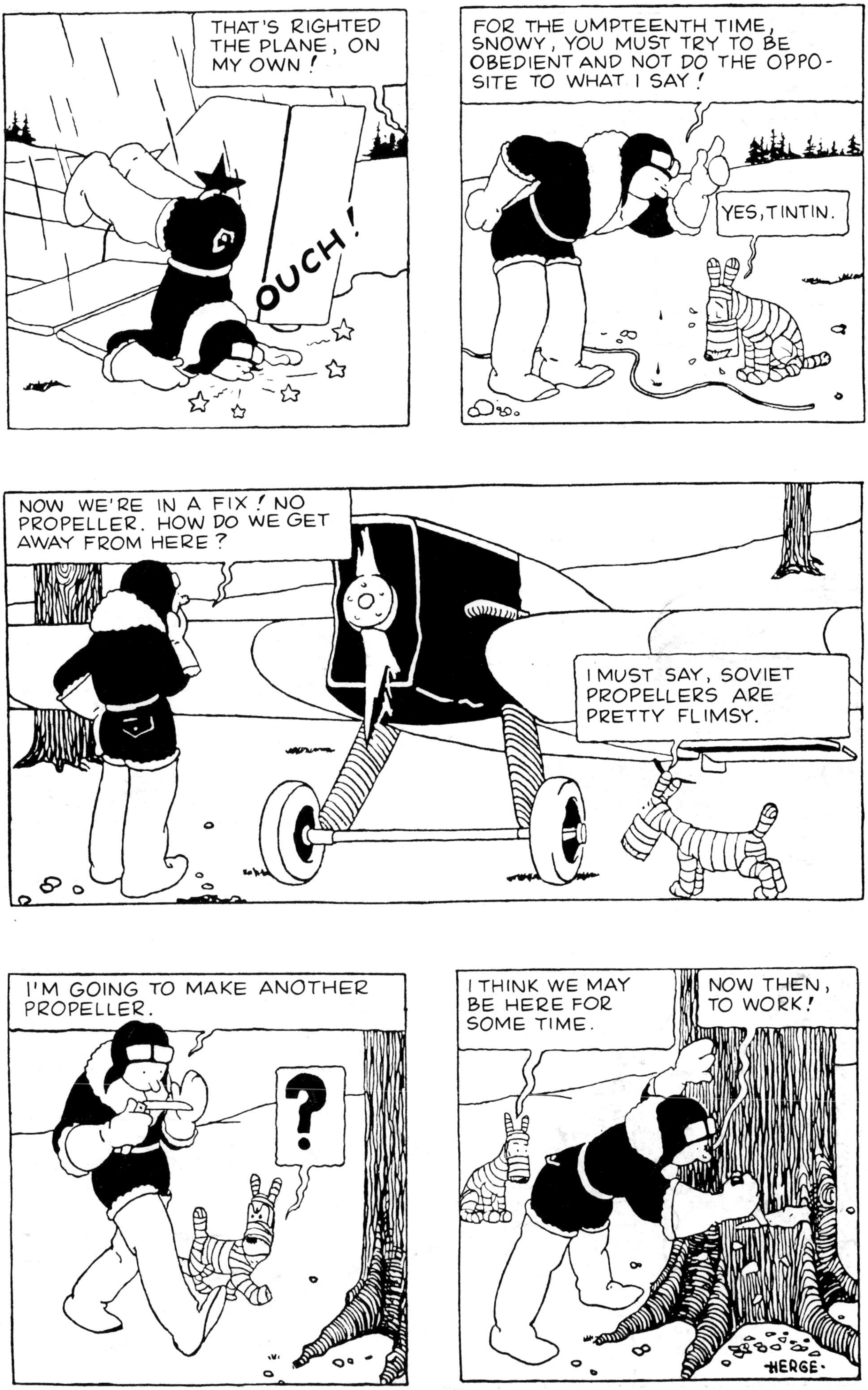

THAT'S RIGHTED THE PLANE, ON MY OWN!
OUCH!
FOR THE UMPTEENTH TIME, SNOWY, YOU MUST TRY TO BE OBEDIENT AND NOT DO THE OPPO-SITE TO WHAT I SAY!
YES, TINTIN.
NOW WE'RE IN A FIX! NO PROPELLER. HOW DO WE GET AWAY FROM HERE?
I MUST SAY, SOVIET PROPELLERS ARE PRETTY FLIMSY.
I'M GOING TO MAKE ANOTHER PROPELLER.
?
I THINK WE MAY BE HERE FOR SOME TIME.
NOW THEN, TO WORK!
HERGE

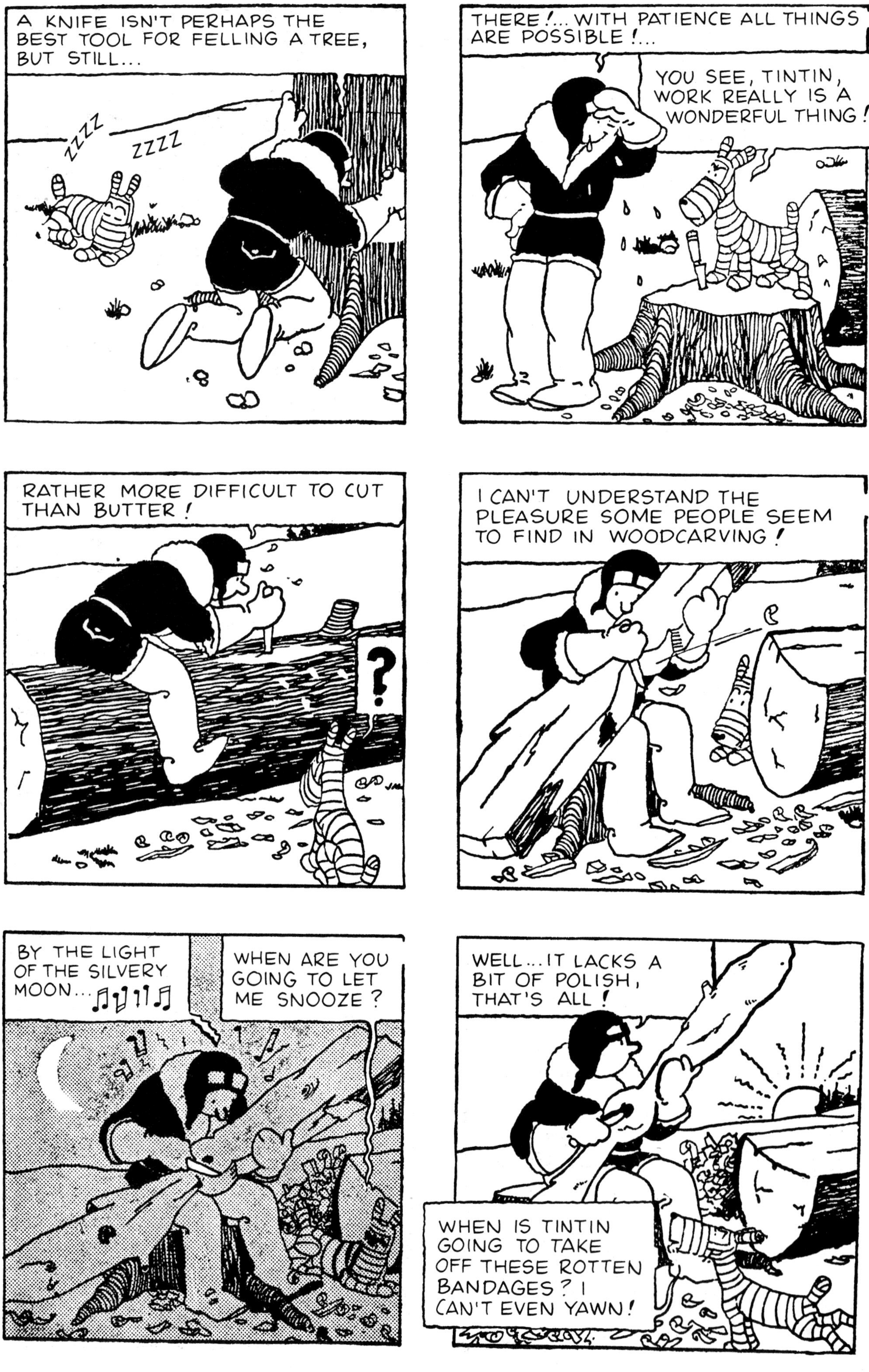
A KNIFE ISN'T PERHAPS THE BEST TOOL FOR FELLING A TREE, BUT STILL...
ZZZZ
ZZZZ
THERE!... WITH PATIENCE ALL THINGS ARE POSSIBLE!...
YOU SEE, TINTIN, WORK REALLY IS A WONDERFUL THING!
RATHER MORE DIFFICULT TO CUT THAN BUTTER!
?
I CAN'T UNDERSTAND THE PLEASURE SOME PEOPLE SEEM TO FIND IN WOODCARVING!
BY THE LIGHT OF THE SILVERY MOON...
WHEN ARE YOU GOING TO LET ME SNOOZE?
WELL... IT LACKS A BIT OF POLISH, THAT'S ALL!
WHEN IS TINTIN GOING TO TAKE OFF THESE ROTTEN BANDAGES? I CAN'T EVEN YAWN!

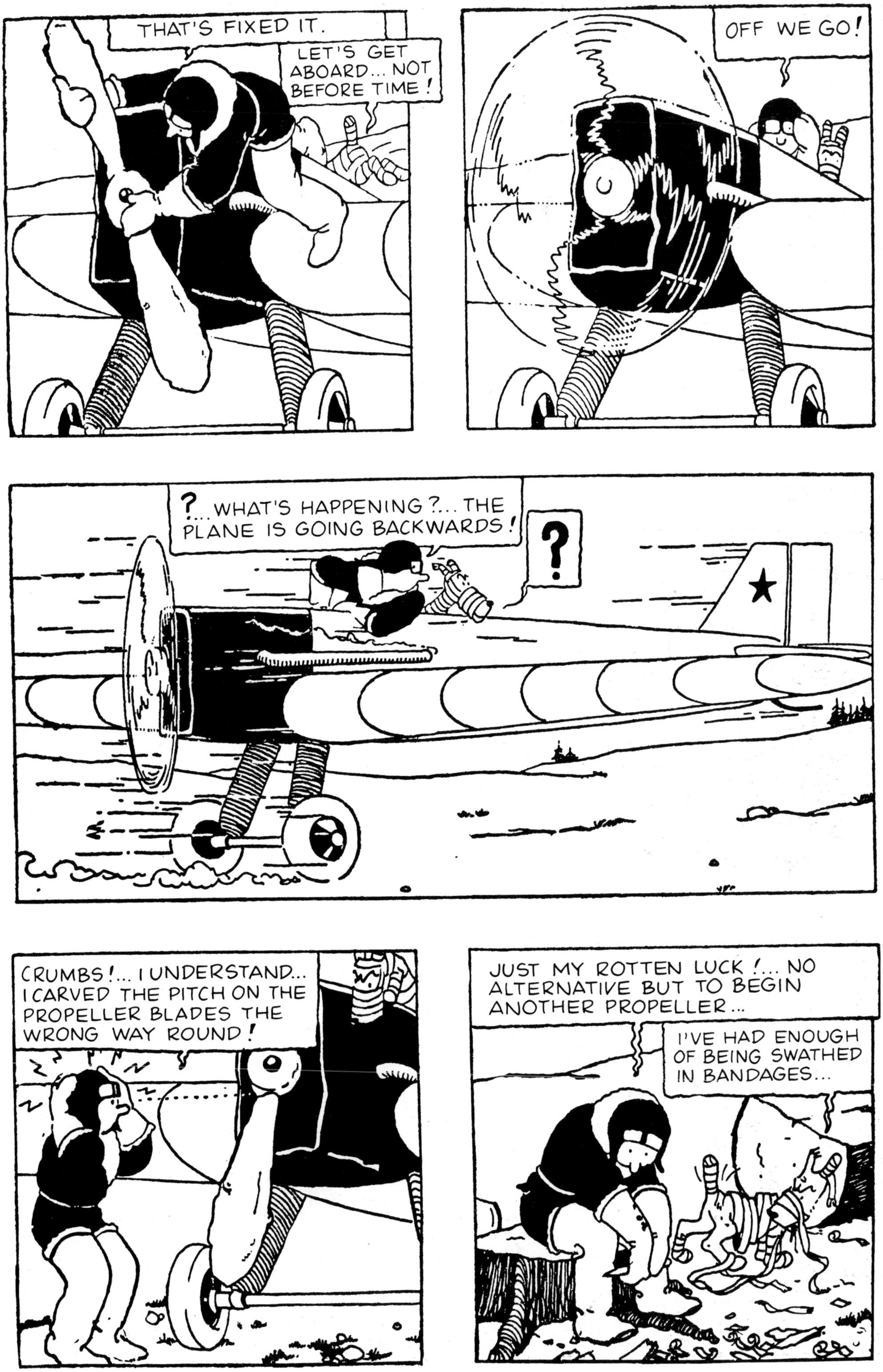
THAT'S FIXED IT.
LET'S GET ABOARD... NOT BEFORE TIME!
OFF WE GO!
?... WHAT'S HAPPENING?... THE PLANE IS GOING BACKWARDS!
?
CRUMBS!... I UNDERSTAND... I CARVED THE PITCH ON THE PROPELLER BLADES THE WRONG WAY ROUND!
JUST MY ROTTEN LUCK!... NO ALTERNATIVE BUT TO BEGIN ANOTHER PROPELLER...
I'VE HAD ENOUGH OF BEING SWATHED IN BANDAGES...

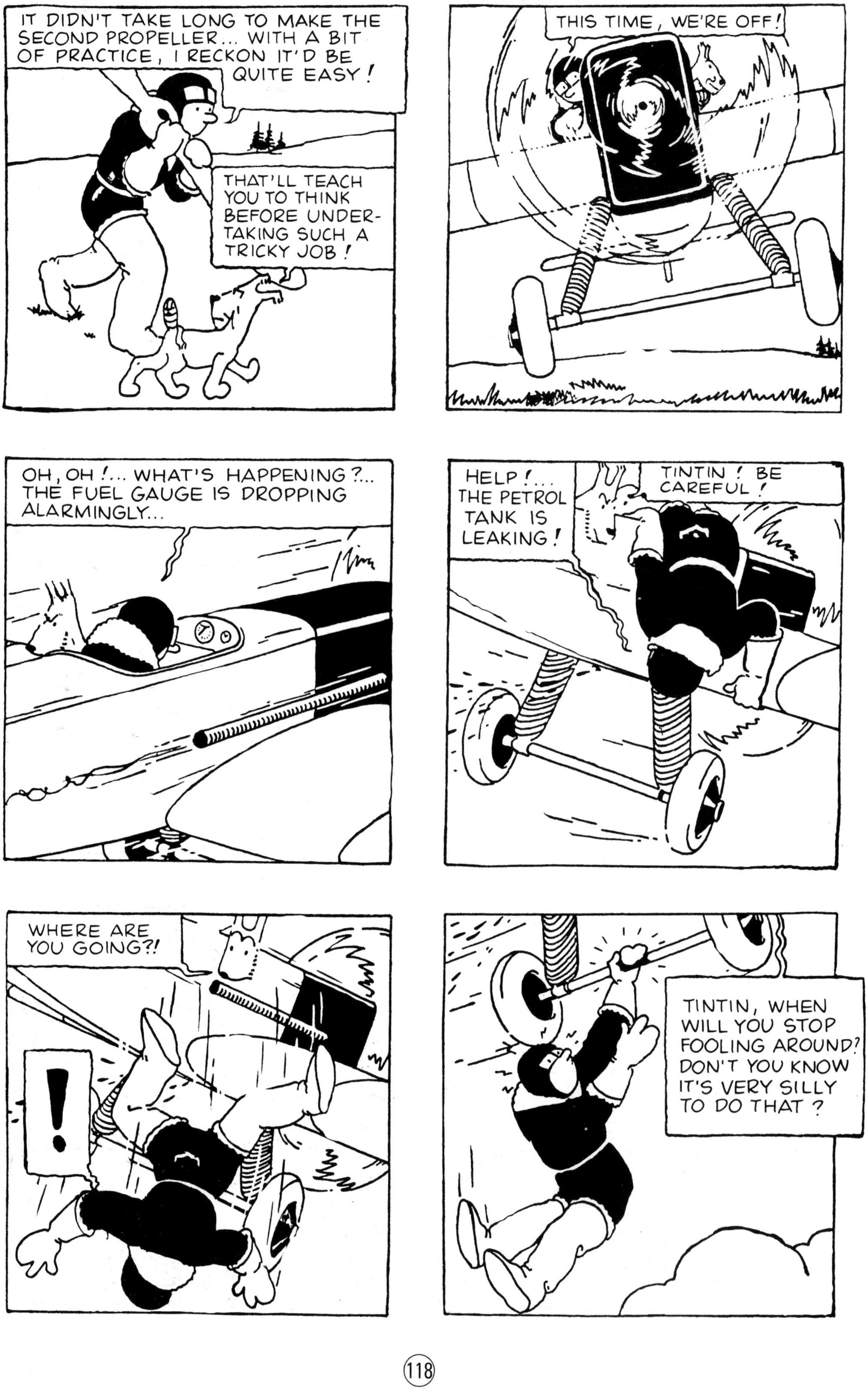
IT DIDN'T TAKE LONG TO MAKE THE SECOND PROPELLER... WITH A BIT OF PRACTICE, I RECKON IT'D BE QUITE EASY!
THAT'LL TEACH YOU TO THINK BEFORE UNDER-TAKING SUCH A TRICKY JOB!
THIS TIME, WE'RE OFF!
OH, OH!... WHAT'S HAPPENING?... THE FUEL GAUGE IS DROPPING ALARMINGLY...
HELP!... THE PETROL TANK IS LEAKING!
TINTIN! BE CAREFUL!
WHERE ARE YOU GOING?!
!
TINTIN, WHEN WILL YOU STOP FOOLING AROUND? DON'T YOU KNOW IT'S VERY SILLY TO DO THAT?

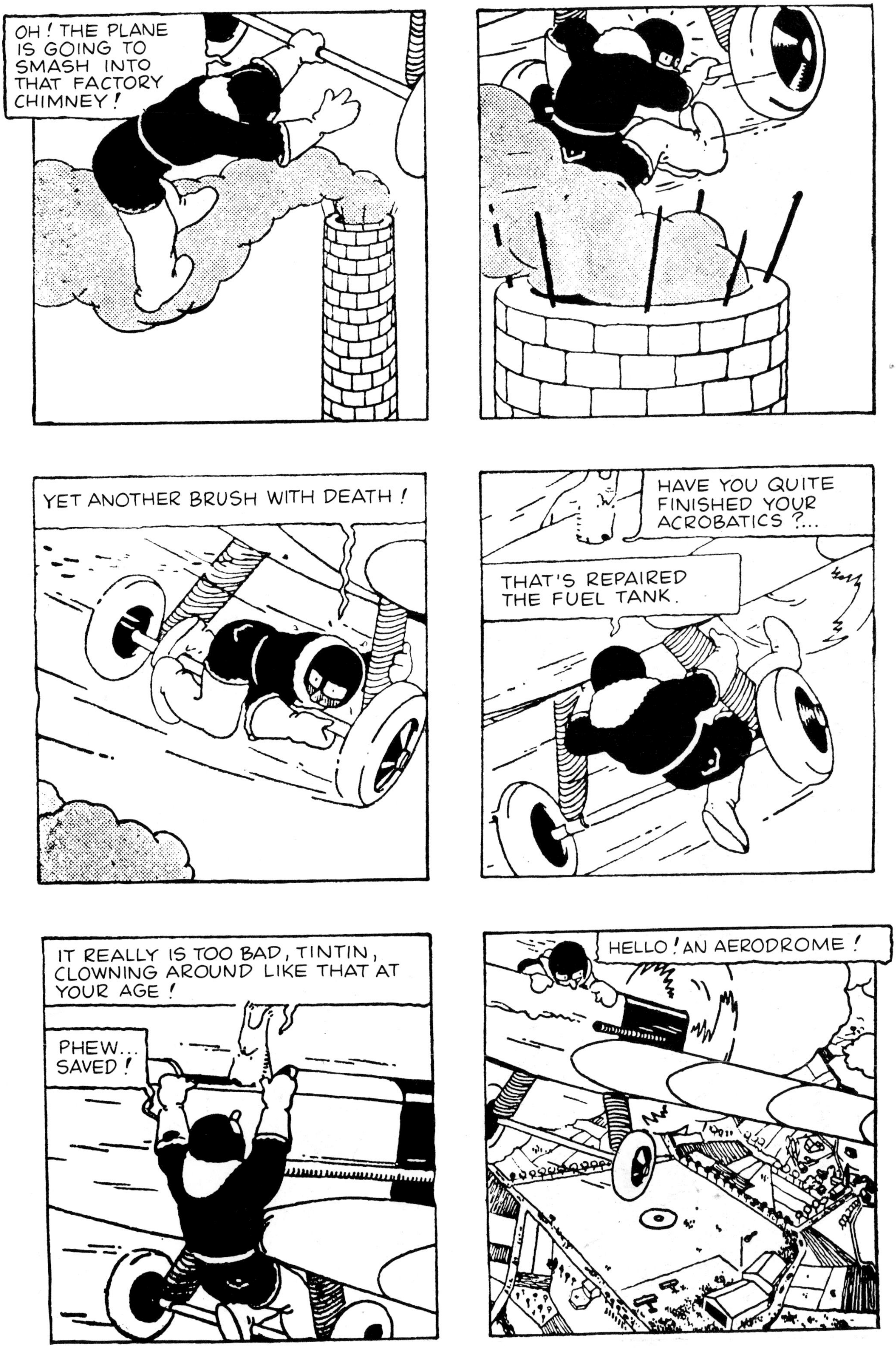
OH! THE PLANE IS GOING TO SMASH INTO THAT FACTORY CHIMNEY!
YET ANOTHER BRUSH WITH DEATH!
HAVE YOU QUITE FINISHED YOUR ACROBATICS?...
THAT'S REPAIRED THE FUEL TANK.
IT REALLY IS TOO BAD, TINTIN, CLOWNING AROUND LIKE THAT AT YOUR AGE!
PHEW... SAVED!
HELLO! AN AERODROME!

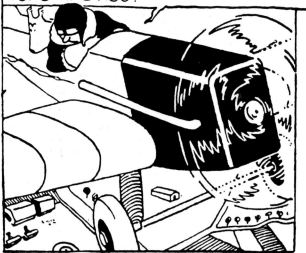

NO MISTAKE !... IT'S THE AERODROME AT TEMPELHOF, NEAR BERLIN ! SO WE CROSSED THE RUSSIAN FRONTIER A LONG TIME AGO !

WE ARE GOING TO LAND... BUT WHY ALL THE PEOPLE ?

WHAT DO THEY WANT ?

HELLO !

HIP... HIP... HOORAY !

THEY'RE VERY KIND...

HIP... HIP... HOORAY !

...WE SALUTE YOU... GLORIOUS HERO OF THE SOUTH POLE TO NORTH POLE FLIGHT, ON YOUR TOUCHDOWN IN BERLIN !

THEY'VE MADE A MISTAKE !

...THE FIRST LEG IS OVER. NOW YOU HAVE TO ACHIEVE THE SECOND... WE WISH YOU GOOD LUCK !

GOOD, EH ?

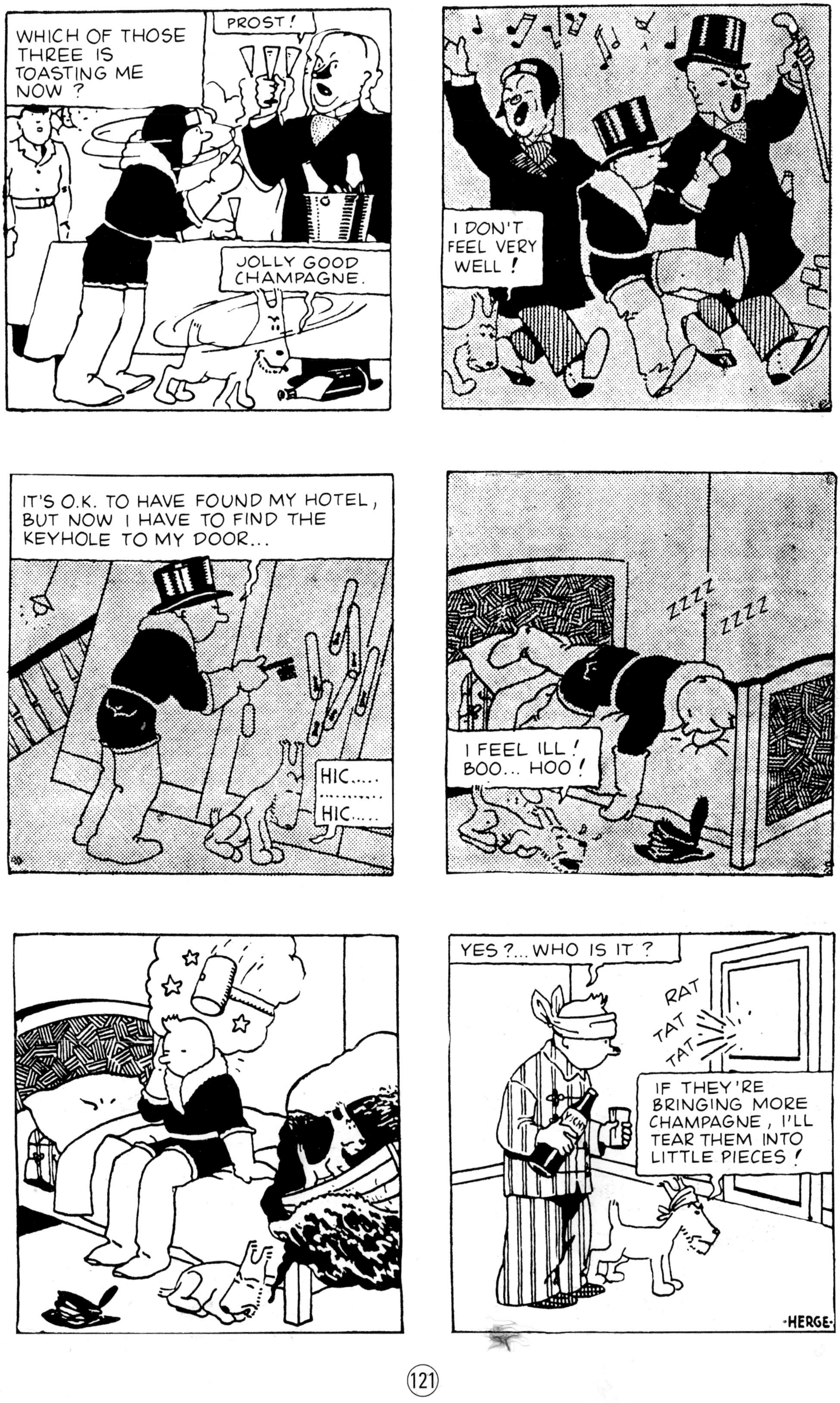
WHICH OF THOSE THREE IS TOASTING ME NOW ?
PROST !
JOLLY GOOD CHAMPAGNE.
I DON'T FEEL VERY WELL !
IT'S O.K. TO HAVE FOUND MY HOTEL, BUT NOW I HAVE TO FIND THE KEYHOLE TO MY DOOR...
HIC.....
HIC.....
ZZZZ
ZZZZ
I FEEL ILL ! BOO... HOO !
YES ?... WHO IS IT ?
RAT
TAT
TAT
IF THEY'RE BRINGING MORE CHAMPAGNE , I'LL TEAR THEM INTO LITTLE PIECES !
VICHY
HERGE

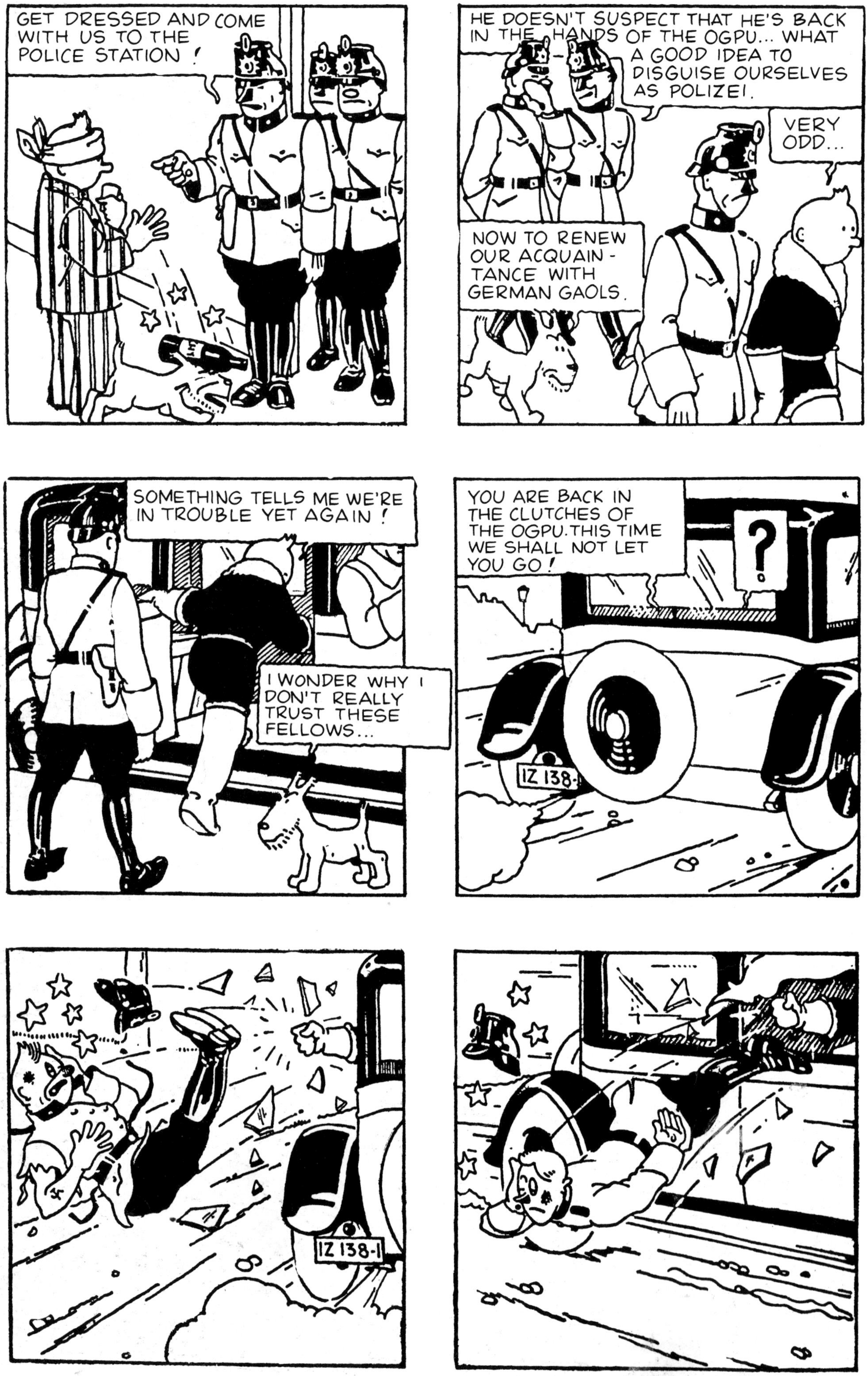
GET DRESSED AND COME WITH US TO THE POLICE STATION !
HE DOESN'T SUSPECT THAT HE'S BACK IN THE HANDS OF THE OGPU... WHAT A GOOD IDEA TO DISGUISE OURSELVES AS POLIZEI.
VERY ODD...
NOW TO RENEW OUR ACQUAIN-TANCE WITH GERMAN GAOLS.
SOMETHING TELLS ME WE'RE IN TROUBLE YET AGAIN !
I WONDER WHY I DON'T REALLY TRUST THESE FELLOWS...
YOU ARE BACK IN THE CLUTCHES OF THE OGPU. THIS TIME WE SHALL NOT LET YOU GO !
?
IZ 138-
IZ 138-1

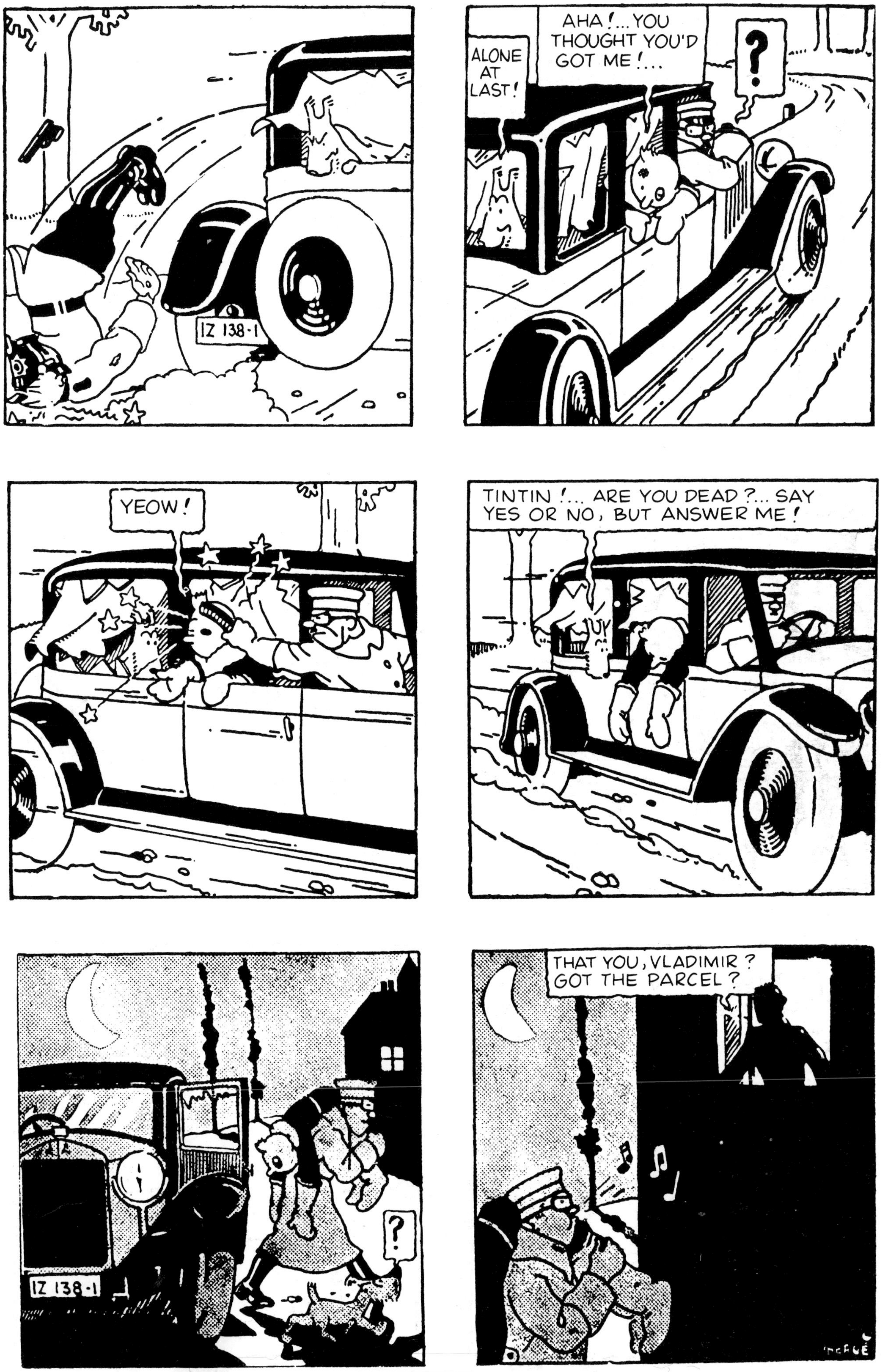

ALONE AT LAST!
AHA!... YOU THOUGHT YOU'D GOT ME!...
?
YEOW!
TINTIN!... ARE YOU DEAD?... SAY YES OR NO, BUT ANSWER ME!
IZ 138-1
?
THAT YOU, VLADIMIR? GOT THE PARCEL?

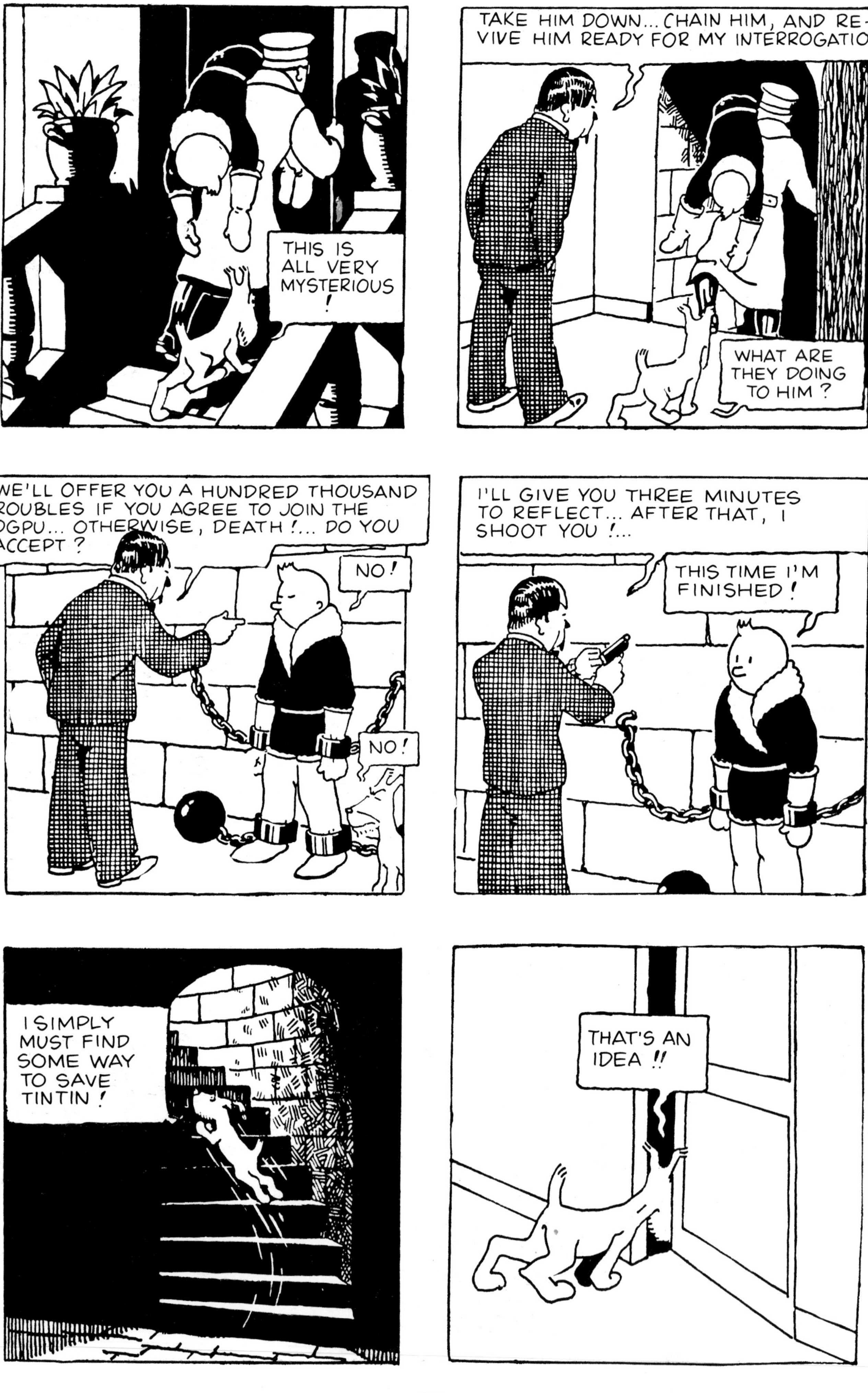
THIS IS ALL VERY MYSTERIOUS !
TAKE HIM DOWN... CHAIN HIM, AND RE-VIVE HIM READY FOR MY INTERROGATION.
WHAT ARE THEY DOING TO HIM ?
WE'LL OFFER YOU A HUNDRED THOUSAND ROUBLES IF YOU AGREE TO JOIN THE OGPU... OTHERWISE, DEATH !... DO YOU ACCEPT ?
NO !
NO !
I'LL GIVE YOU THREE MINUTES TO REFLECT... AFTER THAT, I SHOOT YOU !...
THIS TIME I'M FINISHED !
I SIMPLY MUST FIND SOME WAY TO SAVE TINTIN !
THAT'S AN IDEA !!

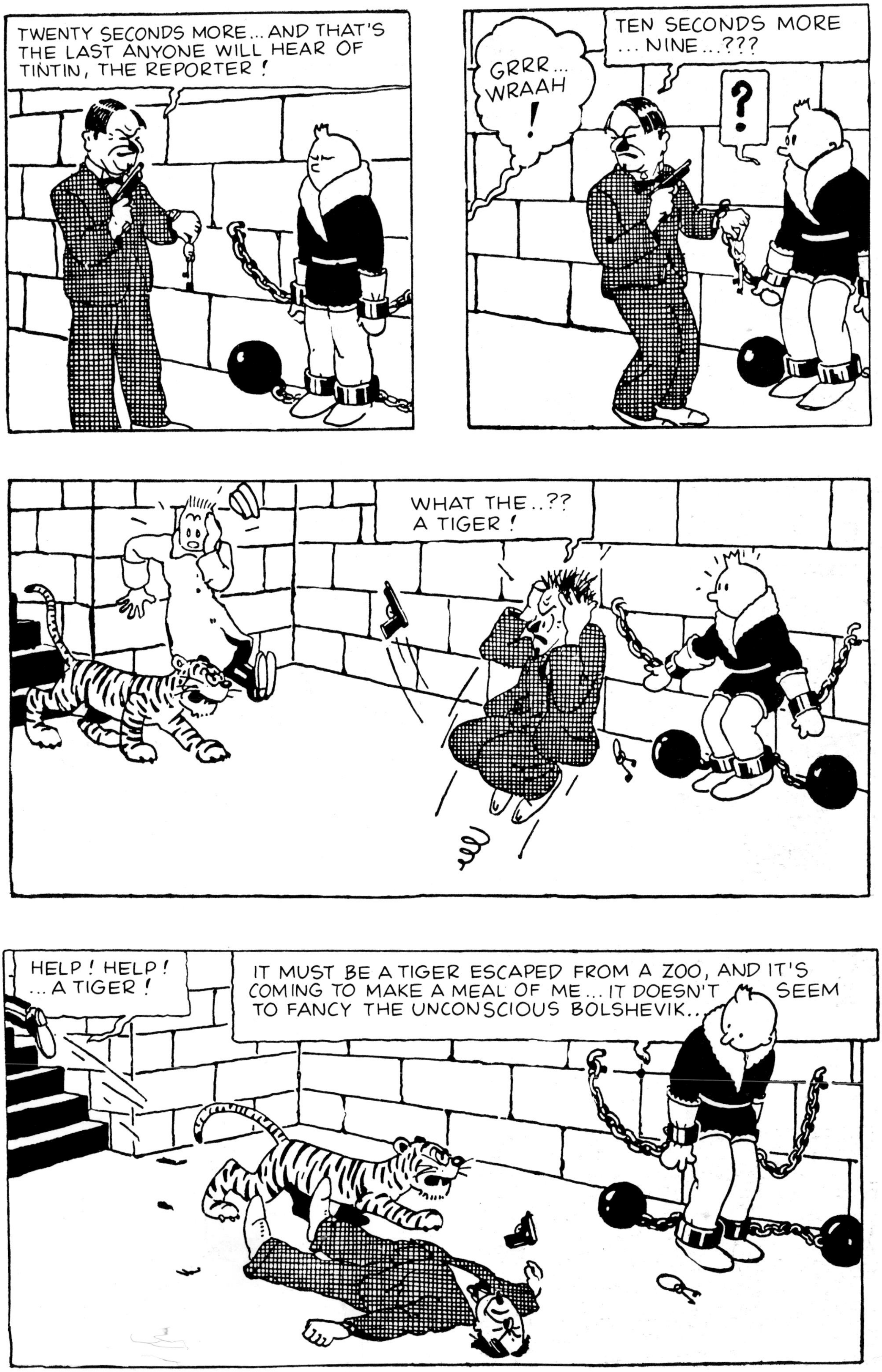
TWENTY SECONDS MORE... AND THAT'S THE LAST ANYONE WILL HEAR OF TINTIN, THE REPORTER !
GRRR... WRAAH !
TEN SECONDS MORE ... NINE...???
?
WHAT THE..?? A TIGER !
HELP ! HELP ! ...A TIGER !
IT MUST BE A TIGER ESCAPED FROM A ZOO, AND IT'S COMING TO MAKE A MEAL OF ME... IT DOESN'T SEEM TO FANCY THE UNCONSCIOUS BOLSHEVIK...

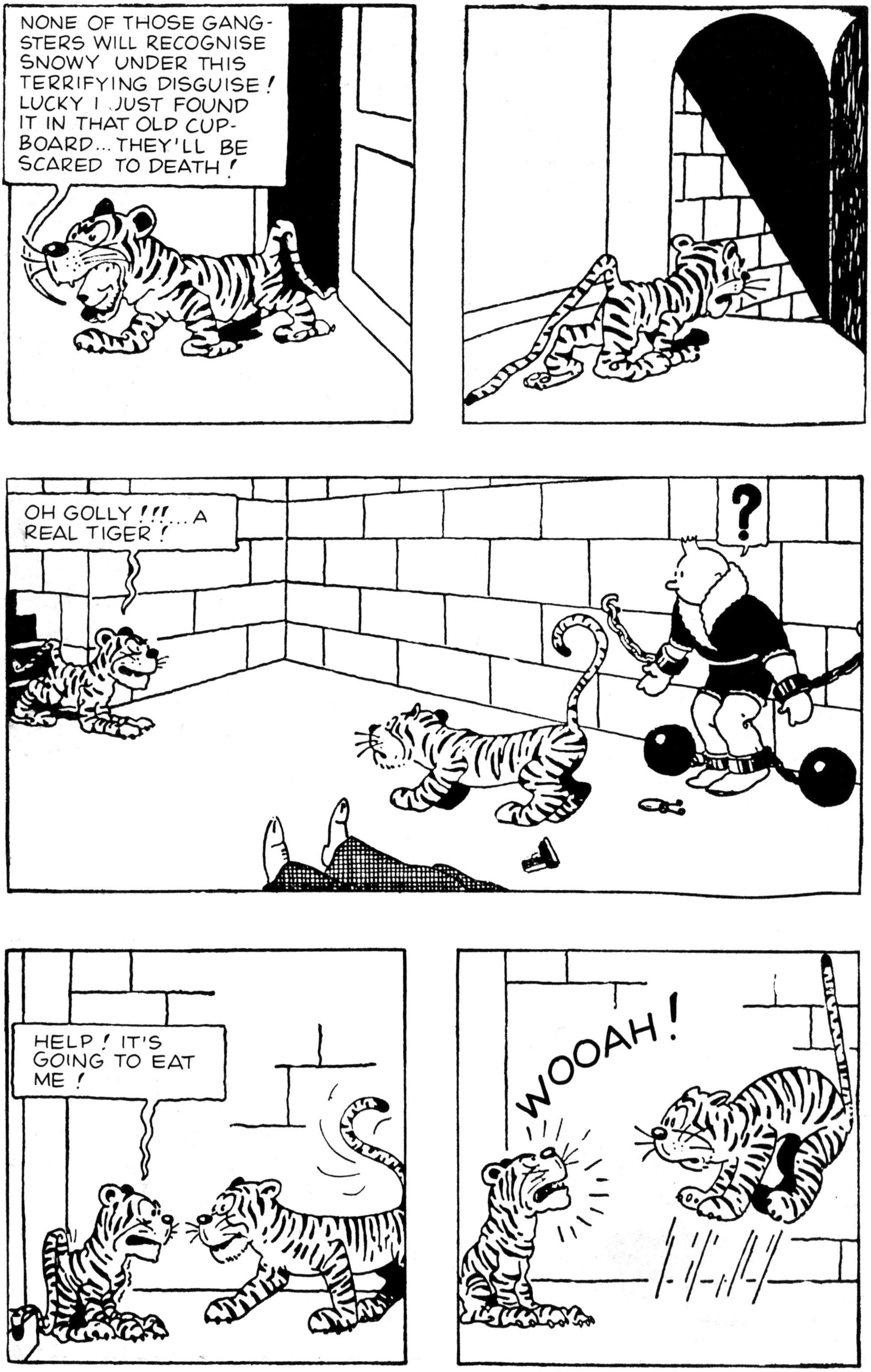
NONE OF THOSE GANGSTERS WILL RECOGNISE SNOWY UNDER THIS TERRIFYING DISGUISE! LUCKY I JUST FOUND IT IN THAT OLD CUPBOARD... THEY'LL BE SCARED TO DEATH!
OH GOLLY!!!... A REAL TIGER!
?
HELP! IT'S GOING TO EAT ME!
WOOAH!

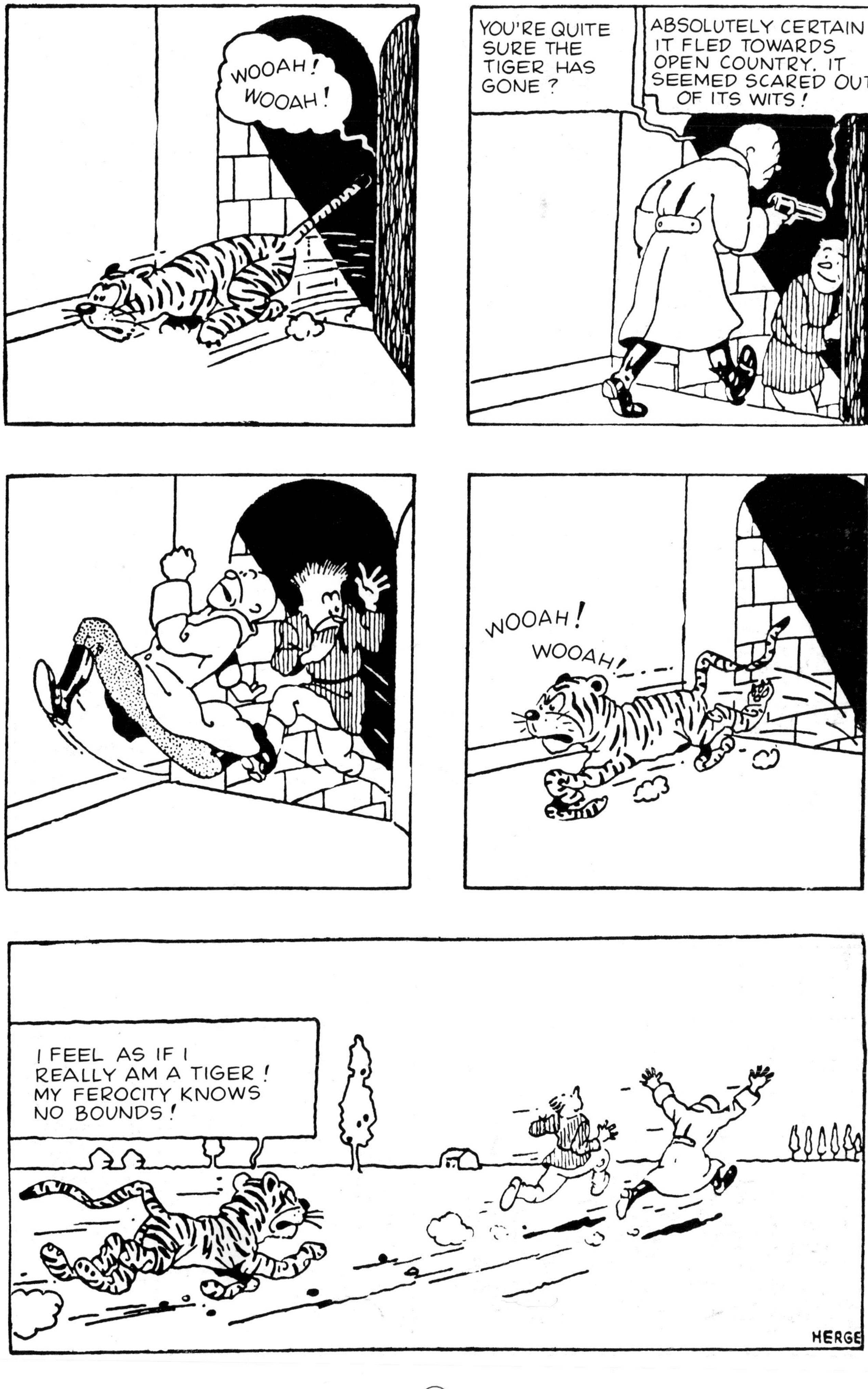
WOOAH! WOOAH!
YOU'RE QUITE SURE THE TIGER HAS GONE?
ABSOLUTELY CERTAIN! IT FLED TOWARDS OPEN COUNTRY. IT SEEMED SCARED OUT OF ITS WITS!
WOOAH! WOOAH!
I FEEL AS IF I REALLY AM A TIGER! MY FEROCITY KNOWS NO BOUNDS!
HERGE

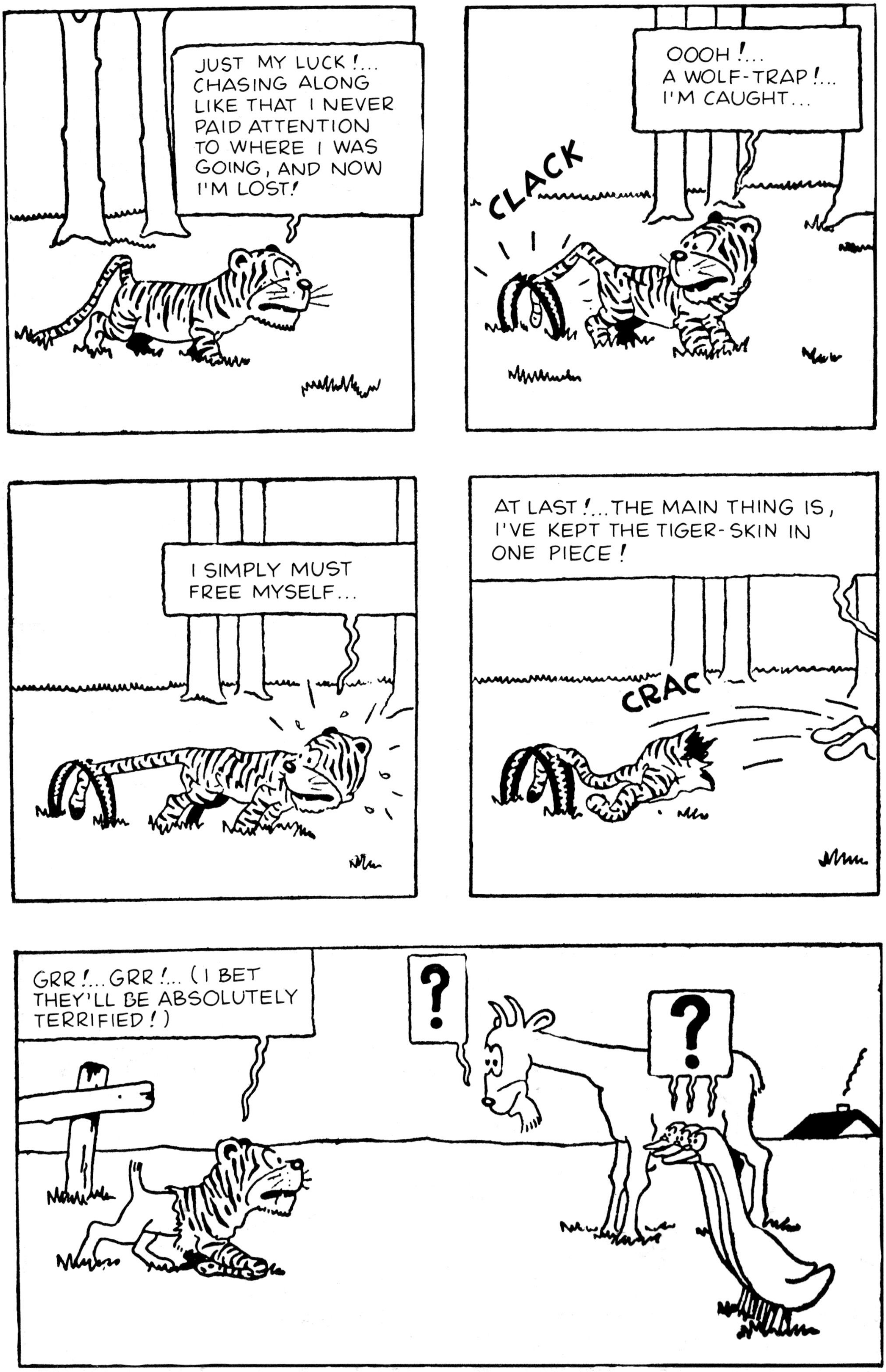
JUST MY LUCK!... CHASING ALONG LIKE THAT I NEVER PAID ATTENTION TO WHERE I WAS GOING, AND NOW I'M LOST!
OOOH!... A WOLF-TRAP!... I'M CAUGHT...
CLACK
I SIMPLY MUST FREE MYSELF...
AT LAST!... THE MAIN THING IS, I'VE KEPT THE TIGER-SKIN IN ONE PIECE!
CRAC
GRR!... GRR!... (I BET THEY'LL BE ABSOLUTELY TERRIFIED!)
?
?

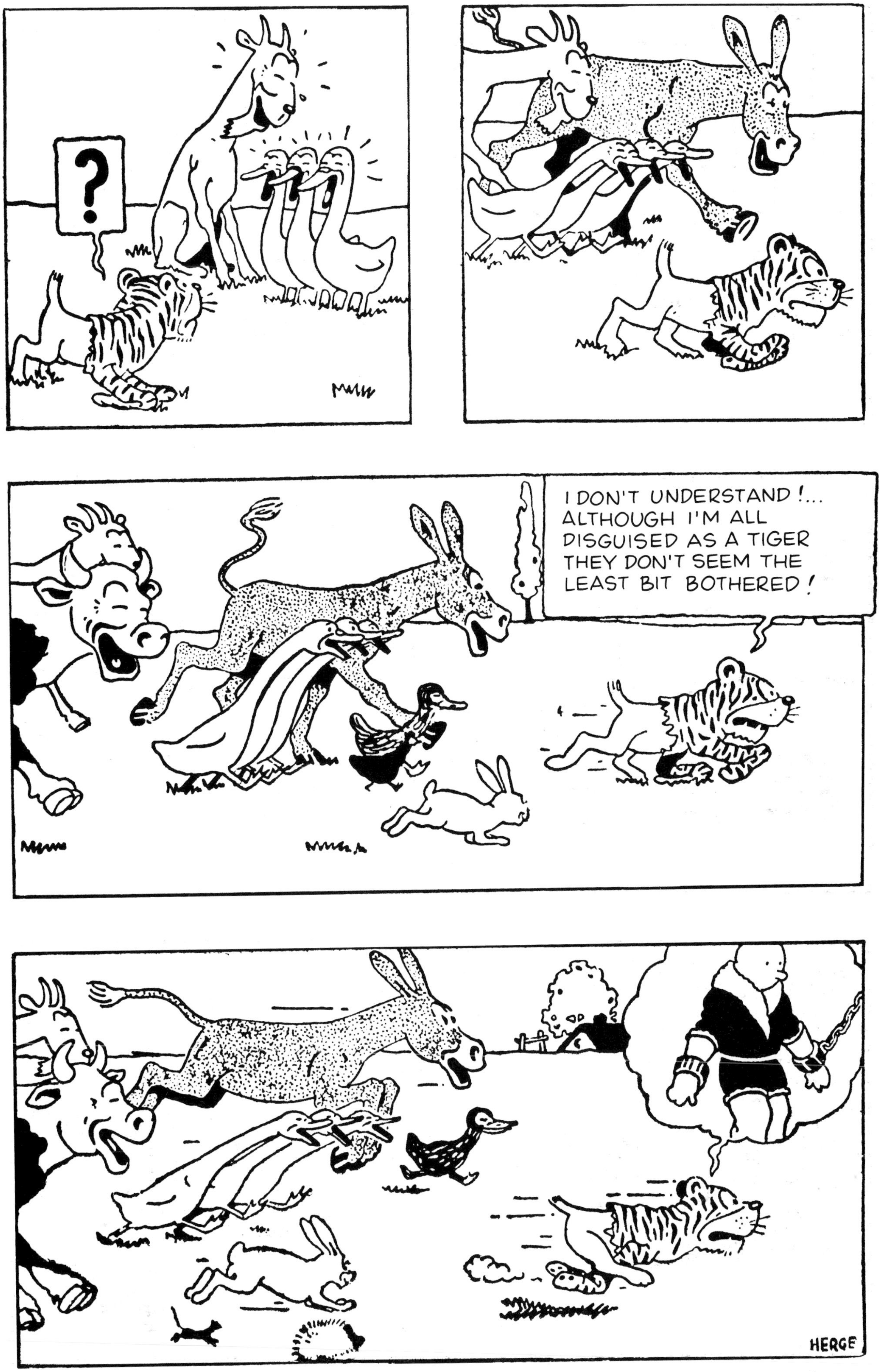
?
I DON'T UNDERSTAND !... ALTHOUGH I'M ALL DISGUISED AS A TIGER THEY DON'T SEEM THE LEAST BIT BOTHERED !
HERGE

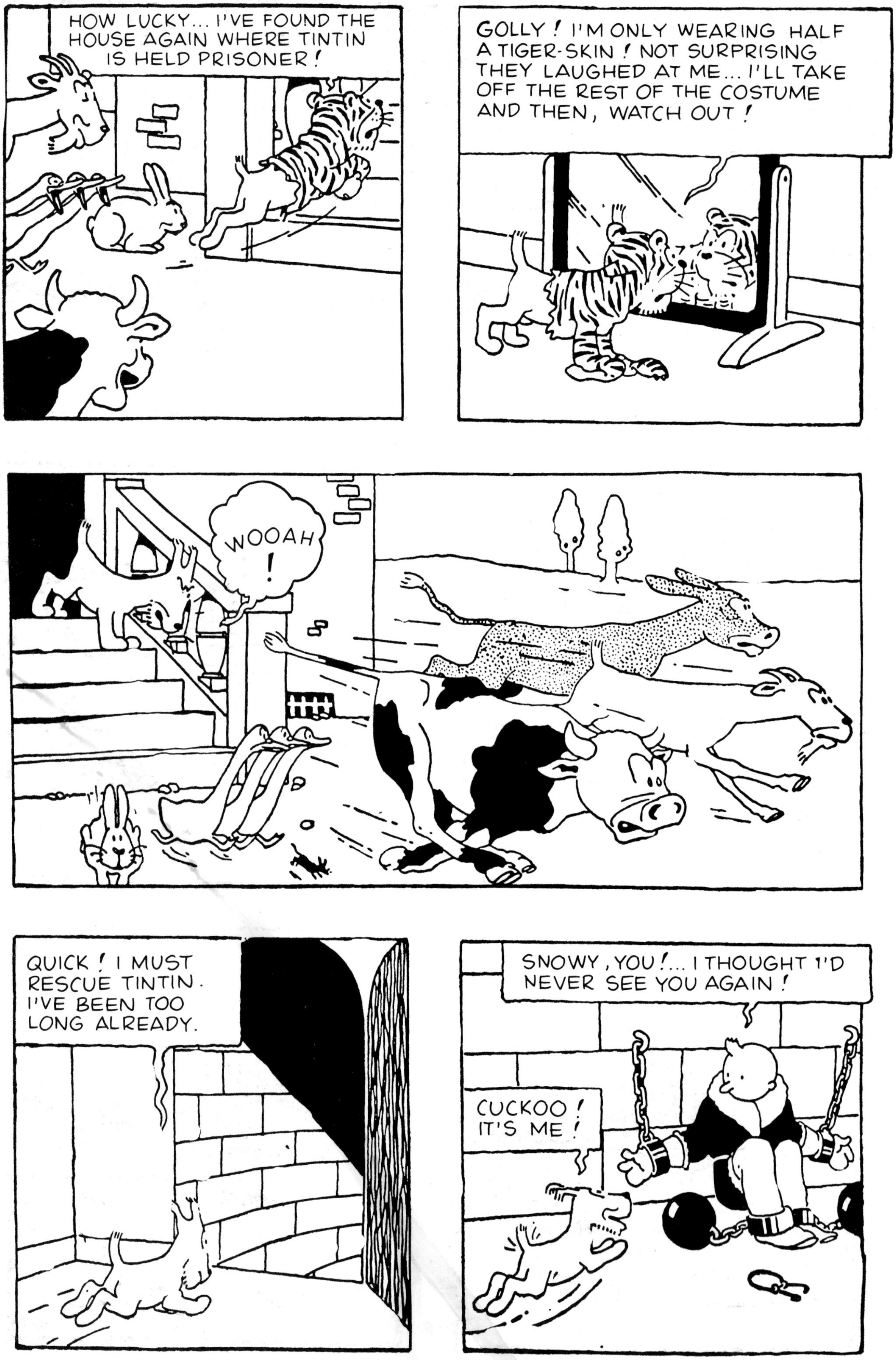
HOW LUCKY... I'VE FOUND THE HOUSE AGAIN WHERE TINTIN IS HELD PRISONER!
GOLLY! I'M ONLY WEARING HALF A TIGER-SKIN! NOT SURPRISING THEY LAUGHED AT ME... I'LL TAKE OFF THE REST OF THE COSTUME AND THEN, WATCH OUT!
WOOAH!
QUICK! I MUST RESCUE TINTIN. I'VE BEEN TOO LONG ALREADY.
SNOWY, YOU!... I THOUGHT I'D NEVER SEE YOU AGAIN!
CUCKOO! IT'S ME!

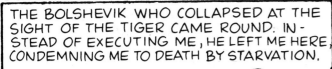

THE BOLSHEVIK WHO COLLAPSED AT THE SIGHT OF THE TIGER CAME ROUND. INSTEAD OF EXECUTING ME, HE LEFT ME HERE, CONDEMNING ME TO DEATH BY STARVATION.

LUCKY THE IDIOT FORGOT TO TAKE HIS KEYS!

ALL RIGHT?...

YES...

FREE!... FREE!...

THANKS TO ME!

BERLIN 15 KM

THREE HOURS' WALK!... THAT'S NOTHING FOR US!

AND THEN WE GO HOME?...

COURAGE, SNOWY!

YES, BUT I'M TERRIBLY THIRSTY.

BERLIN!

AT LAST! NOW TO EAT AND DRINK AND SLEEP.

HERGÉ

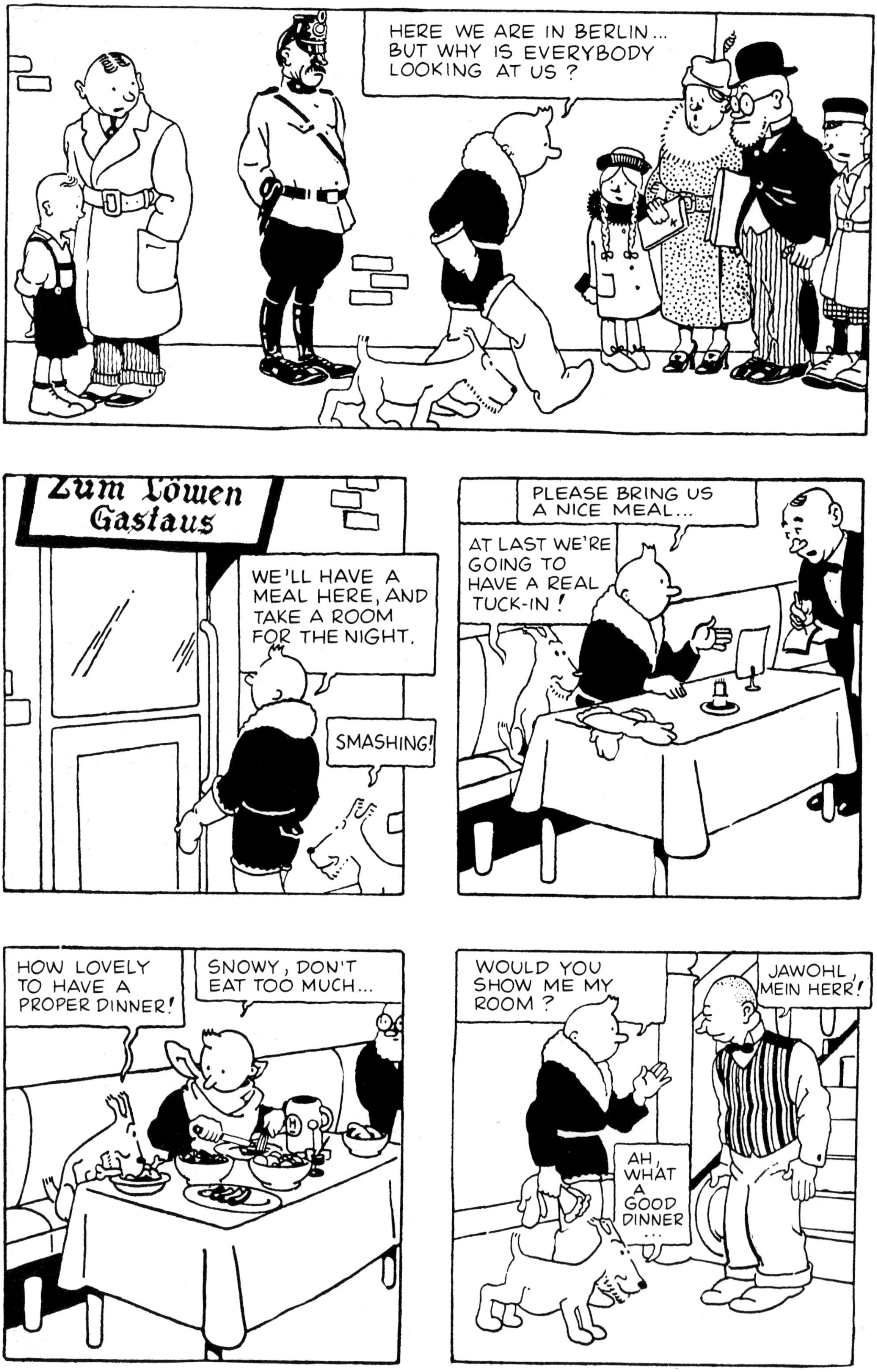
HERE WE ARE IN BERLIN... BUT WHY IS EVERYBODY LOOKING AT US ?
Zum Löwen Gastaus
WE'LL HAVE A MEAL HERE, AND TAKE A ROOM FOR THE NIGHT.
SMASHING!
PLEASE BRING US A NICE MEAL...
AT LAST WE'RE GOING TO HAVE A REAL TUCK-IN !
HOW LOVELY TO HAVE A PROPER DINNER !
SNOWY, DON'T EAT TOO MUCH...
WOULD YOU SHOW ME MY ROOM ?
JAWOHL, MEIN HERR !
AH, WHAT A GOOD DINNER ...

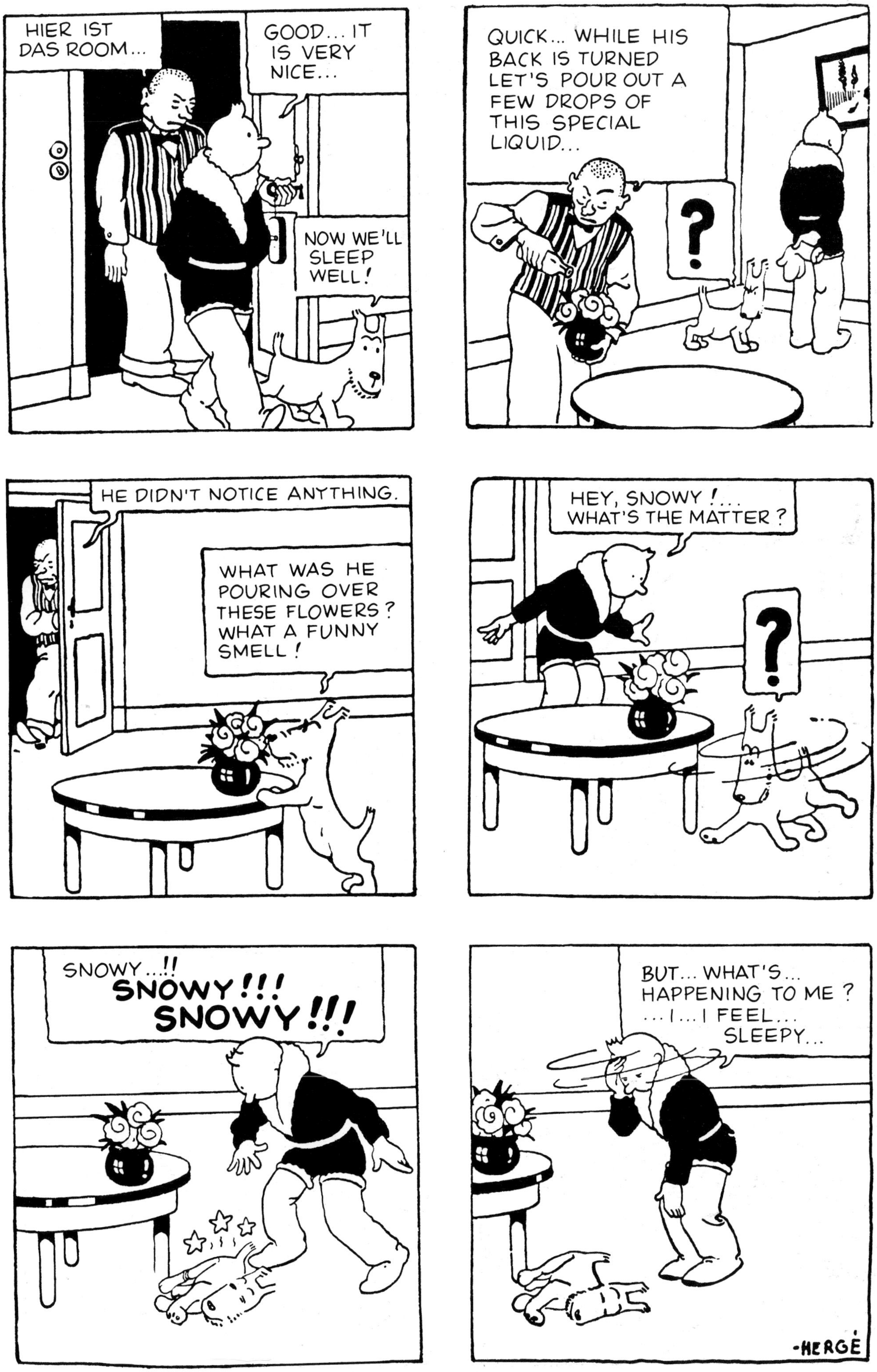
HIER IST DAS ROOM...
GOOD... IT IS VERY NICE...
NOW WE'LL SLEEP WELL!
QUICK... WHILE HIS BACK IS TURNED LET'S POUR OUT A FEW DROPS OF THIS SPECIAL LIQUID...
?
HE DIDN'T NOTICE ANYTHING.
WHAT WAS HE POURING OVER THESE FLOWERS? WHAT A FUNNY SMELL!
HEY, SNOWY!... WHAT'S THE MATTER?
?
SNOWY...!! SNOWY!!! SNOWY!!!
BUT... WHAT'S... HAPPENING TO ME? ...I...I FEEL... SLEEPY...
HERGÉ

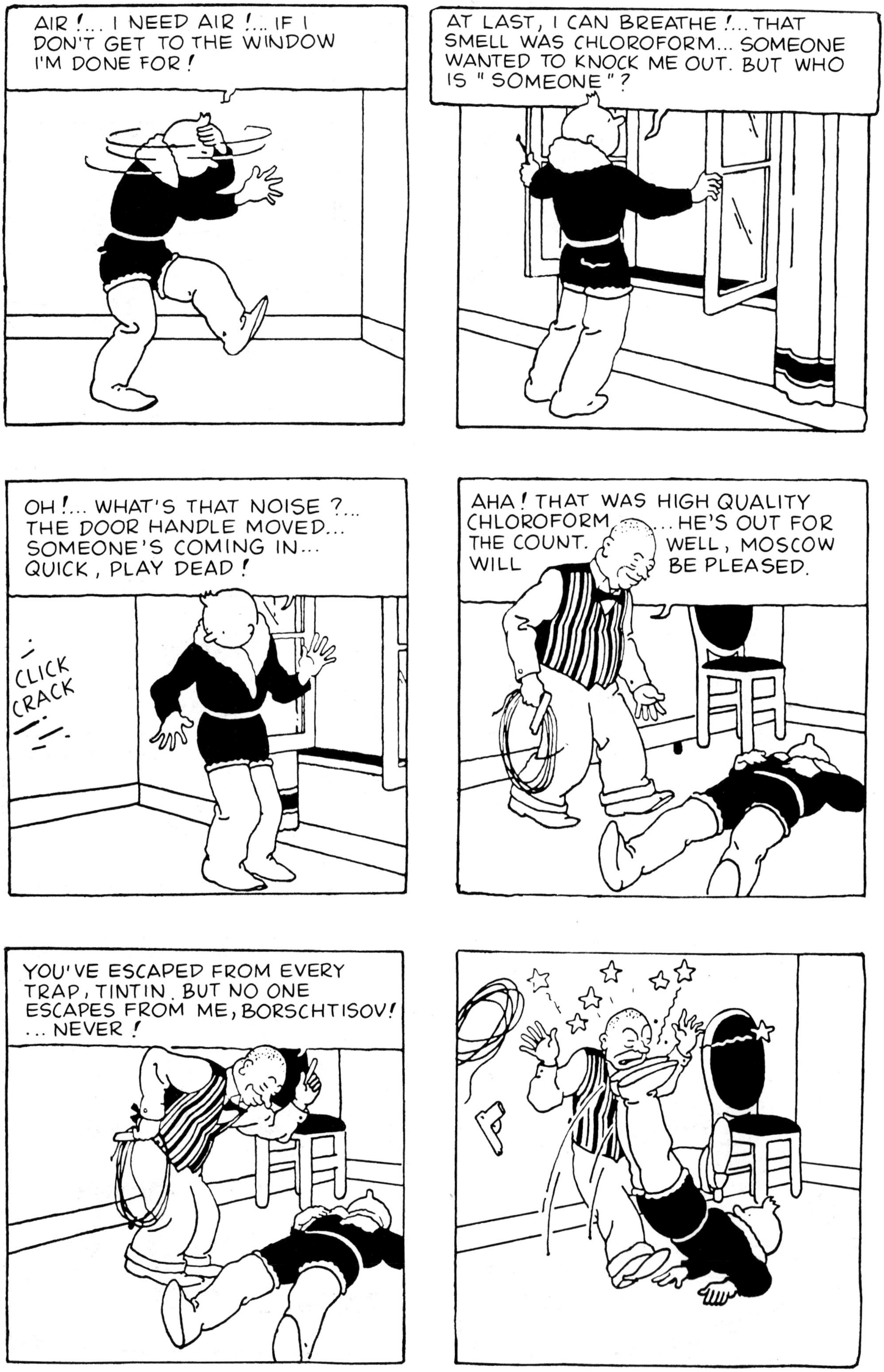
AIR !... I NEED AIR !... IF I DON'T GET TO THE WINDOW I'M DONE FOR !
AT LAST, I CAN BREATHE !... THAT SMELL WAS CHLOROFORM... SOMEONE WANTED TO KNOCK ME OUT. BUT WHO IS "SOMEONE"?
OH !... WHAT'S THAT NOISE ?... THE DOOR HANDLE MOVED... SOMEONE'S COMING IN... QUICK, PLAY DEAD !
CLICK
CRACK
AHA ! THAT WAS HIGH QUALITY CHLOROFORM ... HE'S OUT FOR THE COUNT. WELL, MOSCOW WILL BE PLEASED.
YOU'VE ESCAPED FROM EVERY TRAP, TINTIN. BUT NO ONE ESCAPES FROM ME, BORSCHTISOV! ... NEVER !

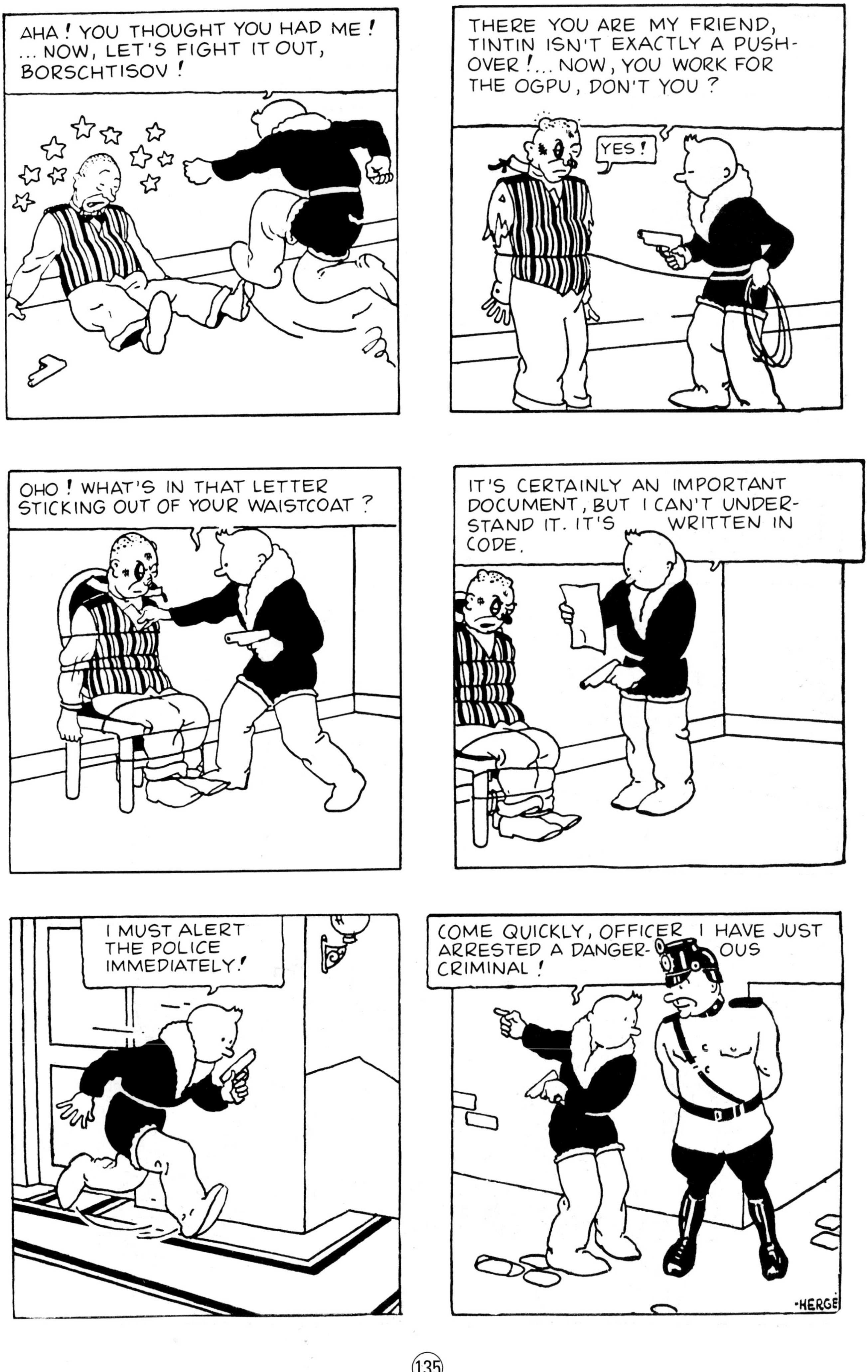
AHA ! YOU THOUGHT YOU HAD ME ! ... NOW, LET'S FIGHT IT OUT, BORSCHTISOV !
THERE YOU ARE MY FRIEND, TINTIN ISN'T EXACTLY A PUSH-OVER !... NOW, YOU WORK FOR THE OGPU, DON'T YOU ?
YES !
OHO ! WHAT'S IN THAT LETTER STICKING OUT OF YOUR WAISTCOAT ?
IT'S CERTAINLY AN IMPORTANT DOCUMENT, BUT I CAN'T UNDER-STAND IT. IT'S WRITTEN IN CODE.
I MUST ALERT THE POLICE IMMEDIATELY !
COME QUICKLY, OFFICER I HAVE JUST ARRESTED A DANGER-OUS CRIMINAL !
HERGÉ

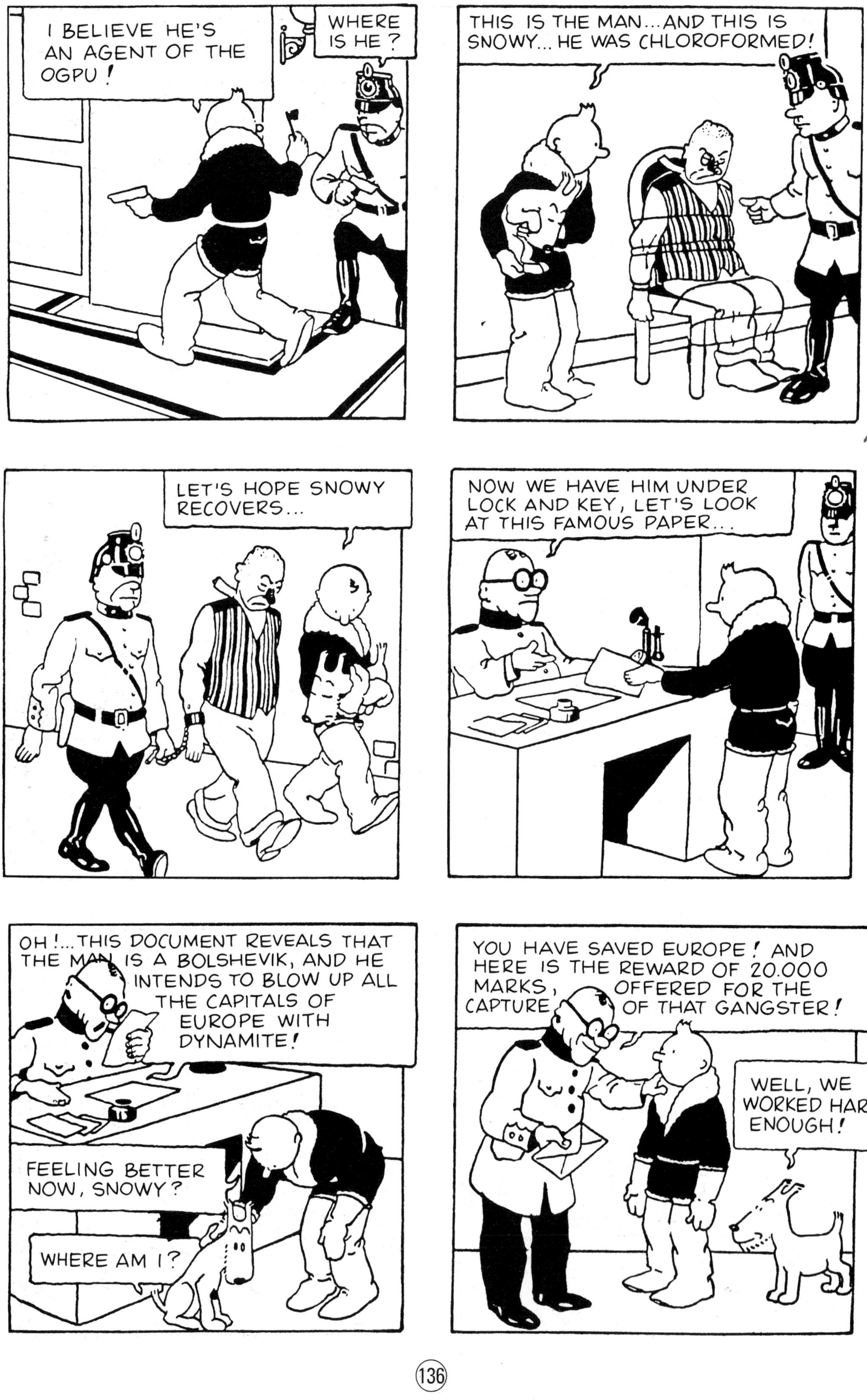
WHERE IS HE ?
I BELIEVE HE'S AN AGENT OF THE OGPU !
THIS IS THE MAN... AND THIS IS SNOWY... HE WAS CHLOROFORMED!
LET'S HOPE SNOWY RECOVERS...
NOW WE HAVE HIM UNDER LOCK AND KEY, LET'S LOOK AT THIS FAMOUS PAPER...
OH !... THIS DOCUMENT REVEALS THAT THE MAN IS A BOLSHEVIK, AND HE INTENDS TO BLOW UP ALL THE CAPITALS OF EUROPE WITH DYNAMITE!
FEELING BETTER NOW, SNOWY ?
WHERE AM I ?
YOU HAVE SAVED EUROPE! AND HERE IS THE REWARD OF 20.000 MARKS, OFFERED FOR THE CAPTURE OF THAT GANGSTER!
WELL, WE WORKED HARD ENOUGH!

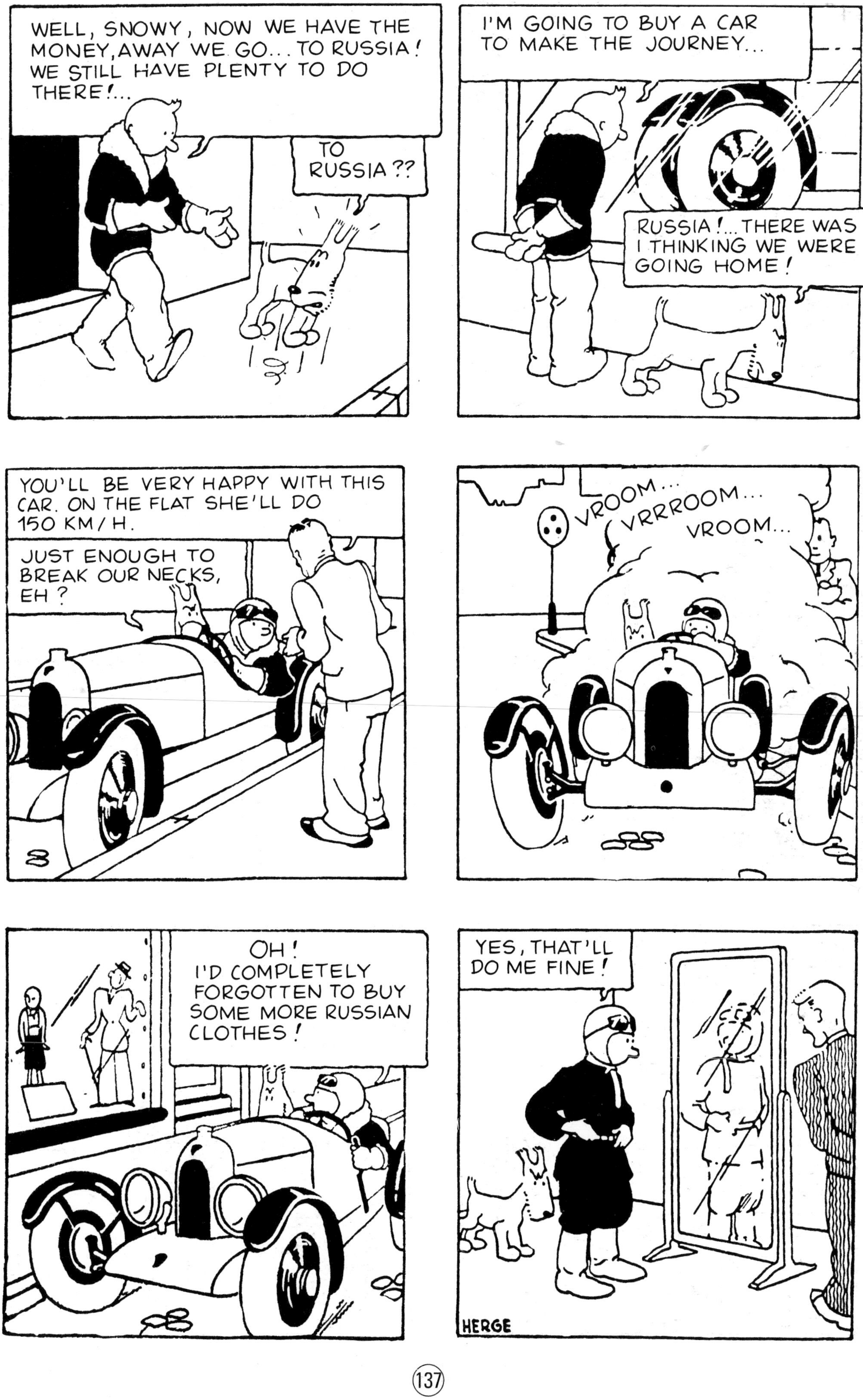
WELL, SNOWY, NOW WE HAVE THE MONEY, AWAY WE GO... TO RUSSIA! WE STILL HAVE PLENTY TO DO THERE!...
TO RUSSIA??
I'M GOING TO BUY A CAR TO MAKE THE JOURNEY...
RUSSIA!... THERE WAS I THINKING WE WERE GOING HOME!
YOU'LL BE VERY HAPPY WITH THIS CAR. ON THE FLAT SHE'LL DO 150 KM/H.
JUST ENOUGH TO BREAK OUR NECKS, EH?
VROOM...
VRRROOM...
VROOM...
OH! I'D COMPLETELY FORGOTTEN TO BUY SOME MORE RUSSIAN CLOTHES!
YES, THAT'LL DO ME FINE!
HERGE

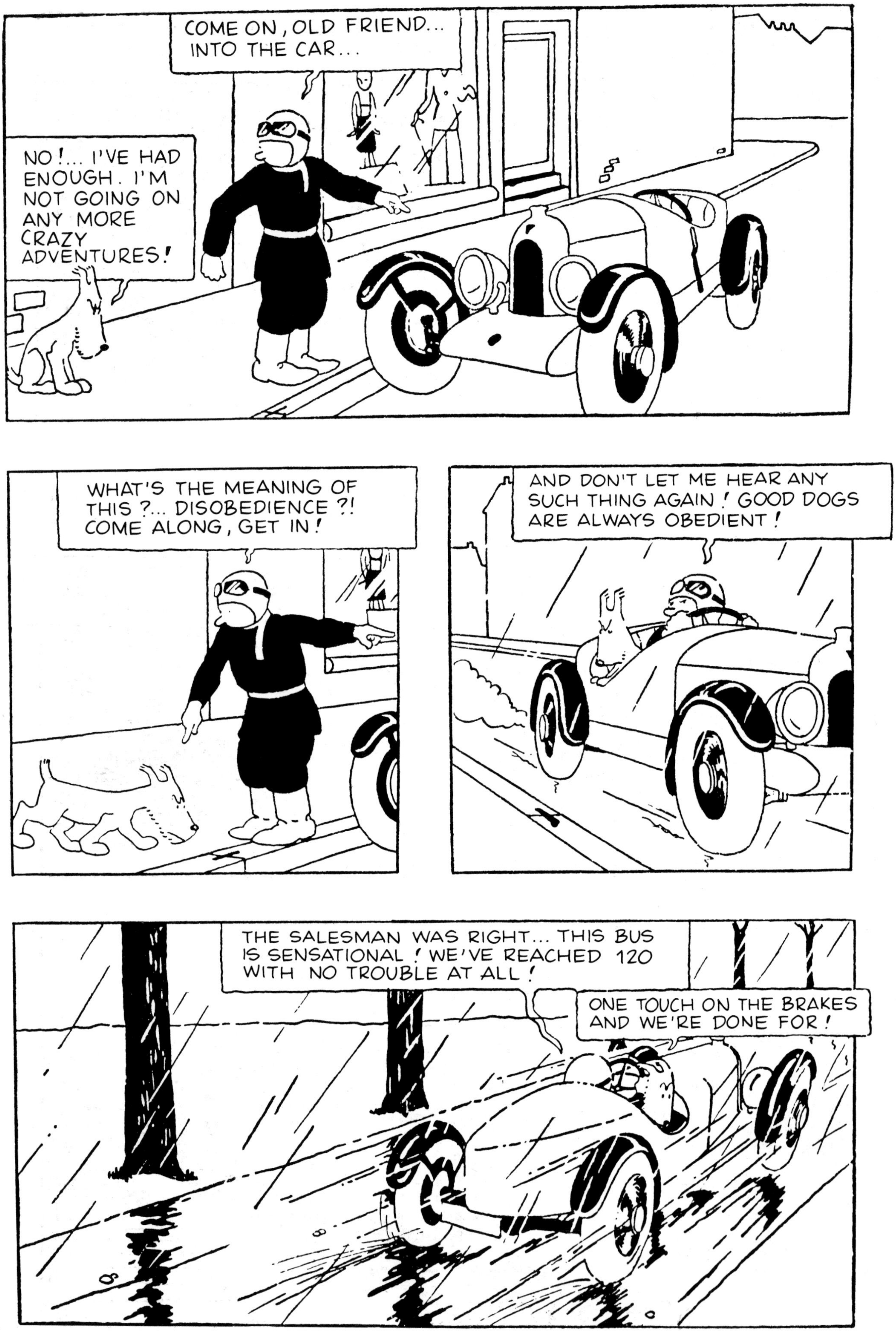
COME ON, OLD FRIEND... INTO THE CAR...
NO!... I'VE HAD ENOUGH. I'M NOT GOING ON ANY MORE CRAZY ADVENTURES!
WHAT'S THE MEANING OF THIS?... DISOBEDIENCE?! COME ALONG, GET IN!
AND DON'T LET ME HEAR ANY SUCH THING AGAIN! GOOD DOGS ARE ALWAYS OBEDIENT!
THE SALESMAN WAS RIGHT... THIS BUS IS SENSATIONAL! WE'VE REACHED 120 WITH NO TROUBLE AT ALL!
ONE TOUCH ON THE BRAKES AND WE'RE DONE FOR!

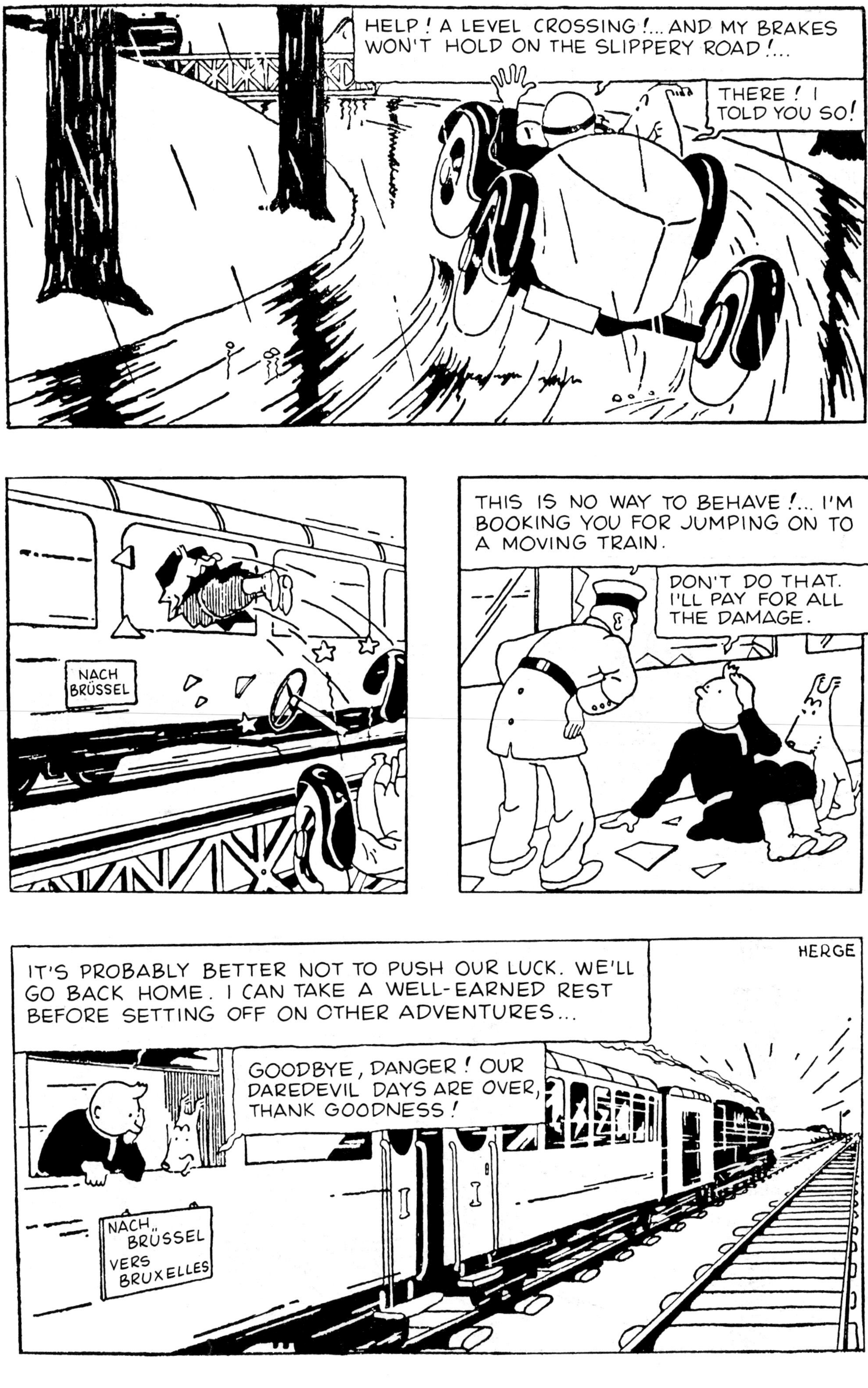
HELP ! A LEVEL CROSSING !... AND MY BRAKES WON'T HOLD ON THE SLIPPERY ROAD !...
THERE ! I TOLD YOU SO !
NACH BRÜSSEL
THIS IS NO WAY TO BEHAVE !... I'M BOOKING YOU FOR JUMPING ON TO A MOVING TRAIN.
DON'T DO THAT. I'LL PAY FOR ALL THE DAMAGE.
HERGE
IT'S PROBABLY BETTER NOT TO PUSH OUR LUCK. WE'LL GO BACK HOME. I CAN TAKE A WELL-EARNED REST BEFORE SETTING OFF ON OTHER ADVENTURES...
GOODBYE, DANGER ! OUR DAREDEVIL DAYS ARE OVER, THANK GOODNESS !
NACH BRÜSSEL VERS BRUXELLES

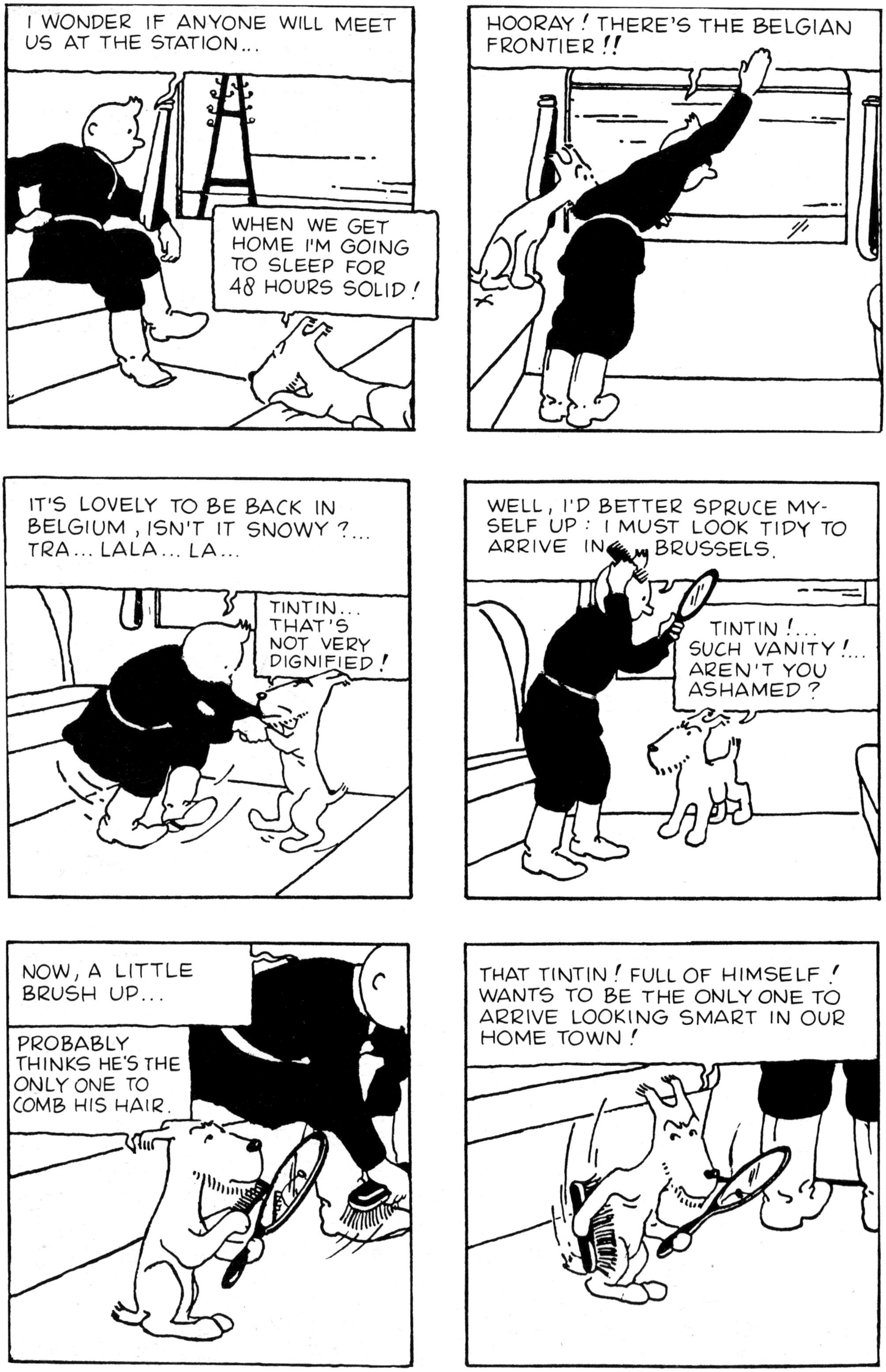
I WONDER IF ANYONE WILL MEET US AT THE STATION...
WHEN WE GET HOME I'M GOING TO SLEEP FOR 48 HOURS SOLID!
HOORAY! THERE'S THE BELGIAN FRONTIER!!
IT'S LOVELY TO BE BACK IN BELGIUM, ISN'T IT SNOWY?... TRA... LALA... LA...
TINTIN... THAT'S NOT VERY DIGNIFIED!
WELL, I'D BETTER SPRUCE MY-SELF UP: I MUST LOOK TIDY TO ARRIVE IN BRUSSELS.
TINTIN!... SUCH VANITY!... AREN'T YOU ASHAMED?
NOW, A LITTLE BRUSH UP...
PROBABLY THINKS HE'S THE ONLY ONE TO COMB HIS HAIR.
THAT TINTIN! FULL OF HIMSELF! WANTS TO BE THE ONLY ONE TO ARRIVE LOOKING SMART IN OUR HOME TOWN!

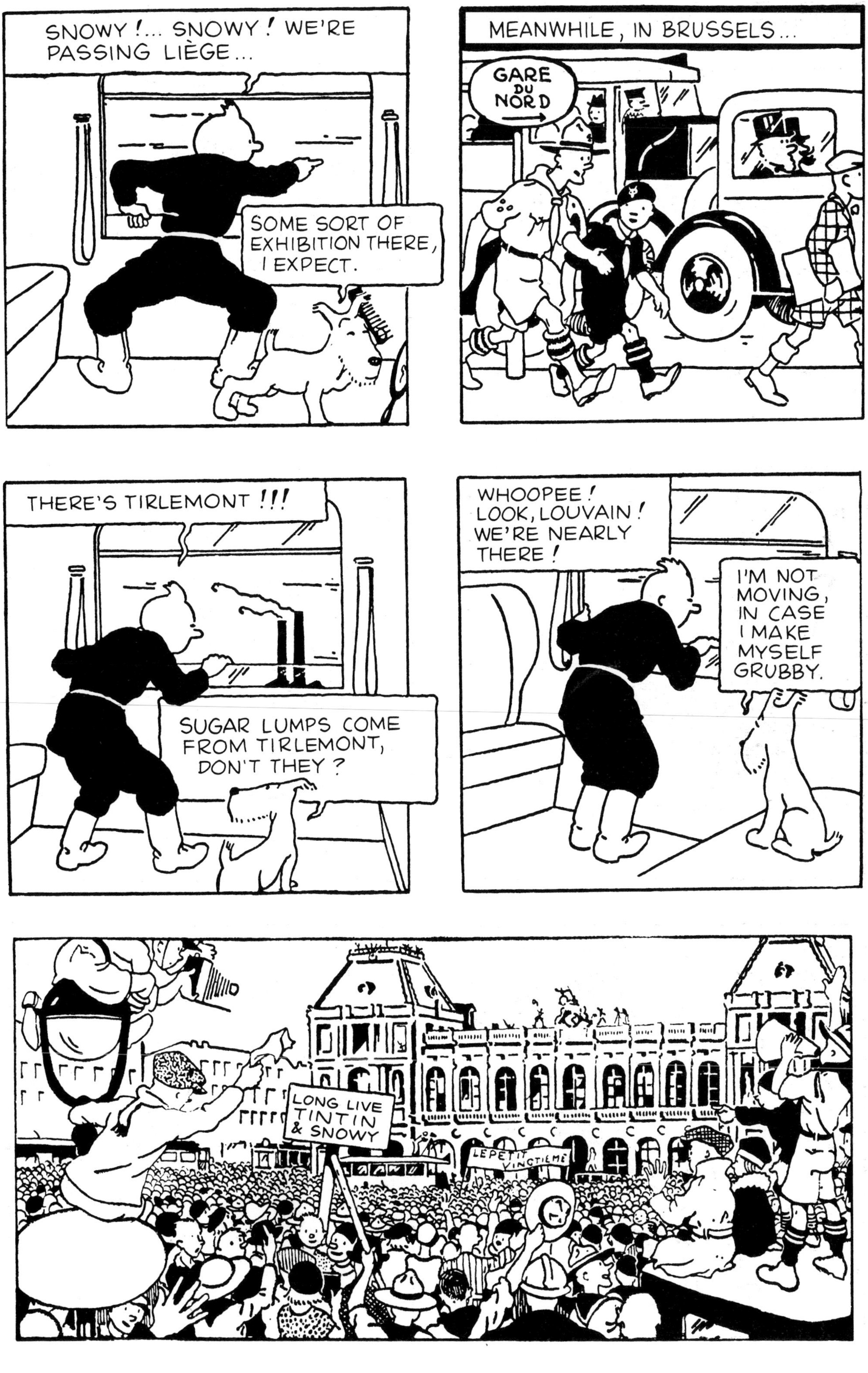

SNOWY !... SNOWY ! WE'RE PASSING LIÈGE...
SOME SORT OF EXHIBITION THERE, I EXPECT.
MEANWHILE, IN BRUSSELS...
GARE DU NORD
THERE'S TIRLEMONT !!!
SUGAR LUMPS COME FROM TIRLEMONT, DON'T THEY ?
WHOOPEE ! LOOK, LOUVAIN ! WE'RE NEARLY THERE !
I'M NOT MOVING, IN CASE I MAKE MYSELF GRUBBY.
LONG LIVE TINTIN & SNOWY
LE PETIT VINGTIÈME